4% famous

DEBORAH SCHOENEMAN

4% famous

A NOVEL

Shaye Areheart Books / New York

Published in the United States by Shaye Areheart Books, an imprint of the Crown Publishing Group, a division of Random House, Inc., New York.
www.crownpublishing.com

Shaye Areheart Books and colophon are trademarks of Random House, Inc.

Library of Congress Cataloging-in-Publication Data
Schoeneman, Deborah, 1977–
4% famous / Deborah Schoeneman.—1st ed.
1. Gossip columnists—Fiction.   2. Manhattan (New York, N.Y.)—Fiction.
I. Title: Four percent famous.   II. Title.
PS3619.C4495A613   2006
813'.6—dc22   2005032258

ISBN 13: 978-0-307-23746-0
ISBN 10: 0-307-23746-X

Printed in the United States of America

DESIGN BY ELINA D. NUDELMAN

10   9   8   7   6   5   4   3   2   1

First Edition

For my parents.

Gossip is the new pornography.

—Woody Allen (*Manhattan*, 1979)

4% famous

seek out the competition

With her new job as the "legs" for a gossip column, Kate Simon often feels as if she's crawling on all fours. There's too much to see and do. Stories to devour and spit back up in bite-sized items for the *New York Examiner* every week. Things to catch up on, things she wishes she already knew as soon as she learns them. It's hard to sleep when you feel as though the whole city is wide awake and feasting.

"I've already been to every party too many times," said Paul Peterson, the column's head, arms, and torso, during her interview two weeks ago. He's forty-two but looks fifty, and his eyes always seem strained, as if pulled open by tiny translucent threads that are slowly losing their elasticity. "Only the themes change. And only slightly."

"The parties must be pretty fun," Kate said, imagining walking down a red carpet with cameras flashing like lightning. Champagne perched on silver trays. Oysters heaped on the buffet.

He laughed. "You can have it."

She hoped he wasn't laughing at her.

Paul asked if she'd always wanted to be a journalist, and she decided to be honest and say she's always wanted to be an investigative reporter. Find the guilty, free the innocent. Comb through files, ring bells and blow whistles.

Hold something in her hands that she could show people when they asked her what she did for a living, something her parents would frame. She has always been inquisitive—okay, even nosy. She just never knew before that it could become a career.

"Well, celebrities can be criminals," said Paul.

The cab pulls up to a town house that looks a little like the *Examiner*'s office nearby but much more expensive. It's got a wrought-iron gate and ivy crawling up the walls to prevent people like Kate from peering in and trying to piece together the story inside, maybe find something to make her feel less envious.

Kate keeps the receipt for her expense report and checks her reflection one last time in her compact. If she were blond, she could be straight out of the opening scene of a chick-lit novel. The sticky August rain has her light brown curls frizzed out electric and unyielding. She tries twisting the mass up in a barrette and leaves just a few strands framing her face. That's better. But even another dab of concealer isn't going to hide the pimple budding on her chin. Why does she always break out at the worst possible times? Kate tries to remove a small stain on her white collared shirt with a tissue and some bottled water while mentally rehearsing her interview questions for the **New Literary Wunderkind** about his book. She stayed up late finishing it last night. At least it gave her something to do besides toss and turn, wondering how she's going to pull this job off.

While Kate waits to check her umbrella in the foyer, she sees a tall guy pushing a mop of sandy-blond hair out of his face as he emerges from the bathroom and stuffs a tape recorder in his blue blazer pocket. He looks as if he could have been thrown out of prep school for smoking pot on the tennis court. He makes a beeline for a white-haired man making a small group laugh across the room. Kate quickly intervenes, stepping in his path.

"Excuse me," he says, looking over her shoulder.

He's got a faint white ring of powder lining his left nostril and he smells like cigarettes. Kate would have missed it if it weren't for her extensive experience helping her college roommate, Zoe Miller of Fifth Avenue, groom during parties.

"Hi, I'm Kate Simon, from the *Examiner*?" she says, making a big show of wiping her nose with the back of her palm.

"Oh, you must be Paul Peterson's new pair of legs," he says, introducing himself as Blake Bradley from *Manhattan* magazine's gossip column. He says it all in one breath, as if his affiliation were his last name. No one ever asks about Kate's predecessor, who left to go to grad school. "Purgatory," is how Paul described the career shift.

"You're friends with Zoe Miller, right?" Blake asks her. "Her mother keeps asking me to look out for you. She's a friend of my mother's."

He's still looking over her shoulder at the white-haired man, who Kate has figured out is Bill Clinton, though she's not sure why the former president would be at a book party. She wishes she had one of those camera cell phones so she could snap a shot for her dad, but that would probably make her look too starstruck. To do this job well, she should pretend she doesn't want to ask every famous person she sees for an autograph. She starts frantically wiping her nose again. She'd rather stay here and help a potential ally than go in that room right now.

"Do you need a tissue?" Blake asks.

"No," she whispers, "but you do."

His eyes widen and he pulls a handkerchief from his pocket and quickly wipes his nose.

"I owe you big-time," he says, putting his arm around her shoulder and guiding her into the living room.

He tells Kate he needs to get a quote from Clinton for an item. "It's always easier if you just find them somewhere instead of dealing with their gatekeepers," he says, excusing himself.

Meanwhile, the New Literary Wunderkind is standing slightly apart from a small group corralled by the hostess, boldface magazine editor Terry Barlow, looking as if he wants to crawl behind the big white curtains. Every few moments he squeezes out a tense smile and says thanks as if he's being prompted by a hidden microphone.

Kate looks at her notepad again, trying to memorize a few questions to ask the author, when she feels a tap on her back. She turns around and sees the most attractive guy at the party smiling at her and her heart hop-scotches. He's the only person here wearing jeans, with a white T-shirt and a black blazer. He's got spiky, short black hair and almost translucent pale green eyes that seem to be taking an X ray of everyone in his path. She swears he can see right through her clothes, hunting for folds of fat, freckles, flaws. She feels her cheeks get hot and hopes he doesn't notice she's blushing. He smiles even bigger.

"Hey, I'm Tim Mack from Column A," he says with the authority of a person who knows he's the life of the party, the neon streak in a room of primary colors. "I saw your name at the bottom of Paul's column last week. Great guy."

Kate's not sure how this guy knows who she is. The *Examiner* doesn't run photos of its writers. Thank God. She can't decide if she should feel flattered or nervous. Paul called Tim Mack the best—Paul used the word *bulldog*—gossip reporter around, and Column A is by far the most-read gossip column. But he doesn't look as if he's doing anything right now but getting buzzed off white wine.

"Relax," he says. Kate tells herself she's got to stop wearing panic as a new accessory. "Blake pointed you out. No one's posted your photo on a blog, and ball-busting Barlow didn't print out napkins with your face or anything. The Teutonic-tempered editrix hasn't thought of that trick yet." He pauses and looks up at the ceiling. "Though I have to say that's not a bad idea."

Does he always talk in alliteration?

"Smile, sweetheart. You've got a good few months to leverage your relative anonymity."

Kate tries to laugh but it comes out more like a cough. Relative anonymity? Relative to whom? She looks over at the New Literary Wunderkind. He's holding a toothpick from a cube of cheese, trying to find a surface to ditch it without anyone noticing. Just as Kate considers walking over to save him, Terry takes his arm to lead him around the room for a round of show-and-tell.

If Kate's going to succeed at gossip enough that she'll be able to get *out* of it one day, she's going to have to get to know some guides. She remembers Zoe telling her the best way to make friends in New York is to at least indirectly compliment what people do for a living. "Feed the ego," is how she put it.

Kate finally breaks her silence and asks Tim if Blake's stepmother is the glamorous decorator Lindsay Bradley, whom she keeps reading about in Column A.

"Ahem." Tim clears his throat and raises an eyebrow. "Blake's stepmonster likes to be called a designer, which is why we call her the **Sugar Daddy Decorator**. Apparently she grew up in an actual trailer park in Arizona but managed to meet a series of increasingly rich boyfriends by decorating their apartments and finding out their secrets, like what they kept in their bedside tables and which meds they were on."

Kate wonders how long it'll be before Lindsay gets pregnant. Zoe says that's the only way the second wives get any money out of the prenup.

"Before she convinced Blake's dad to trade in his wife for a newer model, we used to call her the **Home-Wrecking Hooker**."

Just then Blake comes back grinning. "Bill's the best." He grabs two glasses of white wine from a passing silver tray. "He totally gives it up." Blake doesn't reveal exactly what the former president is giving up.

"Are we done working now?" asks Tim, grabbing a glass of wine in each hand. Kate notices that neither one of the men seems remotely concerned with interviewing the Wunderkind. The object of this parlor game seems to be getting an unrelated item and mentioning that you got it at the party for the book. Maybe the author is smart enough to know that if he's seen but not heard, he can't come off badly in the columns.

Blake tries rearranging the place cards so they can all sit together during lunch, but a stern handler stops him. "Someone planned the tables this way!" she hisses before dashing off to help a camera crew set up a light over Terry's table.

Blake starts heading over to his seat in the front of the room. "Being trailed by a camera crew is the new status symbol," he whispers in Kate's ear, nodding at the cameras.

Kate wishes she could sit with her new friends, but she's stuck with balding and bearded foreign correspondents talking about the "situation in Syria." At Terry's table, Blake's sitting between a powerful politician's daughter and the Wunderkind, who is studying his silverware while being talked at by a deep-pocketed divorcée who likes to be called a Democratic fund-raiser. Tim will later mention that before she was well married and divorced twice, she was found handcuffed to a radiator in Amsterdam by her first husband, who she pretends never existed.

Blake is probably going to ask Terry about the rumors about her magazine folding—which is what Kate is here to do—before Kate can even introduce herself to the editor. He seems to be her columnist pet and Kate wonders if she'll ever get that kind of seat at a party and what she will do if she does. She's not sure if she should try to interview Terry before or after lunch is served, or to not even bother. She feels as if an invisible chain has her locked to her seat.

Tim's real estate is even worse. He's across the room at the table farthest from Terry's, looking miserable next to a woman wearing a low-cut, short black cocktail dress. He'll later explain that she's a baroness, though she was only married to a penniless baron with a big drafty castle in Austria for a few months before he burned all her gowns and locked her in a tower for a week. All she got out of the settlement was the title and a book deal using Terry's agent, who's also at their table.

Tim gets up and stops by Kate's table on his way to the bathroom.

"I'm hearing about who the baroness fucked this summer to get helicopter rides to the Hamptons, while Blake's getting the item I came for," Tim says quickly to Kate without revealing what that item was, but Kate's pretty sure they all came here with the same mission. "At least the food should be good. Terry got some hot new chef named Marco Mancini to make lunch. She probably got him to cater in exchange for exposure because he's got a new restaurant opening up soon. When he becomes a big shot, all her friends will know she got to the guy first."

Tim leaves when the food arrives. Kate is suddenly starving and she's relieved she has something else to focus on because the situation in Syria isn't becoming any friendlier. She tucks into a roasted fig-and-Gorgonzola salad, trying to figure out the ingredients in the delicious dressing.

"Aged Italian balsamic," says a guy in thick glasses sitting across from Kate. "Good enough to put on ice cream."

Kate tries to look busy, afraid he'll ask her about the Middle East. Kate reads all the papers every day and could fumble her way through local or national politics, but Syria is just unfair—it's as if everyone else at the table has a seven-letter Scrabble word and she only has vowels. So far, not one person has mentioned the book being feted today.

"I help Paul Peterson cover parties at the *Examiner*," she tells the man sitting next to her in a brown tweed blazer with arm patches, who looks like a history professor. It will be months before she realizes that he's her dad's favorite political columnist.

"That must be *fun*," he says, sweetly.

"*Fun*," she agrees, nodding and stuffing her mouth with a big bite of salmon covered in sweet-and-sour rhubarb compote. She makes a mental note to ask Zoe, who works at *Gourmet* magazine, about this new chef, Marco Mancini. They should try to get invited to his restaurant opening.

Even though Kate's unsure of what she should be doing she feels a buzz building inside, an electric thrill to be at this party, in a room full of important people she can later brag about meeting—even if she didn't know what to say to them. It reminds her of her job as a hostess one summer in a popular restaurant in Woodstock, where she got the first of many lessons in VIP treatment. She once led Bob Dylan to his favorite table and could hear people hold their breath as he passed. It was a hush that keeps echoing through her ears all these years later.

When Kate gets back to the *Examiner*'s office, a cramped four-story brownstone off Park Avenue, she tells Paul that she met Tim and Blake, who already seemed to be interviewing Terry about her magazine's future, and that the New Literary Wunderkind ducked out before dessert.

"So did you get any items?" he asks, and she shakes her head.

Paul frowns. "You've got to learn how to manage your time and report-ing better. Come up with questions on the spot if you know you're getting scooped. You can't be intimidated by these people."

Kate feels like an amateur for not coming back with anything better, and it's not a good feeling. She's used to impressing people. At school, she got straight A's and had a front-page story in the campus newspaper at least once a week. Competition always bred productivity. How hard could it be to cover parties?

"And Kate," says Paul, looking her straight in the eye. "Be careful how close you get to those guys."

She's not sure how she's supposed to get sources and scoops if she doesn't try to get close to them—they've already proven to be very useful—but if she's too close to them, they're friends, and she's not sup-posed to be friends with her sources. On Kate's first day, Paul took her to lunch and said the most important rule is to never sleep with or accept any kind of favors from sources.

"You can't write about your friends, either," he added, even though none of Kate's friends were remotely newsworthy. Paul, however, is always going to lunch with old friends whom he calls his sources. It doesn't make much sense. Yet.

The first hint of pink sky would be a reliable if unwelcome sign that it's time to go home—if only nightclubs had windows. But Ripe, a cavernous new club that's really just an old club re-opening tonight with a new name and a fresh coat of paint, may as well be a dungeon.

Almost every club in the city gets re-invented every few years after they fall prey to predictable scandals that Tim Mack keeps churning into fod-der. And *they* keep thanking him for it because the items double as adver-tisements. Loyalty is a gossip columnist's best insurance policy, and Tim's loyalty is rewarded tonight with a prime table stocked with bottles of booze and marked with a shiny black-and-white RESERVED FOR VIP sign.

The club's promoter (who loves when he's called a nightlife impresario—promoters never want to be called promoters) keeps feeding Tim items and booze, even a few lines of coke, so everything Tim is thinking and saying seems too sacred, too urgent to waste by going home early or alone.

"Hey, isn't that Kate Simon from the *Examiner*?" Tim asks Blake, pointing at the bar.

Blake nods. "Yeah, that's her," he says. "And the one with the long black hair is her friend Zoe Miller. She's an editorial assistant at *Gourmet*."

"The friend is fucking hot. How do you know her?"

"She's always had a walk-on role in the sitcom of my life."

"Well, I never saw those episodes," says Tim.

Blake runs a hand through his hair. "Zoe is a family friend I've wanted to sleep with for about a decade, but she always has a highly inappropriate boyfriend cockblocking."

"Well, I'm much less appropriate than you are. We should invite them over here," says Tim, pouring drinks for the girls and forgetting about the leggy model/actress, or mattress, lounging at the table. He notices that Kate looks much prettier than she did at Terry Barlow's. She's wearing a short black dress and black leather boots, with her long brown curly hair falling over her shoulders.

Blake's cell phone rings and he ducks under the table to try to have a conversation, probably with Bitchy Bethany. He resurfaces moments later looking like a scolded little boy.

"Sorry, man, I've got to get back to the trenches of domesticity."

"Are you fucking kidding?" Tim looks at his new fancy, free watch. It could probably get about four hundred dollars on eBay. "It's not even one A.M.! The party is just getting good!"

Blake shrugs. "It's the same as every other party."

"We get paid to be the last ones standing!" Tim shouts. "Do you want me to get all the scoop here tonight? And who's going to help me entertain all these lovely ladies?"

The mattresses purr. Most are fresh off the boat from NoWheresVille.

Hot, hungry, and unconnected. Fuck it. Without Blake there's more for Tim. The mattresses will stay for as long as Tim wants—they love having a corner claimed, an indication that they are not just one of the sheep. It turns the girls on to know they're with a VIP who can plug their shampoo commercial or calendar or straight-to-DVD movie or whatever the hell they're doing when they're not partying and rich-husband hunting. Getting your name boldface in Column A is the first toll on the freeway to fame, even if it's a price you could end up paying every time you get on the bridge.

Tim is a popular guy.

Blake throws on his blue blazer and stops briefly to talk to Kate and her hot friend before getting swallowed by the crowd of civilians. Tim almost gets up to ask Kate for an introduction to this sexy Zoe Miller, but the *impresario* bounds over and offers Tim a girl for the night. Tim can picture her now, a RESERVED FOR VIP ribbon wrapped around her tight ticker of a red dress, pushing up her impossibly perfect big, round tits. He's almost drunk enough to pretend she just could really, really like him.

"No thanks," he says instead.

"Just trying to hook a brother up," says the promoter, slapping Tim on the back.

Tim has to decline just in case the promoter ever does something really bad like sell Oxycontin to some kids, at which point the promoter could use the hooker against Tim so he won't write about it. Besides, waking up next to her would feel far worse than any hangover. So he'll go home alone even though he's getting tired of sleeping alone or sleeping with women who probably wouldn't even talk to him if he didn't have an all-access pass to Manhattan.

A few hours later Tim looks around and realizes that it's only him and the guys sweeping the floor and a lone busboy stacking bottles in a sticky bin. Kate and her hot friend are long gone and he didn't even get to say hi or offer them a drink. The music still vibrating through the floor feels like a stream of subways trying to flee the island. He stumbles outside, pleased that he remembered to bring his sunglasses, and folds into a cab.

"I'm going straight to hell," he tells the driver, who turns around and looks at Tim as if he just stabbed someone. "Settle down, pal. Hell's Kitchen."

Tim can't remember which one of his keys opens the front door of his apartment building on West Thirty-sixth Street. He should use those colored plastic things so he doesn't have to fumble with the lock when he gets home drunk most every night. Early morning is more like it. Mornings when men in gray suits and women wearing sneakers with heels in their bags rush past him, filtering out into the streets, where the faintest hint of sun starts reflecting off the shimmery asphalt and stabbing his pale green eyes even through shades. Filtering out to hell, he thinks, squinting.

Summer is the worst season to be single. For the past two months, his only option has been being a houseguest in the Hamptons, which is usually worse than staying in his apartment all weekend, especially because he stays with promoters or publicists—people who expect good press in exchange for a bed, bottomless booze, and nineteen-year-old girls in string bikinis.

At least he's not one of those guys on his way to work, one of those anonymous spokes in the spinning wheel of Manhattan. Sitting in a white office without windows and tasting the morning's deli-cart coffee well after noon, with the *tick tick tick* of the big white clock on the wall for a sound track. A continual countdown to nothing counting. It's Wednesday. He'll catch up on sleep this weekend. Only amateurs go out late on weekend nights—and Tim is not, never has been, an amateur.

At least I'm not them, he thinks again, even though his head feels as if it's leaking brain fluid. He's been working all night and he has a few notes on crumpled napkins in his jeans pocket to prove it. There's got to be a few items in there—if he can read his own handwriting. He'll feel better after a little nap, a shower, a shave, a few cigarettes. Then he'll walk the ten blocks to his desk on the twenty-second floor of a massive monolith of a skyscraper that's home to the *New York Tribune* and Column A. Its ticker outside blares news in electric red letters all day, wrapping around the office, squeezing everyone inside tight to spit out breaking news, faster and better than the red NBC ticker nearby in Rockefeller Center and the blue CNN ticker on the Time Warner building a few blocks uptown. But only the *Tribune* can boast the biggest circulation of any city tabloid. They may not always be right, but they're almost always first.

The news editors with their bulging bellies and big, fat fingers reeking of cigar smoke are always barking at Column A, pushing them to run photos of scantily clad starlets. Sex is still selling.

Column A is the city's, maybe the country's—fucking hell, Manhattan is the center of the media world, so that makes it the *world's*—premiere gossip column. Tim's number two under Charlie Rogers, who's been doing the job for almost two decades and is almost ripe enough at age forty-eight to join the short list of syndicated dinosaurs who still think Liza Minnelli and Elizabeth Taylor are worth reporting on. Which is fine by Tim, who gets to cover pretty much whatever he wants, anyway. Besides, being the guy in charge means you've got to take the fall if the lawyers call. Deal with the crunch of finding a lead item on a summer Friday at four P.M. when everyone newsworthy has fled the stinking streets to one of those beachy bullshit places.

Or at least that's what he tells people when they ask, but the truth is sometimes Tim wants something bad to happen to Charlie so he has to give up the column and Tim can save the day, showing everyone that he could do it better than anyone else if he really had to. Maybe Lyme disease or a broken pelvis. Something curable with a lot of time-consuming treatment.

In the first pale light this morning, the groaning steps leading up to Tim's apartment look dirtier than he remembered. Cigarette butts, empty beer cans, a wet trail of someone's trash trickling down to the basement. Maybe his. Tim wonders if there are any cleaning services he can convince to give him a free maid if he calls them "a celebrity cleaning service" or "maids to the stars" in his column. He can't afford a maid on his $65,000-a-year salary.

He made more money writing for a supermarket tabloid a few years ago, but no one gave him anything for free back then. They didn't return his calls or take him out to lunch at places where burgers cost twenty-five dollars, either. Back then he was bribing maids at the Plaza Hotel to let him into Michael Jackson's room. Finding out that the **Gloved One** (Tim coined that nickname, natch) had clogged his toilet with pages of a magazine. Probably porn. That made for better copy, anyway.

That job was good, but the perks are much better now. Free hotel rooms, free booze, free food, free clothes, free whatever the hell he wants. "Do you know who I am?" actually works, and that's enough to make his friends back in Maryland brag about knowing him in high school.

Tim finally opens the door to his apartment and stumbles over the dirty laundry and old newspapers on the floor. There's *got* to be a maid or a cleaning service that will barter for boldface.

Tim rifles through a stack of mail. More bills. Bills are like magazines: Just when you think you've made it through a month, a whole new batch arrives and you have to start all over again. He peels off his old T-shirt and jeans and lets them fall to the floor, where they'll stew in a rancid heap of smoke and spilled drinks for at least a week until he hauls his laundry down the street. At age thirty-one, he still can't even iron, so his dress shirts go to the cleaner's down the street—**the dry cleaner to the stars!**

He unfolds the cocktail napkins from his jeans pockets. He got decent stuff tonight. The limo driver the promoter hired to ferry around the B-list celebrities gave Tim a ride to the club opening and said a certain aged Hollywood star accused of shooting his wife pissed in the backseat of his limo rather than ask him to pull over for a bathroom. The car service quietly billed him three hundred dollars. That's pretty good, especially because the star's about to go to trial. LOATHED HOLLYWOOD LOTHARIO PISSES OFF CHAUFFEUR. Yeah, it works.

In return for the limo ride and the VIP table, the promoter just wanted a sighting of dueling starlets giving each other hostile looks at the party opening because they're still fighting over the same Hollywood heartbreaker. That kind of sighting means a hot spotlight, seducing the moths of Manhattan who will shell out $325 for a bottle of vodka if it comes with a table reservation at the club of the season.

He calls Charlie's voice mail about the lothario so Charlie can pitch it to the top editors at the eleven A.M. meeting. This way, Tim won't have to write them up until he gets to the office later this afternoon. He swallows an Ambien, washing it down with a beer, and waits for the numbness, the heaviness, that deafening cloud to descend.

Blake exhibited *excellent* self-control at the Ripe opening tonight. He only had four drinks, three lines of coke, and one cigarette, and he's home at one-thirty. Highly unusual, he thinks, almost patting himself on the back when he walks into his Gramercy Park apartment building, wishing again he didn't have a doorman. The guy is pleasant enough but Blake prefers to be the one stocking up on secrets.

Blake got an item at the club opening, which made going out worthwhile.

Tonight Blake learned that a certain boldface fashion designer was supposed to design the club's waitress uniforms, but the owner never paid her, so the waitresses just wore their own black clothes. Now the designer is suing the club owner. An item with a lawsuit is the best kind because it's the easiest to fact-check and clear with *Manhattan* magazine's lawyers. Send one of those cute fact checkers like Alison White down to the courthouse on Centre Street with a pocket full of quarters to Xerox the lawsuit. She's particularly nice to Blake because he gives her the book party invites he doesn't want. Plus, he's the only straight single guy on staff.

Blake will have no problem getting to his office by ten-thirty today, Wednesday, the day before his deadline. The day when everything has to be in decent shape. He's way ahead of the game this week, already having had his lead item confirmed, fact-checked, and copyedited:

Terry Barlow says her new monthly magazine, *Four Weeks*, has been flying off the newsstands. "Our first three issues sold out in every major city," she chirped at a recent lunch she hosted for **Amos Stone Fallow**'s new political novel, *Right Here Right Now*, attended by **Bill Clinton, Kareena Gore Schiff**, and **Salman Rushdie**. However, a company report that will be published next week states that Ms. Barlow's magazine has sold only 25 percent of the ads that its publisher projected. An inside source who leaked the report also tells *Manhattan* magazine that Ms. Barlow's backers may be cutting off her financing as soon as next month if the numbers don't improve. Ms. Barlow's publicist, **Howard Rubenstein**, insists all is well. *"Four Weeks* had the most critically acclaimed launch in recent history," he says. "My client looks forward to building up the brand with a commitment to quality over quantity."

Last year, Terry staffed *Four Weeks* by raiding *Manhattan* magazine's masthead—which means Blake's editors are particularly drunk with Schadenfreude. Plus, divulging Terry's alleged big failure is yet another way to embarrass his dad. He and his new wife, Lindsay, have been dinner-party friends of Terry's ever since she listed them as one of the city's power couples in a special holiday-entertaining issue at her previous magazine. Everyone's got a reason for being in the gossip game, but unlike Blake, no one ever uses the power of the press—and it is power—to strike back at a father who never, ever thinks his son is good enough. It makes perfect sense to Blake and all his shrinks.

The other five items for his column are pretty much set—he's just got to call a few publicists who won't comment. He needs to wait as long as possible to call them, though, until around five P.M. tomorrow, so the publicists won't tip off a daily with their own spin if they don't like the item. Blake's column closes Thursday night, and while for hourly incrementing fees he can make changes up until around 1:30 P.M. on Friday, that still gives a big window for a daily to get a spun version of Blake's item before *Manhattan* magazine is published on Monday. However, any seasoned flack knows that giving one columnist's gossip to another is a surefire way to get blacklisted. Still, if Blake thinks he's being fucked with, he checks it out with Tim, who always warns Blake if he needs to come up with a backup item so he doesn't have to do the Friday-morning scramble, begging everyone in the office for quickly confirmable news and driving his fact checkers crazy.

If he does get scooped by someone else, most likely the indefatigable Robin Pearce at the *Daily Metro*, he's usually prepared and filed in the system a backup item from PETA about plans to throw more red paint at a fashionable celebrity for wearing fur or to run some new ad campaign. Those PETA publicists can be a gossip columnist's best friends during emergencies, even if their items are predictable and self-serving. A backup for the PETA backup is usually from the Learning Annex, which has an aggressive president who always wants to sell more tickets to lectures by people like Donald Trump, so he leaks little things, like which speakers have sold the least tickets.

Blake's been writing *Manhattan* magazine's gossip column for three years and it's all his. By now he knows the basic tricks of the trade. Gossip columnists write about a new nightclub opening and never have to pay for drinks there. They sprinkle a fashion designer's name in a column just twice and get to borrow a four-thousand-dollar suit or gown to better blend in at a five-thousand-dollar-a-plate benefit. To help out Broker A, the gossip columnist may report the $20 million contract Broker A's nemesis at a competing realty firm, Broker B, just got signed for a Fifth Avenue duplex—*before* the buyer meets the co-op board. When the buyer inevitably gets rejected (boards hate learning about potential new neighbors from the columns), Broker A slides in to save the day, selling the buyer a pricier condo. But, of course, Broker A officially declines comment. The day after the item comes out, Broker B invites the columnist out for lunch to make sure the game works in her favor next time.

The most important trick he's learned is glamorization: If you compare someone to an attractive movie star, he or she tends to forgive you. Everyone wants to be pretty and famous. Rich tends to be a bonus track if you've already got the other two working for you. For example, if he writes that a sixty-year-old socialite's husband is leaving her for his twenty-something secretary and describes the socialite as a "dead ringer for Lauren Hutton," the socialite may even become a society source and feed Blake future items to embarrass her ex.

The column is probably the only thing Blake's earned by himself, and it's definitely the only way he has any kind of power over his dad, a Wall Street financier who thinks he and his friends should only be mentioned in the press at birth, marriage, and death. His mother used to know more celebrities, back when his parents were still married, but now she only attends fund-raisers for diseases. His dad got the arts in the divorce. "Diseases have more straight single men, anyway," his mother says. Even with a very big divorce settlement, including a full-floor apartment in a very good building on Fifth Avenue, wealthy uptown women over fifty have a hard time attracting male partners unless the men are in debt or they're gay, with careers that benefit from party-picture exposure.

Gossip is also the only thing Blake has ever done well besides exercise excellent manners, which is more than a little ironic since gossip is anything but polite. Maybe it was his proper upbringing, with Emily Post's manifesto on his bedroom bookshelf, but Blake just knows things, things like sending a hostess flowers the day *after* her dinner party rather than arriving with them (so she doesn't have to fuss with vases and placement during the party) and always writing swift thank-you notes on heavy personalized stationery.

Blake also has perfect eyesight and hearing, but his attention to detail and fact checking, his rarely reporting anything false, means his column is often dull. Too often, Blake figures out that a juicy item is only half true— not true enough for the magazine's lawyers or his fact checkers, especially Alison White—just before it goes to print.

"Trust your instincts, and if something's keeping you up at night worrying, it's probably inaccurate," is the best advice his editor, The Nerd, ever offered. In his ten years as a gossip columnist, Blake's never had to print a correction.

He quietly hangs his blue blazer in the closet and carefully places his shirt and khakis in the laundry bag for the maid his mother bankrolls. "I'm not going to be embarrassed by your mess," she told him, even though she never goes below Fifty-seventh Street. Just the idea that the doorman might think Blake lives in squalor was terrifying enough for her to dispatch her maid downtown.

Bethany thinks the maid is just another way for Blake's mother to keep an eye on him. "I don't understand why you can't hire your own maid," she says, not understanding that his trust fund is tied up in things like railroads and real estate, things she can't use to buy clothes at Barneys. She only knows he gets a big chunk of it when he gets married.

He opens the bedroom door and sees Bethany sound asleep in the big antique bed. She looks tiny, even helpless, enveloped in the thick white comforter, her silky black hair streaked out on the white pillows. He would have had much more luck with one of the cokehead mattresses tonight. If he even tries to kiss her, she'll probably make him sleep on the couch. Still, it's comforting to come home to a warm body in an air-conditioned bedroom. He's an only child and has spent much of his life alone, if you don't count his roommates at boarding school and college.

The bathroom light hits the antique emerald cut diamond set in white gold on Bethany's engagement finger, sending the slightest shiver across the dark wood floor. Her eyelids flutter as if dreams are skating over the black ice of her irises. That's the thing about Bethany. Everything about her looks positively exquisite in the right light. She is the most beautiful woman he's ever dated, and that beauty is another addiction—until she starts being a bitch.

He's been with Bethany for two years. Their mothers are friends from sitting on all the right boards together (Memorial Sloan-Kettering, the New York City Ballet), but Bethany's parents are the opposite of Blake's. Her parents have belonged to the right clubs for decades (the Maidstone, the River Club, the Atlantic Golf Club) and have the right addresses (Southampton, Palm Beach, Park Avenue), but the family fortune is almost gone. If they still owned the castles, they wouldn't be able to heat them. Blake's father, however, earned his fortune the old-fashioned way: through workaholism and the "never enough" disorder perennially plaguing Manhattan's most alpha residents. In New York you have to be extra careful what you wish for. Chances are you'll get it—just as soon as you start wanting something else, something more, instead.

"You're a perfect merger," his mother likes to say about him and Bethany, and it's probably the only idea Blake ever had that she approved of. Sometimes the relationship is too much pressure, but the task of ending it and starting something new is just too daunting. He can only get his trust fund when he marries. Plus, after a night like tonight, watching Tim test out the mattresses, Blake can't help feeling virtuous by coming home to Bethany.

He likes the way Bethany takes the attention off of him when they're out at parties, so he can keep asking instead of answering questions—perhaps the most important social skill any good gossip columnist learns—and more than that, the way other men look at him as if he must be *somebody* when she's around.

He walks into the bathroom, which has two sinks, one for each of them. Powders and perfumes and expensive skin potions from Dr. Stanley Stahl that she uses every morning are piled on her side. His side has a toothbrush, a razor, a bar of soap. He starts the shower, waiting for the room to get steamy. He's got to wash off the smell of smoke and desperation. He studies his reflection. Tim may be more attractive, but Blake's got more hair. He pushes his sandy-blond mop away from his eyes. Most important, Blake's rich, and rich is something Tim will never be.

Kate may have finally had a good night's sleep after passing out when she got home from the Ripe opening, but the hangover wasn't worth it. Each strand of hot sun through her window feels like a poison dart pricking between her eyes.

"Rough day at the office?" asks Nick. He's holding a glass of water and a bottle of Advil.

Kate opens her eyes enough to see the digital clock on her nightstand informing her that it's 8:30 A.M.

"Where did you get that suit?" she asks. When did Nick, her friend from their freshman year at Brown, become a grown-up? He looks like he's been wearing suits to the office for years, and she can't decide if that's a good or a bad thing. She can't remember seeing him in anything but jeans and T-shirts, usually with tons of pens in his pockets that he used for drafting in his architecture classes. She should take a picture and send it to his longtime college girlfriend, Annie, who's starting Stanford Law School in the fall. Annie's been interning at a law firm in California all summer, but Nick tries to talk to her every night before he goes to sleep.

Nick spins around slowly, holding his arms out. "Pierre sent me to Barneys with his credit card. He said if I dress like a little boy, he'll pay me like a little boy."

Pierre Patois is a boldface hotelier who just hired Nick as an assistant. Nick says he wants to learn how the industry works so he can beat guys like Pierre later, after he starts his own design firm.

The loft, a recently converted warehouse that they share, is above a hookah lounge and across the street from a jail, which explains the relatively reasonable rent. Because they're rarely home, it will take them months to figure out that the lounge keeps Egyptian music vibrating through the floors until two A.M. almost every night. But the ceilings are high and the brick walls have a fresh coat of white paint, so the whole place feels a little like a freshly stretched canvas.

"What should we hang on the walls?" Kate asked Nick when they moved in last month.

"Nothing," he answered. "There's too much going on in this city. We've got to give our eyes a rest. Anyway," he said, pushing the couch in the living room against the wall with the windows overlooking the river and the Manhattan skyline, "money can't buy this kind of art."

She downs three Advil with the glass of water.

"I need help," she says, slowly getting up and walking over to her closet.

Nick laughs and sits down on her bed. "You've only worked two parties and already you've got a drinking problem?"

"No, much worse. I have to cover my first society luncheon today, and I have nothing to wear. Zoe's gotten too skinny on Ritalin for me to borrow her stuff. And she threw out everything in my size so she wouldn't have what she called a fat part of her closet."

Kate examines her cramped closet, wishing something perfect were hidden between all the outfits that seem to scream out *college*. Everything looks wrong, especially the two-hundred-dollar navy suit her mom helped her pick out at J. Crew. Zoe had nixed it for the big *Examiner* interview— "unless you want to be someone's assistant."

"You should start making friends with fashion designers," Nick says.

"I'll put that on my to-do list today," she says. That's probably how every- one else in the office manages to look so stylish on their paltry salaries.

Kate throws the navy suit in the back of her closet and pulls on her white button-down blouse with the small hole in the elbow. She steps into the same black pants she wore yesterday, hoping no one notices. Nick doesn't look away while she changes. They've known each other long enough that they may as well be siblings. He's also been happily dating Annie for so long, Kate has ceased to think of him as a sexual being. He's more like a brother with very good taste and judgment.

He walks over and pushes up her sleeve to hide the hole. "Better boring than trashy. And don't worry, all black pants look the same."

"Thanks a lot," she says, heading into the bathroom. She washes her face and brushes her teeth but the hangover hammers on. Kate doesn't have time to try to tame her hair, so she throws her hair up in a barrette, wishing again it would just behave like Zoe's perfectly straight, shiny black mane.

Zoe often calls Kate monochromatic because her light brown hair and eyes and skin all blend together like one big cup of pale coffee.

"You could smuggle yourself in somewhere carrying manila envelopes," Zoe says.

But maybe it's something about that chameleon coloring that has always pushed Kate to want to be noticed and included.

People always wanted Kate around, always wanted to tell her things.

Things often better left unsaid. But as soon as they told her, they'd beg, "Don't tell anyone," knowing she would. They knew she was a natural gossip, but they liked that she cared about the most intimate details of their lives. She could quickly find out anything with just a little targeted research and the knowledge of which questions to ask when. Kate learned quickly that getting any good answer sometimes just takes warming up.

What she never told anyone was that she loved having this power over people. With just a few words, she could embarrass or anoint a friend or enemy. It was addictive and useful. Growing up, Kate was very popular and a little feared, but the pool was never really deep enough.

At Brown, Kate started meeting people from Manhattan, D.C., Boston, L.A. People with expensive cars and summer homes and familiar last names. The children of actors and politicians and glamorous heirs to unglamorous industry fortunes who would arrive on campus by helicopter or in chauffeured BMW sedans. She even briefly dated the son of a prince of a country that no longer had a monarchy, but she still imagined herself getting married one day in a castle, wearing a century-old diamond tiara— until he dumped her for a freshman. It was an early lesson in being careful about what she wished for.

Kate opens up her Chanel compact and blots her face with the powder, then adds lip gloss from Ripe's goodie bag for good measure.

No particular feature of Kate's face is beautiful but each adds up to a nice picture. Still, whenever people tell Kate she's pretty (and people are always telling Kate that she is pretty), she thinks she sounds like something packaged in a factory without windows. No one calls her beautiful or sexy. Just *pretty*.

She picks up her black canvas handbag, which suddenly feels bulky, even though she only packed a pen, her wallet, and a new cell phone. She's probably going to need one of those sleek bags with an expensive logo and endangered-reptile skin. She's probably going to need a whole lot more just to fit in with this job.

On her walk to the subway, she stops by the newsstand, which has become part of her daily ritual, along with getting a medium coffee with skim milk at the coffee cart. Ever since Kate explained to the newsstand guy, Joe, that she's a reporter for the *Examiner*—he couldn't figure out why she bought so many papers every day—he's been calling her Brenda Starr. Kate had to look up the reference and found the old newspaper cartoon about an intrepid reporter. (That's when she learned that you only bold-face people who are alive.) Joe doesn't seem to care that Kate is not glamorous or a redhead, like the cartoon's inspiration, Rita Hayworth. Details are distracting.

The leading man of Brenda's love life was the dashing Basil St. John, a man with an eye patch and a mysterious illness that could be cured only with a serum taken from black orchids growing in the Amazon jungle. Joe always asks Kate if she's found her Basil yet.

"Still hunting," she says, today same as every day.

Tim wonders if he can wear his sunglasses inside the office. Would anyone notice, really? He's still riding high from that scoop he got about the Loathed Hollywood Lothario pissing in the back of a limo, which the news desk teased on the *Tribune*'s cover a week ago. But he can't stretch out that currency longer than a week because there was a slight problem with his big lead item yesterday. Unfortunately, **Latina Lovely Jennifer Lopez** wasn't trying to hide her bump from the paparazzi while lunching at the Ivy.

"Do you just make this shit up?" screamed her manager, who's already switched allegiances to Robin. Robin's column Daily Dish, in the *Daily Metro* tabloid, had a big pretty photo of J.Lo's ass today.

Tim should probably try to report out a tip he got last night about the society pet plastic surgeon Stanley Stahl trying to get his friends to invest in a new skin cream he developed to fade scars. The FDA has yet to give him approval, but he's already building up stock in his publicly traded cosmetics company and the lunching ladies all swear he's some kind of shaman. Even Tim's mom raved for weeks about the $125 bottle of moisturizer Stahl makes, which Tim gave her from a Hampton party gift bag.

"He's going to look like a saint for helping burn victims and kids after serious surgery," whispered a loose-lipped socialite at the benefit Tim stopped by last night. Stahl was the chairman of the event, a fund-raiser to help bring dental surgery to kids of Third World nations. "But he's really just going to make millions from all his face-lift and boob-job clients."

"How about making an appearance before noon?" Charlie, his boss, asks when Tim sits down at his desk, deciding he should take off the shades so the interns don't look at him like he's a serial killer. They stopped being friendly when he started calling them show ponies because they preen around in miniskirts. *Clippity clop clop.* Are the interns still in high school or something? And why can't they make themselves useful by helping him spell Scarlett Johansson's name right just once? At least they know enough to tell Charlie's wife that he's in a meeting whenever she calls in the morning because he didn't make it home the night before.

Tim knows he's late when the sports guys who sit next to the gossip pod ask if Charlie and Tim want to get in on the lunch order, and today is no exception.

"We're ordering pizza, you want one?" asks the baseball reporter. Tim shakes his head. Digesting food seems too challenging right now. At least there's no birthday cake in the office today. There is nothing more revolting than the sports guys sticking their fingers in cheap supermarket cake that always gets smeared all over their desks. In fact, the next time someone asks Tim if he's "involved with any causes," he's going to say he's putting his charitable efforts toward a ban on cake in the office.

Charlie's going to lunch today with the *Examiner*'s resident syndicated dinosaur, a big, brassy old blonde who always wears a strand of gigantic pearls and a pink bow in her hair. Syndicated dinosaurs trademark their style. More branding. The dinosaur's name is Tiffany Gold, which Tim suspects is not her given name. Whenever she sees him she says, "Aren't we the luckieeeeeeest?" drawing out each vowel. Then she giggles like a little girl even though she's pushing seventy. But everyone returns her calls. Loyalty is the gossip columnist's gift that just keeps on giving.

Whenever there's a big marital scandal, the wife goes to Tiffany first. Likewise, any high-profile person who's about to be exposed in a potentially embarrassing light will leak the news to Tiffany in some transparent way. Usually, Tiffany will pretend to have a source who overheard a conversation at a restaurant about the situation, which naturally makes the high-profile person sound completely in control of the spin cycle. It's a cottage industry and she's the queen. She even gets subsidized by a major Wall Street financier who likes to control his gossip column mentions.

Tiffany's counterpart is Robin's boss at the *Daily Metro*, The Suckup, a silver-haired Southern dandy who favors white suits and bow ties and smokes cigars in restaurants without anyone telling him to go outside. He actually gets prominent politicians on the phone to confirm or deny rumors, and he's known for promotional interviews with the big Hollywood stars of the moment. For decades, The Suckup has been luring them—and their publicists, who happen to be his "dear old friends"—to his one-bedroom Upper East Side maisonette with a small garden for some "Southern hospitality," which often includes pitchers of mint juleps and feigned heterosexual flirting.

Tim flips through all his papers. The *Times* and the *Journal*. Boring and boring. *Women's Wear Daily*, which Tim likes to call *Weapons of Women's Destruction*. Pretty pictures of socialites who would rather be called philanthropists and who are only nice to him because they want protection or press when they decide to do something meaningful like launch a handbag line or throw a dinner party.

Reading the Daily Dish sometimes feels like a competitive sport. If they have any decent items, items that make Tim fucking mad to read, the *Tribune* editors yell at Charlie and Tim. Today's going to be a yelling day. Robin has an item about a certain **Hollywood Prince**'s young kids trying to use their dad's car service to pick up drugs on their way home from the airport. The kids said they needed to buy some "headphones." On 126th Street. Meanwhile Daddy and his new young actress bride were vacationing in the Bahamas. Tim knows Robin wrote it for The Suckup's column because the actor's publicist is not a friend of The Suckup's. And Tim is the one who introduced her to the Hollywood Prince's ex-girlfriend, who's still smarting because he ditched her for the glamorous actress. Robin swept the ex up into her orbit—knowing no one gives better items than scorned lovers—by agreeing to go to fragrance-launch parties and ladies' lunches on Madison Avenue, things Tim can't even pretend to care about even though he should, because that's how you get the good stuff.

He doesn't feel like answering his phone yet, so he lets the calls go straight to voice mail while he searches online for cheap fares to somewhere as far away as he can afford. Anywhere people speak English. Tim barely passed high-school Spanish and he doesn't want to go anywhere he can't eavesdrop. Australia. New Zealand. The Canary Islands. Gibraltar. Today there's a deal on American Airlines: $920 round-trip to Sydney, which is about six hundred dollars more than he has in his bank account.

The phone won't stop ringing and now it's one P.M. Time to get the day rolling. He's got no choice, so he picks up the next call and instantly regrets it. A publicist asking if Tim is going to a party at Bergdorf's feting a coffee-table book about accessories next week.

"Send me your headshot!" Tim yells before hanging up. Charlie cackles but doesn't look up from his computer. Store parties are the worst. Particularly if the publicist is running a company on Daddy's credit card and connections.

Their editor, whom they call Tubby, waddles over eating a doughnut he picked up from the sports section's pod. They have at least one box delivered every morning, which holds the guys over until the inevitable cake in the afternoon. Powdered sugar spills down Tubby's shirt, which is stretched across his bulging belly. Between bites, Tubby announces that from now on, they're only allowed to mention a certain blond model/actress from a famous literary family if they call her svelte or sexy. Her lawyers are threatening to sue because Column A keeps chronicling her yo-yo weight and calling her the **Plus-Sized Pinup**.

"It's not our fault she porked out," says Tim, and Charlie cackles again.

Tubby clears his voice loudly. He's not laughing.

Charlie purses his lips and looks down at his computer. "No problem."

sing for your supper

Blake closes his column at seven P.M. on Thursday night, staying an extra hour to make sure his editor, The Nerd, doesn't add any detail that could reveal the source on his item about Victor Goll smoking a joint with a powerful politician's daughter under a table at a fashion designer's birthday party. Blake barely caught a fuck-up on the proofs. The Nerd had changed "according to a source" to "according to a witness" to give the item more gravitas. Blake had to run over to the copy department to change it back on the proofs just minutes before they were shipped off to the printer.

Only a few people could have been the witness who told Blake about the joint, which means if he hadn't fixed it, he'd have to screen his calls on Monday morning when the magazine hits the newsstands. Then he'd have to fire off an apology e-mail to the source (the fashion designer, who would most likely never have the politician's photogenic daughter in the front row again) with plenty of flattery and promises of future press and party pictures to keep the source loyal. Or he'd accidentally answer the phone and have to listen to the yelling, the bullshit, the begging.

"I can't take back what's already in print," he'll say. "But I promise to make it up to you." And they usually call in that promise when they have something stupid they need to promote or hide. But sometimes they switch loyalties and you know right away what you're missing when you read it in a competing column. Blake's been writing his column long enough that he can read almost any gossip column in town and know who's talking to whom. Robin got that Hollywood Prince item yesterday from the actor's psycho ex, whom only Robin can tolerate kissing up to. Tim must be pissed.

Blake's already forty-five minutes late to his father's dinner party, but he takes a little more time to sift through next week's invitations and wait for the Sudafed to start clearing his sinuses. (Whenever he sniffles through dinner, his dad shoots him hostile looks.) Blake gets his favorite fact checker, Alison White, to sort the invitations into different files for each day and lets her RSVP herself to anything she wants to attend, which is usually just boring book parties or literary readings. There's never enough room to write down all the details in his desk calendar, including who's supposed to be coming and which publicist to call to get the gift bag sent over before the party so he doesn't have to carry it around all night if there's something decent in it.

He crumples up an invitation for a party tonight at Bergdorf's. Since when are there coffee-table books about accessories? The invitation has a long list of hosts who love seeing their name in print, even if it's just an invitation. People like Courtney and Edward Schaffer, who constantly invite him to their events and send him boxes of their company's bags every season, which he gives to his maid and his doorman. The Schaffers are one of those New York couples who say they need to be out every night for "work," but they really just don't want to be home alone with each other. They say they never stay at events past eleven o'clock because they need to get home to their son, but what they really need is beauty rest for the next night's pictures. Plus, they know that the photographers tend to stick around only for an hour or so after arrivals.

Today Blake got a white orchid from Courtney Schaffer for running her picture this week. He sends her a thank-you note and keeps the potted plant in the shopping bag to bring home as a gift to Bethany.

deborah schoeneman

"If your girlfriend called the florist, she'd know you didn't buy it," says Alison, always a stickler for facts, walking by his desk at the end of the day.

"Good thinking," he says, removing the sticker with the florist's name from the cellophane wrapping. "Thanks."

Now he's close to an hour late, which is not going to go over well, especially if he blames it on the actor Victor Goll. Blake's father, Steven Bradley, actually has a few famous friends, but Goll is not among them. His dad is friends with people like Dan Aykroyd and Michael Douglas, actors who offer themselves up for lunch on the auction block at the Waldorf to raise money for cancer or Alzheimer's or whatever's the fashionable disease these days. He tells them that his son is a journalist for *Manhattan* magazine without uttering the word *gossip*, as if Blake just wrote features.

Just before the cab pulls up to his dad's building on the corner of Fifth Avenue and Seventy-fourth Street, Blake is tempted to tell the driver to keep driving. Maybe he could find a nice bench in the park and order takeout Chinese. Unapologetically slurp greasy noodles and devour sticky spareribs. He takes a deep breath. At least Bethany's already there to diffuse the attention away from Blake. It's probably the best reason for having a girlfriend.

Blake leaves the orchid with the doorman and tries to make conversation with the elevator operator, who's hired to wear a stiff uniform and push buttons as if the task were beneath the residents.

"It's a hot summer," Blake says, even though it's no different from any year.

"Yes. Lovely." The response probably works for most of the operator's brief conversations. He must hate me, Blake thinks.

The elevator climbs up to the eighth floor and opens up to his dad's foyer, where there's a new big mirror shaped like a lightning bolt, which could very well be the ugliest thing Lindsay's ever convinced his dad to buy during one of their shopping sprees. She keeps encouraging him to buy art made in the sixties to go with the aesthetic she's obsessed with.

Blake tries to make himself a little more presentable. He folds a hand-kerchief so it's square in his pocket and smooths his hair out of his eyes. He'd like to go to the bathroom to wash his face and hands, cleaning off the deadline-day grime of lunch and ink and sweat, but he has no idea where the bathroom is on this floor. His dad bought the duplex penthouse for $7 million last year and then ended up marrying his thirty-four-year-old decorator, Lindsay. Blake has always suspected she made every choice while plotting the merger—particularly the yoga studio, since his dad thinks yoga is "for the lazy."

Before Lindsay, his dad was into old-world charm. Dark wood book-shelves, heavy red velvet curtains, and antique crystal chandeliers used to be his aesthetic, but now it's all sleek and modern, full of Lindsay's hard edges and bright colors.

About twenty people are having drinks in the living room and Blake sticks by the bar. He can't really understand what anyone is talking about. It's as if he's watching a foreign movie without subtitles. He's not sure if he can talk to anyone about anything but celebrities. He overhears two of his father's friends talking about how much they liked a new Hollywood action movie starring one of the mascots, and he feels depressed. He can no longer separate art from life, and it's a real fucking bummer for his spare time. No new book or movie or restaurant or play is safe from the smear of secrets.

Instead of mingling, he downs a scotch and watches Bethany describe her new line of chandelier earrings to one of Lindsay's new clients. She looks up and waves to Blake but continues talking.

Blake needs to apologize for being late. "I was on deadline," he walks over and tells his father, who's standing with two golf buddies, swapping stories about breaking Ivy League varsity sports records. As usual, his father is wearing his uniform of a black suit, a white shirt, and a Hermès tie.

"Is this new?" Blake asks about the Jim Dine collage hanging on the wall, which looks like it could have been pasted together by a kindergartner.

"It's new and very important," says his father, biting into the lemon garnish from his gin-and-tonic and wincing. His father clenches his jaw, muttering something about how you should work late only if you're well compensated. One of the golf guys asks Blake what he was working on.

"He writes for *Manhattan* magazine," says Blake's father quickly, after shooting Blake a steely look. Blake finishes off his second scotch instead of saying anything.

Without even a short pause, his father switches the subject to the new golf pro at the club. Business as usual. Blake decides to find the bathroom for just a little bump to put him in the mood for small talk, but he quickly gets cornered by spacey Grace Miller, Zoe's mother, and Bunny Frank, a socialite who inexplicably wears her blond hair sprayed up and flared back from her face. Sometimes Blake thinks he should just do her a favor and tell her to give the roots a rest. But maybe that's a job for the society publicist she (and most of her clan) hire to ensure regular appearances.

Blake has a sneaking suspicion that Lindsay keeps Bunny around just to feel good about herself since she's thinner and richer, perhaps even smarter. And has better hair. Having Grace around probably makes Lindsay feel pretty good, too. Grace is friendly with Blake's mom and must report back to her about what a perfect hostess Lindsay is.

Grace is already slurring her words and spilling her martini on the new vintage Pucci carpet. She manages to ask Blake if he's met Kate.

"Please show her the ropes," says Grace, and Blake wonders if Grace or her husband helped Kate get the job. He fails to get any TV scoop out of Grace even though her husband, Jack, runs one of the biggest networks. They probably have separate bedrooms, anyway. Blake has heard on more than a few occasions that Jack's having an affair with one of his network's newscasters, but running that item wouldn't be worth losing his sources at the network. Plus, it's a good piece of gossip to hold over his dad. The two men have been close friends since Princeton, where Blake also managed to graduate, thanks to a few generous family donations to the university.

"Blake, my dear," says Bunny, coming in for the kill. "I'm just dying to talk to you about the Alzheimer Gala at the Waldorf in a few months. I'm the chairwoman this year," she says, beaming. But then, like an actor cued for a dramatic scene, she starts telling Blake all about how her grandmother, her *nanna*, died of Alzheimer's, but she always remembered Bunny. The tears roll down Bunny's cheeks and the makeup doesn't even smudge.

"Blake, my dear," she says again. "Please let me take you to lunch at Cipriani next week so we can talk more about my charity work. Maybe it's time for *Manhattan* magazine to do a big story on the city's most influential philanthropists?" She must really want her picture in the magazine to justify her perfectly positioned but pointless existence, Blake thinks. She smiles, dabbing away her tears, and Blake excuses himself and finally goes to the bathroom. He does a bump of coke off his key and splashes cold water on his face. Then he calls in reinforcement.

"SOS," he tells Tim over his cell phone. "If you pick me up in an hour, I'll pay for the cabs and drinks all night. And I've got an eight ball burning a hole in my blazer."

"Way to bury the lede," says Tim. "I'll be right over."

Later, when the doorman interrupts dinner to announce Tim's arrival, Lindsay invites him up, while Blake's father walks over and puts his hands on his son's shoulders, digging into the flesh a little.

"I can't believe your friend ran that item about Stanley Stahl," hisses Blake's father in a voice that sounds like a hiss.

In the centerpiece's candlelight, Blake notices that his dad has dark circles under his eyes. Blake knew the Stahl item was going to come up, since Stanley and his father have been on the same charity boards for years, and they sometimes play golf together in Southampton.

Lindsay claps her hands together in delight when Tim walks in, looking as if he'd rather be trapped at the Bergdorf party tonight.

"Let's play the blind-item game!" Lindsay trills, perhaps overcompensating for the few guests, namely the Wall Street guys, who get particularly uneasy whenever they come across anyone who writes for a gossip column.

The last thing they need is their wife or the IRS to know what they're up to. Even press on a promotion could backfire.

"I love the blind-item game!" echoes Bunny in the same high voice Lindsay just used. "And I've never been lucky enough to play it with a professional!"

At least once a week, Column A publishes a salacious item they call blind because they leave out the person's name so they won't get sued or cut off from a potentially good source who will be thankful enough not to get named.

Blake looks at Tim and shrugs as he sits down next to Lindsay, who's frantically patting a chair where she wants Tim to sit, as if he were a show poodle.

Tim wonders how much he could get if he auctioned himself off at one of those benefits under the category "Tabloid Dinner Entertainment." These assholes might even pay a grand. Tim recognizes a few well-coiffed women from the pages of *Weapons of Mass Destruction*. They're all complaining about having to come into Manhattan from the Hamptons, where they "summer," to see their husbands during the week. Tim wonders if they know that their husbands are probably all having midweek affairs with their yoga instructors, personal trainers, summer associates, or cocktail waitresses.

"The traffic is unbearable," explains Juliette Reed, a brittle-thin woman sitting next to her husband, Mark, who was just on the cover of *Forbes* for making millions selling his wireless-technology company. "But you wouldn't understand."

Tim decides he'll punish Juliette for that snooty statement and never mention her fucking fancy charity for kids allergic to peanuts again in Column A. He motions for the Filipino waiter to bring more wine. If anyone asks about the Stanley Stahl item, Tim will blame Charlie. "My editor" is the easiest scapegoat.

Tim takes another sip of wine. At least the game is easier than chitchat, he thinks when Lindsay motions for him to start.

In his best game-show voice, Tim asks, "Which publicist was recently fired from a big corporate account for openly snorting lines of coke at a Bridgehampton polo match with a certain hard-partying heiress?"

Bunny and Lindsay trip over each other's words, trying to guess first. Everyone knows who the hotel heiress is—who else could it be?—but there are three different answers for the publicist.

"I can't say who it is," says Tim, smiling wickedly. "But Lindsay's not wrong."

"More! More! More!" yells Lindsay, clapping her hands together.

Woof! Woof! Woof! Tim almost shouts.

Blake offers up an item that was killed last week by lawyers for both *Manhattan* magazine and the *Tribune* because the subject is a valuable advertiser. "Which Italian fashion diva jetted into New York this week to have an emergency nose job after her already-altered nose collapsed after a little too much cocaine?"

Lindsay gets it first, prompting Blake's dad to mutter, "I don't know if I should be proud or embarrassed."

Lindsay kisses him on the lips. "Proud! I do due diligence on all my designer investments!"

Blake's dad looks as if he swallowed his lemon garnish.

Dessert is individual fancy fruit tarts that look flawless enough for Tim to wonder if they've been shellacked. At Tim's mom's house they usually just polish off ice cream cartons for dessert. Here, the women take no more than a bite out of their desserts, leaving the rest for their husbands, who seem to consider the task just another tax on being married to someone expensive. When Tim spots Mark Reed digging into his wife's dessert, Mark says, "Don't print this in Column A." Self-important prick.

Tim takes a big bite of his tart before dispatching his next blind item:

"Which former *New York Tribune* columnist, who happens to be the daughter of a major mobster, used to sit on the toilet in a stall in the only women's bathroom, smoking cigarettes and talking on her cell phone?" he asks. No one has any idea. Mobsters are not on their ladder. Blake gets it.

"More! More! More!" yells Lindsay, clapping again.

Woof! Woof! Woof!

Last night Kate went out for drinks with Justin Katz, her old editor at the college newspaper, to celebrate surviving a month on the job. Justin, who's now a tech reporter for the *Wall Street Journal,* knows Lacey, and he helped Kate get the job after graduation in May by putting in a good word.

"But I don't want to be a gossip columnist," she said back then. Her mother is a social worker and her father is a civil rights lawyer. They left Manhattan in 1975 for Woodstock. What would they think?

"Just get your foot in the door. The rest is just a popularity contest for the first few years," he said. "And at least you'll get to go to good parties. The most glamorous thing I do is eat lunch at the Four Seasons."

He asked Kate to meet him at a bar near his office. "I can't be far from my desk," he says. "We don't close the late edition for another few hours and a big tech merger may be announced." His cell phone and BlackBerry hum like mosquitoes while they order drinks. She follows his lead in ordering a dirty martini, because it seems like a grown-up thing to do.

"You better be my first media source," she says after the drinks arrive. She can't stop herself from grimacing after a small sip. He laughs and orders her a glass of white wine.

"That would be like insider trading," he says.

What's the point of having well-connected friends like Justin and her roommate, Nick, if they don't help with items? At what point do people trust you enough to trade secrets even if the secret doesn't immediately help them? Kate's not sure how she's going to figure it out, and she has to stop herself a few times from taking notes while Justin's talking about his job. He's trying to get an interview with Stanley Stahl, a plastic surgeon who was just mentioned in Column A for getting his friends to invest in a new skin cream before he had the FDA approval to market it.

"I have a feeling this guy's going down," says Justin. "But he won't talk."

Kate wonders if she should try to get an item out of this, but she doesn't even know where she'd start, other than with people she knows who are already working on the story, which only makes her feel more competitive. It's not just about breaking stories, it's about beating the competition.

After they've had just one drink the *Journal*'s news desk editor calls Justin to say news of the merger was coming across the AP wires. He heads back to the office quickly to avoid getting scooped by the *New York Times*'s Web site. Kate doubts Paul would ever call her this late about, say, a pending celebrity divorce or a club opening, and she can't help but feel a little envious that Justin is the kind of journalist with real power, someone who can move markets rather than just mollify publicists and keep the socialites in the party pictures. If she were an investigative reporter, she would get these kinds of calls. Calls you have to apologize for taking during dinner even while they make you feel a little smug about being important enough to be getting them.

Instead, she calls Zoe to help her finish off the fresh round of drinks and appetizers they had just ordered before Justin's call. Zoe, who happens to be around the corner on a blind date, is glad to be of service.

"Consider it a double rescue mission," says Zoe, who has spent the past few hours with "yet another single Jewish mama's boy who lives on the Upper West Side and considers himself a real catch."

Kate gets home early enough to read in bed, but now she reads magazines instead of books. Most of the monthly magazines tend to have similar features and they're all starting to blur together. She's just got a dark red Persian carpet she found in her parents' attic for color. She hasn't had any time to get shelves, so her books—mostly crime fiction and anthologies of great magazine journalism—are stacked on the floor.

Paul told Kate she needs to read pretty much every newspaper and magazine that comes out each day to make sure she's not pitching items that have already been reported. Tonight she's got a big stack to plow through. Fortunately, Nick's not home to distract her. He's visiting Annie in California for a long weekend.

A few weeks ago, Kate asked Lacey, the column editor, how she gets through all that reading every day. Lacey advised Kate to just read the headlines and bylines and scan the first few paragraphs, where the news is. "The rest just catches you up." But Kate already feels behind, struggling to catch up on names and faces and terms like *flack,* which she just learned means a publicist. A lede is the first sentence or paragraph of a story, but a lead item is the first of the items that fill a column. If only the job came with a manual.

"And you only have to read book reviews," added Lacey, who usually wears her white-blond hair back in a tight ponytail that pulls the corners of her eyes up as if she were being dragged around on marionette strings. Kate has yet to see Lacey wear the same coat or even carry the same bag more than once. It seems as if everyone at the *Examiner* is secretly rich. There's even an office myth about a fact checker, the heir to a real-estate empire, who never cashed his paychecks.

Kate gets through *Vanity Fair* before falling asleep, so when she answers Paul's phone the next morning, she recognizes the caller's name from her byline on a big investigative story about a murder in Hollywood and its prime suspect, whom Column A has been calling the Loathed Hollywood Lothario.

"Could you tell him Eve called?" the caller asks. "And who are you? I love getting to know Paul's deputies." Eve doesn't use the word *assistant* or *legs,* which makes Kate feel a little taller.

"How about I take you out to lunch and the Manolo Blahnik sample sale next Friday?" Eve asks her.

"He has a sample sale?"

"Honey, no one pays retail."

Even if the five-hundred-dollar pairs of strappy sandals were reduced by 70 percent, she still couldn't afford them, much less walk in them.

Lacey whips around the corner, walking impossibly quickly in her four-inch-heel black boots. "Eve, right?" she says, and Kate nods. "Stay away from her." Her gold bracelets jangle as she starts to talk excitedly with her hands.

"Sure, she's a great fucking writer—probably the best at the seduce-and-destroy game," says Lacey, her speech sounding rehearsed. "She can pry secrets out of anyone. But she tries to befriend every one of Paul's assistants and always offers them sample sales or access. She's dated pretty much every eligible bachelor in New York who's now married, but she's still single and in love with Paul. She almost got Paul's last assistant fired last year by convincing her to reveal Paul's New Year's Eve plans. Eve actually tried to crash his dinner party at Le Cirque, which Paul's wife was less than thrilled about. Eve was so drunk she had to be escorted out by Sirio, who then leaked the whole fiasco to Column A."

"Sirio?" asks Kate.

"Kate," Lacey sighs, hard enough for her bracelets to faintly jangle again. "Sirio Maccioni is the owner of Le Cirque." Kate is not sure when restaurateurs became celebrities and column fodder. "You have to read the gossip columns every day. You have to keep up. Sirio is an easy one. I think he and Donald Trump check in with Column A almost every day."

"What do you mean? People actually call in items about themselves?"

"All the time," says Lacey, inspecting her flawless pale-pink manicure. "So does the entire Hilton family, especially Paris and Nicky's mother. And then she gets mad whenever anyone writes about her daughters misbehaving, as if that weren't the tax on the attention. As if getting big in Japan were just something you got just for subsisting on Red Bull. That's exactly why you shouldn't feel guilty writing about them." She puts her hand on her waist. "They should be thanking us."

Kate answers Paul's phone again and has to pull it away from her ear so she can understand the screeching woman on the other end. "Tell Paul I'm begging for the picture! My knees are bleeding!" a very high-pitched voice yells. "Bleeding!"

Besides writing a gossip column, Paul edits the party picture page, a weekly collage of shiny, smiling New Yorkers who usually hit at least one party a night primarily to get their photo snapped by Patricia Cullen. She gives the *Examiner* first dibs in picking pictures and then services the rest to pretty much every other publication without a staff photographer.

The screecher continues, without pausing to identify herself, "Tell him I let him go to whatever he wants. Plus-one! And now I need this!"

Kate wonders how to turn down the volume on the phone. Maybe she should get one of those headsets, even though Lacey said it makes you look like a telephone operator.

Paul walks by Kate's desk to hand her today's stack of invitations and hears the screeching through her phone. "Meg?" he asks, and Kate shrugs. She has no idea. He takes the receiver out of her hand.

"Meg, stop yelling at Kate," he says, taking his free hand to rub his temple. "Just stop yelling altogether." He listens for a few moments and then says, "Okay, Meg. Whatever you want."

Kate remembers Lacey and Paul advising her to never cave to publicists, that "they need us more than we need them." Kate gives him a quizzical look.

"When it comes to Meg Steiner," he says, hanging up the phone, "resistance is futile."

"But that doesn't mean she always gets what she wants," Lacey yells out from her adjacent office. "We still printed that she traded Stanley Stahl *Star Wars* premiere tickets for free Botox treatments!"

Meg Steiner keeps calling Blake on his cell phone even though she knows he hates that. He's not going to run an item about her lackluster movie screening. There's too much real news this week and he's still punishing her for her behavior at his dad's and Lindsay's wedding. When they were taking vows, Meg whispered a little too loudly to her date, "It should be for richer or richer." And she never gives him any good items. She saves her best gossip for Paul Peterson at the *Examiner*, though she pretends that she's above gossiping. But Blake knows her clients like to see their names and faces in the *Examiner*, so she plays the favor game with Paul. Meg's also harassing Blake because she's been cut off from Column A for lying about her ex-boyfriend's affair with a married Kennedy and, worse, for letting Robin Pearce at the *Daily Metro* get that scoop. Tim and Charlie are enjoying torturing her and it's clearly making her nervous. Her reputation has been destroyed too many times to matter, but her livelihood is another story, especially because skinny publicists with Column A monikers (Andrea Hoffman, **Spinster**; Bessie Gordon, **Bottle Blonde**) are encroaching on territory Meg's been guarding for more than two decades. No one can do anything forever, even if it takes ten years to do anything well.

Blake takes a walk around the office, pausing at Alison White's desk. She has the facts she's checking for next week's issue highlighted in yellow and has made notes in red ink in the margins, everything stacked up in neat piles. The manila folders are labeled and filed. Perfect order. He looks over at his desk. Yesterday's coffee cup, a dead bouquet from Spinster, scraps of paper with scribbled notes. He's got to clean up his act.

Blake walks down the hall, to editor's row. Each editor has a tiny office with one window. Their desks all face out to a long gray-carpeted corridor and carrels of assistants. No doors. No secrets. No color. Even if there were doors, everyone would still be eavesdropping. If someone so much as wonders aloud how a new restaurant is, someone else will inevitably yell back a brief review through the thin walls.

The editor in chief and the managing editor are the only ones with big offices with views of the Midtown skyscrapers, tiny cabs below like toy cars, mini people rushing around to somewhere, anywhere, fast. Catching up. It's hard for Blake to focus on anything but those views whenever he's summoned to explain an exorbitant expense report or an angry letter from a celebrity's lawyer. But he always has an explanation or at least an item to buy back his freedom, though sometimes he wishes he didn't. He knows a well-connected, good gossip columnist is hard to find because anyone really good doesn't want to do it for more than a year or two. Not everyone has a personal reason, like Blake does, for staying on the job.

Blake's last shrink said, "Your career is based on rebelling against your father, and it's the only thing you can do that he has no control over."

"Tell me something I don't already know," Blake said before firing her. That's the great thing about New York. There's quality in the quantity.

"Being with Bethany is another kind of rebellion," said the next shrink. "It's rebelling against yourself because you really just want to fit in with your family and she's exactly the person to do that with. If you marry her, you have an instant acceptable ally who's not either one of your parents."

He fired her, too.

The phone is ringing when Blake gets back to his desk, and it's Heath Frank, Bunny's son, who went to Buckley with Blake before they were shipped out to boarding school.

"Dude," says Heath, who pretends to work in a big corner office at his dad's real-estate company when he's not hunting with sexy brokers for the perfect two-bedroom Tribeca loft. "I hear you're getting *diluted*."

"Diluted?" asks Blake, confused. He hasn't even gotten his trust fund yet. Is his dad getting investigated by the SEC?

Heath cackles. They've always been competitive, all the way back to their sandbox days, when they'd argue about who'd built the bigger castle. "My mom told me that Lindsay's pregnant."

Blake swallows hard and forces out a little laugh that sounds more like a cough. "Oh yeah, we're all really happy about it." Blake bites his lip hard enough to taste blood. Why did he have to hear this news from someone else? And from Heath! For years he's been protecting his dad and his entitled friends and gotten nothing but constant distrust. Maybe it's time for his dad to realize just how useful Blake can be, or how fucked all those golf buddies would be without Blake's thankless deflections of their dirty little secrets. Blake decides he's going to let the next item that comes his way slip through the cracks just so they appreciate him.

Lindsay probably pushed for this baby. In the prenup, it's clearly stated that she gets a lot more money if they have a kid together and get divorced. Blake tries to change the subject. "We should get lunch and play squash at the University Club next week."

Heath knows Blake's tricks too well and he plays right back. "You'd better make sure this new little sibling doesn't get too spoiled. My little stepsister has never even seen the inside of a commercial plane."

Tim wakes up around four A.M. on Tuesday, sitting up straight and screaming, "It's Courteney Cox *Arquette*!" Her publicist always freaks out when they forget, as if the actress's husband's name were anything to show off. Tim hates dreaming about celebrities, but it happens at least once a week, and he figures it must be some kind of sign if they're invading his most personal headspace. It always makes him feel a little violated and also wonder if he's slightly clairvoyant, though none of his dreaming tips have panned out—besides one about Jennifer Lopez and Ben Affleck breaking up, but everyone could see that one coming.

He's lying next to the mattress he brought home last night after a modeling agency party, which was only worth going to for the excessive amounts of quality sushi. Few guests were consuming anything other than cocktails, cocaine, and cigarettes, none of which ever dull Tim's nocturnal appetite. Food always seems disgusting during the day, when he's often nursing a hangover or worse, so he usually leaves the office starving, heading to the party he thinks will have the best food. The mattress looks at him through mascara-stained eyes like a rabid raccoon. He hopes her makeup won't stain his new sheets—it turns out the expensive ones really do feel a lot better, especially if they're free.

"I forgot the Cox," he says, and she giggles.

"What did you write about her husband's cock?"

"I wish," says Tim.

She looks confused. "What?"

"Nothing," he says. "Forget it."

"You have such a demanding job," she says, as if he were a surgeon getting a call from the emergency room. Just like everyone else he brings home, she thinks he does God's work. Fucking him is a consolation prize for not getting a real celebrity, and he's just famous enough for her to brag to her booker or agent or friends who religiously read the column. Tim considers trying to get another blow job. He was too coked up to come from the first one, but now he's too sluggish from the Ambien he took an hour ago when he was tired of tossing and turning, embarrassed about all the effusive conversations he'd had with people right after snorting a huge line at the party last night. He cringes when he remembers running into Charlie and introducing the mattress as his girlfriend.

Tim's jaw aches and he hopes he wasn't grinding it again. He coughs up a bloody green goober and swears to stop smoking until this lingering bronchitis clears up. If Blake hadn't brought Bitchy Bethany to the party, he would have stayed out with Tim, who wouldn't have felt lonely enough to take the mattress home. This is Blake's fault.

Tim wakes up again around eight A.M., wishing he had remembered to close the shades. He's too hungover to get up, so he puts on his sunglasses, which are on his bedside table, to block out the light pouring into the room, giving the dirty piles of laundry and old newspapers a faint, almost pretty, glow. The mattress is in the shower and he vaguely remembers her saying something about an audition for a soap opera this morning and asking him if he knew anyone at that network so he could put in a good word. At least she was good in bed. He loves girls on the Pill. Condoms suck, especially when he's drunk and it's hard enough to get it up. It's too late to ask her name, so he leans over to her open purse on the floor and rifles through her wallet for a license. Danielle Marks of Queens—an address that doesn't quite match up with the real Gucci purse or her fake British accent. She's thirty-three, though he thinks she said she was twenty-eight. Danielle has his business card tucked inside a little pocket of the purse, alongside a bottle of prescription pills, but before he can read what they are, he hears the bathroom doorknob turn and quickly chucks the purse back on the floor.

She walks out toweling off her short bleached-blond hair and Tim wonders why women let their dark roots show. Isn't the whole point to pretend you're a natural? She's got great pert tits. It almost makes up for the dumb tattoo of a Chinese symbol on her lower back. She says it means love but it could mean stupidity for all she knows.

"I can't be late for my audition," she says, and he's pretty sure she's not getting any parts looking the way she does now. But she's in a rush, tearing

around the room and gathering her things. She starts wriggling into a red
G-string that belongs to a different mattress, though Danielle was wearing
red lace panties last night. Hers are under the bed. He's not sure if it's too
late to say something, now that she's pulling on her tight black jeans over
someone else's underwear.

"Hey, you want to go to Holly May's birthday party together?" she asks.
It's two weeks away but Danielle is probably already planning her outfit.

"Sure," he says, even though he doesn't have her phone number or
e-mail and isn't about to exert any energy to get them. But he's fairly sure
he'll be hearing from her soon. If she gets the part, she'll want a boldface
mention, and if she doesn't, she'll want introductions.

"I'll e-mail you," she says.

"Great."

The faint jangle of the chain on his lock as she shuts his door is perhaps
the sweetest sound he's ever heard. He takes off his sunglasses long
enough to read over the notes he took last night on a napkin and call them
into Charlie's voice mail. Tim's favorite item from the night is going to
have to be a blind item. A horny socialite who loves seeing her name in
boldface and who wants press for her upcoming benefit told him that she
used to have an affair with a married senator who ran for president. "We
rolled around in his hotel bed for a few hours," she whispered, her chest
getting a little flushed. "But he couldn't get it up."

He liked the blind item so much, he traded her another little tidbit that
he'd heard from Danielle. "Don't worry, you're in good company," he
said, wondering if she'd ever cheat on her troll of a husband with him.
"JFK Jr. could only get it up in the bathroom of Hyannis Port."

Kate's not sure what the party at the Dior store is for. The publicist,
Bottle Blonde, says she'll be giving out free shoes, which trumps all the
free beauty products and spa certificates Kate has been collecting for
weeks. "Any pair you want," she says.

When Kate tried to ask her about the party, she said something vague about rewarding special customers. Then she e-mailed over a list of "confirmed arrivals" as if it were a movie premiere, and it seems a little strange that the Park Avenue princesses would show up just for a free pair of shoes when they could easily afford any shoes they wanted.

"Their husbands probably have them on a shoe budget," Lacey said when Kate told her about it.

When Kate arrives at the store on East Fifty-seventh Street at the corner of Madison Avenue, she gives her name the way she learned from Tim and Blake, who unfortunately weren't invited to the "girls only" event.

"Kate Simon from the *Examiner*," she says in one breath, and two pretty, thin blondes holding clipboards sing, "So nice to meet you," in a creepy unison. There must be a secret training school for publicists, somewhere they learn to dye their hair and eyebrows bleach blond, slather on fake tanner, and only consume Diet Coke, cocaine, cigarettes, and steamed spinach.

"Have fun!" they sing, offering her a tip sheet detailing which Park Avenue princesses are here. Kate still can't figure out the occasion for the party, and she's only more confused when she sees a deejay spinning records, though no one seems inclined to dance or drink a sweet pink cocktail at 5:30 P.M. on a Monday. Kate's starving but she declines each tray of drinks and sushi, afraid that she'll spill something and have to pay for the damages.

Dozens of women in Chanel jackets and tight designer jeans are tearing open boxes, sticking their skinny legs in the air, and parading in front of the mirrors. The shoes look like they belong behind glass cases in a museum. Kate is surrounded by sharp heels, jewelry dripping off ankle chains, tall soft leather boots laced up on the sides. She wonders what she has in her closet that would look remotely right with any of them. Maybe a pair of black heels? Black heels would go well with anything and Kate doesn't have any. Yes, she needs black heels. Kate picks up a pair of spiky heels that fasten up the back in the style of a bondage corset. The price makes her hands go cold: $860.

A salesgirl brings over a pair in Kate's size, ten, without making any jokes about her big feet. All around her, women with waxed legs and perfect pedicures in colors called Dune Road, Delicacy, and Ballet Slipper slip on size sevens and eights.

Kate tries on the shoes, wishing Zoe or Nick were here to tell her how they looked. Kate thinks they look pretty good; she just hopes she can tolerate the pain to wear them. They have the highest heel of anything she's ever tried on and she feels like an ostrich as she hobbles around a little carpeted corner.

"To! Die! For!" trills Bottle Blonde, running up to Kate and giving her a kiss on both cheeks. She's acting like the sorority sister Kate never had— or wanted. "They totally go with your hair!"

Kate wonders how black shoes go with brown curly hair, but she just smiles and says, "Thanks." Bottle Blonde sweetly asks if Kate would urge Paul to pick one of the party pictures from that day. Kate spots the photographer Patricia Cullen across the room trying on a pair of tall red leather boots. Free advertising must be the reason for the party. Kate wishes there was at least an earnest beard, like a percentage of the proceeds were going to a charity. But no, it's just about materialism.

"Working hard, Kate?" Kate jumps with surprise at someone knowing her name. It's Label Whore, the *Examiner*'s fashion writer, who always flashes the labels of her designer coats and bags to invoke envy. Label Whore tries to smile, but her pumped-up lips are frozen in a half grin that looks a little painful. She's carrying a bag with three shoe boxes and standing with a short, skinny redhead with freckles splashed across her nose. The redhead's nails are chewed down to the quick and she's jabbering away on her cell phone about getting a pair of the $3,500 brown suede boots.

Label Whore introduces the redhead as "Robin Pearce from the *Daily Metro*," and Kate instantly recognizes her name. "You two should know each other."

Robin pulls Kate into a big hug, throwing Kate off balance and nearly crashing into a silver platter of glasses filled with Diet Coke.

"Babe, it's so great to meet you! I've been meaning to take you out for drinks ever since I saw your byline at the bottom of Paul's column last week!" she says, almost shouting. Kate will quickly learn that Robin only likes being friends with people she considers underlings, people she can mentor, or someone like Label Whore, who can offer up designer freebies. Robin thrusts her card into Kate's hand. "We've got to hang out. I'll totally show you the ropes."

"Sure." Kate hands over one of her new business cards, unsure if Robin wants to actually hang out or if this is a professional networking exchange. It feels like elementary school, when you have to invite the entire class to your birthday party because you're stuck with them for the year.

"Why did you pick the cheapest shoes here?" asks Robin, peering into Kate's bag. "Hello? eBay!"

Label Whore nods. "You could still trade them in," she offers, and Kate suddenly wants to stab them both in the face with her new heels for giving her a dose of that lethal Manhattan syndrome, the "never enough" disease. Now she feels like she's settling for $850 shoes when she could have gotten the $3,500 brown boots. Now she'll never be able to enjoy the most expensive shoes she's ever put on her feet because she'll always know she could have had something better.

The next day, Kate shows off the new shoes to Lacey to try to feel better about the freebie.

"You've got to be kidding," says Lacey, shaking her head. "You have to give those back or else the entire newspaper's credibility will be compromised in any coverage we give Dior."

A tiny part of Kate is happy she didn't take the pricier shoes, but a bigger part is mortified that she's being reprimanded after less than a month on the job. She tells Lacey that Label Whore got three free pairs of expensive shoes.

"Well, she's a lost cause," says Lacey. "No one takes her seriously, anyway." Lacey explains that Label Whore's father is the longtime physician of the *Examiner*'s publisher, Henry Carnegie, and has "sacred-cow status."

She didn't even get fired when she once tried to return a free $1,650 designer bag from a fashion PR firm for cash.

It's become somewhat of an office sport to find and spread outlandish stories about Label Whore. A few weeks ago, after Lacey went to get her leg hair removed at some trendy place Label Whore keeps plugging in her column, she was able to top the previous story being circulated about one of Label Whore's breast implants deflating during a step-aerobics class.

"The owner said they hate her so much, whenever she comes in for one of those mini face-lifts that uses currents of energy, half the time they don't even turn the machine on," Lacey had whispered.

Kate puts the shoes back in the bag.

"You don't want to be Label Whore's kind of journalist," adds Lacey, now flipping through *WWD*. "Whenever we need a serious fashion story, we assign it to a freelancer because she's corrupt from all the SWAG."

"SWAG?"

"Shit We All Get. But you didn't hear it from me," adds Lacey. "I'm very comfortable with our frenemy status."

"Frenemy?" Lacey is like a one-woman thesaurus.

"Keep your friends close and your enemies closer," says Lacey, who adds that if Kate ever walks into a party and wants to hide from someone, the first thing she should do is go over and say hello to that person. "But never, ever take your eyes off a frenemy."

All the ladies who lunch were adoring Dior at the fabulous fete PR powerhouse **Bessie Gordon** threw to celebrate the exclusive brand's fall footwear collection. The $3,500 brown suede boots with red stitching were the biggest hit, prompting both cosmetics heiress sisters **Aerin** and **Jane Lauder** to snatch a pair. **Amanda Rockefeller** opted for the more risque $860 spiky black heels styled to resemble a bondage corset. "My husband will love these!" she squealed to the *Daily Metro*'s **Robin Pearce**. "This is the best party of the week!"

Today's one of those days when Tim feels like he's just holding a softball mitt in the air, catching items. There's no shortage of dumped, divorced, or fired gossipers who get a little rush calling Column A with dirty news about whoever recently dumped, divorced, or fired them—even if the rush only lasts about an hour. Today he doesn't have to use the other tricks of the trade, like surfing the blogs for an item to report out or going out to lunch with a publicist or combing through the new batch of closed real-estate deals that get delivered to his desk, compliments of an expensive service the newspaper pays for. Some days it's as easy as reading that Julianne Moore bought a West Village house, complete with the address and price. (The only way he won't print an address is if the celebrity's publicist gives him the address of another star instead, or he gets a threatening letter from a lawyer about a star's dangerous stalker.) Other days he has to work harder, calling up skittish sources and offering, "Tell me about the people you hate so I can help you hate them."

Tim picks up the phone and immediately wishes he'd let the call go straight to voice mail when he hears a chipper woman on the other end.

"Is this Tim Mack from Column A?"

She says she's calling from the human resources department of a stupid celebrity weekly magazine based in New Jersey. It's always a better sign if you get this kind of call from an editor.

"We just love your work and were wondering if you would like to interview to be our new executive editor?"

Any magazine that wants Tim as an executive editor must suck. He hasn't written anything longer than a 150-word item in about five years. And what happened to the old executive editor? Maybe that could be an item.

"What's the salary?" he asks, holding his hand over the receiver while he hacks up a big, bloody ball of phlegm.

"Well, it's a little premature to have that conversation, but rest assured it's in the six figures."

Six figures to work in New Jersey for a shitty magazine where no one would return his calls and where he'd have to show up on time every day? Editing stories about Jessica Simpson's hot new bikini bod? He may be broke and bored but he's not desperate.

"Sorry, I'm pretty happy here," he says, unwrapping a cough drop. "But thanks for thinking of me."

He hangs up and reads an e-mail from one of only five publicists who actually know how to play boldface games, offering him a five-thousand-dollar ticket to a charity event hosted by Julia Stiles next month if he gives the benefit a plug to boost ticket sales. He writes back: "If she gives me a blow job and I get a plus-one, we're on."

Tim picks up the phone again.

"Is this Column A?" asks a woman in a half whisper.

"No sweetheart, it's the FBI."

She doesn't get the joke, so he quickly backtracks, putting on his nice-guy voice.

She says her ex-boyfriend is Andy Billings and that she busted him having an orgy with his staff in the pool of his new Miami hotel last weekend, when he thought she was in New York.

"I like it," says Tim, unsure of her motivation. She says this has happened before, but this was the first time he didn't invite her, and *that* was grounds for the breakup. Sounds like Tim's kind of terms.

"Sweetheart, if you weren't comfortable with it . . ." he says, trying to remember other catchphrases he's read in the *Glamour* on the floor of some mattress's bathroom.

In exchange for the item, she just wants him to go to her edible-lingerie launch party next week and mention that a few celebrities like Pam Anderson have been buying the stuff. And of course, embarrass Andy.

"No problem," says Tim, wondering if she's hunting for a rebound fuck. Andy Billings wouldn't date her if she weren't a nine or ten. At least now Tim's got her cell phone number and e-mail. She'd probably go to a movie premiere with him.

Tim takes a deep breath. Now he's got to call Andy. He wouldn't necessarily call the subject of an item like this, or if he did, he'd wait until seven P.M. and then call his office, knowing it would be too late to get anyone. But Tim needs to play a little fairer than usual this time. Column A needs the hotelier. He often calls in items about his celebrity guests, and he hosts pretty good parties at his hotels, parties Tim and Charlie like being invited to.

Andy's secretary says he's in meetings all day and Tim imagines her as a sexy blonde on her hands and knees under her boss's desk. "Could you please just tell him it's *Tim* from *Column A* calling about his *staff orgy* in Miami?"

In less than a minute Andy is on the horn.

"We're friends, right?" he asks. More like frenemies. If Tim had to pick a hotelier friend, it would be Pierre Patois. His hotels always have big bathtubs with jacuzzi jets.

"Sure," says Tim.

"So let's play," says Andy, knowing how to feed the monster. He offers up an item exchange, saying he knows superstar actor Randy Crowling threw a huge fit at Patois's Miami hotel last weekend. Randy wanted chicken paillard but the kitchen had run out of chicken, so he sent his assistant downstairs to berate the hostess and the maître d' for the shitty service. When they still couldn't get his dinner, he picked up the phone and started screaming at the concierge, who used to work for Andy and spilled the story after asking for a job.

"Randy was screaming shit like, 'How can this be! Can't you do something? Can't you go out and get more chicken?'" says Andy, laughing. "And then when he saw the security camera over the desk, he waved and took a bow!"

It's a decent enough swap. Andy's only a New York celebrity (maybe 10 percent famous) and Randy's an international one (at least 85 percent).

"Oh, and come by any of my hotels for a weekend," says Andy. "My staff would love to take care of you."

"Always a pleasure doing business with you," Tim says sweetly.

He hangs up and starts researching online fares to Miami, thinking about a big hotel suite with a view of the ocean. Room service. Rubbing suntan lotion on some girl's back. If only he knew of a girl he wouldn't want to drown after just one day, maybe he'd actually take the trip.

He checks his e-mail and opens one from Danielle, who has never said anything about leaving his apartment in someone else's red thong. It's full of stupid symbols like ;). She probably used to dot her *i*'s with hearts. Maybe she still does. She says she didn't get the soap opera role, so she really wants to go to Holly May's birthday party to network "with the industry peeps you must know." Peeps? Disgusting neon-colored marshmallow Easter bunnies flash in his head. He e-mails back that he's working that night and doesn't know which parties he has to cover yet.

"Maybe drinks next week," he suggests, without mentioning a date or place.

Nick got Kate and Zoe on the list for Pierre Patois's "gladiator" party to generate buzz for his newest hotel opening in Rome next month.

"You have to swear the party is off the record," Nick insisted.

Kate wonders how she can explain her civilian status to Paul and Lacey, whom she already bragged to about getting invited. They'll expect some good items. It was a coup because gossip columnists are always banned from Pierre's penthouse, but that also means Tim and Blake won't be at the party.

"I swear," she said, looking Nick right in the eyes.

When Zoe and Kate arrive at the downtown loft building that houses Pierre's triplex penthouse, they're greeted outside by two men mounted on horses, playing trumpets. Zoe is wearing a metal bikini with a fur vest and Kate's rented a long white Empress gown with gold embroidery and a fake gold crown atop her curls.

As soon as they get off the elevator, they see a circle of candles, and inside the circle two contortionists writhe around on the floor with what looks like a boa constrictor. There's marble fountains flowing with wine and about fifty people lounging around the living room on pillows, drinking out of silver goblets. Everyone looks vaguely familiar, somewhere between famous and civilian. Zoe points out that the very hot bartenders are Columbia students. "They're the new party trick."

Kate spots Nick across the room wearing a toga fashioned out of what looks like one of her bedsheets. She tries waving to him but he walks slowly by her, indicating that she should follow him into a guest bedroom. Probably so Pierre won't know that they're friends.

He gives her a kiss on the cheek and says she looks great. "I'm glad I could do this for you and Zoe, but I haven't told Pierre that I even know you." He crinkles up his forehead. "I can't have him constantly worrying that I'm leaking shit to you."

Kate feels like a kid crashing a party and her white Empress gown suddenly feels itchy and hot. Nick should trust her. She would never intentionally do anything to jeopardize his job, but maybe he's right. She's in a tricky profession, where you can never really make promises because someone is always breaking them.

He kisses her on the cheek again. "I'll make it up to you. I'll find you an item about a boldface name that's not my boss."

Kate starts to protest, but then his cell phone buzzes and he's off.

Back in the dining room, a guy in a leather tunic is feeding Zoe grapes. She waves Kate over and introduces him, and she immediately recognizes his name. He's the son of a famous novelist, and is known more for his modelizing than his movie producing. Names and faces from parties and magazines are always sticking, even though she's already forgotten where she put her jacket.

"Kate's a writer," says Zoe, who's clenching her jaw a little. She popped two Adderalls in the cab.

Kate glares at her. Zoe better not mess up the first coveted invitation that Kate has procured for them.

A waitress wearing a leather bikini and a big silver headdress with pink feathers offers a platter of oysters with a slimy orange topping that Zoe explains is sea urchin called uni. Zoe shoots one back and closes her eyes, moaning a little. "It's just as good as everyone says it is," she says, explaining it's the new signature dish of a chef named Marco Mancini, who's opening his first restaurant, Coast, next month. He used to be the sous-chef of a two-star place that shut down the week before and apparently he's incredibly hot.

"Hotter than Chris Flemming?" Kate asks. In college they used to watch Chris' Food Network show every Sunday night.

"Much hotter. You've got to get us in to his opening night party. I'm sure I'll be the last one from my office to get an invitation."

Kate hopes Paul won't want to cover the opening. Kate takes an oyster from the tray, inspecting it as if it were from a lab.

"What, are you afraid it will bite?" asks Zoe, nodding at the oyster in Kate's hand. The orange sea urchin has soaked into the briny water, making the meat of the oyster turn an unnatural pale orange hue. Kate only started eating sushi a few years ago. This raw combination may be a little too advanced for her.

"Don't be a baby," says Zoe, sucking back another. "You have no idea what you're missing."

The fear of looking unadventurous overpowers the squeamishness and Kate follows Zoe's lead. The first thing she tastes is a slimy smooth nutty flavor.

"That's the sea urchin," says Zoe. "You're going to be suddenly addicted. I just know it."

Then salty and silky swirl together over her tongue as the oyster slides down her throat, carrying a sweet kick along for the ride.

"Passion fruit at the end, right?" asks Zoe. "A genius combination. If he can make something that tastes this good, just imagine what he must be like in bed."

Kate laughs and then tries to remember what he looks like, but she can't piece the picture together yet.

"We're even thinking of putting him on the cover if the restaurant does well," says Zoe. "He would be the first human on the cover. Usually it's like a turkey or a slice of pie. But *chefs* are New York's new celebrities," she says. "At least that's what my editors say."

"I think he cooked lunch at Terry Barlow's party," says Kate, remembering the way the salmon with rhubarb seemed to melt when it hit her tongue.

"How was the food?"

"Great."

"Probably the same guy. I'm sure he's in full PR mode to generate buzz for the restaurant."

Kate nods slowly. "And Terry's the queen of buzz."

The producer nuzzles Zoe's neck. "It's so cool that you work for *Gourmet*," he says. "When are you going to cook me dinner?"

Kate has never seen Zoe make anything other than reservations in her dad's name. But she's right about the oysters and sea urchin. The producer and Kate each suck one down and then quickly take another and another before the waiter goes back to the kitchen to restock, probably never to return.

Zoe knocks over her goblet and red wine splashes across her legs. The producer starts sopping it up with a napkin and Kate offers to get paper towels. She gets up and goes through the door to the kitchen, where four men in white chef's jackets are darting around steaming pots and sizzling pans. Oven doors slam open and close like shutters in a storm. In the center of it all is a man with black curly hair wearing a white chef's jacket with his name embroidered in dark blue on the lapel. *Marco Mancini. Executive Chef. Coast Restaurant. New York City.*

"This needs salt!" he says, dumping what looks like a blizzard of clear crystals in a steaming dish. His hands, weathered with burns and cuts, look strong enough to lift every piece of furniture in the kitchen in one graceful swoop. He makes everyone else in the room look like a fake plant as he supplies the room with fresh oxygen.

"Yes, Chef!"

"The risotto is burning. Start over! Risotto is like a baby! It cannot be left alone, not for an instant!"

"Yes, Chef!"

"Polenta is supposed to be creamy, not gummy!"

"Yes, Chef!"

And then he looks up, catching her eye. She takes a step back, relieved that the wall is cool and solid behind her. Even in the fluorescent kitchen light his big, dark liquid brown eyes framed by thick lashes look miles long. She feels silly wearing a rented Empress gown and a fake gold crown. In her own clothes she might even feel bold enough to say hello. In this outfit she's just another guest, a drain for expensive food and drinks.

He smiles and shrugs as if to say, *What can I do?* She feels a hot wire slowly weaving through her veins. She wants to say something but she's not sure what. In New York, the first thing you tell people is what you do; then, where you live; and third, where you're from. Even if she could tell him, she doesn't think any of her answers would be particularly impressive. His gaze unlocks and he's back to stirring the risotto.

"Can I help you with something?" asks a waiter, snapping Kate back to reality. She realizes she's been standing with her back against the wall staring at Marco for a few moments too long and she'd better get back to the party. She says she needs paper towels for her friend and the waiter promises to bring them out. Kate wants Marco to look up again, but he's busy garnishing a plate with thin slivers of something white and earthy looking. It's not cheese or chocolate.

Back in the dining room, Kate can't find anything but a wine-stained patch of floor where Zoe was sitting. Stranded, she takes the stairs up a flight to a rooftop garden, and suddenly she's in California or Capri, somewhere far from downtown Manhattan. It's lush with massive trees illuminated from underneath so their leaves look waxy and white. She walks through the garden to enormous glass doors that lead into a room with a crowded concrete dance floor, a deejay booth perched high above. Men wearing tall headdresses and women showing perfectly toned stomachs and arms pulse with the music, raising their swords and goblets to the sky. This is one of those New York moments, Kate thinks, one of those moments you move here for. But to Kate standing there alone, it seems like a scene on television blaring into an empty apartment.

She leaves and walks up another flight of stairs and stops dead when she sees the outdoor pool, a perfect steaming rectangle. An invitation to an exotic dream. She never would have guessed that someone could have such an apartment here in New York. For a moment she can't believe she's here, at the home of someone like Pierre who's figured it all out.

Kate hears a man's voice behind her say "Wow," in a hushed whisper. Exactly what she's thinking. *Wow.* The voice comes closer and soon it's right next to her.

"I never thought anyone lived like this," he says, and she quickly inhales. It's the chef from the kitchen. Marco Mancini, oysters artisan.

"You looked pretty busy just about ten minutes ago," she says, trying to sound casual. His white chef's jacket is stained with what looks like gummy polenta.

"I'm just taking a little breather," he says. "The polenta and the risotto are the only things I really needed to baby-sit." She wonders what else he thinks about besides food. Where is he going and where has he been? How old is he? She wishes she had all the easy questions answered so she could ask him about something worth talking about. "The rest is just following recipes I already made."

Away from the fluorescent kitchen lights his eyes look more like dark pieces of chocolate, the kind that tastes bitter before it's baked.

Kate's crown slips down a little and she steadies it with a bobby pin. "The oysters were delicious."

Marco smiles and runs his hand through the brown curls that hang just over the tips of his ears. Kate notices they have similar hair and briefly fantasizes about how well matched they would be as a couple.

"That's what I like to hear," he says, smiling. "That's what makes it worth it. Knowing that I'm making people happy."

Marco's the first person Kate's met in a while who's doing something for other people's happiness—or at least trying to. If Kate's job ever makes people happy, it's usually only for a week. More often, she makes people feel mad or jealous, which was not the reason she wanted to become a journalist. She suddenly feels an impulse to help Marco, to anoint him as the next buzz-worthy chef in Paul's column.

"I've got to get back to work," he says. "Unlike you, I'm just the hired help. At least for now. Maybe if my new restaurant does well, I'll actually get out of the kitchen and get invited to a party like this."

Kate wants to say that she's also hired help, paid to navigate parties, but she promised Nick. For tonight, she's going to be just another girl at another party.

Marco doesn't seem to be in a hurry to leave. "I like your outfit," he says, and she can feel her cheeks redden. "I like a little left to the imagination."

Kate would have worn one of those bikinis if she had Zoe's body. This may be the only time she's thankful for being a size six, even though she skipped dinner to fit into her dress. Now she's starving. She wishes she had an entire tray of oysters and sea urchin to herself.

"It's almost time for dessert," he says. "Which means it's almost time for me to get out of here. I'm going to try to stop by Holly May's party after this if it's not too late."

Paul got the invitation to the supermodel's annual birthday bash but said he was going to pass this year. "It's always just a few models and mobs of men who think they can date them," he'd said.

"You're friendly with Holly May?" asks Kate.

"Probably as friendly as you are with Pierre."

Kate laughs. "Exactly."

"We share a publicist who says I should go, and I'm doing whatever she says because I'm opening my restaurant next month." Ambition flashes in his eyes like heat lightning. "All the gossip columnists will be there and I need a little exposure to get the big reviews." He swallows as if something is stuck on his Adam's apple. "Did you know that only one out of every five restaurants that open in New York succeeds?"

She shakes her head and he leans back for a moment against the brick wall. "I'm Marco, by the way."

Kate points to his name embroidered on his chef's jacket. "So I see. I'm Kate." Just Kate.

"Lovely to meet you, Kate." He pauses, probably waiting for her to give her affiliation as a last name. "Don't forget to come by the kitchen and tell me what you think of my chocolate almond parfait."

He opens up an exit door. "For the hired help," he says, raising his eyebrows and disappearing down the dark stairway.

An hour later, Kate goes to the kitchen to tell Marco that his crunchy and sweet chocolate almond parfait was her favorite dessert, but he's already gone. The sous-chefs are cleaning up and one of them tells her Marco went home. She's mostly relieved. She's exhausted and the gold spray paint on her cheap sandals is already chipping, revealing the shiny black plastic foundation slicing blisters into her toes. All that glitters may only be gold for a few hours on a $24,000-a-year salary.

It's 1:15 A.M., a perfectly reasonable time to go home, even though Paul would say she should at least stop by Holly May's party. Zoe has vanished, so Kate heads downstairs, deciding to splurge on a cab home. She's not going to ride the subway back to Brooklyn in the costume.

Outside, a horn blares and Nick rolls down the window of Pierre's Town Car. "I've been waiting for you forever."

Kate can't remember a more welcome sight. She slides in next to him, kicking off her shoes and sinking in the leather seat. "I'll take out the trash for a whole week for this."

"Deal."

As the car rolls toward Brooklyn, she tells him how she was trying to say good-bye to Marco Mancini.

Nick laughs. "Take a number."

He's probably right. Why would someone like Marco, someone about to hit his stride, even want to talk to Kate for longer than five minutes at a party? He should date a socialite, one of those women who get photographed for *Vogue* in a size-two borrowed gown at some fund-raising gala they're helping to host.

"Why don't you just find a nice guy who will be good to you? Guys like Marco are very busy trying to get famous. Guys like Pierre and his friends are famous enough to be assholes to anyone who can't help them. Why would you want to deal with that shit?"

Kate tries to explain that she thinks Marco is genuinely talented, and mentions that she wants to find a way to get him press in the *Examiner*.

"Why? So he can owe you one?" asks Nick, lowering his window. Kate can smell autumn creeping into the air, cooling the shadow of summer before she's ready to let it go for a whole year. Winter has always felt like the loneliest season and living in New York will probably not change that. If anything, it will just be harder to navigate the streets and social circuits in hostile weather. "Don't forget to have at least one gray line between work and play."

"I'm worried there are no lines in my job if I want to do it well."

He leans his head back. "That's definitely something to be afraid of."

When they get home, Kate stumbles into the bathroom and sheds her clothes in a heap, turning on the shower and letting the room get steamy. Clean the pores. Heat the lungs. But no matter how much water rinses through the drain, she can't stop thinking about Marco. She soaks her hair in conditioner, hoping to detangle the curls, but once she's out of the shower and standing in the soft white bathrobe from Pierre's hotel, she still can't get a comb through her hair.

Nick comes in to brush his teeth and Kate asks for his help with her hair. He instructs her to sit on the bathtub's edge while he works his fingers and the comb through her mop of wet curls.

"I don't want to hurt you," he says, "but I have to pull before you get dreadlocks."

She tells him to pull as hard as he needs to.

"You look like you're about to cry," he says, putting down the comb. She looks at their reflection in the mirror and asks him to keep going. He works intently, pulling apart strands, gently putting smooth pieces back in place as if he were re-stringing a guitar. She closes her eyes and tilts back her head, falling asleep as his hands work through her hair.

A promoter—whoops, nightlife impressario—reserved Tim a table in the VIP area of Holly May's party at Ripe. Tim scans the room, hunting for an easy item before he gets too wasted to care, and spots the magician David Blaine with his new model girlfriend. Perfect. Tim walks over to the magician to ask him about his new stunt.

"Sorry, dude," he says. "But I'm not David Blaine. I'm Guy Oseary. Happens all the time."

Shit. Tim hates it when he fucks up the faces of the semifamous. B-list blundering is a major occupational hazard. At least Oseary, a music executive and friend of Madonna's, has a good sense of humor about it. The B-listers are usually pleasant enough, buying insurance because they can't afford the bad press, or worse, no press at all.

Tim didn't want to come to the party alone, but he also didn't want to bring a date. That would be like bringing sand to the beach. And Blake already had plans—he was going with Bethany to a stuffy dinner party at that rich asshole Mark Reed's place on Park Avenue. So Tim had agreed to come with Robin from the Daily Dish. She could take care of herself and get herself on the list. Fortunately, she's been busy bopping around the party air-kissing publicists, so she hasn't interfered with his two-hour courtship of Danielle, who's sitting next to him dressed in a skimpy red dress. He's drunk enough to forget why he didn't want to come here with her in the first place, even if Robin says the fake British accent is weird. He's not even sure where she came from or how she got in without his help, but she looks exceptionally hot.

Around 1:45, Robin comes by to point out the back of a tall, curly-haired guy in a white chef's jacket across the room. When he turns around, Tim remembers the face from Terry Barlow's kitchen, even though they didn't meet there. Terry doesn't like to share her new pets.

"My latest target," she says, explaining that he's Marco Mancini, who's opening a new restaurant called Coast soon. He used to cook at a pretty good place Tim went to once before, probably the night it opened. That's the thing about being a gossip columnist: You tend to go to places only two times—when they're born and when they die.

"I know him," says Danielle, pouring Tim another drink. "He used to go out with my friend Jade, who's going to be the hostess at his new restaurant."

Robin raises her eyebrows. "I wonder what his girlfriend Wendy Winter thinks about that." Tim can see Robin mentally updating her files. *Click. Click. Save.*

Spinster, who also reps Holly May, is dragging Marco around as if he were a new toy. If only Tim had Robin's patience for these people, he could probably scoop Robin at the *Daily Metro* every day. Spinster and Marco come toward Tim's table and Marco gives Robin a kiss on the cheek. Spinster makes a big show of kissing Tim on both cheeks and quickly introduces him to Marco.

"I'm a big fan," Marco says, smiling wide enough to show the tops of his gums. Spinster's trained him well. Nothing gets you in Column A faster than flattery.

"Hey! I thought *my* column was your favorite," says Robin, giggling. She always acts like a twelve-year-old when she has a crush, which could be why she never has a relationship that lasts longer than two weeks. At least Tim doesn't have to hear about it anymore all day long at the office, as he used to when they worked together on Column A.

Marco smiles and pours her a drink from their bottles on the table, mixing the vodka with cranberry juice and ice. He winks and tells Robin that she's his favorite.

"Nice to see you again," he says to Danielle, giving her a kiss on the cheek. Tim wonders if they've fucked.

Spinster quickly drags Marco away to meet Holly May. What the hell is going on? Last time Tim checked, chefs were fat, sweaty guys who never left their kitchens, much less partied with supermodels.

"I bet he breaks up with Wendy Winter any day now," says Robin, reapplying a coat of pink lipstick, a ritual Tim now can identify as a precursor to an aggressive flirtation. But it looks as though Robin's got competition. Across the room, Marco feeds Holly May a strawberry and hands her a glass of champagne. Patricia's camera is all over it. Tim scribbles *randy restaurateur* (he can't think of anything punchy to go with *chef*) on a napkin, trying not to notice his dried pink phlegm on one side, and shoves it in his pocket.

A photographer from an online party-picture site stops by their table.

"Tim Mack from Column A, can I get a shot?" he asks, smiling. No one's going to ever buy the picture unless Tim gets embroiled in a scandal, but the attention, the ego shot, seems to be turning Danielle on. She rubs his inner thigh while the flash goes off.

beware of the open bar

Tonight, Kate is covering the opening of Lush, a new lounge in Soho. She has eighty-seven dollars in her bank account and her thousand-dollar share of the rent is due next week, so she expenses the cab to Zoe's apartment. Zoe's parents bought her one-bedroom "maid's quarters" about ten years ago and never got around to breaking down the wall between it and their apartment. So Zoe recently moved in and only pays rent by allowing unannounced parental visits.

Kate walks in the open door—there's no reason for locks if you only share the floor with your parents—pausing to take in the living room's white furniture, dark wood floors, thick white curtains. The glass coffee table is marked with rings from wineglasses and is piled high with new Condé Nast magazines and heavy books of photographs of Zoe's parents' friends' apartments.

Kate makes her way to Zoe's bedroom. "Did you see that item about Marco and Holly May?" Zoe blots her lipstick with a tissue and throws it in the general direction of the trash, missing by a few inches.

Column A is spread out on her bed, so Kate can read the item for the fourth time this week.

Randy restaurateur **Marco Mancini**, who's slated to open the much-hyped Coast next month, was spotted canoodling with leggy lovely **Holly May** at her big birthday bacchanalia at Ripe, where **Madonna** pal **Guy Oseary** berated a reporter for mixing him up with magician **David Blaine**. No word on the where-abouts of the decorating diva girlfriend **Wendy Winter**.

"Great," says Zoe. "Now he's lost to the land of supermodels."

All day Kate hasn't been able to decide if she was happy that he was maybe cheating on his girlfriend, indicating a potential breakup soon, or if she was annoyed that the sous-chef had told her Marco went home after finishing up at Pierre Patois's party.

"They share a publicist," explains Kate, who finds this news reassuring. Coast was mentioned, which means Spinster probably planted the item.

Zoe disappears into her walk-in closet, which is about the same size as Kate's bedroom. "Everyone at work is talking about him. They say his oysters-and-uni recipe is the most innovative dish since Nobu's miso cod."

Kate's never dined at Nobu but it sounds like a big compliment. She wonders aloud if she should pitch a profile of Marco to her bosses at the *Examiner*. It could be a chance to get a byline, and if he really becomes a hit, she'd get credit for being there first, which seems to be the priority of the media game as far as she can tell. Interviewing Marco would also be an excuse to see him again.

"But then if he didn't like what you wrote, you'd ruin your chance with him," says Zoe, brushing her long black hair to a smooth sheen. "You could try to run a picture or something from the opening party. By the way, you've got to get us into that. Everyone in my office wants to go, and I'll never get on the list."

"You think I actually have a chance with Marco Mancini?"

Zoe smiles. "If you get him before you build him up and someone else takes him down, sure."

Kate likes the idea of giving good press to someone worthy of it instead of those self-promoters who call in items about themselves every day. But how is she supposed to help promote someone if she also wants to date him? Lacey and Paul always say Kate can't write about her friends, but how are you supposed to get items and sources and find people worthy of buzz without becoming friends—or more?

Zoe, meanwhile, has moved on to more pressing matters. "What are you wearing tonight?" she asks, ransacking her closet for a perfect outfit for her new perfect size-two figure. It's as if they never left college, where they were always getting ready to hit the bars or host a party. But back then, they were both a size six and would probably have already ordered pizza. Zoe says she's not hungry and Kate pretends she's not, either, but sneaks into the kitchen to drink diet soda. It's the only thing in the fridge besides champagne. Zoe likes things that expire before she tires of them.

Kate would be lying if she didn't say Zoe looked great. It seems that it takes something a little unhealthy to make you look a lot better, be it diet, overexercising, ultraviolet rays, or pills. Cheating, successfully. With her shiny black hair, ironed straight from an expensive, torturous Japanese treatment, and her light blue eyes with thick, dark lashes, Zoe is the kind of woman every guy on campus wanted to date, even if her attention span only allowed her to date someone for two months before getting antsy, cheating, and moving on—a pattern she blames on attention deficit disorder.

"I'm not going to be seen out with you in that," says Zoe, surveying Kate's basic black pants and white button-down shirt. "I have a reputation to maintain." She slips on a red Diane von Furstenberg wrap dress that still has its tags and throws Kate a black dress.

Zoe's mom, Grace—who was once her father's assistant—wanders into the room wearing a white Chinese silk robe and an eye mask filled with cold blue gel to soothe her puffy, unfocused eyes. The blue is the only bright color in the room. "You girls look so pretty," she says slowly.

"Moooooommm!" drawls Zoe, as if she were talking to a small child. "Don't you knock?"

Grace picks up a porcelain statue of a ballet dancer and puts it down softly, as if it might just shatter in her manicured hands if she holds it any longer. "Why don't you girls meet me at Bergdorf's for lunch sometime?" She fusses with the white curtains. "They're so nice to me there. I get free meals because I spend so much on my shoes. Isn't that clever? Frequent-shopping meals!"

Zoe has told Kate that her mother has pretty much knocked herself out on potent downers after getting busted for downgrading Zoe's dad's mistress from first class to coach on a trip they were taking to Hawaii, where he claimed to have business checking out sites for a possible new reality show for his network.

Grace looks at Kate as if she's never seen her before. "Oh, Kate," she says after staring for a few moments, and Kate nods, smiling, trying to be encouraging. "Have you met my dear friend Claire Bradley's son, Blake? He writes a *column* like you do, for *Manhattan* magazine."

Grace doesn't say the word *gossip*. It may as well be an expletive, and suddenly Kate's skin feels caked in grime, like it does after she's been walking around the city on a hot August afternoon. "That Blake is such a doll," continues Grace. "He ran the nicest picture of me from that luncheon in Central Park. I looked so thin in my big white hat." She looks at herself in a mirror on the wall and smoothes her hands over her short black bob.

"It's all about flattering accessories," Grace says as she wanders out again, as if an invisible bell signaled the end of her visit.

"Sorry. The new prescriptions are making her spacey," says Zoe, whose own pill popping is having the opposite effect of making her a hyperactive insomniac.

There's a massive line flanked by velvet ropes at the door of Lush. Blake and Tim flash their press passes and the ropes swing open with some back-thumping from the bouncer.

"Faster than fucking Moses and the Red Sea," says Tim, slapping the bouncer on the back. The laminated pass is only supposed to be used to cut "fire and police lines," but Tim and Blake use it whenever they can.

Blake and the club's owner, Alec Coleman, whom Column A always calls **Manic Millionaire**, were in the same elementary-school class, and one summer weekend before college Blake stayed with Alec's family in East Hampton. They also invited a few girls they knew from the city, and one of them ended up fucking the star of a then-popular television series, who was another houseguest.

"Everyone's going to be jealous of you in the morning," the actor told the girl, boasting that Alec's mom, her friend, and Alec's older sister had all hit on him the night before. Sure enough, in the morning, Alec's mom barged in wearing a negligee, demanding that the actor get ready to play tennis. The girl stayed in bed, eating cherries and spitting the pits out on the night table, while Alec's mom dressed the actor in whites. Blake peered into the bedroom on his way to the bathroom. Their pretty blond friend's lips were stained scarlet. Juice dripped down on the white sheets.

"Don't tell anyone," she told Blake when she finally got up, but he knew she meant "tell everyone," which is what he did. People who say "Don't tell anyone" mean tell someone, or else why would they tell anyone at all?

Y ou have to get one of those," Zoe tells Kate as the red velvet ropes part at Lush for two guys flashing laminated passes. Kate thinks the guys may be Tim and Blake, but they breezed past her so quickly, she's not sure, and she doesn't want to shout out their names in case she's wrong.

Zoe makes Kate flash her business card and the bouncer lets them in. "You should have told me who you were," he said, smiling as he opens the door for them.

Zoe smirks. "I told you so."

Lush's owner, Alec Coleman, bounds toward them in an extra-white tuxedo flashing extra-white teeth. "My father told me his father owns a G5," Zoe whispers, raising a freshly plucked eyebrow that Kate should probably tell her is just a tad too thin.

"Kate Simon from the *Examiner*! I'm so glad you made it!" he says, pushing his big designer sunglasses up on his head. "And you're so much cuter than Paul, even though he is a very close family friend." Alec is a little short, but his muscles bulge beneath his jacket as if he works out every day with a trainer.

"My own Lois Lane!" says Alec, pulling Kate close, and she wonders how many cartoon characters she'll be compared to in this job. She's suddenly exhausted by his energy and wishes she were home watching a movie with Nick and Annie, who's visiting for a few days even though she's spent most of her time studying at their kitchen table. Maybe giving herself a pedicure and imagining that parties like this would be more than just a frat-party semiformal with better dresses.

"Bring over a bottle of Cristal!" he orders a waitress. The drink menu says the bottle costs $625 and Kate slips the menu in her purse. She has yet to learn that the prices are standard.

Across the room, she spots Tim from Column A wearing jeans and an old Ramones T-shirt. He's with Blake, who keeps pushing his sandy-blond hair out of his eyes, and Kate thinks she sees a tape recorder sticking out of the pocket of his blue blazer.

"So, why did you name this place Lush?" she asks Alec, thinking it's a dumb question as soon as it comes out of her mouth. Lush is not a theme. And Alec does not seem like someone worthy of press. He was just born into this. It's too easy for him. He expects the attention.

"Well, it's sexy and rich and we're all drunk, baby!" he yells, high-fiving a friend at a nearby table. Zoe coughs to hide her laugh. Moving on.

Zoe knows half the people in the room and keeps a running commentary about who's had a nose job, whose parents rent their apartment instead of owning it, who has a house in West Hampton—which is apparently the wrong Hampton.

"See that girl with the Louis Vuitton handbag? She told everyone she went to Canyon Ranch in Arizona for a month, but she really went to Cirque Lodge in Utah!"

"Is Cirque Lodge a cheaper spa?"

"No!" Zoe laughs. "It's cushy rehab, where you take Pilates classes and get facials. And anyone who's anyone goes there. It's where Nicole Richie kicked heroin and MK started eating again, at least temporarily." Kate thinks Zoe would do a better job working on a gossip column than being an assistant at *Gourmet*. She's been in training since she could read. For years she's been paying attention to the little things that suddenly seem to matter.

The drinks are nice and strong at Lush. Tim will write them up a decent enough item about the opening party, especially because there's a relatively impressive crowd. The celebs probably flew in from L.A. on the Coleman family Gulfstream. Leo DiCaprio and Robert De Niro's son are sitting up on a banquette, wearing baseball caps and kind of swaying back and forth, occasionally waving their hands in the air. Keith Richards's hot blond daughters are slinking around a table full of older guys wearing Gucci and Hermes belt buckles.

Tim glances over at the bar and spots Kate from the *Examiner* with her hot friend, Zoe, who's wearing a red wrap dress. Tim has always wanted to fuck a rich girl in one of those little plaid private school skirts, and she probably has one.

"You want to finally meet Zoe Miller?" asks Blake, noting Tim's interest and pouring them each a drink from their bottle on the RESERVED FOR VIP table. "Apparently Kate hasn't figured out that she's bottle-service-worthy yet."

Tim runs his hands through his hair and sits up straight. "Ready whenever you are."

Blake walks up to the girls and points out their table to them. Tim smiles big and waves them over, holding up two drinks for them.

"Ladies," says Tim as they approach, "welcome to the soul-sucking world of free cocktails."

Zoe smiles and takes her drink. "I hate waiting on line."

"Stick with me and you'll never have to," says Tim, kissing her on the back of her palm. "Tim Mack from Column A. Pleased to make your acquaintance."

"Do your parents know where you are?" Blake asks Zoe, sitting down across from her.

Zoe laughs. "Let's hope not."

Tim studies her face, trying to pretend he doesn't know the answer to the question he's about to ask. "Are you Jack Miller's daughter?" Jack Miller hates Column A, even if he takes Charlie out to lunch once a year. Tim's not sure if this will make it harder or easier for him to get Zoe into bed.

She cocks her head. "Do you want me to be?"

Blake laughs. Tim becomes determined. He *will* get her into bed. If he knew Kate had hot friends like Zoe, he would have made more of an effort to hang out with her.

"Hey, how do you get a press pass, and does it always work to cut lines?" asks Kate, looking sweet and confused with a tiny dash of competitive.

"Did you tell them who you were at the door?" asks Tim.

Zoe finishes her drink. "*I* had to," she says. "Kate's a little shy. But at least she had a business card."

"Your managing editor should have the form to get a press pass," says Blake.

"Get one immediately. The first trick of the trade is never stand on line," says Tim, pouring Zoe another drink.

Tim knows he's drunk enough, and plus he's got to pose for a photo spread about the city's gossip columnists for *Gotham* magazine in the morning, but he pours himself another drink, anyway.

Then he wraps his arm around Kate. "Welcome to the playground, sweetheart. Just watch out for the bullies, and don't get picked last for any teams."

"If she knows what's good for her, she'll stay away from you," says Blake, putting his arm around Kate's other shoulder.

Zoe pulls out her camera phone. "Aren't you guys cute! The three gossipteers."

Tim suddenly spots Danielle's stupid Chinese-symbol tattoo peeking out from her low-slung jeans across the room. She's beginning to freak him out. She e-mailed him a link to the WireImage.com photo of them from Holly May's birthday party asking him to run it in Column A. Deluded and desperate is a scary combination. He's got to get out of here before he convinces himself it would be worth it to take her home.

He pulls his arm off Kate's shoulder and shoves his napkins with notes in his jeans pocket. "Do you ladies have cards?" he asks. "I just remembered I have to get up early tomorrow morning."

"Before eleven?" asks Blake, looking a little confused. Tim shoots a look in Danielle's direction so Blake will get the hint. It works.

"Oh, right—sorry, man," says Blake. "I should have reminded you. That photo shoot."

"Are you guys being shot for the *Gotham* magazine spread, too?" asks Kate, twirling one of her brown curls. She's pretty but not Tim's type.

"No choice. It's good for the column and the magazine," says Blake. "Just make sure they do your hair and makeup or else you'll look like shit."

Tim takes Kate's and Zoe's cards and hands them his. "How about we all meet up at the Tom Cruise premiere next week?"

"If I can steal Paul's invite, I'm in," says Kate.

"And if you can't, we'll get you in," says Tim, slipping into the crowd right as Danielle sees him and starts heading over. He narrowly escapes out into the September night, which has a welcoming, familiar crispness. When he hears a siren shrieking, for no discernible reason he briefly thinks the police are chasing him and considers sprinting down the street, but it's an ambulance, not a police car, and suddenly it's screeching to a stop in front of Lush. Alec Coleman and one of his hot cocktail waitresses stumble outside.

"I'm fine! I'm fine!" Alec screams. "I have a prescription!"

The bouncers lead him toward the ambulance, holding a bloodstained white cloth napkin to a cut on his head while he yells, "You can't treat me like this! My father has a plane!"

Alec looks like a bloated penguin in his white tux. "Oh no," he says when he sees Tim. "Not you!"

Tim comes closer. He's known Alec and his parents for years. They're firmly in the camp that believes that all press is good press. They even rat out their allegedly good friends to make items work in their favor just for sport.

As he's carried into the ambulance, Alec shouts, "Did you see we got Leo and Gisele here?"

"A-list," says Tim, trying not to laugh.

"Don't screw me on this!" Alec yells just before the ambulance doors close. "If you write a nice item, I promise you can ride in the jet to Miami whenever you want! Fuck it, let's go to Capri! Ibiza! Skiing in Gstaaaaaaaaaad?"

As the ambulance speeds down the street, Tim's phone vibrates. He takes it out of his pocket and tastes the panic at the back of his throat when he sees the 111-222-333 number, which means it's the office calling. There's still another hour before the late-edition deadline.

"We got a problem," says Charlie, skipping the small talk, and Tim thinks this is it. He's getting fired for any number of things, though he's not sure what finally did him in.

"They killed the lead about Randy Crowling." Charlie and Tim may never know why, but it probably has something to do with the publisher's son being old friends with the short-fused star. Tim smiles. Perfect. It's one of those rare nights when Tim can prove to be useful. He does know what's going on in the city and he's got Charlie's back, and that should let Tim coast through the next time he gets in trouble.

"Pretty fucking good," says Charlie when Tim tells him about Alec's grand exit. "But not worth losing his parents. Slip on the kid gloves."

The alarm buzzes and Kate instantly regrets being anywhere but in her own bed. She should have gone straight home from Lush, but Zoe insisted on going to Marquee with Todd Slattery, the movie studio publicist she was making out with at the bar, and his friend, **Opportunistic Actor**. Kate would have gone home after that, but the cabbie refused to take her to Brooklyn, so she ended up in the actor's bed. She never knew cabs could do that, but she was too drunk to argue and Todd had already spirited Zoe away in a Town Car.

The actor pulls her in close. "Last night was fun."

She mumbles in agreement. She's wearing what must be his sweatpants and an old T-shirt. She looks at the cheaply framed poster of Edvard Munch's painting *The Scream* and thinks she could be back at college, but there's bleating traffic below and *Dianetics* on his bookshelf. Marco Mancini's face suddenly pops into her mind and she wishes she were waking up next to him instead, even though that will probably never happen. He probably lives in an old brownstone with a backyard. Fruit in a bowl. Flowers in a vase. She hasn't even worked up the nerve to pitch Lacey a profile on him, but already Kate is crafting his storyline.

She can't remember anything after meeting Opportunistic Actor at the bar, but she hopes she got enough quotes to write up the party. It's deadline day at the *Examiner* and Kate has to be at the office at nine-thirty, which is early in the media world, where calls usually don't get made until noon. But she can't go into the office wearing Zoe's black dress, which is rumpled on the floor. There's no time to go home to Brooklyn, from his Midtown apartment. She quickly says good-bye and, on her way out, checks a piece of mail. She wants to look him up on IMDB.com.

Kate tears through Midtown looking for any open stores and finally dashes into Banana Republic in Grand Central Station, desperate for a new, fast morning-after outfit. College walks of shame were so much easier and cheaper, she thinks as she speed-walks through the store.

Later this morning she has to pose with Paul for the photo shoot of gossip columnists, so she can't just grab a T-shirt. She remembers Blake's advice to make sure someone does her hair and makeup, but it seems like a ridiculous request in the daylight. She grabs a green button-down shirt that she tries to throw over Zoe's black dress, but the dress still smells like last night. She quickly finds a brown skirt that sort of goes with her black boots and changes into the new outfit in the dressing room, paying on her way out—with her parents' credit card, which she's only supposed to use for emergencies.

In the subway to the office uptown, she opens up the papers she bought at the newsstand outside the store. Justin left her a message last night, saying she should look for his byline tomorrow, so she starts with the *Journal*. She quickly finds his story on the cover of the Marketplace section. It's about that Park Avenue plastic surgeon he was talking about, Stanley Stahl. Justin's sources say Stahl sold the bulk of his shares of his company's stock twenty-four hours before the FDA issued a statement refusing to approve his new skin cream—without telling any shareholders, who were hit hard after the announcement this morning. The SEC may launch an investigation for potential insider trading. Kate's impressed; she wishes she could pursue this kind of story. There must be many more pieces of this puzzle to sort out, like who tipped Stahl off about the FDA's decision, and who lost money? Someone famous or at least controversial must be involved, and that would make it a great *Examiner* story. Stahl must have some boldface friends. But how can Kate compete when she doesn't even know where to start?

Blake can't believe he agreed to be at the office early for this stupid photo shoot. Who cares what gossip columnists look like? Isn't the whole point that they be anonymous? But the magazine's aggressive publicist made him do it. "Exposure of you means exposure for us," she chirped.

It's only nine o'clock but he's already got a message on his voice mail from a big-time divorce lawyer, which means the rumor of the pending separation of a socialite couple is probably true. High-profile couples' lawyers tend to try to spin separations in the press to benefit their clients' settlement. "We want to defuse the rumors and we trust you," says the lawyer on Blake's machine. Perfect. Nice and easy.

He got a call from his dad an hour earlier, saying Blake should read about Stanley Stahl in the *Journal*, and sure enough, it looks like the guy's going down. But Blake hopes The Nerd doesn't want an item about it. He went to boarding school with Stahl's daughter and doesn't want to piss her off. "I didn't invest in him but plenty of my friends did," said his dad's message. "I hope you'll be sensitive to the circumstances." If only Blake had broken that story.

When the photographer arrives, Blake leads him to The Nerd's office, which Blake pretends is his. There's no reason for anyone to know that he shares a carrel of four desks, even if he has his own fax machine. Press is a matter of perception, after all. No one else is at work yet, so the silent dark hallways are a little eerie, as if ghosts of conversations and editors past are haunting every corner.

Blake keeps saying "prunes" whenever the photographer snaps a photo. The Olsen twins' manager told Blake that the twins always do that for the cameras. It's how they look a little pouty and serious at the same time.

"Prunes," says Blake.

Charlie calls and wakes Tim up to say Alec Coleman sent them over a case of expensive scotch. "To thank us for our *friendship*."

"Great," croaks Tim, his voice coated with the cigarettes he smoked last night in front of the television. His throat is sore from coughing through the night until he downed a bottle of Nyquil, which actually gave him a nice buzz. He'd stayed up until three o'clock watching the Weather Channel in various countries and imagining drinking icy cocktails with fresh coconut and pineapple. If he had a thousand dollars, he would ask for two weeks off to go to Australia, where it was supposed to be a hundred degrees today near the Great Barrier Reef in Cairns, a city the weatherman pronounced like *Cans*, which made Tim crave a six-pack. Tim pictured the coral, electric orange under the transparent turquoise ocean, and dolphins swimming in a dive boat's wake. At least that's how it looked on the Discovery Channel. Maybe the fares will go down on Monday. Maybe he can find a junket to a new hotel there. He recently heard something about Ivana Trump building a resort in the South Pacific. Or maybe the Loathed Hollywood Lothario's lawyers will actually sue for libel and Tim can spend his severance on a one-way plane ticket.

"By the way," says Charlie, reeling Tim in from his day dreaming, "you slept through that photo shoot. I tried to call you three times."

Tim checks his cell phone's "missed call" log. Confirmed.

"Who cares?" says Tim, trying to sound like he doesn't.

"Well, you would if you ever wanted to do anything else."

"You know of any jobs with better perks?" Maybe he should have taken that glossy tabloid magazine job, even if it was in New Jersey.

"And Tubby wants to talk to you."

"About?"

Charlie swallows loudly. "I don't think that item you wrote about the Loathed Hollywood Lothario went over all that well with his lawyers, now that the murder charges against him have been dropped. The wife's boyfriend's now the main suspect. So the paper is facing defamation of character on two counts. They said he never pissed on his seat *or* killed his wife."

They'll never win. The paper has an army of lawyers to squash threats. Still, it doesn't look good for Tim to constantly be lectured about his sourcing.

Tim pulls the covers up to his nose. If his bedroom had wallpaper, it would say *YOU'RE FUCKED* in big, red, repeating bold letters.

"One more thing," says Charlie, sighing. "You may have started the Stanley Stahl coverage, but we got trounced by the *Journal* today, which everyone here is pissed about."

Tim's relieved to finally hang up. His eyes scan the floor for some clean clothes and they stop on a monogrammed fluffy white robe from Pierre. He gets out of bed and pulls it out of the shopping bag and slips it on, tightly fastening the belt.

Tim checks his cell phone and finds a text message from Danielle: WE NEED TO TALK! He feels like she's yelling at him through the phone. She probably just wants to go to the Tom Cruise premiere next week. He's got to find civilians to date. Mattresses are liabilities.

Walking around in the bright white robe makes Tim feel a little like a ghost. Is he really here? He spreads out his fingers in front of his face. An ink pad's red angry splotch on his wrist reminds him of the party he was at last night. He's also got a mystery bruise on his arm, and studying it makes him vaguely remember getting thrown out of the dive bar, actually ending up on his ass outside, but he quickly pushes the picture back into a deeper file in his throbbing head.

Tim adds a splash of Kahlúa to the coffee he ordered from the deli. It's going to be a long day.

Lacey gives Kate a funny look when she arrives at the office.

"Morning-after outfit?" she asks, handing Kate a pair of scissors. "You may want to confiscate the evidence."

Kate can feel her cheeks getting hot. She quickly sits down at her desk, diving into the rest of today's newspapers, and gets a shot of envy mixed with panic when she reads Column A:

Manic Millionaire Alec Coleman left the opening party for his new hot club, Lush, a little earlier than expected—in an ambulance. "I worked so hard on the fantastic opening party that I passed out from the stress," he told us from his hospital bed early this morning, where he was recovering from stitches to his head where he hit a banquette. "But I made every effort to make sure my VIPs, like **Lindsay** and **Leo** and **Keith Richards's** daughters, were well taken care of all night," he added. "I'll do anything to guarantee the success of my A-list new club."

Lacey says Kate has to call Alec for more news after reading Kate's 150-word item about the party, which has no mention of Alec's incident.

"First of all, I don't believe stress made him pass out. Plus, we can't just follow Column A, and now it's too late to cover another party."

Kate's not sure how to get Alec's phone number. He's not a celebrity, so she can't use a service that Paul subscribes to, aptly called celebrity service. Paul's the only staff member who subscribes to the pricey service and he's only allowed four calls per day, which the fact checkers usually use up, anyway. Kate tries Zoe, who doesn't have Alec's number either, but she says her mom talked to Mrs. Coleman, who says he passed out from popping Quaaludes from his dad's medicine cabinet.

"Well, that would advance the story, wouldn't it?" says Lacey when Kate updates her. "But you still need to talk to him."

Kate's about to give up on getting the number when Lacey suggests calling information, which seems like an obvious step, though Kate didn't think of it herself.

"Hello, Lois Lane," Alec says when she gets him on the first try. "Did you have a good time last night? Did your photographer get good shots of my mom? You know, she's friendly with Henry Carnegie. He's like my godfather." Paul warned Kate that everyone claims a close tie with Carnegie, but the publisher's sacred-cow list is actually very short—and it doesn't include the Coleman family.

"How are you?" she asks, slowly. "I read in Column A that you, um, had a little problem last night."

"It must be a slow news day."

"Well, it's a deadline day."

He pauses, sucking in his breath. "Okay, Lois Lane, let's play. I'll give you something better and you leave me alone, maybe get Paul to run a pretty picture from my party on his page."

"Um, okay," she says, unsure if it really is okay. Do they teach these things in journalism school? (Why doesn't she know anyone who even knows anyone who went to journalism school?) Kate remembers Paul warning her to never make any promises.

"Well, the nightclub Moola is about to close and the investors were the last to know," Alec whispers, even though he's at home, probably alone.

He says a prominent gallery owner and an actor are among the pissed-off investors, and Moola's owner was last spotted couch-surfing in Beverly Hills. "Call me back if you need more, my masseuse is here—that fall did a number on my back!"

Kate feels like she's been given a secret key. She rushes to tell Paul and Lacey about the Moola lead. "I think it could be a great feature!" she says.

"Kate, you're only twenty-two," says Lacey. "You'll have plenty of time to write features later. Beware of the meteoric rise. For now focus on writing your first item. Start by calling every investor, find the owner, and don't forget to call Moola's listed phone number. Everyone has to know that we're giving them the chance to confirm, deny, or comment."

The hours seem to fly by as Kate reports the story out, but she's suddenly exhausted after they ship the magazine. She sinks into a cab back to Brooklyn, which she can expense since she worked late. Rain slicks against the windows and the city looks blurred and clean. When you're in transit, no one can stop you and you don't have to even answer the phone. You have vectors someone else is paid to navigate.

When the cab pulls up to her building, she gives the driver a big tip for not trying to talk and letting her just enjoy the silence. Inside, Nick is lying asleep on the couch while the television news blares, washing a white glare across his face. Kate turns it off and gently tries to wake him so he can sleep in his bed.

Nick's shaggy brown hair is matted to his face and his eyes are red because he fell asleep with his contact lenses in again. She pushes him toward the bathroom.

"What glamorous jobs we have," says Nick.

Kate laughs, even though she's a little startled by her pale and tired reflection in the toothpaste-speckled bathroom mirror. She looks like she's aged five years since graduation. "Very glamorous."

They walk out of the bathroom and head to their bedrooms across the hall from each other. Nick leaves his door open just a tiny crack. It's not an invitation, and even if it were, Kate wouldn't widen it. It's just their way of saying this is better than being alone. Faintly, she can hear him telling Annie on the phone that he misses her and he's disappointed she can't come visit again anytime soon.

"How are we going to make this work if we only see each other once every two months?" he asks in a loud whisper.

Eight hours later, they wake up more rested than they've been in weeks. It's Saturday morning and they're not hung over. It didn't even occur to them that last night was Friday night, which used to be their big night out in college. "I think people go out for brunch," he offers when Kate wonders what they're supposed to do on an early weekend morning.

They throw on jeans and sneakers and Nick wears the old Yankees baseball cap that he had on the day they met at the freshman dorm.

They head to the corner diner and Kate spreads her usual armful of newspapers out on the table after they order. If she doesn't read the papers before noon, she starts panicking that she's missed something that Lacey will ask her about Monday morning.

"Reading the papers with you is a competitive sport," says Nick, laughing when Kate complains that Column A ran an item that she found out was false after a few phone calls. Apparently Column A doesn't have fact checkers and doesn't follow Lacey's rule that you have to call everyone involved in a story. The waitress keeps pouring coffee and they keep sitting there, reading section after section with warm sun streaming in from the windows. The bacon is overcooked and the coffee bitter, but it doesn't matter.

After breakfast they go to the grocery store for the first time since they moved in four months ago. It seems that maybe this is what they would do if they didn't have such consuming jobs.

"We have to start doing something to be healthier," Nick says. "I don't think I've eaten anything that was made anywhere but in a restaurant kitchen in months."

It sounds like a New Year's Eve resolution that will last a week, but right now Kate is willing to play along. There's no reason they can't have control over their lives, even if that control is only over what they eat. In the produce section, Kate watches a couple buying lettuce. These two must go grocery shopping every weekend, she thinks. They're in sweatpants, carrying newspapers and books in tote bags, and Kate feels a little stirring of jealousy, even though she knows that's not what she wants to be.

Kate goes into the dairy section and starts grabbing eggs, milk, juice. Things with an expiration date in the near future. She can almost feel all the alcohol and cigarette smoke from the past weeks seep out her skin and evaporate in the cool refrigerator air. This is where things are kept safe from rot and mold, at least for a week or two. Enough time to recover, get some rest, slow down.

Nick comes down the aisle, arms full of paper towels and toilet paper. He takes one look at Kate's cart and starts laughing. "Are you nuts? That will all go bad before we even remember to open the fridge again."

Before Kate can protest, he starts putting back the milk, the eggs, the orange juice. He takes the cheese out of her hands and puts it on the shelf.

"Come on, Kate," he says, sounding a little like her dad used to when she wanted too many new toys at the store. He puts his hand on her shoulder. "We're going to have to go out and be glamorous for a long time before we can start staying home."

Blake spent much of the morning pounding water. He stayed up late again blowing lines with Bethany and her friends who own a big loft in Soho. It was a combination of semifamiliar faces of strangers and a few people he has semihated for years. No one seemed in any rush to go home, and there was no mention of any kind of work in the morning. It feels like a fifteen-pound weight is pressing down on his sinuses even though he popped four Sudafeds when he woke up.

When he gets to his desk, clutching his latté like a lifeline, he starts with the *Examiner* and immediately gets hit with the familiar dread when he reads the first paragraph of a long item he knows he should have had. Kate seems to have gotten the hang of her job pretty fast:

The name Moola once epitomized fin de siècle New York nightlife. It was the place where the celebrity of that moment, **Leonardo DiCaprio**, often celebrated his post-*Titanic* fame in the ridiculously exclusive third-floor VIP room, the place that a steady stream of gossip-column items depicted as almost too hip and happening to be true. But none of those past glories were reflected in the terse recorded announcement that played for anyone who dialed the club's main number yesterday. Moola's closing and the club's boldface investors are the last to know.

Fin de siècle? Kate's only twenty-two. Fresh off the upstate boat. Paul must be editing her pretty heavily, but still, it's a solid scoop. Blake's phone rings. The Nerd must have also just read the column.

"Can I see you in my office now?" he says with a voice stiffer than cardboard.

Blake takes a deep breath and heads down the hall. He tries to look appropriately contrite while being badgered by The Nerd about getting scooped on the Moola item. A few years ago Blake would have had more acute column envy, but now he just wants this little meeting to end. Maybe it's the coke residue still coursing through his system, or maybe he's just getting tired of writing the same stories. Mad Libs for media whores. Just fill in the name of the nightclub closing or the hotel opening and the person fighting over the debts left behind. Wash. Rinse. Repeat.

The Nerd pushes his glasses up on his nose. "Who is this Kate Simon, anyway?"

He's probably wondering if they should hire her. That's the thing about being scooped by someone who must get half of Blake's salary. The Nerd looks particularly pissed about this one. The editor in chief must have yelled at him this morning. Everything about *Manhattan* magazine is top down, with usually at least one buffer between the editor in chief and the reporters, unless you do something really wrong like write something that pisses off an advertiser, or worse, the publisher's friend.

Blake offers up another item, the one about the socialite couple getting divorced.

"I'm beginning to forgive you," says The Nerd, leaning back in his chair. His glasses slip down his nose and he leaves them there. He's still pissed.

"But stay on that Moola item. Maybe we can advance it for next week."

don't confuse attention with affection

Who wants another Bellini?" asks Zoe, because Bellinis are what you're supposed to drink at Cipriani 42nd Street, a cavernous old bank transformed into an elegant catering hall. Kate thinks it's one of those grand New York places that feels like a set from an old movie.

The three gossipteers plus Zoe are getting drunk after watching the world premiere of the new mediocre but expensive Tom Cruise movie. Paul wanted to go but had to hand over his tickets and press passes to Kate at the last minute because his son came down with a fever. Kate wonders if Paul's column would be more interesting if he still made the party rounds the way he did a decade ago. Almost every other gossip columnist Kate has met is single and dating someone much younger who really, really likes to go to parties. Or married and cheating with someone much younger who really, really likes to go to parties.

It turned out that Kate, Zoe, Tim, Blake, and Robin were all sitting in the same row (on the left side, toward the back of the orchestra) at the Ziegfeld, along with every other gossip columnist in town. They had to wait an hour while the theater filled up, with the most famous people arriving last. The syndicated dinosaurs like Tiffany Gold and The Suckup were in the center sixth row, standing up until the lights went down to flaunt their hard-earned status. Tiffany was wearing a powder-blue kimono-type dress because the movie was filmed in Japan, Kate guessed. The Suckup was in a white suit and a red bow tie, waving his hand at the wrist as if he were riding on a parade float.

"Please don't let that be us in thirty years," said Tim, and Kate felt a shudder shock her spine.

They finish their Bellinis and head into the after-party fray, holding notepads and tape recorders while Zoe flirts with Todd Slattery, that guy she went home with after the Lush opening, who's thankfully not with Opportunistic Actor tonight. He had called Kate earlier, fishing to be her plus-one for the after-party.

"Let's get this party started," says Blake, taking his tape recorder out of his blue blazer pocket.

The clipboard chicks usher them to the VIP area and make a big show of kissing Tim and Blake on each cheek. Blake introduces Kate to the queen clipboard chick, who scurries off to find Tom Cruise.

One of her minions asks the three to pose for a photo for WireImage .com and the guys sandwich Kate between them, wrapping their arms over her shoulders. "Yeah, like anyone's going to run a picture of us unless we're in some scandal," says Tim, laughing.

"But appealing to our narcissism isn't a bad tactic," adds Blake, handing a business card to the photographer.

Kate wishes she were wearing some makeup. She doesn't know yet that most everyone who appears on the Web site knows to wear plenty of face powder. Plus, they know to pose with one foot in front of the other. If you turn sideways—the way she did—your arms look enormous. You look thinnest if you put your hands on your hips.

A pretty actress who hasn't had a decent part in about five years walks by and gives Tim a big hug, her cleavage practically bursting out of her tight dress.

Tim shrugs. "We've all got our B-list pets," he tells Kate once the actress is gone. "They come through when we have a Friday-afternoon dry spell and I plug their shit when they need it. Plus, they're item slot machines after a few drinks. They don't even know all the shit they have stored up."

No one is whispering anything to Kate. No kisses from famous people or even publicists. She has no idea what to ask anyone or how to even get anyone to talk to her and her tape recorder. Tim's now talking to Tom Cruise and Blake's cornered the leading lady, who's so thin her shoulder blades stick out of her bare back like bony wings.

Kim Cattrall is leaning against the wall as if she needs a little break. She could be worth a quote, thinks Kate, taking a deep breath and heading over. A clipboard chick suddenly appears at her side with a tight smile. Kate explains that she's writing up the party for the *Examiner*.

"Just two questions," she says sternly, as if there's a line of reporters waiting to interview the actress.

Up close, Kim's skin has an orange tint, as if she's been doused with fake tanner or, worse, has jaundice. She looks much better on camera. But she's a pro on the party circuit and she throws Kate a few lines about how Tom Cruise was her first celebrity crush.

When Kate finishes the interview, Blake grabs her hand.

"Come on," he says. "We're getting out of here."

Tim has Zoe's hand and they run out of Cipriani, pausing only to pick up the heavy gift bags by the door. Kate wonders if it's okay that she got only one celebrity quote, and it had nothing to do with the movie. Should she have tried to talk to Tom?

Tim thinks not. "By the time you close your column, we'll already have covered the shit out of this party," he says, and grabs an extra bag. "We're doing you a favor by getting you out of here now."

In the cab, they tear apart the gift bags. Tim downs everyone's mini vodka bottles, throwing the empty bottles out the window and scattering shards of glass across the street. Kate offers the red nail polish to the driver in case he has a wife or daughter. He smiles and tucks it in his pocket.

"Where are we going?" Kate asks as they pass Penn Station. It's 11:11 P.M. She makes a wish that she'll get a feature story in the *Examiner* soon, something to prove that she can do something other than interview the people desperate to be interviewed, people the editors never want to hear from, anyway. Since everything happens so fast, she's also nervous that if she stops to think about one item for too long, she'll miss the next one.

"After hours," answers Tim, before kissing Zoe's neck.

They pull up to a door with no sign, just a red lightbulb burning over the entrance. Kate wonders if she'll ever know New York the way these guys do.

Inside is a dark room with video games, old couches, and a motor-cycle—it could be a suburban basement, and Tim and Blake act like they own it. Tim goes to get free drinks and Blake focuses on the jukebox. It suddenly doesn't matter where the celebrities in the city are and what they're doing. A big bear of a bearded man named Tony introduces himself as the owner of the bar, South, which is clearly the guys' after-hours spot, and pounds the guys on the back, stuffing drink tickets in their pockets. He thanks Tim for running an item the previous week about a *Saturday Night Live* cast member making out in South's bathroom with a girl who wasn't his fashion designer girlfriend.

"Tony, I'll trade you free advertising for free drinks anytime!" says Tim. Then Tony whispers something to Tim.

Tim writes something down on a napkin on the bar and shoves it in his back pocket. In two days an item will appear in Column A about a certain respected *fighting* actor joining the *club* at South for bringing a fan to her knees in the bathroom.

Kate's starting to catch on that Tim's trick is to always seem to be blow-ing off work, but in fact, he's always working.

"You Can't Always Get What You Want" by the Rolling Stones comes on and Blake starts dancing around as if he were alone in his bedroom with the shades drawn, sandy-blond hair flopping in his face. "Yes I can!" he keeps shouting over the chorus. "Yes I can!"

They all start dancing and Kate thinks for the first time that this city feels like home, or at least a college campus where you can always find your friends late at night if you know where to look. Kate feels like she's part of a legion of snoops who are always the last ones standing at the parties—and get paid for it.

"I want to show you something," says Blake, dragging Kate down the dark stairs by the bathroom. The cracked concrete floor is muddy with beer, cheap vodka, cigarette butts, empty plastic cups, making a mess of Blake's khaki cuffs. It's a good thing she's wearing a dress. He leads her past an old photo booth covered with photo stickers of him and Tim on various late nights with marginally attractive women adorned with body pierces, tattoos, and dark eyeliner. Blake pushes aside a tattered green couch and opens a hidden cellar door, revealing a small room with a long card table. They sit down in folding metal chairs.

"Welcome to the clubhouse," he says, offering her a line of coke, and she takes it, inhaling the chemical powder that drips back to her tonsils and instantly makes her feel like spilling all her secrets.

She shakes her head and lets her hair fall out of its clip. She runs her fingers through the knots and notices that he's still staring at her. "What?"

"Kate, you're pretty," he says, taking a hand to her cheek. "Don't you think we should kiss? Make out a little to get it out of the way?"

He's grinding his teeth and Kate knows he'll regret this conversation in the morning. Blake is supposed to be the polite one. Besides, Kate would much rather have Blake as an ally than as a two-week fling. He's already told her about his girlfriend, Bethany. Kate won't help someone cheat.

She pulls away and he sits back in his chair and sighs. Then he smiles and she thinks maybe this was a test. "Okay, well, I tried. And if you change your mind . . ."

She knows this is going to sound like one of those lines you don't mean, but in this case she actually does mean it. "I really like you. How about we stay friends for a long, long time?"

Blake smiles. "Fair enough," he says, shaking her hand as if they were meeting for the first time, and instantly the polite Blake is back.

Kate's ready to go home, but she's not sure how these guys ever decide to call it a night. She doesn't want them to think she can't keep up.

"I really have to get home," she says, wondering how she'll ever fall asleep with her heart pounding like a jackhammer through concrete.

"How about I give you an item if you stay out a little longer," says Blake, chopping up a small chunk of cocaine with his laminated press pass.

"Why would you give me an item if you could use it yourself?"

"Because I can't. And you'll trade me another one back when I need it."

After snorting another line, he says the movie producer Harry Stein was airlifted out of St. Barts last week and is now at an Upper East Side hospital.

"The *Times* said he has a bacterial infection, but my father and step-monster were having dinner with Harry and his wife in St. Barts the night before, and they say the real problem is that his testicle blew up like a balloon from the infection," says Blake, pushing his hair out of his eyes and shoving his little Ziploc bag back in his blue blazer pocket.

"Can we print that kind of thing?" she asks, suddenly feeling a little rush. There are certain people Lacey particularly likes bringing down, and Harry Stein is at the top of the list.

"Well, I can't, because my dad will kill me," he says, lighting up a cigarette. "But you should go for it."

"How do I confirm it?"

He laughs, taking a long drag of his cigarette. "It's not going to be easy, but it'll be worth it. I'm sure Lacey will be impressed if you can pull it off."

Kate wants to show her gratitude but she doesn't have any fresh intelligence.

"You should write something about this new chef, Marco Mancini," she says, blurting it out before deciding if sharing her current obsession would help or harm her—or make it so someone will steal him away.

"The guy opening that restaurant Coast in two weeks? I just got that invite. Why?"

"My sources say he's the one to watch," says Kate. He doesn't have to know her only source is Zoe. Kate wonders if she should be giving away her idea, but it seems safer in someone else's hands. And if Blake ends up writing something about Marco or Coast, she can always claim credit later.

"I'll look into it," he says. "Do you know the guy?"

Kate shakes her head.

"So you've just decided to become his fairy publicist mother?" Blake asks.

"No, I—" Kate takes a deep breath, turning away from the table with the coke on it. "No, I just thought it could be a good tip for you."

Blake raises his glass. "Well, then," he says. "To playing trade." Kate clinks her glass against his.

On their way back upstairs, Kate stops in the bathroom to call her voice mail so she won't forget any of the Harry Stein details, practicing for the first time a trick she learned from Blake at Terry Barlow's party.

"Harry Stein. Testicles. Balloon. St. Barts," she whispers into her cell phone. Trying not to touch anything in the filthy bathroom, she re-applies her lipstick and stares at her reflection. The hair, the eyes, the lips are all the same, but there's something more coarse than comfortable, as if each flake of tobacco, each grain of alcohol, each crystal of cocaine consumed tonight were molting beneath her skin.

Upstairs, Tim says Zoe is at the deli buying more cigarettes, probably pissed off that Tim didn't offer to go get them for her. He's already failing her tests. Blake is focusing on picking more songs on the jukebox. Beyoncé's "Crazy in Love" comes on and Blake starts dancing again.

Kate sits down on the couch next to Tim, kicking off her new shoes and rubbing her pinched toes. "So do we need to go out like this every night to make a name for ourselves?"

"Yes and no," says Tim, draining his drink. Ice cubes rattle around the empty short glass, fighting their fate. "You should just want to be four percent famous."

Kate's not sure if it's the drinks or the drugs or even the threat of dawn, but Tim is making some sense. She'd rather have 4 percent than no percent. Nothing would be worse than no percent.

"I thought Andy Warhol said everyone will be famous for fifteen minutes," she finally says.

"But that's not true. Everyone won't be famous for fifteen minutes. Everyone is a lot of people, and being famous for only fifteen minutes doesn't get you very far. Maybe like a quarter of one percent of the whole population will ever be famous, if only for a quarter of an hour." He pounds his fist on the table, sending someone's cell phone clattering to the dirty cement floor. No one seems to notice.

The equation still sounds vaguely familiar. "I think there's a movie from the seventies called *The Seven-Per-Cent Solution*," she says, remembering that the title had something to do with the amount of cocaine Sherlock Holmes consumed. Would that be more or less than what she just did with Blake downstairs?

"Hello? Are you listening? I'm not talking about *movies* here. I'm talking about boundaries! What I'm saying is all of us"—he stretches out both hands—"we all—well, at least me and you and all the people we run around with—*should* want to be just four percent famous. That's not cover-of-tabloids famous or so famous you can't walk down the street without being mobbed. But it's famous enough for a certain slice of the population to know your name, to want to sit next to you at dinner, and for you to have something at least relatively interesting to say. For your face to look slightly familiar but not be a usual suspect on party-picture pages. Famous enough to get good tables and free shit but not have to pay the tax of living under the microscope. Famous enough that people will always tell you, even if it's a lie, that they loved your last column or you looked great on TV or they can't wait to catch up. Famous enough that someone will always hire you to leverage that four percent because you can occasionally take it higher. Four percent famous, baby. Four percent!"

Blake looks over at them, shrugs, and goes back to dumping quarters in the jukebox.

"Four percent!" shouts Tim. "Any more and you know it can't last."

He polishes off his drink and orders another.

"Forty percent is bullshit! Someone—no, *I*—will *knock you down*. Hell, I'll suck the piss right out of you. Make you pay for it. But if you've just got four percent, people aren't going to worry about you stealing the fucking spotlight. Four percent famous is enough to feed the ego without having the ego fuck you," Tim yells, knocking over his fresh beer as he waves his hands in the air again.

"Can I get another beer?" he yells out to no one in particular. He looks around the bar where they've been hanging out for hours, as if taking in the damp cement floor, the tattered furniture, and the toilet seat hanging precariously over the bar for the first time. "Where was I?"

"Four percent . . . famous," says Kate slowly.

"Right. If you settle for just four percent, you don't always want fame so badly, the desperation disfigures your face like Botox-resistant wrinkles. If you shoot for four, you may get four, or even forty, but if you want anything more than fifty, you're totally fucked. You end up selling out, imploding, combusting, melting down, just another late-night television special starring yours truly. Watch the fucking shows, people!" he screams out, but the place is empty save for the two of them, the bartender, and Blake. "It's all the same story."

Tim leans in close and belches, letting Kate smell every drink he's consumed tonight.

"So who is four percent famous?" asks Kate.

"Well, first you have to think about the whole goddamn world. Four percent famous means a Sherpa in Nepal or a surfer in Sydney has never heard of you. But a soccer mom may have. That hotel guy dating Uma Thurman is a good example. He's got a big loft, a hot girlfriend, and goes to all the good parties, but will you ever see his face on the cover of a magazine? No! He'll never be more than twenty percent because he's not trying to be, and he pays a publicist thousands of dollars every month to keep him out of the columns unless it benefits him."

Zoe walks back in with two packs of cigarettes and Blake calls her over to the jukebox and asks for quarters. Tim doesn't notice.

"But don't actors need to shoot for a hundred percent?" Kate asks.

"Not if they want to keep getting good work. Once you're over eighty-five percent, it doesn't matter what you're shooting for. But to get there, you should want something more than a high fame quotient. You should want quality and endurance. You should want something more than fame if you want it to last."

Kate wonders if she'll ever work up the nerve to interview anyone more than 1 percent famous. "So who's a hundred percent?"

"Well, that Sherpa will probably know of Bill Clinton. Madonna. Michael Jackson."

"Who's fifty percent?"

"Kate!" He's starting to slur his words and his eyes are tearing from a coughing fit. He lights up a cigarette. "You're missing the point. It's an equation of instinct. It's not about the math. It's about the machine!"

Zoe walks over, wobbling in her new satin red heels that are half soaked with whatever's flooding the floor.

"What are you guys talking about?" she asks, sitting down on Tim's lap and wrapping her arm around his neck.

"Just work stuff," he says. "Tricks of the trade."

Tim and Zoe stumble out of South around dawn. "I need to bring my sunglasses when I go out with you guys," she says, squinting at the shiny specks in the sidewalk.

"More fun than going out with Todd Slattery, right?"

"I'm not going out with Todd Slattery."

"Good. I'd hate to see you date someone who got a nose and a chin job to look like Ben Affleck."

Zoe laughs. "Really?"

"Really. I know everyone's dirty little secrets."

Tim easily hails them a cab and asks Zoe for her address, but she says she wants to go back to his place. She doesn't want to go back to her apartment. She's probably worried what the doorman would think, or worse, that they'll run into her dad getting up early for work.

By the time the cab pulls up to Tim's, they can barely keep their hands off each other long enough for Tim to pay the driver. He briefly wonders if he can expense the cab because Zoe may be good for future tips about her dad's frenemies. Tim manages to distract Zoe, pushing her up against the wall and kissing her hard enough on the lips so she doesn't see the fat rat scampering across the stairs. He fumbles with his keys. Tomorrow he'll send an intern to get those colored plastic things.

Inside his apartment, Tim pushes a pile of newspapers to the floor—or what should be the floor under the dirty clothes and empty beer cans and liquor bottles—to clear a spot on the couch. As he unhooks Zoe's pale-pink lacey bra, he wonders if she has any items he could use tomorrow. He's going to get to work late again. Her dad must have some scoop. He runs his hands down her smooth white skin, which looks as if it's never seen the sun. Private-school girls like Zoe sit on the beach under big straw hats. He lifts her up—she can't weigh much more than 110 pounds—and carries her into the next room, where he throws her down on his bed, but he still can't get that excited about her and has to down half a bottle of Nyquil to ease a sudden, decidedly unsexy, coughing fit.

"Maybe you should give up smoking at least until that cough gets better," she says.

He lights a cigarette and inhales deeply, blowing out smoke rings. "Nobody likes a quitter."

She asks him if he needs to come down a little and he nods. They each take an Ambien and lie down. They want each other—really, they do—but the chemical cocktail coursing through their bloodstreams is slowing down their hearts and making them sweat cold through the sheets.

Zoe wakes up early the next morning, saying something about having to be at the office for a tasting by a new chef. His head feels as if it's leaking brain fluid again. Next time he won't get as fucked up. Next time they'll actually have sex. She says something about a morning-after outfit and Tim thinks she says the morning-after pill, which doesn't make any sense.

"Early-morning shopping at Banana Republic is the best fashion tip Kate ever had," she explains.

Zoe quietly walks around the apartment, gingerly sidestepping the old take-out Chinese food containers and junk mail on the floor. She pulls on a pair of red lacey underwear, but they're about a size too big. Shit. From across the room Tim realizes it's Danielle's. If he had a maid, this would never happen. Zoe takes them off and looks at the tag, scowling.

"I would never buy lingerie at Victoria's Secret," she says, throwing them back on the floor and giving her smooth, long black hair a flip. She seems most offended by the lackluster label.

"But I like you much, much more," he says, coming over and taking her face in his hands and kissing her. "Much, much more."

Zoe laughs as if she could care less. She has more important things to worry about than her predecessors. She is only interested in right now. She gives up looking for her underwear and throws on her dress and her stained shoes. On her way out, she leaves him her phone number and the number for her cleaning lady. Zoe is a woman with initiative. Zoe is not a mattress. Tim feels as if something slightly rusty came unhinged in him sometime before dawn, and he's not sure if he should feel excited or scared. He just knows he feels something, and that alone is more than he would have expected.

B renda Starr! You're late today!" says Joe later that morning. "You must have been out at the Tom Cruise movie premiere!" He holds up a photo in the Daily Dish of the star walking the red carpet at the Ziegfeld. Kate remembers seeing the tabloid's photographer lunging over a velvet rope to get the shot and then getting yelled at by Cruise's publicist for not asking permission first. When she looks carefully at the photo in Joe's hands, she spots half of Tim's face in the background. Two percent famous?

Joe wants to hear all about the party, so Kate tells him about interviewing Kim Cattrall.

"She's so over," he says sadly, putting his hand on his bulging belly. He makes sure Kate takes her receipt, knowing that she can expense the publications.

"You following this Stanley Stahl scoop?" asks Joe, tugging on Kate's scarf. "Your friend at Column A reported today that the guy's got famous friends who may also get charged for selling off their stock before the FDA verdict. It sounds like a good story to me."

"You and every other reporter in town," says Kate, worried that the scandal keeps getting bigger. Paul's been working on it but he can't get anywhere, either. No one knows which of Stahl's boldface friends are getting charged because no indictments have been filed yet.

"Met your Basil yet?" Joe yells out predictably as Kate walks away.

"Find me black orchids first, then I'll find the guy," she shouts over her shoulder. She turns back around. "What's the use of finding him if I'm going to be busy trying to save him the whole time?"

When Kate finally gets to the office, she tries to transcribe her interview with Kim Cattrall. She puts the mini cassette in the recorder but Kim's voice sounds garbled, as if she's underwater. Kate opens up the recorder and the tape unspools all over her fingers. At least the actress didn't say anything good, but Kate still has to cover for herself.

"Happens to the best of us," says Gavin, the sportswriter who sits next to Kate. "That's why you need a digital one like mine." He holds up a tiny little device, one that could easily slip into a pocket. Kate writes down the make and model and hopes she can expense it.

Kate walks into Lacey and Paul's office and tells them she saw Tim and Blake at the premiere party last night at Cipriani. "They're both covering it before we go to press," she says, hoping this means she's off the hook.

"Well, did you get anything you think they didn't get?" asks Lacey.

"I interviewed Kim Cattrall."

They look even less impressed than Joe did.

"Did she give you an item?" asks Lacey, and Kate shakes her head.

"Well, did you have a good time?" asks Paul. Kate notes that he's wearing a nice suit even though he's not covering any events tonight.

"Definitely," says Kate. "Tim and Blake are really fun."

"So I've heard," says Lacey, who raises her eyebrows and shoots Paul a worried look when she thinks Kate's not looking.

Kate has to come up with an item, and fast, so they don't think she's just using her job to create a social life. "Harry Stein's testicles blew up like a balloon last week in St. Barts," she suddenly tells them. "That's why he's in the hospital now, even though his flack says it's a bacterial infection."

They both look right at Kate and start grinning.

"I love it," says Paul, raising his eyebrows. "And better your name on the item than mine."

Lacey nods. "First do a Nexis search and make sure nothing else has been written about this. Then call his rep, Todd Slattery. But be careful," she says, writing down Todd's phone number. "He can be a real asshole."

Kate remembers Todd as one of Zoe's conquests but doesn't mention the connection to Lacey. She goes back to her desk and does some research. No reports of Harry's testicles on Nexis.

Kate gets interruped by a phone call from Zoe, who wants to share her outtakes from last night at Tim's. "I have never seen a messier apartment," she tells Kate. "It's borderline pathological. I gave him my cleaning lady's phone number and said he should only call me after he calls her."

Kate tries to explain that she's on deadline but Zoe keeps chatting.

"Well, he couldn't get it up after all the coke, so we just made out for a while."

Zoe sounds as if she's popped a few Ritalins already, and it's only 2:30 P.M.

"He's definitely not boyfriend material."

"Because he's a gossip columnist with a drinking problem or because his apartment is a disaster?"

"Because I am not looking for Mr. Right right now," she says.

Kate wonders if Mr. Right would be repelled by a gossip columnist. Zoe's still rambling on about Tim, and Kate hopes this inevitable uncoupling doesn't ruin her new relationship with him.

"I said I'd go to Da Silvano with him on Sunday for dinner," Zoe is saying. "The publicist is giving him a free meal for running a sighting of Sarah Jessica Parker there."

"Well, Sunday night means he probably has at least another girlfriend,"

Kate says gently, to try to manage Zoe's expectations a little. There's nothing worse than thinking you're in control of a relationship when the opposite is true. And Kate is pretty sure Tim keeps his nights busy with pretty publicists and aspiring models.

"At least I'll get a table at Da Silvano without waiting for an hour."

Lacey walks by with a jangle of bracelets and Kate remembers her mission for the day.

"Hey, do you know a guy named Todd Slattery?"

"Of course I do. He's that guy I was making out with at Lush, and we went to Bungalow 8 with him and his friend, that actor." *That's* why his name sounded familiar—Kate has got to get better with these details. "A total asshole, never called me back. But he's a great kisser with a very nice apartment in the West Village. Oh, and Tim told me Todd got a nose and a chin job to look like Ben Affleck."

"Really?"

"Really. He's a wealth of information. Hanging out with Tim is like reading a couture gossip column."

Kate tries calling Lenox Hill Hospital, where Blake said Harry Stein was, but they won't tell her anything. And Blake won't ask his mother any more questions.

"But trust me, it's true," he says when Kate calls him later that day. "The only thing my mother lies about is her age."

She calls Tim, too, but he says he hasn't heard anything, besides that Harry's sick with a bacterial infection. "And hey, watch out for Todd Slattery, he's a real asshole."

"Thanks. So how's your day going?" she asks him, not wanting him to think she was just calling for help. But she doesn't really want him talking to her about Zoe, either.

"I think it's going to have to be a PETA day."

A few hours later, Lacey says Kate should just call Todd already. Deadline is approaching. Kate dials the number slowly and prays for voice mail, but he picks up.

"Hi, um, this is Kate Simon from the *Examiner*."

"Oh, hi. You're a friend of Zoe Miller's right?"

Shit. He remembered. But he doesn't sound like an asshole. "Well, I'm actually calling you about an item I'm working on about Harry Stein."

"Oh no, did he put someone in a headlock again?" he asks, laughing. Easy.

"Not exactly."

"So, what's up? I know you guys are on deadline today."

Kate gets ready to type whatever he's saying, but she wishes she were asking a better question.

"Well . . ." she stammers. "This is a little weird, but I heard that he's actually in the hospital because, well . . ." She pauses. "Because his, um, his testicle blew up like a balloon."

Todd doesn't utter a word, but he's breathing heavily.

"Um, I heard from a solid source that, well, um, his testicle blew up like a balloon and—"

He cuts her off, yelling, "Are you fucking kidding? Please tell me you're fucking kidding!" Now he's shouting so loudly that Gavin can hear every word next to her. "You. Must. Be. Kidding. What you do for a living is fucking despicable. You are the bottom of the bottom feeders. Do you know *anything*?"

Kate swallows hard and tries to not cry.

"I'm just trying to do my job," she says, echoing what she's heard Paul say. "Will you confirm, deny, or comment?"

"You're going to be very sorry you asked me this," he barks, slamming down the phone.

Her desk feels cool against her hot cheek as she puts her head down and all but crumbles. "You've got to pay your dues, kid," says Gavin, echoing what the *Examiner*'s editor in chief, whom they all call The Principal, always says. "We all do."

About an hour later, the phone rings again and Kate jumps, praying that it's not Todd. Perhaps even scarier, it's The Principal. Paul and Lacey she can handle by now. The Principal is still terrifying and probably always will be.

"Come into my office," he says, and she starts panicking, knowing it's about the Harry Stein item. Would he fire her for this?

Kate hasn't been in The Principal's office since the day she interviewed for the job, and the brief walk there feels miles long. She sits down on the leather couch, after pushing away a stack of newspapers to make room. He shuts his door. She counts seven bottles of scotch on a high bookshelf.

"Kate," he says, pausing. "You shouldn't have asked Todd Slattery about Harry Stein's testicles." He's not laughing. "He can make access very tough on us in the future."

"But Lacey and Paul said you would want this item." She hopes telling him that doesn't sell them out.

"Well, I would," he says, staring out of his window, "but there are some political complications."

"Complications?"

"I'd rather not get into it," he says, rubbing his temples. "But suffice it to say Paul's friend Eve is also my friend." Frenemy? "Hell, she's got friends everywhere. She's very close with Harry and called me from his hospital room to give me a hard time." He sighs. "Let's just drop it. And don't trade it to Column A or *Manhattan* magazine. Our prints are already all over it."

Kate thought the editors at the *Examiner* played by the rules. If the top brass here is worried about protecting a well-connected writer at a rival publication, is there any way to write a gossip column that's fair? Why does she have to protect Eve, who's never done anything for Kate? She wishes there were a manual filled with diagrams and flow charts and percent-famous equations. Something to indicate the risks of pissing off person A if you're trying to protect person B, that kind of thing. All she knows now is that there's a lot she doesn't know, and no one's going to explain it to her because the answers are not always fair.

A producer from VH1 wants Tim to come in for a screen test. Tim's been doing these stupid talking head shows for years, shows where they pretty much give you a script of tidbits from Column A to read as they flash footage of celebrities dancing on banquettes and driving around in fancy cars. It doesn't necessarily matter if the gossip is true. Airing the right footage takes priority. Everyone just wants to see celebrities looking glamorous or awful. Only the extreme images matter. The sound bites just move the pictures along.

A few weeks ago, during a long taping in a hot room without windows, Tim tried to tell the producer that Natalie Portman didn't buy a condo in a new Gramercy Park tower, as per the script, that the developers were just trying to hype the new building as a celebrity magnet. Instead, the actress had bought in the West Village. But they already had shot the outside of the building, so Tim had to go along with it.

As much as Tim hates the tapings, and the makeup that never really comes off with the Baby Wipes they give you after, he likes the attention. Whenever any of his friends or family sees him on television, they call right away, leaving messages like, "You're famous!" and "Don't forget about the little people!" He's the most famous person any of them know. At his high-school reunion everyone kept asking him questions about celebrities, thinking he was actually close with them. At least he didn't have to talk about himself or hear about their new houses with yards and second babies.

Now the network is casting a new show with a permanent cast rather than a rotating cast of talking heads. "Most people are too afraid of offending someone to be as funny as you are," the producer says. Tim decides to take that as a compliment.

Tim is e-mailing and catching up on today's papers, not really paying attention to the phone conversation until the producer drops the bomb. "And we'd pay you."

Tim stops typing. "How much?"

"About twenty-five thousand for the year."

He puts on his nice voice, the one he uses with a first-time source. "Greaaaat."

"Greaaaat! I'll have someone call you to set up a screen test next week."

Even reading Robin's item today about Bruce Springsteen forgetting the words to "Born to Run" onstage doesn't faze Tim, who wonders if maybe this VH1 thing could turn into a career, maybe one that would pay for plane tickets to New Zealand or Fiji. Television pays much more than print, and he knows he looks good and sounds funny on those dumb shows—just as long as he doesn't get too fucked up the night before.

He picks up the new issue of *Gotham* magazine and his heartbeat quickens when he sees it's the issue with the spread on gossip columnists. He flips open to it and curses himself for sleeping through the shoot. His mom would have wanted to add it to her scrapbook and show her friends at the beauty parlor. Blake looks smart and sophisticated, posing in a suit at his desk—or someone's desk. A little blurry photo of Tim drinking a beer out of a bottle is superimposed on the corner of the Column A page. It must be that WireImage.com photo from Holly May's birthday party. Danielle's red skirt is partially draped over his leg. His quote about how being a gossip columnist is like "Christmas on acid" is the pull quote, big and bold in the center of the page. (It's a description of fame he stole from Lara Flynn Boyle.) He rips out the piece to send home to his mom. She'll still be proud. He's the only member of his family to ever appear in a magazine.

Blake's father's secretary calls Blake at work, saying she's got his father on the line.

"Punch him through," says Blake, annoyed that his father never calls directly, as if that minute of waiting for his son to answer is too precious to spare.

"An intern just showed me the new issue of *Gotham* magazine," Blake's father says coolly, each word coated with a thin skin of ice, "and I happened to see you on one of those stupid shows about celebrities at the gym this morning. Twice in one day is double what I would like."

Why does his father pay for a trainer to watch him watch television while running on the treadmill? "I wasn't aware I had to clear all press with you," says Blake, flipping open to the article himself. He thinks he looks okay, sitting at The Nerd's desk.

"I just don't understand why you don't get off that column. I could help you get a job at *Forbes*. You could write about something of substance like the stock market."

"Maybe I like my job," says Blake, tired of having the same conversation every few weeks. "Maybe I'm good at it."

"Maybe by the time you grow up you won't be able to get another job. Maybe you will have put me and your inheritance in danger and then you'll actually have to live off ninety thousand dollars a year. Do you ever think about that? Do you ever think about me? As if I need any more scrutiny."

Blake wonders just what kind of scrutiny his dad thinks he's under. Maybe he's just worked up, now that Stanley Stahl's going to trial, charged with insider trading. That's the kind of thing that makes Blake's dad and his friends tremble. *It could happen to me,* they think. It's probably the only time his dad's friends are interesting to watch. Whoever said Edith Wharton skewered her social set because she was bored knew what he was talking about.

"Did you ever call that editor I know at *Business Week*? Don't miss out on opportunities just because you don't want me to help you."

Blake wants to blurt out that he wants to write a book. Leave town. Get something on his own for once. His dad doesn't know anyone in the book publishing industry. But Blake's not sure what he would write about even if he could write about something more substantive than Jessica Simpson's marital woes. Gossip has become as involuntary and blinding as sneezing.

Kate calls Nick at work and asks him for his opinion of the *Gotham* magazine spread. He asks her to hold while he finds Pierre's copy and then he comes back on the phone.

"Truth?" he asks.

"Truth."

"Well, I'm not so sure you should be doing stuff like this," he says. "Especially if you still want to be an investigative reporter. Anonymity would probably work more in your favor."

She decides not to send it home to her parents.

"I'm just doing this until I get a better job. It's not like I want to be a gossip columnist forever," she says, more than a little defensively.

"Well then, you need to be careful of the company you keep. People in New York care much more about what you're doing now than what you say you'll be doing in a few years."

One of the show ponies clip-clops over to tell Tim he has a visitor in the lobby. You would think they worked at the CIA for all the security people had to clear to get to the newsroom.

"Another singing telegram?" he asks. Last week the PR firm behind a new strip club opening near Times Square sent over four dancers dressed like French maids to serve up steak *au poivre* as a promo for the club's steak house—as if anyone would go there for the food. It made the sports guys' week and earned Tim and Charlie free courtside tickets to a Knicks game.

The pony shakes her ponytail and shrugs. "Some girl with a fake British accent."

"Short blond hair? Looks kind of crazy?"

The show pony nods and puts her hand on her cute little hip. "Definitely crazy."

Tim grabs his cigarettes and heads downstairs. Delusional Danielle is not getting the hint. How many more times does he have to blow her off? He made a drinks date and canceled it and hasn't responded to any of her calls or e-mails. Doesn't she have any girlfriends to stop her from this kind of humiliation?

When he gets to the lobby, Danielle gives him a big smile. She's dressed for a nightclub in tight black leather pants, high heels, an off-the-shoulder black sweater, and big silver earrings. He doesn't tell her she has lipstick on her teeth and a smile like a sociopath.

"What are you doing here?" he asks, motioning for her to walk outside with him. They stand under the red news ticker and Tim tries to resist the urge to read it instead of looking at Danielle. He lights a cigarette and offers her one but she shakes her head. She looks weathered in the early-afternoon sun and Tim's a little worried an editor may see them and think she's a hooker.

"I saw you on TV last night! You were great. They must pay you a lot to do that, right?"

Tim is usually pretty good at reading people, but he has no clue what this crazy chick wants from him. "What did you say you were doing here?"

"Well, I was just in the area and—"

"Doing what? Auditioning for Broadway?"

She laughs and touches his shoulder. He imagines her finger could burn a hole the size of a dime through his skin. He has got to get rid of her for good.

"Listen, Danielle, I'm sorry if I wasn't clear, but this isn't working for me."

She sighs and crosses her arms over her chest, pushing her pale tits up through her low neckline. It occurs to Tim that she's under the false impression that he's a real catch, that he actually is some kind of celebrity.

"Well, that's not going to work this time," she says, giving him a weird grin, as if she's holding a surprise behind her back. "We have some important decisions to make."

She looks happy, even a little jazzed. He motions for her to follow him down the street, toward Times Square. He doesn't want anyone to see him talking to her.

Danielle grabs his arm and leans in close, as if he were escorting her to a prom. "Tim," she says in a loud, excited whisper, "I'm pregnant."

Guys in helmets are digging up concrete with jackhammers down the street. Somewhere nearby an ambulance wails. A woman wearing a placard shoves yellow fliers into their hands.

"What?"

She didn't just say that.

"We're pregnant," she says, smiling big this time, revealing the wide lipstick smear on her front tooth.

Tim feels like taking that jackhammer to his head. No, he wants to take the jackhammer to her stomach or push her down a flight of stairs. The ambulance careens around the corner, heading right for them with lights flashing. He wants to insist it can't be his. Demand a DNA test. Call her a delusional psycho bitch. But Tim has had enough experience to know when he's being lied to.

He puts his hands over his ears. "I can't hear you!" he shouts, wishing the ambulance would stop for him, scoop him up on a gurney, and spirit him away to a cool, clean, white bed. "I can't hear a word you're saying."

don't sleep with sources

Blake meets his mother in front of an antiques show at the uptown armory because she doesn't want to walk in alone. "What will people think?" she asks, and he stops himself from saying, "They already know you're alone."

The only thing being passed around is white wine and envy. He should have gone with the cute fact checker, Alison White, to the book party at Elaine's. He hates working a society event on an empty stomach—everyone looks that much more miserable.

They wander through the aisles and Blake hopes Lindsay's not here. That's the last thing his mother needs. The new wife is always the old wife's worst nightmare—a glamorized, upgraded version of herself. Fortunately Lindsay is more into modern decor.

Blake has his tape recorder in his pocket, and it feels heavier than a fifty-pound weight. He's supposed to write up the show for his party-picture page, but he feels frozen at his mother's side, stuck in the role of the Upper East Side son, trying to avoid the gaze of socialites he's managed to offend in his column—even though he always compares them to beautiful movie stars.

Maybe he'll get something at his next stop, the opening of a restaurant called Coast. Kate e-mailed him twice to tell him to meet her there, and she's not even covering it. He remembers her talking about the chef that night at South, a tip Blake promptly forgot all about until now. He'll go if only because he promised Tim wingman support—he's going to ask Zoe to go as his date.

His phone rings and he goes to the hallway to answer it. His mother hates it when he talks on the phone in public. It's Bethany calling from a jewelry show in L.A. "Why don't you look at headboards for us," she says.

Blake wants to say, *Don't be so sure you're a permanent fixture.* The thought of buying more things for *them* instead of *him* is only going to make this harder. But he's too tired and hungry to even think that through right now. "Okay."

Bethany asks if he's made reservations yet for all the double dates he's dreading this weekend. Blake's not sure when their relationship started to be about forging other relationships together. He can't remember the last time they ate dinner alone.

Girls like Zoe take a little more work than mattresses and Tim can't decide if that's a good thing. He can't stop picturing her in a bikini on a tropical beach, somewhere that takes at least eight hours to fly to.

He's been spending his mornings carefully crafting e-mails to her so he won't call and say something stupid he can't erase. And he needs a distraction from Danielle's increasing barrage of e-mails asking him for money and baby name ideas and to sign up for Lamaze class with her. Lamaze? She's got to be kidding. She's not kidding.

He's not doing shit until he's got a DNA test, which he's going to have to try to explain to her. He doesn't care if he has to rip a hair from the baby's head to know for sure.

Danielle's official line is that the antibiotics she'd been taking must have interfered with the Pill and that's why she got pregnant. He should have checked that prescription bottle he found in her purse. He could have looked up the prescription to see if it actually does interfere with birth control; to figure out if Danielle lies about everything or if there was something he could have done to get out of this jail without paying bail.

"I can't have another abortion," she'd told him as they walked into Times Square that day she informed him of the pregnancy. Another? Tim remembers hoping some major news would break on the ticker so he'd have an excuse to run away. "I'm thirty-three. This may be my last chance."

"I thought you were twenty-eight," he'd said.

"I thought you would be excited about this."

I'm a fucking moron! Zoe will never want to date someone who would be dumb enough to fuck a desperate mattress without a condom.

But realistically, Zoe couldn't know. She's probably just not interested in a poor hack who's never going to be on the same rung as the people he writes about. He'd have to stop writing about them to ever be one of them. She could have her pick of rich guys who could fly her around and take her to four-star restaurants without having to endure an annoying publicist's visit to the table in lieu of a check. But maybe, just maybe, an invitation to the opening of Coast, a new restaurant in the West Village, could be irresistible bait. It's the event of the week and he knows she doesn't have an invitation. Only the top editors at *Gourmet* would be invited. He's got a whole book full of hot, easy women who'd go anywhere with him at just a few hours' notice. His chick-ionary, he calls it. He flips through it quickly just to remind himself, though each name is like another itch on his arm, something nagging he doesn't want to flare up again. He wants to bring Zoe.

But for now, he's got to file this blind item, one of the best he's written in weeks:

Which blockbuster actor is trying to squash a rumor about his dark past now that he's married to a squeaky-clean actress? We hear he just paid off a busty, young deaf woman who he had his way with in a nightclub bathroom years ago, boasting to his pals, "I did her a favor!" and imitating the way she talks. She was shopping around a book proposal that the actor preemptively optioned to produce as a movie that we doubt will ever get the green light.

That was fun. But now what? Fuck it. Tim caves and calls Zoe at work. It's not as if he doesn't make much harder calls all day long. She sounds slightly breathless when she answers and he imagines her shiny dark black hair falling over her bony shoulders, those big red lips, the way the skin around her collarbone gets flushed when she gets excited.

"Hey, it's Tim Mack from Column A," he says, instantly wishing he hadn't introduced himself the way he does when he calls people for comment.

"It's about time you *called*."

"Well, you never returned my last e-mail."

"An e-mail that sounds like a Column A item is not the same thing as a phone call. After almost leaving your apartment in someone else's *cheap* underwear, I thought I deserved a call."

She probably wouldn't believe he was doing research to start a lingerie line. So he just goes for it, asking her if she wants to go with him to the opening of Coast. The chef is that guy Marco Mancini, who seems to be popping up everywhere, ready to explode. Tim hopes Danielle won't weasel her way in, which she could do since her friend is the hostess Marco used to fuck. This island is too small.

"It's a little short notice," she says, and he wishes he had called her last week. She pauses for maybe three seconds before blurting out, "I'm already going with Kate but you can come with us."

"That's cool," he says, slightly relieved that he doesn't have to deal with the pressure of a real date. It's just an event and events are easy. If nothing else, it will take his mind off the lawsuit the Loathed Hollywood Lothario's lawyers just faxed over. He's going to have to show it to Tubby, but it can wait a day. It could have easily been buried under the stack of papers piling up on the fax. Faxing is for syndicated dinosaurs' assistants.

Wow. Everyone's here," says Zoe as they walk into the Coast opening party. She points out various chefs and informs Kate of their Zagat guide status and the number of *New York Times*–awarded stars they've gotten. "I told you we would want to be here."

Tim steers them to the bar and points out Marco Mancini's girlfriend, the decorator Wendy Winter, who's holding on to Marco's arm as if they were at a grand ball. Tim leans in close to the girls. "I heard Marco fucked his hostess on his roof last week."

Kate suddenly looks very interested. "How good is your source?"

It's probably the only thing Danielle is good for. "Well, where there's smoke . . ."

"Which one is the hostess?"

Tim nods toward a striking Asian woman in a clingy black dress. Complimenting curves in all the right places—the kind of woman who makes Kate feel clumsy.

Kate drops her pen and gives a nervous little laugh. What's she so nervous about? She takes out her notepad like a novice.

"You're seriously not going to use it as an item?" Tim asks.

The *Examiner* would never run an item like that, but Kate seems fascinated. A waiter with a tray of roasted figs stuffed with Gorgonzola on mesclun greens walks by.

"Hey, buddy, over here!" shouts Tim, and the waiter circles back. "The food better be good for all the hype."

If *he* knows about Marco fucking the hostess on the roof, there's a pretty good chance Marco's going to find out about the baby. Tim's not taking any chances.

Kate considers asking Marco's publicist, Spinster, for a formal introduction to the chef. "She's trying to break into the food world," Zoe explains about Spinster, who's wearing a ruby-encrused lobster brooch on her black silk blouse. "I hear she's been asking every chef in town out to lunch, promising to make them celebrities, with TV shows and cookware lines. But of course she can't represent them all. Most of them hate each other."

Zoe flutters off to make sure her editors from *Gourmet* see that she somehow got invited to the party, leaving Kate and Tim to attack the hors d'oeuvres as soon as they come out of the kitchen.

"Chef's special," says a handsome waiter, presenting them with a familiar tray of slimy orange stuff inside an oyster. "Oysters with sea urchin and passion fruit nectar."

"It looks like something that comes out of my nose after a big night," says Tim. "Does it taste like snot, too?"

The waiter tries to look like Tim has asked a reasonable question. "Uni is sea urchin."

"That's disgusting," says Tim. "Sushi is still a stretch for me."

"You're disgusting," Kate says, sucking the whole thing back as if it were a shot of tequila, the way Zoe showed her how at Pierre's party. It's just as delicious as it was then, with a texture of slippery mango slice and a salty aftertaste, as if it were dipped in summer. Tim tries one after watching her reaction and then they try to finish off the platter, but the waiter moves away after they each devour three.

They move even closer to the kitchen door. That's always the best place to stake out at a party if you're hungry—until the waiters start sidestepping you so they don't have to refill their trays immediately.

"No wonder his hostess fucks him," says Tim, smacking his lips.

"You don't know that's true," Kate says, even though she barely knows Marco. She hasn't decided if she should introduce herself with her affiliation this time around. She picks up another glass of champagne and wanders with Tim around the foodies and the freeloaders, pausing to consult with Robin about upcoming events that promise to have a similar spread of gourmet food and free-flowing booze.

Blake, who arrived minutes before, joins them and points out a ubiquitous party crasher with wild gray hair, named Shaggy, who's refusing to let his photograph be taken by Patricia Cullen, who's now snapping celebrity chef Bobby Flay tasting the shrimp ceviche. The baroness whom Kate first saw at Terry Barlow's party hovers by the bar wearing an extremely short skirt and flirting with the maître d' from the Four Seasons.

Across the room, Marco appears and he's all smiles and *kiss kiss hello I'm so glad you could make it* while being interviewed by a skinny *New York Times* food writer. Zoe tells Tim that the writer gave a glowing review to a new restaurant partly owned by a four-star chef who gave the writer, in turn, a gushing blurb for her new cookbook. In a few days that item will turn up in Column A. The writer will end up being picked on for a year by Tim, who makes a sport of turning people who treasure their anonymity into boldface names.

Kate hears metal clinking against glass. Marco is standing on a stair leading up to the second-floor dining room. Terry Barlow is standing with him, enthusiastically tapping a knife against a wineglass and smiling fakely as if she were on television, even though her camera crew isn't here.

"If everyone could just be quiet for a moment, I promise I'll send out extra trays of desserts," Marco says, flashing a warm smile. The room falls silent enough for Kate to hear someone's cell phone vibrate inside a handbag. "There are a few people I really need to thank for helping me realize my dream of having my own restaurant. Without them, none of this would be possible. It takes a tremendous amount of faith and support to open a restaurant in New York, where there are about eighteen thousand restaurants and a thousand new ones every year. Only one out of five of those succeed. I believe the team behind Coast is a recipe for success."

Kate feels a little electric spark hit her heart when she remembers hearing this statistic at Pierre's party, where she met Marco. She feels like the only one invited to the dress rehearsal for a big Broadway play. While he thanks his investors and staff members by name, Kate imagines what his lips would taste like. He must be a great kisser.

"I got into this crazy business to make people happy," Marco continues, "and seeing so many people I adore look genuinely happy tonight makes me feel extremely proud. So eat, drink, and be merry. But take notes and tell me what you think of the recipes. I trust all of your palettes and I'm counting on you to put me to the test. Please come back and visit once we're up and running." He laughs. "But do me a favor and wait a few weeks so we can iron out all the wrinkles."

The room breaks into applause.

"Sweets for the sweet! *Salut!*" shouts Marco, holding up his glass. Suddenly waiters materialize seemingly out of nowhere, holding trays of shimmery champagne. Everyone grabs a glass and holds it up to the sky.

"Salut!" the crowd roars, like a delicate and deliberate chant.

A few moments later, Kate loses track of Marco. The room feels a few degrees colder in his absence.

She asks a waiter to direct her to the bathroom and wishes she hadn't already drank three glasses of champagne. The stairs seem a little blurry. She looks straight down so she won't trip, and also to avoid the publicist Todd Slattery, who's coming down the stairs behind her. She hopes he doesn't remember what she looks like, but that *Gotham* magazine spread probably reminded him. It is his job, after all, to keep track of such things. Kate pushes through the first door she sees, which turns out not to be the bathroom. It's the entrance to a hallway. She should turn around but she can't help wandering a bit when she hears deep breathing, like the kind you're supposed to do in yoga class, coming from inside an office.

Marco, the missing man of the hour, is sitting with his eyes closed behind a cluttered chrome desk, taking deep, even breaths. Maybe he's napping? Kate tries to tiptoe back to the hallway but crashes into a rack of white chef's jackets, sending hangers clattering to the cement floor.

Marco's eyes slowly blink open, and they're even more stunning than she remembered. She's not sure if it's their warmth or all the oysters with sea urchin she just ate, but Kate feels like something is trying to jump out of her chest.

"Didn't we meet at Pierre Patois's party?" he finally asks.

She realizes she's been holding her breath and slowly exhales. "I'm surprised you remember."

"I never forget a beautiful face." Beautiful? She feels her cheeks getting flushed. "But what are you doing in my office?" he asks, slightly more curious, even amused, than angry.

Paul taught Kate that every good reporter answers a question with another question. "Aren't you the host of the party upstairs?"

He looks at her carefully and smiles perhaps the biggest smile she's ever seen, which is much more startling up close than from across the room when he was giving the toast. Everything about him makes her think about eating chocolate, which she read somewhere was an aphrodisiac, and she wonders how much you have to eat before you feel the same emotions as love. "I asked you first."

"Okay, but if I tell, you have to tell," Kate says, and he nods, grinning. "I'm hiding from someone who's mad about something I almost wrote in my column." She shrugs, trying to make a joke of it, as if dodging bullets at parties is part of her routine.

"I can't imagine what you'd be doing if you actually ran the item," he says. "And what column is yours?" He sits forward in his chair. "I never asked what you did."

"Kate Simon from the *Examiner*," she says, extending her hand as she walks into his office.

"Ms. Simon, I'm a subscriber!" he says, perhaps a little too quickly. He must know that every journalist, especially gossip columnists, wants to hear that people know who they are. "I'm a huge fan!"

His hands are a little sweaty, but his grip is strong. "Thanks. I guess."

"You guess?"

"Well, I kind of hate people thinking I'm a gossip columnist." She stuffs her hands into her pockets.

"What kind of gossip are you?" he asks.

"What do you mean?"

"Well, the ones I've met either want you to feel sorry for them and help them do their job or they want to entertain you with gossip about other people so you'll feel like they're on your team. The scary ones are out for blood."

"I'd rather be known as a journalist."

"What's the difference? Besides, everyone reads the gossip column first. You should be proud."

"I barely know what I'm doing," she says. "I just want to be an investigative reporter one day, but I can't be too picky about my first job out of college." She leans against the wall. "Now it's your turn. What are you hiding from?"

"Everything. Everyone." He looks much younger than thirty-two, which is still older than any other man who has made Kate feel jittery like this. "Just needed a little break from all the small talk," he says, rubbing his temples. "It gets a little overwhelming. That guy Tim Mack from Column A is here, and I want to kill him for that item that called me 'the randy restaurateur.'" He rolls his eyes. "My girlfriend didn't speak to me for a week."

"Your staff told me you went home that night," she says.

"Had I known that you would have gone looking for me, I might have stuck around." Would he have brought her to Holly May's party? Kate coughs so she'll have an excuse for her cheeks reddening. "And my sous-chefs are under strict instructions to tell anyone who asks that I went home after a job."

He's got deep shadows under those liquid chocolate eyes. But when he smiles again, she almost forgets what she has to ask him. She almost forgets his party is weaving on upstairs without either one of them.

"So why were you breathing that way?"

"Aha, can't withhold anything from a gossip columnist. . . ."

"Journalist."

"Same thing," he says, smiling even wider.

He stands up and walks toward her, and she tries to catch her breath. He looks at her as if he's been waiting to get her alone all night. It's the kind of look that women tell their friends about, trying to figure out what it means.

"In the interest of full disclosure"—Kate notes that Spinster has him well trained already—"I was meditating. But that's off the record."

Marco is not the kind of person Kate would have expected to mediate. Meditation is for people like her parents, who once took her to a monastery in Woodstock for a meditation workshop, where you kneel on cushions for hours, just staring straight ahead. She kept changing positions, stomping her legs to stop them from tingling. She never could keep still.

He bites the inside of his lower lip. "Well, let's just say it was necessary."

"The stress of the hostess and your girlfriend in the same room?"

He steps back as if she just hurled something sharp at him and immediately Kate wishes she could take it back, but there's no delete or escape button within reach.

"So, you really are a gossip columnist!"

"I'm sorry. I shouldn't make jokes like that."

He sits back down at his desk and looks down at a pile of papers, which he pushes into a corner with a sweep of the hand. Whatever valve she caught open has sealed up tight. "No, no. I appreciate your candor. But I'm certainly not confirming or denying anything about my personal life, especially with a professional gossip. But, you should know not to believe everything you hear."

Tim may exaggerate, but he doesn't make things up from scratch. Where there's smoke . . .

"It's questions like that that keep me hiding out down here, trying to calm down."

"Does it make them go away?" Kate thought she was the only person in New York who would rather hide in a basement than work a party. She thought she was missing the gene for schmoozing, that smooth ability to talk to anyone about anything for five minutes and then find a polite out, like "Can I get you another drink?"

"Obviously not," he says, "but sometimes at parties like this one I get a little anxious and it's hard to breathe. I wanted to prevent anything like my panic attack this afternoon when the chairs and flowers still hadn't arrived. Oh, and I haven't slept in about a week." He laughs again but it's a nervous laugh, a laugh that says he's not having any fun. "Maybe you could write that the people at the party are waiting, actually hoping, that Coast fails so they can feel better about themselves?"

"I thought they were your friends?"

He asks Kate how long she's been in New York and laughs when she says just a few months. He pauses, biting his lower lip again.

"The people who like me the least are drinking my champagne the fastest, and they're the ones I have to be the nicest to if I'm going to get the reviews I'll need over the next few months." He leans back in his chair and runs his hand through his hair. "Most of the people upstairs went to fancy prep schools and colleges. They start networking in kindergarten, when I was living in Italy with parents who never learned English."

Kate wishes they could stay right here talking, but his eyes are already darting behind her. He wants more than 4 percent, he wants all of it, she thinks, and he's the first person she's met who just may deserve it.

"I'm sorry," he says. "I'd like to stay and hide in here with you all night, but I really should get back to working my party." He stands up. "Not that I want to, or that I really know how. . . ."

"You seem to know what you're doing, at least much better than I do," says Kate, wanting this to last a little longer.

"I'm not so sure, but now I know that at least someone else didn't get any secret memos on how to do it," he says. "You leave first and I'll follow. We don't want anyone to get the wrong idea."

Kate thinks she should drink some water, sober up, and see if Marco still wants to talk to her back at the party, when he really has nothing to gain by talking to her anymore. He's put in his requisite ten minutes of face time with a gossip columnist. Hired help.

When Kate gets back upstairs, Tim says she missed the action.

"Terrence Kielbrant just chucked an oyster shell at Chris Flemming! It was awesome."

Zoe explains that Chris accused Terrence, a newly minted three-star chef, of stealing a recipe for a shot glass filled with both hot and cold liquid, which Chris actually ripped off from a famous restaurant in Spain.

Now Chris and Marco are posing for a photo, both probably trying to think of something funny to say into Blake's tape recorder about the spat. Spinster is coaching from the sidelines like a cheerleader.

"Don't worry, I saved some scoop for you," Zoe says to Kate quickly. "Chris's Food Network show is being canceled because his girlfriend, who's also the producer, caught him cheating on her with his coat-check girl, who he brought here as his date. Classy, huh?"

It's beginning to seem as if getting trapped is sometimes the only way to escape.

The floor at South is starting to tilt, so Tim slouches down lower on the couch. The beer sloshing down his throat tastes like water through a rusty pipe after all that expensive champagne at Coast. He gives Zoe a big, sloppy kiss.

"Bethany," Blake says, throwing his blazer back on after putting five dollars' worth of quarters in the jukebox to play the same songs he always plays. The Rolling Stones' "You Can't Always Get What You Want" starts up once again and Tim's starting to think the song may not actually be his own sound track after all, even though every other time he's heard it, he thinks it's the gospel.

Tim pulls Zoe in close so he can feel all of her pressed up against his chest. She smiles, kissing his neck. He puts his hand on her neck and tilts her face up to his. He kisses her again and wishes he weren't sweating so much. Her hair falls in her face, into their mouths, and he tucks it away behind her ears.

"I like you," he says. Three simple words he hasn't said to anyone else in he can't remember how long. They take a breath. "I like you," he says again. That's the most Tim has ever felt for anyone. Love is a flight that keeps getting delayed for Tim. But it would probably get grounded for good if Zoe knew about Danielle.

"Come on," Tim says, grabbing their coats and leading her outside with his hand on the small of her back.

They hail a cab and immediately start kissing again. Tim wants this to go slowly, to last through the cold months, in fact to last long enough that he'll maybe have someone to go away with for summer weekends when everyone flees the city. He shouldn't even be thinking that far in the future, but he likes this girl. And plotting the distant future is easier than worrying about tomorrow morning.

Zoe says her parents are away and they should go back to her place. Tim wants to see how she and the other half live, so he says sure, but when they pull up to the solid limestone fortress uptown, he starts feeling anxious. Why would Zoe want to date him? She doesn't even need Column A to promote anything. If she's not using him, then what does she like about him? And how fast would she run away if she knew about Danielle?

"I like you," he says again, and she laughs.

"Careful or it will go to my head."

The doorman lets them in and gives Tim the slightest once-over, but Zoe wouldn't bring him back if the doorman were a spy. She's smarter than that. As the elevator climbs, it briefly occurs to Tim that maybe Zoe wants to freak her parents out by getting busted for being with him, a rich-kid rebellion strategy he's learned from observing Blake.

"Don't worry," she says, feeling his fingers tighten around her smooth palm. He tries not to act too impressed as she leads him through her living room. Everything's white and he's a little afraid to even sit down.

"Can I fix you a drink?" she asks when they stop in the kitchen. She looks good even under the unforgiving fluorescent light. He must look like shit. He hasn't slept more than six hours in the past two days.

There's nothing but diet soda and champagne in the fridge. "Have any scotch?" he asks, and she opens a cabinet stocked with only the finest booze. The ice cubes clink against the short glass and make a little lullaby hiss when the amber liquid hits them. He could get used to this.

They take their drinks back to the living room, where Zoe asks Tim to put some music on the stereo. She's got a few old newspapers stacked up on the glass-topped coffee table and Tim likes knowing she must read his column every day. He's already part of her routine.

"What kind of music do you want to hear?" he asks, thinking maybe some jazz. Something that means this cocktail hour is going to be short.

She says she's never actually used the new stereo her dad got her as a college graduation present. It's a mass of tiny lights and wires. The speakers aren't even attached. He plugs them in and scans her CD collection. Lots of Madonna. No jazz.

"I know," she says. "It's embarrassing."

Prince is the best he can do. If they last until Christmas, he'll get his guy at Apple to send an iPod for her customized with Tim's favorite playlists. Tim stifles a yawn when he sits back down next to her, pulling her legs on his lap so she's sitting sideways.

"No yawning!" she shrieks, shaking him when he nods off for a moment. It's so quiet and clean here he could sleep for a week.

She rolls her legs off his lap and walks over to an antique dark-wood desk that she's probably only ever used to write checks with Daddy's money, if she doesn't already have an accountant to do that. She takes a silver case out of a small drawer.

"Cigarette?" asks Tim, thinking that's what she's going for and offering her a lit one.

"I've got something better," she says, returning with a little bag of coke, a razor, and a silver spoonlike hook that she holds up. "It's an antique," she says. "It used to be an ear cleaner in some Ethiopian tribe. My mother brought it back from a charity trip that was yet another excuse for her to buy shit without feeling guilty."

Tim wants to say no, let's just go to bed. Maybe a bottle of wine. Not this. He's got his screen test tomorrow for VH1. He's got to catch up on some rest. But she's already cut out four neat lines and he barely hesitates before taking the Ethiopian trinket from her. She turns up the music and they start dancing around her living room, which has swiftly transformed into their private nightclub high above Fifth Avenue.

When they're breathless and sweaty, they collapse on her bed. He starts kissing her neck, gently pulling off her silky black tank top, which looks like a negligee, and it slides silently off the bed. He's not sure just who started the trend of wearing underwear as outwear, but he likes it.

"Want a Xanax?" she asks, wondering if he needs to come down a little. But the coke was good, much better than the shit he usually gets. He feels just fine. Great, even. The clock next to her bed says 3:33 A.M. Before long they're a tangle of limbs. He pulls her hair a little and she moans, begging him for it. She wants him. He hopes it's not just the drugs that make her want him as he slides inside her, holding still for a moment as she presses her fingers into his back, trying to bring him in even closer.

It's noon and Tim still isn't at work or answering his cell phone. Blake wants to know how the VH1 screen test went and he needs a phone number for an item he's working on. He got a weird call this morning from a girl he knew at boarding school. She said her friend's maid found a dead body in a closet in a Palm Beach mansion owned by a banking dynasty heir, someone who was in Blake's dad's eating club at Princeton. If he calls the Palm Beach police, the story will break in the local papers before *Manhattan* magazine comes out, but if he asks his dad for the guy's number, Blake will get the lecture again about leaving his dad's friends alone. Money, power, and murder are always good ingredients for an item that will get picked up by the other papers and land Blake on television.

Tim finally calls back to say he's just leaving Zoe's apartment. Even though there's a trace of a long night in his voice, he sounds a little lighter—as if he's been on vacation.

"Did you fuck her this time?" asks Blake.

"You want to see the videotape?"

"You're kidding!"

"I'm kidding."

Blake figures Tim slept through the VH1 screen test and isn't sure if it's a good topic to bring up. Maybe Charlie has the banking heir's number?

"I blew off that screen test," says Tim before Blake can mention it. "It's bullshit, anyway."

"I thought they were going to pay you if you got it."

"Yeah, but I'd have to give up Column A. Tubby won't let me do both because I'd have to tape three times a week during the afternoons, including Fridays."

Blake takes a swig of his coffee and swallows loudly instead of saying anything.

"If you were in bed with Zoe Miller all morning, you would blow it off, too."

Kate wakes up late on the morning she has to cover a breakfast charity event at the Pierre hotel, so she quickly hops in a cab, hoping that oversleeping is a legitimate excuse for expensing the eighteen-dollar cab from Brooklyn. There's no time to stop for the papers, so she doesn't get to catch up on the news until she's sitting at her desk at 11:30 A.M. It's almost too late to start with today's news, so she just skims the cover sections of the *New York Times* and reads Tim's column. Kate flips to Robin's column last. There's a photo of Marco sandwiched between Chris Flemming and Bobby Flay at some benefit for kids with food allergies.

Marco's smiling big, broader than the other chefs. They're all in white jackets, and Marco looks as though an anxiety attack is the last thing on his mind. The guy sitting next to Kate is reading his own paper, pausing over the same picture. She wants to tell him how she found Marco meditating at his restaurant opening, wants to tell someone, anyone, that she knows this man in 3-D.

Robin's got an item about a publishing mogul and a prominent art dealer being investigated for selling off shares of Stanley Stahl's company before the FDA verdict. Kate feels anger burning lantern bright somewhere near her stomach. She should have had that item. Maybe if she weren't so distracted by Marco, she could get her work done.

And yet she still can't stop thinking about him when she gets to the office, even though she has calls to return, party schedules to plot, e-mails to answer. She replays again last night's meeting him at the Coast opening, trying to remember the details.

Kate feels as though she's doing something slightly unethical, but she can't stop herself from searching online for information about Marco, as if he were a profile subject she was preparing to interview—that is, if she ever got to write profiles. She pulls up a bunch of Web pages with his recipes that make her stomach almost rumble. Salmon with rhubarb. Sea urchin with raw oysters. She can almost taste the flavors and textures, and the tiny taste buds in her mouth start tingling a little. She finds a photo of Marco and Wendy Winter at a Bridgehampton polo match this summer. His arm is over her shoulder and they're both smiling the way couples smile after a long day together in the sun. Love in the time of the Hamptons.

"You're hard at work," says Lacey, making Kate jump and quickly close the Web page. "Please don't tell me you're e-stalking Marco Mancini."

Kate turns to face her. "I'm not e-stalking Marco Mancini."

Lacey raises her thin blond eyebrows, dyed to match her hair. "Kate, he's charming and cute, but he's a phony. A very ambitious phony."

Lacey quickly walks away and returns with the *Daily Metro*, opened to Robin's column. "But it looks like your man could use a better publicist today."

Decorating Diva **Wendy Winter** gave randy restaurateur **Marco Mancini** the boot after dating him for six months. We hear she got tired of his canoodling with a certain sexy minx.

Kate has to think of the dead mice in the traps in her living room to stop from smiling. Lacey tosses the paper in the trash. Kate has yet to see anyone recycle anything at the office.

"But don't get any ideas. Find a nice normal guy your own age." Kate wonders if Lacey actually thinks Kate has a chance with Marco.

Ever since she began this job, Kate's started to think that everyone else in the industry is listening to her thoughts. Once you start thinking about someone or something, everyone else seems to be doing the same. Before Terry Barlow's party, she had never heard of Marco Mancini. Now she can't stop thinking about him and it seems like she's not alone.

Minutes later Lacey calls Kate, even though they sit just a few feet apart. "You'd better nail down a lead soon," she says. "Paul just called in sick."

Kate wonders what could be wrong with Paul that he'd miss deadline day, but she shouldn't waste any time trying to figure it out. She looks over her notes from last night and decides not to mention anything about Marco and his hostess. Instead, she starts reporting out the Chris Flemming tip from Zoe. The chef may as well be a rock star for the amount of anxiety Kate's feeling now that she actually has to call him.

"Chef, you want Chef?" the person on the other end of the phone asks before screaming, "Chef! Some girl from the *Examiner*!"

When he picks up the phone, she tries her best to sound casual.

"Hi, Chris, this is Kate Simon from the *Examiner* and I'm working on an item about you for my column."

Chefs are among the half-famous people in New York who are quick to learn the names of all the gossip columnists. Items generate buzz even after the reviews run, and buzz brings customers. "Hey, Kate! Great to hear from you. Love the column. What are you working on?"

She wishes he didn't sound so nice and helpful. "Well, I'm also a big fan of your cooking. I had a great meal at your restaurant a few months ago," she says. Zoe's mom took them there to celebrate Zoe's birthday.

"Why didn't you tell me you were coming in?" he booms. "I would have taken care of you!"

That's the secret of all these fancy restaurants, she's learning. Suck up to the chef for the star treatment and watch the tourists spend a fortune after reading a glowing review of the food and service they'll never get.

"Thanks for the offer, but I hope you'll still want me to come in after I ask you this." She pauses and hears a knife chopping in swift, rhythmic motions in the background.

"Hit me!" he says, just like on his show when someone asks him a cooking question.

"Well, I hear your show is being canceled and you broke up with your girlfriend, who was the producer."

He pauses and then clears his throat. "Oh, come on, Kate, what kind of item is that? That's news? Who's going to care about my love life?"

"Chefs are New York's new celebrities," she says, echoing something Zoe said. "People actually do care. It's just a short item and I'll mention your restaurant."

"Can you say I'm shopping a show to the Style Network?" he asks, which is as good as a confirmation, since he didn't deny it. "And come on in anytime and taste my new menu! I'd love to have you in," he adds, resuming his slightly robotic television voice.

Tim could have gone home with a mattress tonight but he just wasn't in the mood, especially after spending the past few nights sleeping next to Zoe, waking up when she tossed and turned and occasionally running to the bathroom so she wouldn't hear him coughing. He liked opening his eyes a little and watching the muscles on her smooth white back clench up and relax again when she drifted back to sleep. If only Danielle would fall down a flight of steep stairs, Tim could actually enjoy this.

Maybe Zoe does have a *work thing* tonight. Or maybe she has a thing with someone who does something better than gossip for work. Or maybe she's figured out that she's too good for him—that he's stuck on a roller coaster that keeps looping around the same scenes. It gets old pretty fast, honey, even if you like heights.

He throws his smoky clothes in a heap and unwraps the napkins he stashed with his items in his back pocket. There's some stuff to work with here. Just the kind of trash Charlie loves. He calls in the items to Charlie's voice mail, cracks open a beer, and turns on the television. Suddenly his face flashes on the screen.

"I look like shit," he says aloud. He's got to remember to wear bold colors when he tapes these things. He looks pasty and pale feeding the camera bullshit about how Natalie Portman bought a condo in that new Gramercy Park tower. The show will be on heavy circulation for months.

Maybe he shouldn't have fucked up that screen test. He may need a new job if the Loathed Hollywood Lothario's lawyers get their way. Tubby didn't take it particularly well that Tim couldn't remember which car service the driver who told him worked for.

"So you've got nothing to back up the item?" Tubby asked, his cheeks turning red. "How many times are you going to fuck us on this? Do you feel like answering to the big guys about this? Do you?"

The libel suit against the paper wouldn't be such a big deal if Tim hadn't already fucked up a few other times in the past few months. Tubby even made him attend a libel seminar for new reporters, which was boring and embarrassing, particularly when he saw the show ponies swapping notes about him.

"Not exactly," said Tim, wondering why this actor doesn't have bigger issues to worry about than suing a tabloid, which will be expensive and probably futile.

"Well, 'not exactly' is not exactly going to save your ass," said Tubby.

Tim puts a tape in the VCR so he can record the show for his mom. She'll lie and say he looked great. Mothers are the most loyal publicists.

Tim cracks open another beer and sits on his couch in his boxers, watching himself make puns about people he's never met, people he acts like he's known forever. The television is the only light in the apartment and its light flickers across his face, a faint flash to remind him he's still here.

Meet us at Lush," yells Tim over his cell phone, as if it were an order. It's 8:15 P.M. on a Tuesday, two weeks after the Coast opening. Tim and Blake are at fashion designer Jackie Joseph's baby shower.

"A baby shower at Lush?" asks Kate.

"Everyone's doing it! Get down here!" he shouts, and she can hear Blake saying, "Tell her we put her on the list!"

Kate was looking forward to an early night to catch up on sleep. She'd been thinking that maybe she'd even go running in the morning. If she woke up early enough, she could run a few miles over the Brooklyn Bridge, racing toward the shiny skyline. But Nick is in California with Annie, and meeting the guys for a few drinks would be better than going home alone. She also could use a good item.

Kate redirects the cab to Lush, deciding not to call Zoe. She has no idea who the guys are with and doesn't want to start answering questions about Tim. At least not yet. Not until Zoe decides if this is something that will hold her attention for longer than two weeks.

There's a line outside, and the same big bouncer from the opening party is guarding the door. Kate now knows the drill and flashes her new press pass. He recognizes her and smiles, even kisses her on both cheeks as if she were a regular.

The club is still pristine white and Kate thinks the crowd looks pretty good. People are dancing and drinking and it's a place she would actually come to with Zoe just for fun, especially now that she knows she can always get in.

She spots Blake and Tim at a table littered with bottles of booze and presents and a bunch of girls with blow-dried hair and spray-on tans. A skinny, short one with an enormous pregnant belly is holding court, unwrapping presents and throwing ribbons in her hair. She's also drinking champagne.

"That's Jackie Joseph," says Blake, pouring Kate a glass of vodka and cranberry juice. "Her dad's the big movie director Julian Joseph and she makes jeans." Kate recognizes the brand. Jackie Jeans. Zoe has three or four pairs of the three-hundred-dollar pants with a *JJ* embroidered on the back pocket.

When the waitress stops by the table, Kate asks for a Diet Coke and Blake looks at her a little funny. "Try something stronger," he says. "You should stick around, I hear Jessica Simpson is stopping by."

Robin rushes over, a fiery assault of of red curls and freckles.

"Babe! You never called me back!" she says, and Kate can't tell if Robin's wired or just always battery operated. "We got to hang out." She talks so fast, it's hard to catch everything she's saying. "Us girls have to stick together!"

"Don't go scaring her now, Robin," says Tim, pouring himself another drink.

"Scaring her? I have to protect her from you lowlifes!" she says, winking at Kate.

Kate finally heads to the bathroom to catch her breath, but even there she can't get any peace. She feels a buzz, as if she's had a few too many drinks. Exhausting or not, this job is fun. But then two women talking loudly outside the stalls while they re-apply their makeup catch her attention.

"If you really need press, just fuck Tim Mack," says the woman with the whiney voice who's talking to a short woman wearing a sparkly red tank top who Kate can see through the crack in the bathroom door. They didn't seem to notice Kate walk in and lock herself in a stall.

"It's totally worth it," says the first woman, snapping shut what sounds like a metal handbag buckle. "Never underestimate the power of the two-week relationship," she says. "You can use it for years."

Kate hears the door close behind them and emerges from her stall. This thing with Zoe and Tim probably can't last more than a few weeks. But there's no reason, at least not yet, to tell her anything about Tim.

When Kate goes back to the table—adorned with a big black RESERVED sign in the center—it's even more packed. Blake is dancing on a booth and she climbs up next to him. He puts his arm around her as if he were a protective older brother who dragged her to a party when he was supposed to be baby-sitting. Everyone's sweaty and shiny, reaching their hands to the ceiling.

"*Uh oh, uh oh, uh oh, oh no no,*" sings Beyoncé. "*So crazy.*"

Opportunistic Actor spots Kate and rushes up to her, giving her a kiss on both cheeks. He asks why she hasn't called him back and says there's a cool party next week they should attend together. He extends his hand to Tim, introducing himself and saying he loves Column A, the same way he told Kate he loved the *Examiner*.

Robin motions for Kate to join her on her side of the table. "Let's dance!" she shrieks. There are so many people on the banquette, Kate tries stepping across the table, thinking it must be sturdy, but she never makes it to the other side. The sound is like a crystal chandelier falling, shattering into thousands of shards on an unforgiving, empty ballroom floor. Bottles collide midair, breaking into jagged pieces, and Kate's crashed in the middle of it. The music keeps playing like a sound track.

Robin cups her hand over her mouth, wide-eyed. "Are you okay?" she asks, and Kate tries to smile but she can already feel a bruise spreading across her butt. Tim is laughing so hard, he's crying. Blake offers his hand, but before he can pull her up, two bouncers grab her.

"It was an accident! I'm fine!" Kate says, trying to shout over the music. "I'm sober!" she adds, which is the embarrassing truth.

She wishes Zoe or Nick were here to help her get up, to tell her everything is going to be fine.

"You are not fine and you're not welcome here," says the bouncer who kissed her on both cheeks on her way in. He and the other bouncer carry her to the door and toss her out so hard she actually stumbles into the street.

Kate pulls out her cell phone and calls Blake to ask him to look for her coat.

"What?" he asks, yelling above the club's music and the muffled mob of people probably still dancing on the banquette as the glass gets cleaned up, swept into dustbins and tied up in big black trash bags.

"You okay?"

Kate says she's fine but he still can't hear her.

"I'm fine!" she finally screams, drawing stares from the people waiting outside Lush's velvet ropes across the street, who probably think otherwise.

"Great exit!" yells Blake.

No one's coming to get her. No old friend or new boyfriend. No allies. Tim and Blake probably think she can take care of herself, which is usually true. Kate takes a deep breath and rolls back her shoulders. At least she hasn't been on the job long enough for someone to recognize her.

She digs through the purse Zoe lent her after declaring Kate's black canvas bag inappropriate for eveningwear. Kate has her phone, her reporter's pad, a pen, and the new $250 digital tape recorder she asked her parents to buy for her. Even extra batteries. But nothing important like keys.

And then, as if on cue, Alec Coleman, the Manic Millionaire, walks out of the bar—with Dylan Frye, the star of an old television sitcom that Kate used to watch religiously in high school. He was probably her first celebrity crush and now she almost wishes she never saw him in the flesh. The fantasy was much hotter than the reality. He's shorter than she imagined, they always are, and he's got deep wrinkles around his eyes. He hasn't had a decent role since the show was canceled a few years ago, after it became too unbelievable that all the characters had been living on a fictional college campus for eight years.

She tries to duck into a doorway but Alec's car is parked right in front of it. There's no escape.

"Quite an exit, Lois Lane," Alec says, laughing. Maybe she's not banned from his club after all. "How's that going to look in Column A tomorrow?"

She says columnists can't attack one of their own—hoping it's true.

"Well, you're welcome back anytime, especially if you put on a show like that. It's all fun and games when something gets broken."

She tries to smile, to shrug off the incident as if maybe she even did it on purpose.

Alec's driver opens up the back door of a black BMW sedan and Dylan slides in first. Alec walks over and takes her hand and pulls her into the car after him. Instead of the rough polyester of cabs, the backseat is buttery light brown leather. It even feels heated and Kate suddenly wants to tilt her head back and close her eyes and wake up under her thick white down comforter. Alec orders the driver to go buy Dylan another pack of cigarettes.

"Dylan, meet my future girlfriend, the lovely Kate Simon."

Kate wishes she could say something smart and memorable but she just manages a nervous laugh as she extends her hand, wishing she could stop gnawing her cuticles to the quick. Alec reeks of expensive cologne that's making her queasy and his spiky hair is shiny and stiff with too much gel.

Dylan says something to Alec about a "mission being unaccomplished," but Kate has no idea what they're talking about.

"Are you guys working on something together?" she asks.

Alec laughs.

"Let's just say my good friend Alec is helping me work *it*," says Dylan, putting his arm around Alec's shoulder. It doesn't seem as though they want to continue the conversation, so Kate changes the subject.

"I've always been a big fan," she says, immediately feeling like an idiot. Why, why would she say something so stupid? Paul says you're always supposed to act as if celebrities are just normal people who work hard. Never, *ever* say you're a fan.

"Thanks," says Dylan, lighting his last cigarette and rolling down his window. He makes no facial expression, gives no indication that he's annoyed or flattered. It's as if his face is a slab of clay. But Kate still feels a little thrill at meeting someone who at least used to be very famous.

Suddenly Alec lunges forward and tries to stick his tongue down Kate's throat—perhaps the fare for the ride home. Before Kate can pull away, Robin and Label Whore walk out of Lush and spot them. They're both wearing Jackie Johnson jeans.

Alec rolls down his window. "Hi, my favorite girls!" he yells to them. "Have you met my new girlfriend, Kate?" Kate wants to vanish but can do nothing but laugh and wave, hoping they're too drunk to remember this in the morning.

"Glad you survived!" says Robin, sucking on a cigarette. The orange tip lights up Label Whore's face, revealing a subtle smirk. Since Dylan's on the far side of the seat, he can't be seen easily, so they probably just assume he's a civilian. Before Kate can make it clear that she's not Alec's new girlfriend, a car service pulls up and Label Whore and Robin hop in.

"Since when do journalists have cars and drivers?" asks Alec as his chauffeur returns and they take off. Kate agrees to join them for a nightcap while she figures out what to do about her lost keys.

Alec's downtown duplex is massive, modern, and mostly decorated with sharp chrome furniture that looks similar to the furniture at Lush. If Kate had Alec's kind of money, she'd decorate the place with antiques, a long dark wood dining table, and deep red Persian rugs. Whenever she's somewhere really nice and expensive, the first thing she does is figure out what she would do differently if she had that kind of money. The exercise always puts her a little more at ease.

Dylan settles in front of the plasma television while Alec gives her a little tour, pointing out a signed Warhol in the living room. Women probably love him for the loft, and Kate's hardly surprised when he says he just broke up with an actress who moved in after dating him for just a week.

"They always do!" yells Dylan from the living room. Among the framed pictures in the living room is a shot of his actress ex-girlfriend on a sailboat. He says he gave her money for a year after they broke up so she could have the lifestyle she grew accustomed to while they were dating. Then he discovered that she'd been shopping online with his credit cards and he cut her off.

Alec tells Kate to ignore Dylan, as if she could. "You want an item?" Alec asks, and Kate feels like a dog waiting for a bone. He looks jazzed, excited to play the game he knows well. Kate realizes that Robin has probably spent the night here at least once.

He tells her that a very wealthy banker—"But I can't say who!"—is to be thrown off the board of the Guggenheim Museum for being involved in an art tax scandal that's about to break. "My dad's on the board, too," he boasts. Alec is one of those gossip-world gold mines Lacey and Paul are always telling Kate to befriend, someone who gets excited feeding the machine, who constantly feels the need to trade for protection and press or just in order to know he is useful.

Kate isn't sure if Lacey or Paul will have any idea what Alec's talking about, but it sounds promising. She ducks into the bathroom and calls her office voice mail, whispering the tip. When she emerges, Dylan has retired to the guest bedroom. Alec pulls her into his bedroom and starts trying to kiss her again. What are a few kisses for items, anyway? It's just kissing. But then Kate thinks of the publicists she overheard in the Lush bathroom and turns her head away.

He's too drunk and she's too exhausted to do anything but quickly get enveloped in the soft, cool pillows. Hours later, there's a knock at the door.

"Come in, Mr. Juan!" yells Alec. The sun is filtering through the electronic white blinds that Kate can't remember closing. A stocky Filipino brings in a tray of coffee, juice, and yogurt with berries. He's also got all the daily newspapers. It's like room service but better.

"This is Kate," says Alec. "She's the nice one at the *Examiner* who wrote the story about Moola closing. And she didn't write about the little 'ludes episode. We love her. Okay, bye now, Mr. Juan. I'll be ready for my massage in about an hour."

It takes a few minutes for Kate to register what just happened. She wonders if Mr. Juan also brought a tray to Dylan, who probably thinks Kate slept with Alec. So much for getting any respect from what she hoped was her first B-list celebrity friend.

It's eight-thirty and she has to meet Paul at Patricia Cullen's studio in forty-five minutes to pick out party pictures for this week's column. She wants to just go back to bed, but Alec is flipping through the papers, seemingly unaware of her existence. Fragments of the previous night roll through her mind like a grainy black-and-white movie.

"I can't believe I fell on the table," she wails, burying her head in a soft pillow. Marco flashes into her mind, and she's suddenly relieved he wasn't at Lush last night to see her even though she had hoped to run into him there.

"Lois Lane!" Alec looks up from reading Column A. "It just means you were having a good time." She wants to ask him more about his tip about the Guggenheim board member, but in the sober morning sun, she's afraid he'll make her promise not to report it out. She knows it's the perfect *Examiner* story.

He points his finger to a picture of Stanley Stahl. "I can't believe no one's reporting that his daughter is being investigated now because he sold her three million shares before the FDA verdict."

He leans over for a kiss but she turns her head so his lips just catch her cheek. She's got two tips already this morning and that's double what she had last week.

Manhattan magazine, "The Insider" by Blake Bradley

Academy Award-winning director **Julian Joseph** has optioned the rights to Literary Wunderkind **Amos Stone Fallow**'s best-selling political novel, *Right Here Right Now*, and faded television star **Dylan Frye** is trying to beat out **Tobey Maguire** for the lead role with some old-fashioned tactics. "Dylan's been sucking up big-time to **Jackie Joseph**," says a source about Frye's recent courting of Joseph's fashion-designer daughter, who recently hosted a party at Lush to celebrate the launch of her new denim line, which is popular with the celebrity set, including **Jessica Simpson**. "He's been stopping by all her events trying to get Jackie to go on a date with him. It's pathetic." Frye's publicist says the actor "has been friends with Jackie Joseph for years and would welcome any opportunity to work with her immensely talented father."

Blake agreed to meet his father at the University Club (or, as he calls it, the U) for breakfast even though he can't remember them ever having breakfast together, not even when he was a little kid. Now that Blake thinks about it, he can't remember his father ever consuming anything but coffee in the morning.

"How about drinks instead?" he offered on the phone when his father called early in the morning to ask him, when Blake felt as if a large animal was squatting on his sinuses.

"No, I have to be in black tie like a fucking usher at the ungodly hour of seven P.M. for some museum dinner that's costing me the price of a private jet to Sun Valley."

Blake pictured his father sitting at his big wood desk, which used to seem miles long all those years ago. "Is breakfast too much to ask?" his father said. "I know you don't need to be in the office before ten."

Whenever Blake enters the University Club—built in 1900 by the legendary architectural firm McKim, Mead & White, which also designed his dad's apartment building—he feels transported back to old New York, when gossip columns were glamorous, when they mattered more. Back then, there weren't any Web sites or television stations devoted to breaking personal news about public people. I'm part of a dying breed, Blake thinks with a little pride as he walks up to the grand entrance under a navy blue awning.

He looks for his father in the soaring lobby flecked with gold leaf and old money. A man in a dark suit appears out of the marble shadows to inform Blake that his father is upstairs in the game room, and Blake thinks it's the same guy who once threw Bethany out for wearing jeans, even though she insisted they were three-hundred-dollar Jackie Joseph jeans.

His father is sitting next to the table with the backgammon board, wearing his signature outfit—a black suit, a white shirt, and an Hermès tie—and leafing through the *Wall Street Journal*, looking paler and thinner than usual.

"Mark Reed got a great blow job today," he says as Blake approaches, pointing to Justin Katz's article in the *Journal*. "He must have bought that kid an apartment or something to get the kid gloves. But now Mark's taped on the target for shooting. A very stupid move for someone so smart."

Blake orders coffee and scrambled eggs. An untouched croissant is in front of his father, who orders his second espresso and keeps his arms crossed over his chest. When the waiter brightly suggests that they "peruse" the buffet, Blake's father gives an icy glare. "Do I look like I feel like *perusing* the buffet?" he asks. Steven Bradley likes structure, order, and boundaries. Buffets make him nervous.

His lips become a thin pale line. "It's not good for anyone that Mark's getting this kind of press. First Stanley, now Mark."

"All press is good press," says Blake, dumping a sugar in his coffee, even though he doesn't necessarily believe that's true. He just likes to make his father stew.

"Not when it comes to Wall Street. All press is not good in my book, and now the SEC and the IRS are going to be combing through Mark's finances, checking every detail of his trying to take the company public with my bank. Do you have any idea how bad this could turn out for me?"

How could this be something bad for his dad? His father looks around the library-quiet room, probably relieved that he doesn't see anyone he knows. This is where he goes when he doesn't want to be seen, when he has to have meetings with friends who have been fired or investigated. Friends he needs to make a show of going out in public with, even though he doesn't want to be seen with them. People like Martha Stewart and Dennis Kozlowski, who would make too much of a stir at the Four Seasons Grill Room, people who his father knows will surely rise again.

"Blake," he says, locking eyes with his son. "I need you to do me a favor."

"Reservations at Per Se for Thanksgiving?"

He purses his lips again so tight they almost turn white. "I need you to tell me immediately if any columnists you know start asking questions about Mark."

"You want to tell me why?"

He relaxes his lips, and the blood floods back in. "What you don't know can't hurt you. Or me."

Fair enough. "What do you want me to say if someone asks me about it?"

His father polishes off his espresso. He has the same look on his face he did fifteen years ago when he told Blake that he and Blake's mom were getting divorced. (But Blake already knew. When he came home from boarding school for Thanksgiving dinner—at the Carlyle Hotel—there were two thick envelopes on the front table from different law firms, one addressed to each parent. His dad was about to make partner and every other partner dumped his first wife before getting the promotion. It's much cheaper that way, and the second wives are more willing to sign a prenup.)

"Tell them you don't know anything, which won't be a lie. Then call me immediately so I can act quickly. Planning is power."

His father has always been a big-plan guy. "Is everything going to be okay?" asks Blake, even though just asking that question usually means everything is anything but okay.

"Yes, of course. I'm just taking a few precautions. This Justin Katz at the *Journal* wants to interview me for some story about 'Wall Street's power art collectors.' Apparently Mark gave him the idea by bragging a little too much about his new Damien Hirst." He takes a sip of water and winces when it must have hit his cavities. Money can't buy good teeth. "Now this guy wants to ask me all sorts of questions I don't want to answer. I told my assistant to tell him to stop calling."

Blake's eggs are sticking to the back of his throat. He suddenly remembers finding it strange last winter that his dad shipped crates of art, which Lindsay probably made him buy, to the airport in Sun Valley, Idaho, only to have them promptly whisked back to New York, on the jet he part-owns, to end up in the house in Southampton. By summer, Lindsay was throwing dinner parties every weekend to show off the two big new acquisitions: a cartoon painting by Roy Lichtenstein of a woman drowning in a sea of tears, and a giant silver-and-black silkscreen self-portrait of Andy Warhol that took up an entire wall in the den.

The only reason Blake knew about the art being shipped back and forth is because he and Bethany were at the Sun Valley house on the day the pilot called to confirm the pickup with the houseboy, who was at the store when Blake took the message. Blake hadn't told his father they were going to the house, and the houseboy seemed a little alarmed at their surprise visit, which Blake didn't think much of then because the houseboy tends to get alarmed at stupid shit, like making butternut squash soup when his dad wanted minestrone.

"How about giving me a little notice next time you want to use the house?" his father asked when he found out about Blake's being there. He had used his tense tone, the same one he used to schedule the breakfast this morning. The one that says more than he's saying.

Blake takes a sip of icy water and feels it slam against the nerve in his back molar. The eggs now feel like they're trapped somewhere between his throat and stomach. His father swiftly changes the subject, and they spend the duration of the meal talking about Lindsay's plans for a pink seersucker nursery in the Southampton house.

Before he leaves, Blake asks his father for a favor in return. He wants the number of the banking dynasty heir, the one in Palm Beach with the body in the closet. He still hasn't repeated that tip.

"So you heard," says his father. There must be some truth to the story, Blake suddenly realizes. His father lowers his voice and leans forward. "I hear it was a gardener who was having an affair with the young wife. The body was hanging in the closet for four days before the maid found him. That's what the old lady who lives next door told Lindsay, who decorated the house."

"Can I call her?"

"Blake." His father sighs. "I'm not your source on this. I'm not going to help your career as a gossip colunnist."

"But—"

"But—let me finish—even I know this is a good story. I'll help you, but you have to promise to try to turn this into a magazine feature if you're not going to take that job at *Forbes*. It's got all the right ingredients and I want to see you write something besides a little item."

Blake would love to write a feature. He hopes he remembers how. His dad is right. This is a perfect *Manhattan* magazine story. The banking heir also has an apartment on Fifth Avenue, where he often throws Republican Party fund-raising dinner parties. He's part of the New York power structure, even if he spends the winters in Palm Beach. Blake says he can't make any promises but he'll try, and his dad agrees to call him later with the contact information.

And then he's off to work, leaving Blake feeling fidgety at 9:30 A.M. It's too early to go to the office, so he heads downstairs to the locker room. The University Club is one of the few places in the city where you can swim in the nude. The pool is reserved for men only, even though women were allowed to join the club in the eighties. Under a painted trompe l'oeil sky, fresh water flows from the mouth of a brass lion's head, filling the pool, which could never meet Olympic standards—which is precisely what Blake likes most about it. A few saggy old pale men are swimming slow laps and sliding up the edge on their bellies like sea otters when Blake dives in, but he doesn't know any of them. The pool is one of the few places in New York where silence is the only sustainable option.

Blake used to be on the swim team back in boarding school. It was the only athletic thing he wanted to do, since he wasn't really a team player. The best thing about swimming is it's just you and the water—there's no ball or baton or surfboard or skis. Goggles would be nice today, but since he doesn't have any, he opens his eyes underwater, feeling the sting of chemicals. The blurry white wall at the other end seems miles away. Each time he reaches it, he feels a sense of accomplishment, even though he's struggling to catch his breath. He's going to—he has to—give up smoking tomorrow. He keeps diving back underwater where it's safe. Where no one's looking to find him. Where the weight of water makes everything feel clean.

Kate manages to escape Alec's grasp in time for work, but not early enough to stop home in Brooklyn first. As soon as she walks out of the building—avoiding the doorman's gaze—she calls information for the nearest Banana Republic. A few blocks later, she races into the store and buys a coral-colored sweater and matching skirt: seventy-six dollars on her parents' credit card. Maybe she should start keeping a change of clothes under her desk. Impulsive evenings are getting expensive and increasingly difficult to explain to her parents.

"Very Palm Beach," says Paul when Kate arrives at Patricia's studio in the basement of a brownstone in Chelsea. Five or six people in their early twenties wearing only black are running around with cameras, coffees, and computer discs. "Vampire Inc.," whispers Paul in Kate's ear. The walls are covered with framed party pictures, a carefully posed world where every-one is dressed up and smiling and having fun—a world that Kate now knows looks better in pictures than in real life. In the bathroom, there's a big glossy print of Holly May in lacey lingerie at eye level to the toilet. Kate's reflection in the mirror above the sink is anything but pretty. She spreads concealer under her bloodshot eyes and over a fresh spray of pimples on her chin.

"Rough morning," she tells Paul, clutching her coffee as she emerges from the bathroom. She offers up Alec's tip about the Guggenheim board member as an excuse. Paul looks excited and says they'll try to report it out later today, even though it sounds like it'll be hard to crack. Wall Street guys are the hardest to deal with. They have no motivation for press. Their egos are usually satisfied by their lavish spending on vacation homes and the means to get there.

Patricia walks in looking as if she were heading out to a cocktail party. She's wearing a black sleeveless dress and tall leather boots. "Sorry, I haven't been to bed yet," she says by means of explanation for the heavy eye makeup and jewelry at the early hour. Kate pictures her hanging upside down to sleep. She always has a young assistant walking behind her and carrying her heavy camera because years spent toting it to parties have caused nerve damage and stress injuries to her wrist.

Patricia leads them into a room with six computers, where an assistant wearing black leather pants with a thick silver wallet chain hands Paul a list of all the parties they've covered during the past week. It's like a mini map of the city, chronicled with photos that tell very little about anything other than what people were wearing and just how many parties they hit in one night. Stacked up by the door are envelopes of discs for publicists, who will try to send them to every party-picture page in town so they can get their clients plugged. Sometimes publicists hire Patricia for events, hoping the pictures end up in the *Examiner*, even though Paul assigns her a few parties to cover every week. It's a racket and no one seems to have figured out the cheaper option: Convince Paul to assign the party to Patricia.

Paul explains to Kate that eventually she'll be able to feel as if she's already attended a party just by seeing the names on the host committee. The party pictures just reinforce this. It's the same faces every week in different outfits and new accessories or hairstyles. There are certain party fixtures—the omnipresent "celebrity mothers" of Diddy, Lindsay Lohan, and Drew Barrymore—whom Lacey has banned from their party-picture page for being overexposed and underwhelming. Reality-television stars may as well be invisible. Sometimes certain social climbers will appear at more than three parties in the same night. Don't they have anything else to do?

Just by going through Patricia's pictures every week, Paul can figure out who's looking for a spouse upgrade and who's cheating. And who needs free clothes, namely the socialites hanging on the arms of gay designers like Zac Posen, Peter Som, Zang Toi, and Douglas Hannant. Of course, having a walker is also in the designers' interests. Spread that name all over the city so well-heeled women in Dallas and Chicago will think they need to shell out thousands for a dress because all the fashionable women in New York do.

They start with a cancer benefit at the Four Seasons.

"How about this one?" says Patricia, pointing out a shot of Spinster with the socialite Bunny Frank. "Even though Bunny does that unfortunate thing with her hair."

"Patricia, you know we don't run pictures of publicists," says Paul, sounding rehearsed, as if he has the same conversation with her every week.

"How about that one?" Kate asks, pointing out one of Blake and his mom in an elegant dark blue dress at the antiques show.

"We don't run pictures of other gossip columnists, either," he says, using a similar tone. Kate realizes that publicists and gossip columnists are on the same party-picture tier. "We're not famous for anything but playing with other people's fame." Her cheeks get hot. She should have known that. But he picks one of Blake's father and Mark Reed, explaining a bit of payback. "For a guy who always begged to be left out of my column, he sure seemed happy to talk to the *Journal*."

Paul skips over a fragrance launch party and another coffee-table book party at Bergdorf's. "No more store parties, Patricia," he says, leaning back in his chair. "I'm tired of the frozen mannequin look. The people in the pictures we choose have to be doing something besides smiling. And we can't run the same people every week.

"Hang on," he says when he sees a picture of Holly May deejaying a fashion party. He also picks a shot of Blaine Trump in a swirl of bright pink taffeta dancing with a principal at the New York City Ballet. "At least they're doing something," says Paul, leaning back again and closing his eyes for a moment.

"Are we having fun yet?" he asks Kate, who's not sure what else to do but nod. It seems like the fun part of these parties is looking at the pictures and feeling relieved you weren't there.

Tim liked the way people looked at him when he walked down the theater's aisle with Zoe tonight. They noticed that she's not just some mattress pimping for press. Much better than his usual fare. Zoe's got class. She would never get a tattoo of a Chinese symbol that may or may not mean "love," or show up at his office unannounced.

"Your job is fun," said Zoe. "And at least no one has introduced me tonight as Jack Miller's daughter."

"You're fun," said Tim, completely serious.

But then the show started, which was not fun at all. The best part of Broadway premieres is waiting to see which critic nods off first. Watching the first big dance number was as stimulating as watching Tubby scarf doughnuts. At least the *Times*' theater critic was snoring. Tim had his item.

"I have a confession," Zoe whispered in his ear after about ten minutes. "I hate musicals."

He laughed and grabbed her hand and led them out of the theater, which the producer would give Tim hell about tomorrow, but fuck them. Fuck them all. The only point of going to shit like this is to work or meet girls, and he's already got an item and the best girl there.

As they walk through Times Square, Tim wraps his coat around Zoe, who's shivering in the November air. Her breath puffs out of her glossy lips.

"What should we do now?" she asks. If he had any money in the bank, he'd hail a cab to the airport. He'd take her to a soft white beach with clear warm water. He'd buy her a string bikini and rub suntan lotion on her back, careful to get every inch.

"You want to meet Kate and Nick downtown at that art thing?" she offers.

Just then Tim looks up and sees a blue neon sign. It sets off one of those cartoon lightbulbs in his head.

"I've got a better idea," he says, pulling her down the block, even though she's stumbling in her heels.

"Slow down! I'm wearing Manolos!" He lifts her up on his back, only putting her down when they get to the reception desk of Pierre's flagship hotel. It's almost eerily quiet in the lobby with all its white couches and white orchids on dark wood tables.

Tim presents his new VIP card to the receptionist, who flashes a smile and types something into her computer. His freebie was technically supposed to be for a suite in Miami, but apparently it doesn't matter. Tim loves that people who work in hotels don't ask any questions.

"I love it!" Zoe yells when they walk into the sprawling suite with floor-to-ceiling panoramic views. She kicks off her heels and runs over to the windows, pressing her arms out on either side as if they were wings.

Tim inspects the minibar and pulls out a bottle of champagne, shaking it up and spraying it all over the floor and on Zoe's dress.

"I guess we're going to have to get you out of that before you catch a cold," he says, sliding her dress over her head so she's standing in front of the glass wall overlooking the blinking neon city thirty stories below in just white lace panties. He picks her up again and throws her down on the big fluffy white bed. Pillows slide to the floor, a cushion to the inevitable fall.

He quickly shimmies out of his jeans as she hungrily pulls his shirt off, wrapping her legs around his waist, squeezing him tight. A girl like Zoe deserves this even if he can only give it to her for one night. Zoe is most concerned with right now, anyway. She doesn't want to be any percent famous, because she doesn't know what it feels like to climb. She just likes the view from the top.

So, Kate, how are things going with the Manic Millionaire?" asks Label Whore, pouring two packets of Equal in her coffee in the office kitchen. She's wearing a fuzzy pink sweater and a pair of dark Jackie Joseph jeans with the Dior boots she must have decided not to sell on eBay. Her lips look extra big and stiff with fresh collagen.

"He's a good source," Kate says, popping a few M&M's from the vending machine in her mouth, knowing Label Whore is mentally calculating the calories and enjoying her sugar envy, though she probably considers Kate at least two dress sizes too big.

About an hour later, after Kate's heard from Nick about how Zoe and Tim trashed the penthouse suite at Pierre's Times Square hotel—"They drank the entire minibar, smeared up all the windows with fingerprints, and broke the bathtub jets"—Kate gets a call from The Principal's assistant, saying he wants to see her in his office in five minutes.

"Anything bad?" she asks, her hands suddenly feeling cold and clammy.

"I really don't know, but he's not in a great mood today."

The Principal slams his door behind Kate when she gets there, and he looks mad. His cheeks are redder than usual, as if his blood is about to boil through his skin.

"Kate, I'm about to have a conversation with you that is going to be very difficult, but trust me, you'll thank me for it eventually."

Difficult? Her mind races through anything she may have screwed up. Maybe they lost an advertiser or she forgot to call someone for a comment and now they're threatening to sue for libel?

He looks her in the eye and holds her gaze for a few moments before he asks about the nature of her relationship with Alec Coleman.

"He's an acquaintance I just met," she says slowly, surprised. "Why?"

"Kate, I want you to understand that it is corrupt to be *involved* with any of your sources or subjects."

Label Whore's smirk pops into Kate's head like a slide on a projector. "But I—"

"I don't want to hear the details. I don't care if you started dating him, or whatever it is you're doing with him, before or after you wrote about Moola closing. What's important is we can't have this newspaper's credibility compromised." He pauses and Kate feels a rope twist through her stomach. "Your source was an investor in that club."

Tim and Blake probably don't get these lectures.

"We can't have *people* saying you're sleeping with your subjects," The Principal goes on. "We can't have our impartiality compromised." He says she should have thought of the *Examiner*'s best interests and passed the tip on to someone "impartial" like Label Whore.

Kate wants to scream, *No fair*. She never did anything but kiss Alec, but more than that, he's now turned into her best source. Everyone complimented her item this week about Stanley Stahl's daughter being investigated, but she can't admit how she got that now. And she probably shouldn't even bother following up on his tip about the Guggenheim board member being involved in an art scandal. There's probably a good story there, but she doesn't want to get fired. Besides, she already made a few calls but didn't get anywhere.

How are you supposed to cultivate sources like Alec without doing something slightly unethical? Shouldn't gossip columns have a more flexible set of rules?

He slowly clears his throat. "Kate, let's save ourselves any more embarrassment. I don't want to hear the details and I don't want you to lie to me. I just don't want you to do it again. You're not working for a tabloid."

She starts counting in her head so she won't start crying. It helps to focus on something else. One, two, three, four, five . . .

"If you worked anywhere else, the editor would probably fire you. Or put you on the sanitation beat." He looks up at his scotch shelf. "Consider this a very serious warning."

She wants to tell him that she never slept with Alec, that this rumor is just a rumor. She wants to say she doesn't want to be in gossip anymore. She doesn't want to be playing a game of telephone all day—when pieces of truth get tangled up in the cords and the connections go fuzzy in the circle of familiar strangers. She can't live like this, always wondering if someone's a friend, a frenemy, a foe, or a source. But she sits still and silent like a chastised child and keeps counting.

She gets rescued when his assistant walks in to say Henry Carnegie is on the phone.

"Okay, kid," he says, motioning for Kate to leave the office.

Kate walks quickly by Label Whore's desk and suddenly has the urge to slam a stapler against her head, but she keeps walking down the stairs to the building's only private bathroom and locks the door. She sinks down to the chipped cold tiles and tries to catch her breath, tries to do anything but cry. An arm attached to a bunch of jangling bracelets knocks on the door with determination.

Kate doesn't want Lacey, the perfect editor with the perfect ponytail and perfect handbag, to see her melted on the floor like this, but she lets her in. She's not leaving anytime soon.

Lacey locks the door behind her and gives Kate a hug that makes her start crying even harder. "Kate, you're going to get past this. Screwing up is the only way to learn how not to do it again." Lacey hands her a tissue. "It means you're doing a good job if someone is trying to take you down."

Kate tries to explain what happened with Alec, but Lacey doesn't let her finish. She probably doesn't want to hear the other tip about the

Guggenheim board member, either. "The details don't matter anymore," she says.

"Well, no one seems to know the only one interesting detail. I got to meet Dylan Frye," she laughs, hiccupping to a cough.

Lacey laughs. "Did you sleep with him, too?"

"No!" Now they're both laughing. "It's too hard to explain. . . ."

"You'll tell me later. And no matter what really happened, this is an important lesson for you to learn now."

Lacey leaves and brings back Kate's things so she can go straight home. "Take the rest of the day off," says Lacey. "Go to a movie, do something anonymous. That always makes me feel better."

It's only a little after twelve noon, but all Kate really wants to do is crawl under her white comforter, where it's warm and safe and no one can find her, or expect something from her.

After Blake finishes looking over the proofs of his column, he starts researching what's been written about his father's art collection. It's 8:30 P.M. The top editors are still working, though, drinking the free margaritas expensed to the magazine every deadline night so they can read their proofs in a slightly altered state. He just wants to go home to bed but he keeps researching, knowing there's something waiting to be found about his dad's new Warhol and Lichtenstein in Southampton. An assistant e-mails everyone, announcing that dinner has arrived.

"You want a slice of pizza?" asks Alison on her way to the kitchen.

Blake thought women didn't eat pizza anymore. "No thanks," he says, surveying the carnage of a day's worth of junk-food wrappers on his desk. "I have highly desirable dinner reservations."

She raises her eyebrows and walks away.

Blake finally gives up for tonight. He's too hungry and he doesn't want to order from the one decent place where the office has a house account. As is the case with reporting all good stories, he's going to have to do some reporting with people instead of computers. He checks his e-mail for the last time and gets a message that sends a little shudder down his spine. It's from Justin Katz, that guy from the *Journal:*

> Hey, I would love to pick your brain for a feature I'm working on about the intersection of the art world and Wall Street. Lunch at Michael's any day next week?

Blake tastes those eggs again from the University Club, as if they're still trapped in his throat. He hates the expression "pick your brain." It makes him think of a dental instrument clawing inside his head. He also hates anything to do with lunching at any industry canteen where he always runs into people he usually tries to avoid. He also hates people who forward e-mail messages, but he forwards this one to his dad. Just to show how useful he can be when he wants to be.

He can almost hear the conversation Justin would want to have. It would start with something like "What's your favorite of your dad's paintings?" It would end with something like "Can you suggest any other people I should talk to about their art and how much they pay for it?"

No, Blake won't go to lunch. He'll schedule it and then cancel it, citing a vague deadline. And then he'll cancel the next time, saying he's got a dentist appointment or something. Then Justin will stop trying. It's better that Blake's dad didn't say what he was hiding, but unfortunately, Blake's figured most of it out already. If he had to write the item right now, he'd probably be at least 65 percent accurate. His dad did something wrong, something that other big guys like Mark Reed are also doing. It has to do with buying art and shipping it on their jets. Greed is the cancer eating away at their better judgment.

Blake decides to do a little more research and scans the Web sites of some of Lindsay's favorite galleries to see if his dad is identified as the buyer of any Pop Art since last winter—or if anything looks like what ended up at their house in Southampton by way of Sun Valley. Unfortunately, Google isn't God and Blake's not getting anywhere. He wishes he could ask an intern to do the research, but he can't risk anyone knowing what's going on with his family.

Alison reappears holding a slice of pizza for him. "Just in case you change your mind."

She saw right through the dinner bluff. His stomach rumbles and he takes the greasy paper plate. "Thanks."

"What are you still doing here? I thought we closed your column. Don't tell me you're changing something."

Does this girl have to verify everything? "No, I'm just catching up on e-mails," he says, as if he doesn't check his in-box at least every ten minutes. He washes down a bite of pizza with soda and two Sudafeds, trying to vaporize the elephant that's been squatting on his sinuses all day.

"Do you have a cold or something?" she asks.

"Just sinus pressure."

"Why don't you get it checked out? Maybe you have a sinus infection. I used to get those when I was little when I had a cold. It feels like hell. Do your teeth hurt? Because the tops of your teeth may hurt if it's a sinus infection."

"My teeth always hurt." All a doctor is going to do is tell Blake to stop doing coke.

She shrugs and, before heading back to her desk, says something about closing the cover story. Maybe it's her jeans, but her ass looks particularly good tonight. More likely it's the Stockholm syndrome, Blake rationalizes.

The Web sites must have all been updated in the past few months because none of them show anything that looks like what's in the Southampton house. But there are plenty of photos of art by Lindsay's favorite artists that seems to have been bought and sold in the past few years, without any mention of the buyers or exact prices. It's too late to call his source at Sotheby's, who may know something—she's probably out sipping cocktails at the Four Seasons with clients—so Blake shuts down his computer for the night with an unsettling feeling. There's a story here and he knows he's close. Perhaps more unsettling, he's not sure what to feel. A tiny part of him wouldn't mind seeing his dad get nailed for something related to Lindsay's pushiness for trophy pieces she can show off to her friends. But

Blake doesn't really want any trouble for his dad. Whatever's going on, he's going to make his dad fess up because Blake hates nothing more than being the last to know. And better he know what's going on before Tim and Robin and everyone else jump on the story.

Blake needs to relax before dealing with Bethany at home, so he walks into a Barnes & Nobles, where everything is perfectly organized with structure and boundaries. He always leaves with a heavy bag filled with books that sit uncracked on his bedside table until Bethany banishes them to the bookshelf in the living room, a reservoir of detoured virtuous intent.

He walks down the fiction aisles, wishing he could spend his days inventing characters and plots instead of relying on dubious facts and sources and confirming half-secrets with questionable agendas. By now he's figured out how people slither through plots and twists. They're all so predictable.

Blake has always wanted to write a book, but all the good stories have already been written. What's left to invent? What could he possibly write that wouldn't cost him sources or friends? People like having writers around because people want to be immortalized—but only if they come off well in the end.

He wanders into the magazine section and almost feels a gravitational pull toward the rack of art publications. His hands go cold when he picks up one that's always on his dad's coffee table and flips to a section on the big sales of the previous year. There's a photo of the big black-and-silver silkscreen of Andy Warhol that a Chelsea gallery sold to a "private collector" for $4 million. Blake wipes the sweat stinging his eyes with the sleeve of his navy blazer.

To think that just a few months ago he actually asked for that same Warhol when his dad died. It may be the very reason his father seems paranoid about ending up in the gossip columns. Blake hasn't pieced together the whole story yet, but he knows he's on to something. "Trust your instincts" was the best piece of journalism advice he ever got, and right now Blake's instincts feel hot and prickly, as if he's an animal awaiting a storm.

He sits down on the thin carpet and leans against a rack of magazines. The possibility of getting his dad out of something feels like speeding down an empty Long Island Expressway to Southampton late at night, maybe one A.M. on Friday morning or Sunday at eleven P.M. A time for feeling smug and entitled.

It's all coming together, he thinks. Blake relaxes his lips, which he's been pursing together until they turned white, and can almost taste blood. He's about to be needed for the first time.

promotions can be traps

"K ate, we have a little problem here," says The Principal. This is the second time he's called her into his office this week. Lacey is already there and Kate starts counting to one hundred to keep her composure.

"You're not ready for this, but right now I don't have a choice," he says, looking down at the coffee-stained carpet that was allegedly once pale pink. "Paul's jumping ship to *Vanity Fair*."

Kate pictures all of them lost at sea, tall icy waves creeping close, desperate for a rescue boat, a buoy, some tether. Even his offer to raise her salary to thirty-four thousand dollars doesn't make her feel any better.

Suddenly it makes sense why Paul has been wearing a suit more often, and why media reporters have been calling all morning to talk to him. Eve's been calling three times a day, but Kate never suspected this. She never thought anyone on his tier got out of gossip alive.

"I tried to keep him, but I just can't afford to match Condé Nast's offer," says The Principal.

"We need you to help out with the column," says Lacey, twirling her ponytail. "Until we find a suitable replacement."

"*If* we can find a suitable replacement," says The Principal. "You have no idea how many unsuitable candidates I've considered. They've been trying to poach Paul for years."

Kate wants to crawl under the couch and hide, even though a small part of her is starting to feel like celebrating. Someone once told her that to get a coveted column, someone has to die. And no one ever comes back to the *Examiner* after jumping ship.

"Kate . . . you're getting a big break," The Principal says slowly. "You're not nearly experienced enough to take over for Paul, but I really don't have a choice. The column needs to get written and I can't spare anyone else here."

"And we think you can do it," says Lacey, sounding like she only half means it. "Your item about Stanley Stahl's daughter is exactly the kind of story we want you to be getting."

"But," Kate says softly, "I'm not sure I want to be a professional gossip." She doesn't tell them that the item was against the rules because it came from Alec Coleman. *Gossip columnist* sounds like a dirty word. She pictures a lifetime of nightcrawling with Tim and Blake, taking notes under the dinner table with people who wouldn't have invited her had it not been for the press or protection she could provide.

But most people her age are assistants or fact checkers. This could be her big break, and it may never come around again. It *would* be nice to have her name on those invitations, Kate thinks to herself—even if Zoe's father calls gossip columnists the media's bottom feeders.

"Listen, you'll be the youngest columnist in New York," says The Principal. "It's a job every other kid your age would love to have. I'm asking you to go to parties, cultivate sources—with a relatively generous expense account—and break news for us," he says. Lacey is bouncing one leg up and down on the other.

"And we'll try to hire someone else to help you," says The Principal. "Let me know if you have any ideas."

"But what if I get pigeonholed as a gossip columnist?" What if she turns out like Tim and Blake?

"Kate, you're twenty-two. You could go to jail for two years and it still wouldn't hurt your career," says Lacey.

The Principal looks Kate in the eye. "Just remember the rules. Don't sleep with anyone you write about. Or anyone close to anyone you write about. No taking gifts. If an orchid from the Schaffers arrives, send it back." He pauses to be sure he has her complete attention. "Do your best, make a name for yourself, and you'll thank me later."

As Kate walks back to her desk, The Principal's words start sinking in. This is what everyone calls the right place at the right time, but she wishes she didn't have a knot tightening in her throat, snaking down her lungs, and making it hard to inhale.

Vanity Fair sent out a press release this morning about Paul coming on board, so she's already got an e-mail from Blake asking her about it. She goes to the downstairs bathroom and calls him on her cell phone and tells him she's going to fill in temporarily. "You want a new column?" she asks, and he laughs.

She says she's not sure *she* wants it.

"You'll quickly learn it's much better to be queen than a lady-in-waiting," he says. "But you'd better be careful. Robin probably already has a hit out on you."

Kate will never survive without Paul Peterson," says Robin, polishing off her first vodka gimlet of the night.

Tim agreed to meet with her before she headed off to a movie premiere because he knew she'd find him at the bar across the street from the office anyway, and as much as he hates to admit it, he likes Robin's company. It almost always makes him feel a little better about himself. She's a less successful, less popular version of him.

But now he's regretting agreeing to the drink date. She's pretty worked up. "I mean, she's fucking twenty-two and fresh off the boat from Woodstock. Hello? That place hasn't been on the radar since the sixties."

"Ethan Hawke and Bob Dylan have houses up there."

"Shut up," says Robin, trying to light a cigarette but getting stopped by the bartender. "Who cares about Ethan post Uma? And Dylan is so twenty years ago."

When Blake called Tim this afternoon to share the news, Blake said he didn't think Kate would be much of a threat. Tim's not so sure. And he's just as pissed off as Robin that he wasn't offered the job. He should have at least been called in for an interview, even if he probably wouldn't have taken it. Column A is a much more powerful column. Still, it would have been nice to use for salary leverage and to remind his editors that he's a desired commodity.

He takes a sip of his beer. "I actually think she's pretty good."

"Hello? Are you paying any attention to me?" asks Robin, banging her empty glass on the table. She flips her red hair as if it were an exclamation point. "I can't believe they haven't called me for an interview yet."

She orders them another round and gets back to what's on her mind. Robin is focused and willful. Robin makes plans. Robin doesn't care about little details. She sees opportunities as big shiny pictures and finds ways to insert herself in the frames.

"Well, I want that column, and you know I'd be better at it than she could ever be."

"Play nice, Robin."

She gives him a steely look. Gossip columnists may come and go, jumping ship or vanishing into purgatory, but the two of them are here to stay.

"You have no idea how nice I'm playing with you."

Tim is suddenly suspicious. "Excuse me?"

"That mattress Danielle, the one from Holly May's birthday party?"

It feels as if brain fluid is pouring out his ears, soaking the table, and oozing into a radioactive puddle by his feet.

Robin stops twirling her red hair around her finger and leans in closer. "We don't have to talk about it, but she called me."

This is not something Tim really feels like talking about, but he's also starting to feel much warmer toward Robin. He's wanted to talk about this with someone, anyone, but he's been too afraid to let the secret out. But he knows Robin protects her sources, and he's got enough blackmail shit on her to keep her quiet.

"I told her she should do herself a favor and shut the fuck up," says Robin.

Tim drains his glass. He wonders if he can use this to get out of paying child support. Trying to plant an item in a rival column must be a kind of extortion. "Thanks."

"I owe you for letting me copy all the numbers in Charlie's Rolodex before I left."

Tim knew that favor would come in handy one day.

"I don't think she'll be trying to plant it anywhere else, but you better watch out. This isn't something you can keep quiet, and you're going to look like a real asshole if you don't at least spin it right."

He sighs. It's a conversation he's had with plenty of people when he calls for confirmation or comment, but right now he just can't give Robin either. He's not ready to accept defeat.

A publicist who represents the National Arts Club, a century-old institution on Gramercy Park, has invited Kate there for drinks and offered a free dinner for any of her friends who wanted to join her afterward.

"We want to give you a membership," the publicist says over glasses of red wine and cheese cubes during cocktail hour. He and Kate are the only people there under fifty years old. "We need fresh blood."

He explains that the club was founded in 1898 by a veteran literary and art critic for the *New York Times*. "The membership committee wants to attract today's young journalists."

Kate smiles. It's great that she's getting something just for being her and not from the favor bank.

"The committee also wouldn't mind a few sightings of our celebrity members occasionally, just to keep the club current," he says. Maybe she was wrong. "Martin Scorsese, Dennis Hopper, Robert Redford, and Uma

Thurman are members, and you may witness something press-worthy involving them if you spend some time here."

Kate wonders where this membership falls on the sliding-ethics scale. Better or worse than the Dior shoes? It will last much longer than the shoes, and they're not exactly expecting any coverage. The publicist just said it would be *nice*.

Zoe arrives first for dinner and they sit down and order right away because Nick called to say he'd just make it in time for dessert. Zoe instructs Kate to order safe club food, like duck or steak. "Stay away from anything Asian."

While they're tucking into their spinach salads, Zoe says she thinks Tim is hiding something from her. "When he was in the shower the other morning, I checked the missed-calls log on his cell phone and there were a ton from someone named Dan. Have you ever heard him mention a Dan?"

Kate shakes her head. "Maybe a brother or an old friend?"

Zoe takes a sip of wine. "I think he's an only child, and why would an old friend call at two or three in the morning?"

"Drug dealer?"

"Shhh!" says Zoe, looking around the room at their fellow diners, mainly quiet seniors. Fresh blood isn't supposed to be toxic. "His dealer's name is Kenny."

"Why were you looking in his phone?"

Zoe rolls her eyes and pushes up the sleeves of her red cashmere sweater. "Like I have to explain that to you. You taught me that trick."

The waiter brings their duck, which they agree is not nearly as sweet or tender as the duck at the Coast opening. The mention of Marco's restaurant sports Kate's interest.

"I keep expecting to bump into him," Kate says, scanning the room.

"It will happen," says Zoe. "Everyone at work is talking about him. He's about to explode and be one of those people you suddenly see and hear about everywhere. Like Harry Potter for the foodie set."

"You think he's that talented?"

"Definitely. Talented and charming. Double potential."

"I'll look out for this Dan if you promise to look out for any foodie events where Marco might be."

They clink their wineglasses together. "Deal," says Zoe.

Nick finally shows up in time to order dessert. Zoe insists that they all get the house specialty, sweet potato pie, but she runs off to meet Tim before it even arrives at the table.

"I can't believe you're letting her date that guy," says Nick, looking exhausted after a long day's work, which included a business dinner with Pierre and the architect of his new Miami hotel. He loosens his tie.

"What do you mean, *letting* her?"

"Forget it." He takes a bite of the pie. "I'm too tired to have anything but a pleasant conversation right now."

"Finish what you just started."

He puts his fork down. "Okay, fine. I think you should take a moment to consider that this setup may not turn out to be in anyone's best interests. Tim is a fun guy to see at parties, and he can help you professionally, but do you really want Zoe dating a guy best known for being wasted at parties and reporting hurtful, half-true rumors about famous people?"

Kate sighs. The pie crust tastes slightly chewy, as if it's been sitting on a shelf for a week.

"Hey, don't get me wrong, we should all be having fun now. I just think you should be careful about promoting this relationship, if that's what it is by now. You girls should stay away from guys in the public eye, and that goes for your little crush on that cook, too." Nick smiles. "You should find someone who's doing something interesting, but not someone who needs a lot of attention for it."

Kate laughs. "Someone like you if you were single?"

He suddenly looks very serious. "I may be soon."

Kate almost spits out her pie. "What? I thought you and Annie were the perfect couple."

He sighs. "Well, we were. For three years on a college campus. But the long distance plus insane working hours are taking their toll. I can barely remember what she looks like. It just doesn't seem realistic to stay in a relationship with someone three thousand miles away who's living a completely different life."

Kate's not sure how to feel. Part of her wants Annie and Nick to stay together because if he were dating a lot, she'd see him even less. But a bigger part would like it if they were both single and could keep each other company on holidays and birthdays and all those times it really sucks to be single in New York.

"Maybe you should try breaking up and seeing how much you miss each other? If it's terrible, you could always get back together?"

Nick shakes his head. "I've never been a believer in the on-again, off-again relationship," he says. "I'm an all-or-nothing kind of guy, and I don't think our situation is going to get any better in the near future."

"Well, let me know if I can do anything to help."

He laughs. "How about introducing me to some of those mattresses you keep talking about? Maybe I can lure them with free hotel rooms."

They head to the bar for a last drink, and while Kate orders, Nick suddenly looks up.

"Amazing," he says, taking in the bright green-and-yellow stained-glass dome ceiling. "I think it's a Donald MacDonald. I love his work."

Their necks tilt back as Nick explains the craftsmanship to Kate, who can't believe she didn't notice the cathedral dome this entire evening. She suddenly has the urge to jump up and run her hands along the ridges, feel the smooth intersections of colors and lines, but of course, they could never jump that high. Besides, the view wouldn't be nearly as striking from up there.

Charlie hangs up the phone and asks Tim, "You hear anything weird about Blake's dad and Mark Reed and some other big guys being investigated for illegally shipping antiques on private planes?"

"Why is it illegal to ship something on a private plane if it's not drugs or guns or anything fun like that?"

"If I knew that I'd be a fucking lawyer. I just know they broke a law."

Tim doesn't follow what goes on in the business world. He has no interest unless a CEO is fucking his secretary or maxing out his credit card at a strip club. Last month he did an item about a big bank keeping a pied-à-terre in Midtown where the partners could take their mistresses. That was fun. An ugly divorce is usually pretty good, too, especially if Ron Perelman is involved. The Stanley Stahl scandal is great because more boldface New Yorkers keep getting busted for cashing in their stock before the FDA verdict. But taxes and technicalities bore the shit out of him. And something about Charlie's tip sounds off. A game of telephone involving dozens of half-deaf ears.

"I don't know, Blake's dad is into tacky modern art these days. But you want me to ask Blake about it?"

"If you think he'll help, sure. But don't do anything to set off any alarms before I nail this down."

I can tell you in no uncertain terms that my dad is definitely not buying antiques," Blake says when Tim calls. "The oldest fixture to grace his apartment is my grandmother."

"Okay, forget the antiques. Chalk that up to Column A percentage error. Anything going on with taxes? Where there's smoke there—"

Blake cuts Tim off. "Save the speech for the civilians." He pushes his hair out of his eyes and straightens up in his chair. It's days like today when he wishes his dad were a dentist or a history professor. "My dad will definitely not take an official call from you or Charlie, and he will sic his lawyers on you if you fuck with him."

"So what do you want me to do? It's Friday and we're getting desperate. We've only got enough shit to fill Saturday's and Sunday's pages now, and Monday won't take a vacation."

So Blake feeds the monster, giving up an item about a powerful fashion editor's boyfriend cheating on her with a ballerina. It was posing a problem for him, anyway, since *Manhattan* magazine's fashion writer has been friends with the editor for decades and doesn't want to piss her off.

"Nice one," says Tim, typing the item into his computer. He'll call the rep for the editor's magazine after six P.M., when everyone will have left for the weekend.

Kate pulls open the heavy brass doors of Coast and smells pungent tropical flowers too exotic for Manhattan. Massive glass vases of bright birds-of-paradise and red ginger are splayed out against the dark red walls like dozens of slender jeweled fingers. She didn't notice them at the opening party—there were too many people then to actually see the space. And everyone was just trying to figure out who else was there rather than where they actually were. She checks out the menu for the first time, too: They only serve a seventy-five-dollar prix fixe. Her parents would never, ever spend that kind of money at a restaurant. When she was growing up, they considered the twenty-three dollars their favorite Chinese restaurant charged for the lobster entrée exorbitant. A waiter brings Kate a glass of cool champagne and she settles back in a plush red-velvet chair, watching the quiet curtain of water stream down the fountain separating the dining room and the reception area, dulling the clinking sound of silver against white china. She could get used to this.

Tonight Kate is finally having her first date with Marco, which only took three weeks to plan. They had a few false starts. When your job involves hitting at least two events a night or catering to VIPs with 8:30 P.M. reservations, planning a date—and this is seeming more and more like a date—has more challenges than usual. By now Kate knows Marco's assistant's direct dial by memory. It all started when she called to thank him for the box of chocolate truffles he sent to thank her for the item about his new pastry chef last month, before he went to Italy for Christmas.

"Eat one every night," he said about the dozens of buttery-rich chocolates. "It's a recipe for sweet dreams." Kate's not sure about that, but she followed his orders and thought about him with each velvety bite.

The restaurant is packed and Marco is working the room as if he were Bill Clinton, looking everyone in the eye, touching elbows and shoulders. Smiling big and remembering names. In here he's 95 percent famous.

The sexy hostess picks up the phone and, after hanging up, tells Kate to meet Marco in the black Lincoln Town Car outside, dispatching the directions without looking up from the reservations book. Kate wonders why he doesn't just come and get her, but she guesses he likes to keep his personal and professional lives separate. In any case, it's certainly a step up from her last date, where she had to meet the guy on a rainy corner outside a restaurant and wait an hour to get a table by the bathroom.

She slips into the idling car feeling like a princess, or at least one of those New York heiresses with a bottomless bank account. A chauffeured car must be the greatest Manhattan luxury. No bursting blisters on the walk home from the subway.

Marco exits through the service entrance, wearing a buttery brown leather jacket that looks a lot like the one Ralph Lauren was wearing inside tonight. Tomorrow she'll tell Tim he should run a sighting of the designer dining at Coast.

"Hey, beautiful," he says, kissing her on both cheeks. She thought he was only going for one cheek, so their heads almost collide. This is the second time he's called her beautiful, and she can't help but feel a quiver dart down her spine. He takes a bottle of chilled champagne from the back of the seat and pours two glasses as if they were in a romantic comedy—the gesture seems a little rehearsed, almost a parody, but charming nonetheless. When he rolls up his sleeves to open the bottle, she notices a faint pink scar snaking up his wrist, the kind of scar that's not from a simple surgery or a skiing accident. It's a scar with a story, but before she can ask about it, he rolls back his sleeve quickly as if his skin were hot to the touch. The only things people tell you right away are the things not really worth knowing.

Marco answers his cell phone and starts talking numbers with a Coast manager, simultaneously pulling out a BlackBerry and sending an e-mail.

deborah schoeneman

Kate keeps sipping champagne, a kind of consolation prize for conversation, and looking out the window with the same intensity as if she were watching a movie. He takes another call and she checks her own cell phone. Still, no messages. He mouths "Sorry" and keeps talking on his phone. But now he's looking at her and she can feel his chocolate eyes melting on her legs even when she's staring out the window.

"I liked you right when I met you," he says, snapping shut his phone as the car stops. Kate decides just to smile and tries to take a deep breath and the car speeds downtown—seeming to effortlessly hover just above the potholes.

The driver opens the door for Kate, and Marco takes her arm, escorting her inside the restaurant Nobu. Small birch logs with wooden branches stick out from skinny trunks, creating a kind of canopy as they're whisked to a booth by the window. Rupert Murdoch and his wife are across the room. Last week Kate ran an item about how a rival South American media baron makes his assistant go to the gym where Murdoch works out just to see how much weight he lifts so the South American can make sure he lifts more. The assistant, who went to college with Kate, told her the story a few weeks ago at a mutual friend's party. He didn't know enough yet to say it was off the record.

Marco tells Kate that Nobu Matsuhisa wanted to serve sake in traditional wooden boxes, but one of his investors, Robert De Niro, kept spilling the sake all over his face when he drank it that way, so they settled for the tiny cups. Kate tries the rice wine for the first time, expecting to grimace but finding the clear liquid cleaner and sweeter than she expected. The small cups seem to have no bottom and the sake quickly starts tasting like water.

Marco asks if Kate's hungry and she nods, smiling. They don't have menus but he tells the waiter they want a six-course tasting menu, including plenty of sea urchin, which he tells Kate is called uni.

"A woman who can really eat is really sexy," says Marco, looking Kate right in the eye.

The first course is slivers of yellowtail, dotted with tiny circular cuts of jalapeño pepper. Marco bites into a silky slice of fish and sighs, closing his eyes and focusing on the flavors in his mouth. He tells her that the secret to flavor is combining sweet, sour, bitter, and salty—the only flavors the taste buds recognize. It's done perfectly in this dish, one of Nobu's most famous, he explains. Kate thinks, but doesn't say, that those flavors could also describe how she feels about living in New York.

"Did you know that bluefin tuna can swim from here to Japan in just a month?" he asks as she bites into a piece of the purple-red fish, which dissolves almost instantly on her tongue. He says the tuna are being studied behind thick glass walls in the Monterey aquarium, right near where he grew up after his family moved from Italy when he was ten years old. They don't need to eat for a week and their scales are always flawless silver. "The perfect animal," he says. He talks about tuna the way Tim talks about Jessica Simpson.

"But every time tuna is kept in captivity," he goes on, "they get a little growth under their mouths. It's harmless but no one knows why they get it." He laughs.

The uni is next, and it's slimy and wonderful, a nutty-sweet sea taste sliding down her throat. Marco tells her it's an aphrodisiac and Kate's not sure if it's the uni or his leg against hers that's making her body temperature rise.

Between courses, he teaches her how to better hold chopsticks, squeezing the tips up high so the delicate pieces of fish are clamped perfectly. It's a technique he learned in Japan. Then he demonstrates how to suck out the brains—"the best part"—of a raw shrimp head, putting the eyes, antennae and all, in his mouth and crunching down. Kate can't look at the beady black eyes, but she doesn't want Marco to think she's a wimp, so she just goes ahead and pops it in her mouth. And he's right—a delicious, concentrated shrimp taste like an ocean musk runs across her tongue.

"Nobu is really a nice guy," says Marco, between bites. "He's probably the only one in the industry who doesn't cheat on his wife."

"No one else is faithful?" The best sources are embedded.

"Want me to tell you which hotels they bring their mistresses to?"

Her eyes get wide. "Yes!" She knows Lacey would love to hear about it, too.

He tells her, then continues with a story about a certain three-star chef who can only get aroused at an S&M chamber above his Zagat-top-rated restaurant.

Maybe it's the sake or maybe she's just emboldened by his leaking all these secrets, but she wants to know one of his. "Why did you and Wendy Winter break up?"

He sighs and carefully blots his lips with his napkin. "Wendy is forty and wants to get married and have kids and I don't," he says, and for the first time since she graduated, Kate feels that her youth is an asset.

"You don't ever, or you don't want to with her?"

"Not now, and not with her. Marriage is a flawed institution and every married man I know cheats," he says.

She thinks about the captive tuna behind the glass.

"I have no interest in making my personal life official," he explains. "I already deal with enough paperwork."

His take on marriage sounds rehearsed, a perfectly crafted script to any woman he dates—and she's not sure she believes it.

"My parents don't cheat on each other," she offers, biting into a silky piece of miso cod. "They're really in love."

"That's what you think. Men can't be faithful."

"Maybe you can't be, but my father is. I know it." Kate thinks of her parents spending summer afternoons in their garden and taking walks down to the creek. They probably wouldn't like her dating Marco. "Just find someone nice," they always say.

"Well, that's rare," he says, as if he doesn't believe her.

Every dessert on the menu arrives at the table. "It's an industry trick," explains Marco, conveniently changing the subject. "It's the cheapest way to spoil VIPs." A long skinny plate of ice cream scoops coated in gooey rice. A molten chocolate cake in a bento box with green-tea ice cream to cut the sweetness. There's no check at the end, but Marco asks the waiter to charge them for the tea so he can leave a tip. Kate spies the receipt: one hundred dollars.

Marco puts his hand on the small of her back, leading her out of the restaurant as if they've been out to dinner countless times. Outside, the car is waiting—it must cost a fortune to have it idle by the curb—and the driver opens the door. Kate stumbles inside, sinking into the soft dark leather seats.

"So cute, you're falling asleep, " Marco says, pulling her in to his chest, which makes a perfect cradle for her head. He unclips her hair, playing with her long, loose, and knotty curls.

He insists on driving her back to Brooklyn and she wants to tell the driver, *Just keep driving. Cross another bridge, take us somewhere far from here. Make tonight last a little longer.*

But the ride is over too soon. There's only traffic when you're rushing to get somewhere, and only clear roads at times like this, when you just want to savor being between destinations. Kate wants to ask him in but the loft is messy with the mousetraps and dirty dishes and bags of trash outside the door. And you can only start something once.

"Are you going to invite me in?" he asks.

Kate shakes her head and grabs the door before the driver can open it. "Thanks for a wonderful night."

She jumps out of the car and runs up the stairs. She knows if she were to turn around, she'd never hold her ground.

New York Examiner, "Off the Record"
by Paul Peterson with Kate Simon

The Chambers Hotel has replaced Blue Ribbon restaurant as the late-night choice for celebrity chefs. And they're ordering room service instead of raw bar. A well-placed source says a certain three-star Italian chef has been quietly checking into Midtown's Chambers Hotel after his popular kitchen closes—and before he goes home to his wealthy wife and kids. The maître d' of a longtime power-lunching canteen also hangs a DO NOT DISTURB sign at the hotel when he has trysts with his wife and their occasional third partner, a certain woman around town with a royal title and a dark past.

There's a bottle of Tim's favorite vodka on his desk when he gets to the office at ten A.M. Kate must have had something to do with it. A few nights ago they had a conversation about why he prefers the brand. The card says it's from Marco, a present for running a sighting of Ralph Lauren dining at Coast, and for not calling Marco the "randy restaurateur." Good enough incentive to kill off that nickname.

When Charlie walks in half an hour later, he looks closely at Tim, probably wondering if he's early today because he stayed up all night. But it's Charlie who's wearing the same clothes he wore yesterday, and his wife has called twice already looking for him. Tim clarifies that he just had a low-key night with Zoe. They had dinner at a bistro on the Upper East Side where, refreshingly, Tim didn't recognize anyone and no one came over to talk about the new dumb thing they were doing. The anonymity was almost worth the $120 bill he'll try to expense.

Charlie sits down at his desk facing Tim's in the corner cubicle and starts checking his phone messages. "You're not sick or anything?"

"Just a little sick of going out late, I think."

"Well, that should help!" Charlie cackles, nodding at the bottle of vodka. "But I had a more useful night. I had dinner with my best Wall Street source," he says. Tim knows that source was fired from a major bank for having an affair with his secretary and that Charlie's night probably included at least one other "social obligation," as he'll tell his wife. "It looks like Steven Bradley, along with a bunch of other big masters of the universe, are being investigated for shipping art they buy here commercially to airports near their vacation homes and then shipping it back here on their own jets to evade New York sales tax." Charlie looks very pleased. He loves breaking society scandals. "As if they can't afford it."

Tim feels the blood rushing out of his head. "Maybe I can get Blake's dad to talk if we leave him out of it."

"Blake's dad *is* the story."

"Can't Mark Reed be the story? He just made three hundred million taking his company public."

"Thanks to Steven Bradley." Charlie raises his eyebrows. "And if we don't name Blake's dad, Justin Katz at the *Journal* will. They're on the story, too. You know as well as I do that we have to do something to defuse the rumor, to show that we were there first."

It's the same speech that Tim gives his skittish sources. They should just have it on tape.

Tim grabs his cell phone and says he's going out for coffee. Once he's a few blocks from the office, he calls Blake and skips the small talk. "Charlie says it's an art tax your father didn't pay and there's an investigation and *Journal* is on it, too. We have to do something, so you want to tell me what to do?"

Tim can faintly hear Blake taking notes with a pen instead of typing. He must not want Tim to know he's reporting back to his dad. "Trade?"

"You're going to have to do a little better than that."

"Spin?"

"Spin away, but do it fast. I can only hold this for a day at the most. If the week stays slow, it could end up on the cover, and then it's really out of my hands."

Blake has something in the bank that his dad said to use only for emergencies, something that should really be in Blake's column.

"Mark Reed just bought that thirty-million Picasso at Sotheby's," he says. All the art reporters and gossip columnists have been trying to find out who bought the painting, even floating "usual suspect" names like Paul Allen, Lily Safra, and Steve Wynn as potential purchasers.

"This should buy you a few days, but you'd better come up with an official line," Tim says. "You can't just bury this one alive."

Whenever he thinks about his dad, Blake faintly tastes those eggs from the University Club. He takes a sip of his lukewarm deli coffee, which feels as if it's burning a hole through his stomach. He calls his dad and gets his longtime secretary, who always blathers on about bullshit for too long. Why, why does he always have to go through someone to talk to his father?

"It's urgent," he says, and he's quickly punched through.

His dad always says small talk is for people who have too much time and too little to say. "Who knows?" he quickly asks Blake.

"Column A and the *Journal*."

For a minute there's just silence, and then Blake hears the rustle of papers, and his father swears and sighs at the same time. Blake suddenly knows exactly what to do. This is his game and he flips the switch to autopilot. He tells his father to fess up and pay whatever taxes he owes immediately. And he gives him the number for the publicist whom powerful men call when they're in trouble—for which they pay at least thirty thousand dollars a month.

"There's no use lying about it," Blake says. "Everyone else is going to lie and you're going to look like the good guy after the shock wave subsides, which will be in about two weeks."

His dad doesn't say anything.

"And if you don't fess up and pay whatever you owe," Blake continues, "they're going to start digging through everything, and do you want that? If Bill Clinton had fessed up about Monica, he wouldn't have been *impeached*."

"I should never have let Lindsay drag me to those galleries in Chelsea," his dad whisper-hisses, even though he has a massive corner office.

"It doesn't matter how or why this happened. You're just wasting time and energy trying to figure it out. It's not history, it's the reaction to history that matters."

"But what about the firm and our friends and the Guggenheim board?" asks his dad, sounding angry, which means he's really sad.

"Memories are short but they better hear about it from you first."

His dad pauses. "Thanks," he says quietly. He clears his voice. "But I'm not giving anything to those assholes at Column A. I know Tim's your friend but they call Lindsay those terrible names. I just can't cooperate with those people."

Blake looks out his window. The streets and tiny cars and people four-teen stories below look freshly scrubbed, as if they've been washed with weeks of rain. As if it were already spring. As if something buried under layers of ice and snow was slowly starting to grow.

When Kate gets to the office she starts plowing through the day's papers, trying to catch up quickly so she can move on to the stack of fat monthly magazines that have also arrived today. She skims the *Wall Street Journal,* which she does every morning in case Justin has a story. He reads all her stuff, so she should read his. Professional courtesy for personal friends. The bonus is she's actually learning something about business, which is a lot like the gossip game but with much more money at stake.

Kate gasps when she reads the headline. BRADLEY'S $3 MILLION BLUNDER.

"Isn't that Blake from *Manhattan* magazine's dad?" ask Gavin the sportswriter, peering over Kate's shoulder.

Before Kate can answer, Lacey comes careening toward their desks, with a jangle of bracelets announcing her arrival.

"You've got the connections to advance that story," says Lacey. Kate's confused. She thought she wasn't supposed to report on anyone she knew. Have the rules changed now that it's her column?

"What are you waiting for?" asks Lacey. "You're on deadline!"

Gavin shrugs and goes back to his computer. Kate starts looking through the notebook on her desk that she uses to write down her phone messages. It's pretty much unintelligible. But then sees a note she wrote to herself: *Museum board scandal. Art tax.* She remembers calling in that message to her voice mail from Alec's bathroom the night she broke all those glasses at Lush. She taps in a search to Nexis, and indeed, Alec's dad helped Steven Bradley get his seat on the Guggenheim board. A quick search of the museum's Web site reveals a board roster now without Steven Bradley, even though he was honored at a recent gala, where he sat with Michael Douglas, Catherine Zeta-Jones, and Dan and Donna

Aykroyd. Kate searches the site's archives and the "cached" sites on Google and finds a board roster from a few months ago. Sure enough, Steven Bradley and Mark Reed are on that one. Her heartbeat quickens and she's not sure if it's racing with panic or excitement.

She has to call Blake before she does anything else. Paul always said "try your best to go directly to the source."

"Please say you're not calling about my dad," is the first thing Blake says when he answers his phone.

Kate tries to stay focused and reads the script she drafted on her notepad in case she gets too nervous to remember what to ask. She says she wants to give Blake a "heads-up" that she's working on an item about his dad and Mark Reed getting thrown off the museum board. *Heads-up* sounded better out of Paul's mouth.

"Do you really need to do this?" he asks.

"I'm sorry but I do," she says, sounding far more confident than she feels. "Now that Paul's gone, I have to deliver."

"Well, better you than someone else." That must mean Kate doesn't have to worry about being scooped by Tim or Robin. "But it's important to clarify that my dad has admitted his mistake and paid the three million he owes, plus he gave another two hundred fifty thousand to the Art Heals charity for inner-city school kids. Mark is still saying he's innocent and he's probably going to have to go to trial."

"If you confirm the museum tip, I'll be sure to mention that," she says, thankful that he can't see her fingers trembling.

"Just on background, yes. They asked him to step down and he did. But you didn't hear it from me. You're going to have to call my dad's publicist for the official statement."

Tim was out too late at someone's downtown loft doing lines with a sexy sculptress, the young owner of a new art gallery, and the recently divorced heir of a pharmaceutical fortune. Tim was under the false impression that if he was the last one standing, the sculptress, who needed to promote her show next month, would end up going home with him, even though he was too preoccupied thinking about Zoe to flirt with any significant enthusiasm. He was by far the most attractive and the poorest of the men left standing at the party. Rich guys tend to sweat just sitting around, and there was a lot of sweating in that room. But as soon as the heir mentioned that he's looking for art to redecorate his Bedford estate, the sculptress immediately switched her focus and slowly moved her leg away from Tim's. It's probably what he deserves for telling Zoe he couldn't get a plus-one to the art-opening dinner he went to earlier. She probably knows that's bullshit. He just was worried Danielle might show up, because she claims she used to date the restaurant's modelizing owner.

He should have called in sick. Charlie comes back from the morning editorial meeting looking like someone punched him a few times in the stomach before whacking him over the head for good measure.

"We should have run with that item about Steven Bradley," he says. "It was bad enough when the *Journal* kicked our ass last week, but now the suits are really pissed off."

Charlie throws a copy of the *Examiner* on Tim's desk, then sits down and starts working his phone. Tim opens up to Kate's column and almost gasps.

The Guggenheim Museum has quietly asked two of its top donors to step down from the board of directors. Last week, Fifth Avenue financier Steven Bradley and tech mogul Mark Reed were asked to resign, as their art world reputations have been damaged by recent allegations of tax fraud from illegally shipping paintings back to New York on their private jets to avoid paying sales tax. They also had to rescind over $4 million combined in pledges to the museum's acquisitions and education departments. While Bradley is cooperating with the authorities, Reed remains under investigation and sources say he could be charged in the next few weeks. "This has been one of the greatest moral dilemmas to plague our institution, and our programs are going to suffer," says the museum's mouthpiece.

Kate had advanced the story and dug up tension at a venerable New York institution. Not bad for a cub reporter who's been playing the naive card.

Clear and present danger, indeed. And Blake's dad comes off like a much better guy than Mark Reed, so Blake probably isn't even mad. Fuck them both. As Blake's best friend and a writer for Column A, Tim should have had that story handed to him on a fucking silver platter. Why save the milk of sacred cows if someone else is going to drink it?

He calls Blake at work. "What else did she know?" Tim asks him. Blake must have given her the item as a diversion from something bigger she was on to. Something Tim should now get. It's only fair.

"She didn't need my help."

"So you're commending her? She's just going to keep scooping me even without your help? Great. That makes me feel just fucking great." Tim slams down his phone, and when it immediately starts ringing again, he picks it up, thinking it's Blake with a peace offering.

He should be so lucky.

"My office," barks Tubby, loud enough to echo down the hall. "Now."

When Tim gets there, Tubby slams the door behind him, and Tim sinks into the small gray couch. "We got our ass kicked by the *Journal* last week and today by that shitty money-losing paper on a story that should have been ours. But nooooo, you wanted to protect your little friend over at *Manhattan* magazine, who I shouldn't have to remind you is a competitor."

Tubby doesn't wait for an excuse or an explanation.

"You smell of booze and cigarettes again. You're probably still wasted from whatever you were doing last night. I'm telling you, Tim, you'd better be getting good—no, *great*—items out of this lifestyle you've carved out for yourself. I don't want the lame excuse that you're just doing your job when you're actually fucking up your job. Do you see Charlie stumbling in here wasted? Do you?"

Tim shakes his head.

"Exactly. So get your shit together. This is officially your second warning for being late, drunk, and protecting your friends. And you know what that means, don't you?"

He wants an answer this time.

"Yes," says Tim. "Three times and I'm out."

Tubby bites into a powdered doughnut on his desk, leaving a white dusting on his black blazer. He's going to let it stay there. Fat fuck. The sports guys got two whole boxes today, but just one bite made Tim feel like puking earlier this morning.

"You know what just kills me the most?" asks Tubby, but this is not a question Tim knows the answer to yet. "Do you?

Tim shakes his head and looks down at the carpet.

"If you would just pull yourself together, if you would do your job, you'd be the best damn gossip columnist in this city. When you decide to actually work, you're the best I've ever seen, and I've been here twenty years." Tim tries to picture where *he'll* be in twenty years, but his brain feels numb. "I'm getting fucking tired of dealing with these lawyers threatening to sue us for libel, and you're never coming up with any decent explanations. We could lose one day and then we'd all be fucked."

Tubby gulps down his coffee. Tim's stomach hurts just thinking about the syrupy sweet concoction.

"So get back there and make it up to us," says Tubby. "You're only as good as your—"

"Last story." It's where the record of the sound track of his life starts skipping.

"So go get a fucking story, get me something we can tease on the cover—and make sure it's true. And don't forget I'm still waiting for something, anything, about that fucking Hollywood Lothario. Get that source on the record!"

W hen were you going to mention that my future father-in-law is a *criminal?*" shouts Bethany as soon as Blake walks into their apartment.

Bethany and her friends don't read the *Journal,* so she missed last week's story, but she must have read Kate's story today. She's been leaving increasingly hostile messages for him all day, but he turned off his cell phone after he talked to his dad so Blake wouldn't have to deal with her. His dad seemed okay with the *Examiner* story, even though he was surprised he didn't get any calls about it. Blake didn't say that people always pretend they didn't read something bad about you even though they almost always do.

Bethany walks toward him, looking like a doll shaken up by a bratty little girl. Flushed porcelain cheeks, long silky black hair with errant strands all akimbo. Black ice irises. Long, pale fingers that look like they've never seen the sun. "Blake, what are people going to say?"

Blake pours himself a glass of scotch and adds two ice cubes. He takes off his blue blazer and his black shoes and sits down on the fluffy white couch that looks much softer than it feels.

"Calm down," he says. "It's not like he killed anyone or blew someone's retirement fund."

"But he *lied*," she says, standing above him, scowling. She's wearing a pendant made of sapphire and diamond serpents, and Blake wishes it would come alive and bite her.

"Bethany, you lie all the time."

"Not about important things! Not on my tax forms!"

"That's because you don't have any money to lie about."

Her eyes get big at this and her mouth goes slack. She slumps down on the white chair facing Blake and he notices there's a little coke residue on the glass table. He runs his finger over it and rubs the powder on his gums. Bethany's jaw is working like she's wired, but he pretends not to notice.

"My mother's worried we're going to get thrown out of the Southampton Bathing Corporation."

"You should. That place is racist, anti-Semitic, homophobic, and perhaps worst of all, boring."

"But where would we play tennis in the summer?" she asks, as if this is a legitimate question. Blake gives her a cold stare and runs his finger over the table again, but there's no more coke. Maybe he should order some. Or better yet, some pot. He's anxious enough.

"That may be the dumbest question you've ever asked," he says.

She gets up and stomps over to the window as if she were wearing four-inch-high stilettos, but she's barefoot and actually looks smaller than Blake remembers. In a tiny voice to match, Bethany says, "Well, how about another dumb question? Are we still going to the benefit at the Guggenheim? Because if we are, I need to reserve something from Donna Karan's spring collection before all the fashion editors get the best stuff."

She's still waiting for his response and perhaps she's realizing how ridiculous she sounds. Maybe it's the coke or maybe she's really worried about her dress and tennis. Or maybe the future is much easier to plan for than today. Bethany sinks down on the floor, probably scared that her mother is wrong and it may actually not be just as easy to marry someone rich as it is to marry someone poor.

Blake puts back on his blue blazer. He grabs his red cashmere scarf from the closet because winter is rolling in with this storm. Bethany looks up at him, black mascara streaming down her face in wet raccoon rivulets.

"What are you doing?" she asks in her wounded animal voice, which usually makes him melt and do whatever she wants.

Another dumb question. Blake leaves and gently closes the door without saying anything. She'll never follow him into the lobby, where someone could see her like this. Bethany demands privacy when she comes undone, which is just one of the reasons everyone thinks he's lucky to be dating her. They don't know any better.

His dad's probably still awake. Maybe he'll crash in the guest room. He's not coming back until she stops asking dumb questions—and that could take a very, very long time.

It's been a month since the dinner at Nobu, and Kate can't help but feel antsy. When is Marco going to call? Was dinner a date or just networking? Could he be too busy at Coast for a personal life? To quell her urge to call him, Kate researches him online. It worked for Blake's dad and the museum. She hopes Blake wasn't pissed off about the story. She's been afraid to call or e-mail him since it came out earlier this week.

"If anything, he should thank you for making Mark Reed seem like the greedy bastard," Lacey had said.

Kate stops just short of going down to the courthouse at 60 Centre Street to type Marco's name into a computer they have there to pull up any lawsuits, the way she sometimes does when she's working on an item. Or sometimes she just goes down there to type in the names of the usual suspects, who are more often than not embroiled in some suit, which makes for good copy. Paul also taught her how to research people on the city's Web sites to find out if they've registered for any renovation permits, bought a condo or town house, or registered to buy or rent a private jet. With a little patience, you can find out practically anything—and people still wonder how she gets their phone number or address.

But nothing has been written about the scar on Marco's arm. No record of any accidents or fights or bad cooking burns. His press clips only mention his restaurants and his graduating from culinary school and various charity events where he's donated gourmet meals. Someone may as well have taken a fat eraser to his files, leaving only the boring and predictable facts.

The phone rings and she nearly jumps, as if Lacey or The Principal can see her through the receiver, wasting her day on a background check for no professional purpose.

"Hey," says Marco, and for a moment she panics, thinking he, too, can somehow see her snooping. The nearby sounds of other phones ringing and fingers clicking on keyboards go mute, making his voice the only sound she can hear.

"It's really great to hear from you," she says, trying to remember to breathe. What took him so long?

"When do I get to see you again? I really enjoyed dinner with you and it's been way too long."

Maybe it was a date. Maybe he really is that busy. "It was probably the best meal I've ever had," she says.

"Well, that's because you've never eaten a proper meal at my restaurant." Kate wonders if *proper* means *free*.

He invites her to bring a few friends to Coast this weekend. "How about Tim and Blake and your friend from *Gourmet?*"

"Sounds perfect," she says, briefly wondering if he just wants press for the restaurant. But he has Spinster for that.

"So, I'll see you Saturday, then," he says, and Kate can't help hoping they'll spend Saturday night together. Maybe they'll brunch on Sunday before strolling through Soho shops and end up spending the whole day together, ordering take-out Chinese Sunday night and watching movies in bed the way couples do when they don't want a date to end, when they don't want to go back to their lives, perhaps out of fear that they'll never find that cozy comfort again. Planning the future is one of the few ways to pretend you can control the present, or what comes between the present and the near-future—those impressionable moments that can never be anything but improvisational.

As Blake's cab pulls up to Coast, he remembers that it used to be a fancy French restaurant. Almost every restaurant in New York used to be something else, and no matter how many coats of fresh paint get layered on the walls, it still sometimes smells like its past. Many restaurants open up in a space still haunted by the previous occupant's downfall, and that always makes for a decent item. Nothing closes or opens without a backstory.

Blake's dad celebrated his birthday here fifteen years ago. Blake remembers his mother's speech being just a few words. In retrospect, he should have heard that she was saying good-bye. His dad was about to make partner and he wanted to make a new life for his new money, but she was perfectly happy with their life the way it was.

"Here's to another great year of great health and golf," she said, before quickly sitting back down and immediately picking up her fork to push her food around her plate.

He's got to break up with Bethany. Every time she calls his dad a criminal,

Blake imagines putting a red cross through another day on the calendar, marking a day closer to ending it with her. He's just not sure when the final day will be, and he wishes he could pay his dad's divorce lawyer to do it for him. Now Blake understands why it's worth the price for a chance at something better. Places and especially people don't ever really change.

As Blake hands his coat to the pretty blond hostess, Marco comes up the stairs to the dining room and heads over. He's wearing a clean white chef's jacket with his name embroidered in blue on the lapel.

"Hey, man, sorry to hear about your dad," says Marco, apparently unaware of the city's cardinal rule about pretending no one read the item you wish was never printed. "But for what it's worth, I think Kate's item made your dad sound like the good guy."

"Thanks," says Blake, who can't decide if Marco is naive or calculating. But he still wants to change the subject.

"How's the restaurant?"

"Great, thanks," says Marco, flashing a telegenic smile. "The review in your magazine really helped. Every table tonight is booked and they haven't even saved one or two for VIP emergencies. Now I'm just waiting for the *Times* to weigh in."

"What's next?" Blake could use an item and he doesn't feel like stopping by Bungalow 8 tonight.

Marco says he's looking for investors for a chain of Coasts and he wants to get some kind of cooking or entertaining television show.

"That doesn't sound like something Daniel Boulud or Eric Ripert would go after," says Blake, seeing if mentioning two of the top Zagat-rated chefs elicits any envy.

"Who says I want to be them? Why can't I be a chef and an entrepreneur? Why can't I be groundbreaking? What if I want to be Martha Stewart *and* Daniel Boulud?"

Blake smiles. "Go for it." He doesn't say that, more often that not, someone trying to be groundbreaking just ends up flying headfirst from the clouds, and no one ever forgets that bloody fall to concrete. It seems Marco wants something that doesn't exist, and for good reason. A quality chef is not supposed to be a salesman. Blake recognizes the faint glint in Marco's eyes. It's the glint of someone who may just get most of what he wants, even if he ends up not wanting it anymore. Blake can always spot the moths of Manhattan, hitting the window screens again and again through the night.

Kate wonders what Blake and Marco were talking about before they all sat down, and she can't help but feel a little competitive, as if Marco should be loyal to just her if he's planting an item.

The waiter says there's no use for menus because Marco has designed a special tasting course for them.

"Impressive," Zoe whispers in Kate's ear.

Kate can almost make out blurry white figures behind the opaque glass partition between the dining room and kitchen and wonders if one of them is Marco, carefully crafting dishes for them.

They each get a small square of salmon with a jellylike yellow top. *"Amuse-bouche,"* explains the waiter as it slides down Kate's throat like something coated in silk.

"Orgasmic," sighs Zoe. "You could eat like this every night if you married Marco."

Kate laughs. "I don't know about marriage, but I wouldn't mind going out with him again."

Blake looks up, a little alarmed. "Who's getting married?"

Tim laughs. "Not you, I hope." He drains his drink and picks up his fork with a full fist, as if he's grabbing a gardening tool, and Kate notices Zoe slightly wince.

The next dish is white truffle risotto, which intrigues Kate, who has never eaten truffles before.

"They're so expensive, it's like eating gold," says Zoe.

The truffles taste like earth and sweat, a musky night next to someone you want. "This tastes like . . . sex!" Kate tells Marco when he stops by the table.

"I knew I liked you," he says, giving her a little kiss on the cheek before dashing off to another table.

The entreés are served with a flourish under silver domes: a sweet duck in a cherry glaze, a buttery-smooth sea bass over spinach, a steak over creamy mashed potatoes laced with black truffles, and a soft salmon with warm rhubarb compote that she remembers from Terry Barlow's lunch last summer. Kate should feel exhilarated by the new flavors and textures, but a tiny fear starts creeping up through her heart, a fear that she's being spoiled. If she gets used to this and it's taken away, she'll always know what she's missing. It almost makes her want to walk out right now.

They get every dessert on the menu and the table fills up with a buffet of bright sweets. "The chef's trick," says Kate.

"And now you're the expert?" asks Zoe.

Two desserts are set in front of Kate. A smooth lemon tart and the same chocolate hazelnut torte she tried at Pierre's gladiator party.

"You should be wearing a tiara," says Blake.

Tim asks for the check. He says it's bad luck to expect that anything is free, even though it usually is, because anytime he's done that, he's gotten stuck with a bill that he can't always expense. The waiter says dinner is a "gift" from Marco, but he's nowhere to be found to thank. Kate suggests they wait at the bar even though she doesn't want to drink anymore. She's already tipsy and she wants to sober up so she can tell Marco what she thought of the meal.

After about ten minutes, the maître d' pulls her aside with apologies from Marco, who had to leave. He doesn't offer any explanation.

"Did he say I should meet him somewhere else?"

"Something came up," he says slowly, carefully annunciating each word.

Zoe comes over and takes Kate's arm. Blake and Tim follow behind her. "He wouldn't invite you in with your friends if he didn't like you."

"Or he's busy fucking his hot ex-hostess," says Tim. Zoe tells him to shut up.

"Or he just wanted us *all* here for press," says Blake. No one says anything, but the *all* rings through Kate's ears at a shrill, high pitch.

In the cab back to Brooklyn, Kate wonders if she did or said something wrong. Maybe what Tim said about the check was true. Maybe she expected too much and so she got nothing more than what he promised, a great meal. But she knows Marco likes her. He kept saying it. If not, he would have invited Spinster to sit with them. Right?

"How was your big date?" Nick asks, rubbing his bloodshot eyes when she walks into their apartment. It's eleven-thirty and he's just finished painting their new kitchen cabinets. He's got white paint on his jeans and even a smear on his cheek.

She brings him a towel for his face and tells him about the musky white truffles and the nutty sea urchin sliding down her throat. Sweet, sour, salty, and bitter. Kate tries to describe every taste and texture with the precision of a scientist but she still feels like she's describing the sky to a blind man.

"That sounds just a little more glamorous than my night," he says, washing off paintbrushes in the sink. Now they'll be able to unpack their kitchen stuff from the brown boxes in the hall, even if they never have time to use any of it. "Everyone got what they wanted."

Kate hopes that what she's doing with Marco is more than trading. Suddenly she feels queasy, as if she were teetering on a sailboat in a storm. She runs down the hall and doubles over the toilet just in time. All those new textures and tastes well right up and out, splashing into the toilet in angry red splotches. Bitter the second time around.

Nick brings her a glass of water and kneels down at her side, pulling her hair away from her face.

"I'm fine," she tries to insist, retching again. "I just got carried away at dinner. . . ."

He kneels down next to her. "Well, I hope your nights with Marco start ending better."

"If I have any more."

"You will," he says, handing her a towel. "You will. Just try not to get carried away."

Blake orders blueberry pancakes this time at the University Club. His father orders a bagel, which is unusual. Even stranger, he spreads cream cheese and strawberry jam over it and actually starts eating it. And then he says nothing. Blake pours syrup over his pancakes, watching his father mentally calculate the calories. He wonders if his dad is becoming one of those people his friends don't want to be seen with at popular breakfast places like the Regency and the Carlyle.

"I had a great dinner Friday night," Blake says. Food is one of his father's new hobbies.

"Oh?"

Blake describes the oysters and sea urchin, the caviar, the rhubarb compote over the wild salmon.

"I love rhubarb," says his father, who adds that he's dining at Coast next week with Lindsay and the Millers. Zoe's mom is out of rehab again. If Blake didn't know better, he would think Jack Miller could have leaked the museum shit to Kate, but Jack hates gossip even more than Blake's dad.

His dad puts down his jam-covered knife and looks up at Blake. "I traded immunity to testify against Mark," he blurts out.

"That's not a bad deal."

"That's what my lawyers said."

Blake reassures his father that Mark's lawyer will make sure he only goes to a country club jail for a few months. Somewhere near a good golf course. "*If* it comes to that."

"What if he goes to real jail?" his father asks. "What happens then? Will he ever get his old life back? It's not like he killed anyone."

But Mark isn't their concern. "You're not going to jail," Blake says, wanting to put his hand on his father's forearm, but deciding against it.

His father looks down at the sesame seeds on his plate and wipes his hands and lips with the white cloth napkin. He clears his voice. "The bank asked me to retire before the end of the year."

Blake is floored. He can't remember a time when his father wasn't working all the time, when the bank wasn't the last thing on his mind when he went to sleep and the first thing when he woke up in the morning. When he wasn't worrying that a younger guy was going to get a bigger bonus even though no one ever did.

"But the thing is," he says with a smile spreading across his face, "I've never felt better."

Maybe the trick to getting what you really want, thinks Blake, is to stop trying to get what you think you've always really wanted. Blake looks closely at his father. The circles under his eyes are gone and his cheeks have a rosy glow as if he's just worked out. He looks better than ever and Blake wonders if this is what he would look like if he got to leave the party early.

K ate picks up her phone, expecting it to be the clipboard chick calling in an item from her event at Bergdorf's last night, since they didn't even send Patricia to photograph it. But it's Marco.

"Did you like the lemon tart?" he asks, and Kate can almost taste the tangy creamy concoction lingering on her tongue.

"Sweet and sour and bitter," she says, trying to kill the quiver in her voice.

"Sneaked some salt in, too. The equation never fails."

Kate wants to tell him how *balanced* she found the salmon with rhubarb, but Lacey comes up behind her and says in an even, calm voice that means she's anything but calm, "You've got exactly two hours to deliver a lead."

Marco can hear her through the receiver and laughs. "Another quiet day at the office?"

"Actually, much more tranquil than usual."

"Can I help?"

He sounds like he genuinely wants to, but if he becomes a source, he becomes someone whom Kate shouldn't be dating.

"Off the record, and you didn't hear this from me," he starts. Spinster must be earning her keep, teaching him that the best way to get favorable press is to give up items, a diversion, about other people. He pauses. "How am I doing?"

"Great. Don't let me stop you."

He says Cipriani is opening a new restaurant in Donald Trump's new condos project. A recipe of money, power, and food—a potential lead item. The new place will surely, even swiftly, become a Manhattan power nexus, and that is exactly the kind of stuff the *Examiner* wants to cover. Paul taught Kate to always call Trump's longtime secretary, Norma Foerderer, for confirmation or a quote from the developer. She's better than any publicist because she always gets what you need by deadline.

"Does anyone else know?" Kate asks Marco. That's the first question Lacey will ask. If the story breaks somewhere else, most likely in Column A, it will be more embarrassing than a weak lead.

"I only know because my investor was the only other person approached about the space. So it's an exclusive. Hurry up and make your calls!"

"How can I thank you?" she asks. "Any famous people misbehaving at Coast yet? Celebrities asking you to hold the butter? Star sightings?"

"We don't hold the butter for anyone. There's butter on everything. Even the silverware."

"Well, that's an item!"

"I don't *need* an item," he says, pausing. "But I *want* to have dinner with you again. Just you. And I don't want to cook it."

Tim pulls Zoe in for a kiss even though she's wearing dark red lipstick. It leaves a trail across his lips. He thinks maybe he could get used to this. Until there's a loud knock on the door and a man's voice booms through the hallway.

"Honey? Are you home?"

"Shit," says Zoe, wiping the lipstick from his lips so quickly he wonders if she left a bruise. "Daddy?"

A free apartment may not be worth living next door to your parents— especially if they have a set of keys. Tim hears the door's bolt click open and wishes there were a trapdoor in the floor or an eject button through the roof. Jack Miller may take Charlie to lunch at the Four Seasons once a year, but he is not a friend of Column A. And he's probably not pleased about the blind item they recently ran about him and his mistress vacationing in Mustique while his wife was in rehab.

"You must be Tim," Jack says, walking toward Tim with his hand outstretched. He gives a firm handshake, maybe too firm. Tim almost winces before pulling away his hand. Jack Miller looks forty even though he's probably more like sixty. Fucking a thirty-year-old anchorwoman could do that to you. He's got a full head of silver hair, and the veins on the insides of his forearms pulse as if he's recently bench-pressed under the watchful eye of an expensive trainer. Over the years, Tim has interviewed all types of celebrities, including politicians, models, and movie stars, but the only people who intimidate him are the very rich, who don't need press. Jack Miller is the kind of guy who reads Column A every day only to make sure he's not in it. He puts his arm around his daughter and she gives him a kiss on the cheek.

"What are you doing back in New York already?" she asks, without showing any irritation at him for barging into her apartment. He says he's in town meeting with a few chefs. He's trying to cast a prime-time cooking show with a telegenic young chef. "Entertaining and cooking," he explains. "Think Jamie Oliver meets Martha Stewart at a trendy restaurant in New York City. I think we're calling it *The Good Life*."

"Catchy," says Tim.

Jack waves a finger in the air. "That's off the record for now, though!"

Woof! Woof!

Zoe's dad says he'll be dining at Chris Flemming's restaurant and checking out any other potential chefs for the show.

"You kids get out a lot," he says. "Have any ideas? We're trying to cast this before the new year."

"Of course I have ideas, Daddy. I work at *Gourmet*, remember? The job you got me?"

"Your boss is hardly letting me forget it."

Zoe starts pitching Marco as if she were on his payroll.

"What do you think of him?" Jack asks Tim, who says he agrees with everything Zoe says. He doesn't really care. He only thinks of food as an accessory for alcohol.

"Well, I think I'm supposed to eat there with the Bradleys next week. Maybe you want to be my date, honey?"

Zoe says sure, sounds fun, and Tim wonders what Jack knows about Blake's dad's art scandal, and if the Millers were Kate's source on the museum story. Maybe he's just making a big show of going somewhere public just to prove he's standing by his friend. They probably have a few million tied up together in some investment. These kinds of guys are rarely just friends for friendship's sake.

"Don't wait up, Daddy," Zoe says, running off to her bedroom to get her purse and, Tim hopes, some high-quality drugs.

"It's nice to meet you," Tim tells Jack to fill the awkward silence. "You've got quite a lovely daughter."

Jack puts a firm hand on Tim's shoulder, smiles, and starts talking through clenched teeth. "If you do anything to make her any less lovely, I'll make sure you never get another byline again."

Tim can't believe he's actually being threatened by the head of a major television network. So much for getting any tips. That's another thing about dating someone with rich parents: There's always a steep tax.

He's still smiling. "I know you heard me. Just remember this, my game trumps your game any day. I don't need you at all. I have built something that's going to last much longer than you."

Tim wants to say something, but it feels as if a transfusion of ice just hit his bloodstream and he actually shudders. No wonder this guy has climbed so high on the entertainment industry ladder. He's got skin thicker and more resilient than rubber tires.

"And I bet you don't even have any kind of life plan but to keep living off your dirty little job, which for some reason my daughter finds impressive."

Tim opens his mouth but then closes it again. Maybe he should at least think of a life plan that sounds better than nothing. Something besides waiting for Charlie to vanish.

"Honey, you look fantastic," says Jack, snapping back into "nice dad" mode as Zoe walks back in the room.

"Ready to go?" she asks Tim brightly.

Ⅎow come you didn't ask me to be your date to the library benefit?" Marco asks Kate over the phone a few days after the event. Patricia snapped a few shots of Kate with Nick, whom she brought so she could work and they turned up on Patricia's website. Maybe Marco's e-stalking her, too? Wanting to refresh his memory of what she looks like before their second date tonight?

"Who's your boyfriend?"

Kate explains that Nick is her platonic roommate and default benefit date.

"So you're telling me you live with your boyfriend?"

Kate laughs. "I don't have a boyfriend!"

"You want one?" he asks, laughing, and Kate tries to laugh, too, so she won't say something stupid.

Hours later she walks into Coast and is hit with more than the sweet, pungent smell of tropical flowers. There's a buzz weaving through the room, one of those sound frequencies that you're not sure is just in your ears. The new pretty blond hostess tells Kate that the restaurant just heard that they got three stars from the *Times* in the review coming out tomorrow. Kate tries to act surprised, as if she hadn't already told Marco. After he spent about a week worrying about it, she asked the new pair of legs at the party column to give her a hint about the review. Her e-mail: "He's got nothing to worry about. Wink. Wink. Wink."

The hostess hands Kate a copy of the review downloaded from the newspaper's Web site. "A star is born," is the first line of the review, which also mentions the critic spending much of the meal moaning with pleasure at Marco's combinations of sweet, salty, sour, and bitter. It makes no mention of what Kate knows, that Marco was getting his hair cut the first time the reviewer showed up and, as soon as someone called to tell him she was there, he ran twenty blocks in the rain to get to her table, pretending he had just been working on recipes in his office.

Champagne is being uncorked by the case, and she sees Marco posing for a photo with the model Holly May, who's sitting at a table with what looks like four other models. Spinster is setting up the shot. Kate suddenly feels fat and awkward. She hopes they do something inappropriate that she can report or farm out to Blake or Tim. She wonders if Holly May would be here if she didn't share a publicist with Marco. But by now Kate knows that everyone trying to get attention needs at least one celebrity friend.

And then she spots Zoe waving her arms in the air, beckoning Kate to her table, where she's sitting with her dad and the Bradleys. Kate recognizes the very pregnant Lindsay from a recent spread in *W* magazine about babies being the season's must-have accessory ("Better than a Louis Vuitton baguette!"). It's a story that Lacey says runs every other year.

Kate hopes Steven Bradley won't give her a hard time for writing about him getting booted off the museum board, but Zoe's smart enough to avoid that topic. Kate catches Marco's eye as he poses for another photo with Holly May. He winks and smiles at her and holds up a finger to say he'll be over in just a moment. Zoe introduces Kate to Blake's dad and Lindsay, and Zoe's dad gives Kate a kiss on the cheek.

Zoe casually whispers in Kate's ear, "My dad is checking out Marco to potentially cast him in a prime-time cooking show, but Marco doesn't know it yet. Chris Flemming is the other major contender."

They're all working through their entrees with the zeal of explorers finding unchartered territory.

Steven Bradley leans in close to Kate. "You did all right by me," he says.

Kate wants to hug him, but no one else heard what he just whispered, so she just smiles and says thanks quietly.

"This is the best meal I've ever had, and I'm not just saying that because I'm eating for two," says Lindsay, who looks like she dressed for a theme party circa 1965 with her frosted lipstick, high ponytail, white high boots, and short Pucci maternity dress.

"It's making me think maybe I should have a new career in the restaurant business," says Blake's dad. "Just look at how packed this place is."

Zoe announces to the table that Kate is going out to a late dinner tonight with Marco, making Kate's cheeks suddenly feel hot.

"Very lucky girl," says Lindsay.

"No wonder he's been getting such great press," says Zoe's dad.

Lindsay cocks her head to the side and asks if Marco has ever been married. Kate says no and Lindsay squints her eyes.

"Really?" she asks. "I could have sworn someone told me he was."

Kate shakes her head. "Definitely not," she says. "I'm sure of it."

Kate excuses herself to the bathroom when she sees Marco heading toward the stairs to his office. She takes the same route she took on Coast's opening night, half expecting to see him hiding out, trying to stave off another panic attack. But instead she finds him on his computer. He tells her he's e-mailing the *Times* review to relatives in Italy.

"Congratulations," she says, and he breaks into a big, bold smile. He gets up and runs over and gives her a big hug. "I can hardly believe it," he says, pulling away.

She's still tingling from his embrace. "You must be thrilled."

"Yes, but . . ."

"But what?"

"I'm also waiting to find out if I scored the *Gourmet* cover. They're supposed to tell me next week. And I'm also worried that the *Tribune* may only give me two stars next week."

"Isn't it enough to be happy with what you have tonight?"

"I know, I have a problem." The "never enough" disease. The epidemic of Manhattan. Something even black orchids could never cure.

"Well, you do know that my friend Zoe Miller from *Gourmet* is here with her dad, who's—"

"Not Jack Miller?" he almost shouts. "I can't believe my hostess didn't put a VIP star next to that table! My agents say he's looking to cast a television show that sounds perfect for me!"

He has agents?

His eyes get big. "You are an angel!" He grabs Kate's hand. "Come on!"

They run back upstairs and Marco invites Zoe's table into the kitchen to celebrate the review. The cooks are popping open champagne bottles, spraying it all over themselves now that dinner service is mostly over. Kate catches a glimpse of her reflection in a gleaming stainless-steel countertop. She looks happy. Zoe helps herself to a handful of white truffle shavings. Marco's busy handing out cigars and slapping backs.

"That's one charming boyfriend you've got," Lindsay whispers in Kate's ear. "Careful or else you'll get spoiled. Because, honey, spoiled is just another word for rotten."

Blake hangs up his cell phone. "Marco charmed the pants off all of them, especially Lindsay, who wants him to cater their anniversary party. And my dad called Kate sweet," he tells Tim.

"She's pretty good. I don't think we gave her enough credit. She broke the scoop about the museum and your dad *still* likes her?"

They're at South, half-hitting on the decent-looking bartender just for sport. At least Tim knows that Zoe didn't bring a date to dinner.

"Are Kate's pants off yet?" he asks Blake.

"Sources say it's imminent."

"I hope we get more free meals out of it," says Tim, ordering another round and lighting up a cigarette even though he's wearing a nicotine patch.

"Well, I bet we'll be getting whatever we want from the randy restaura-teur if he's got any skeletons he wants to keep in the closet," says Blake.

"It's not a question of 'if.'"

Tim's cell phone vibrates. He looks at the screen and ignores it.

"Is Dan a new guy working for Kenny?" asks Blake, reading the caller ID over his shoulder.

Tim closes his eyes and rubs his temples with his fingertips. "Dan is not a drug dealer."

"So who is he?"

"*She.*"

"Okay, who is she? Don't worry, I won't tell Kate if you're worried about it getting back to Zoe."

"It's a little more complicated than that," says Tim. "And I blame you."

Blake raises his eyebrows. "'Complicated' is always interesting—and I'm not taking any blame until I know who she is."

"Remember that mattress Danielle?"

"Great tits; bad tattoo?"

Tim nods.

"It meant love or something corny like that?"

"Right." Tim takes a deep drag of his cigarette. "She seemed kind of nuts—right?"

"I'd have to agree with that assessment," says Blake. "Is she stalking?"

Tim looks up as if waiting for a rope to be lowered from the sky. He sighs. "It's all fun and games until you lose at your own game."

Hey, beautiful," says Marco, sliding in close to Kate in the car he had waiting outside the restaurant. Kate again followed the hostess's in-structions to meet him in the car rather than walk out of the restaurant with him, even though very few people were still left celebrating in the kitchen.

Lacey says you have to meet with a profile subject at least three times before you can form an accurate opinion. Her theory is that people don't stop acting until the third meeting. And while this is only the third time Kate has been alone with Marco, she can't help but think she'll never know where he's going or where he's been.

He tells her he'll finally be able to get some sleep now that he got three stars. "Each star can boost your business twenty-five percent," he says. "It's exactly what I needed, and maybe it impressed Jack Miller enough to want to cast me in his show." Kate feels pleased, and wonders if she deserves a commission for bringing Marco and Jack Miller together.

He pauses. "Now I can spend my nights worrying about that."

Kate says she put in a good word with Zoe's dad. She likes feeling helpful, needed, even wanted.

He smiles. "You know, I liked you right away," he says, once again touching her cheek. Maybe he knew, right away, that liking her would have bonuses, like meeting Jack Miller. But right now he's looking at her as if he just likes her for being her, and the air feels pumped with extra oxygen.

They pull up to Rao's, a legendary Italian restaurant in Harlem where Marco says you can only get a table if you're a mobster or a friend of the owner—and he and Marco are from the same small town in Italy. "Are you wearing your bulletproof vest?" he jokes. They spot the actor Alfonse Paquino inside at the bar and Kate ducks, thinking she should start carrying around a baseball cap and sunglasses. She explains that Alfonse once spit at her at a benefit at the Four Seasons when she tried to interview him for an item about his recent split from his longtime girlfriend.

"Poor baby," says Marco, pulling her into a hug that she wishes lasted a little bit longer. "Your job is so dangerous." He grins and says he happens to know that Paquino is renting the $3,500-a-night suite at the Rhigha Royal, a fancy and discreet Midtown hotel. "That's for him being mean to you," Marco says with a wink.

After a burst of hugs and smiles and Italian words, they're quickly seated and Marco orders in fluent Italian. Before long the table is cluttered with more dishes than they could possibly finish. Kate starts asking him about his life story, and to her delight, he lifts up the curtain without any hesitation. He explains that was born in a small town in Italy but moved to California with his parents and sister when he was ten years old. After high school he went back to Italy for cooking school and to work in restaurants. "Food was my first love," he says, smiling. When he was twenty-five, he moved to New York.

Kate asks if he liked living in Italy the second time. He shakes his head. "I would never move back there," he says, looking down at his hands. "New York is my only home."

Marco squeezes lemon over a plate of fried calamari with a strong, quick hand and takes small bites of each dish, his eyes lighting up whenever he likes something. He feeds Kate spoonfuls of his favorites. They have multiple appetizers on the table, but he insists they don't have to finish everything, calling the meal research. But she can't stop eating even though her stomach feels as if it is about to burst.

"This is how I grew up," he says. "Big family dinners with this exact food."

Kate talks about her Thanksgivings with tofu instead of turkey, brown rice instead of mashed potatoes, and her parents going on and off macrobiotic and vegan diets all her life.

Marco laughs. "Sounds traumatic."

"Do you have a close family?" she asks, and he's suddenly quiet.

"Well, I did," he says. "But my mother died of cancer about ten years ago. My father had a heart attack about a month after they took her off the respirator." He takes a bite of calamari. "My sister and I had a pretty big fight a while ago over a decision I made that she didn't approve of. It's a long story I don't really feel like getting into."

"I'm sorry," she says, wishing she could think of a better response.

The waiter refills their glasses with red wine and Marco takes a sip. Kate notices that he only holds the stem of his wineglass, so she takes her hand off the big bowl of her own glass. Whatever his fight with his sister is about, it seems almost more unsettling to him than losing his parents. At what point in a new relationship—that is, if they're in fact having a relationship—can you start asking the questions the other person may not want to answer?

The waiter brings over five entrées and Marco smiles at the welcome interruption. "Now food is my family," he says, showing Kate how to spread the bone marrow from osso buco on toast for a silky and smoky rich taste. Kate's not sure how many different kinds of wine are in the numerous glasses in front of her. It's hard to keep track of all the regions Marco mentions. She keeps nodding and sipping, pretending that all the red and white liquid hasn't blended into one long gulp.

"Look at the legs on this one," he says, holding up a glass with red streaks down the sides of the mouth. "Full bodied."

Kate takes a sip of hers. "Full bodied," she repeats, trying to mimic his tone.

He laughs. "Ok, that's enough of Wines 101 for tonight. Let's move on to something more visceral. Dessert."

"My favorite."

After sampling a bite of every dessert, they walk out, his arm wrapped around her shoulder. He had asked for the bill but he just got a bunch of smiles and Italian words. They tumble into the car and start kissing and she nods when he asks if they should head to his place. She expected he would live in a West Village brownstone or a Tribeca loft, the kind of place she dreams about owning one day. Instead, they pull up to a white brick building in Chelsea with a bar on the ground floor.

"Glamorous, right?" he asks.

"More glamorous than my old warehouse across the street from a jail in Brooklyn."

"I've been wanting to move since the day I moved in here, but I just can't seem to find the time or energy to move. Besides, I'm sure the market's going to soften soon. It can't keep going up."

"Oh, but it can," says Kate, who keeps writing about insanely expensive apartments selling in her column.

"Well, maybe you can help me look," he says, and she smiles. She likes to feel needed.

They continue kissing in the elevator and don't stop until he unlocks his door with keys he leaves under the mat—because he always loses them, he explains, which Kate finds a little surprising. He seems so organized conducting all the pieces of his moving kitchen every night. She'll learn soon enough that people who are trying to live in the public eye often let their personal lives slip into disarray as their public image becomes increasingly scripted.

Kate thinks she should go home. She should leave now when he most wants her, when he almost has her. But every inch of her wants to stay here with him, to let him lead her to the bedroom, to sink into the soft sheets of his unmade bed.

He pulls off each piece of her clothing slowly and carefully, as if he were peeling an orange, taking extra care to separate the white skin from the flesh. Her jean skirt slides to the floor, quickly followed by her white cashmere sweater, the one with the hole in the elbow. She runs her fingers over his wiry chest hair, over his strong back, and feels each muscle tighten and then relax under her fingertips. Every movement is soft and urgent at the same time—a recipe she didn't know existed before tonight.

Kate's mind is telling her to make him wait but she can't resist. Each doubt escapes out her pores until her mind goes white, letting her body lead. He quickly, smoothly slides into her, moaning as they lock into each other as if they've done this a million times before, as if they are finally talking and listening to each other.

Hours later, the gentle Saturday-morning sun streams across the river into Kate's eyes. She doesn't remember either of them falling asleep but Marco is soundly snoring. She smiles at his snoring. She sees a pimple on his back and finds it comforting. It's nice to know he has imperfections that only she can see.

She's still tingling from last night but suddenly she's wide awake. She decides she wants to do something for him. She's going to make breakfast.

She quietly rolls out of bed and tiptoes to the kitchen. It's full of gleaming new equipment, which he'll later tell her was a gift for his endorsing a brand of kitchenware in an ad. The fridge only has bottles of champagne and white wine and condiments with French labels. *He must never cook at home.* He's got tons of take-out menus, though, so Kate dials up the deli, ordering eggs, coffee, milk, green peppers, onions, and cheese. "Keep it simple" is what Marco always says in interviews about cooking.

Marco is still snoring loudly and Kate thinks he must have taken a sleeping pill at some point during the night. She tries to clear off a little space from his dining-room table, which is piled high with old magazines and newspapers, gift bags from parties, and a stack of old cookbooks with well-worn spines. She doesn't want to pry but she can't help but open an envelope of pictures even though she shouldn't.

They are pictures of Wendy Winter and Marco. It seems to be his birthday and it looks as though she's made him a cake. Kate can't stop her fingers from hunting. She opens another package of pictures and it looks like Italy, but then she hears him stirring and quickly puts them back on the table.

After the delivery guy comes and goes, Kate starts working on breakfast. She chops up the onions and peppers and starts sautéing them. Do scrambled eggs need milk?

"Are you trying to steal my job?" asks Marco, surprising her by wandering into the kitchen looking amused.

She jumps, nearly cutting her finger with the knife.

"I just thought you probably don't get cooked for very often," she says. He puts his hand over hers and shows her how to rock the knife back and forth on the cutting board.

"Well, you're right about that. But please tell me what exactly are you making?"

She starts explaining but he puts his finger to her lips and clears space on the cutting board. He takes a clove of garlic and mashes it under a spoon, before mincing it up. "You want to mash it first. It releases the flavor," he says, dispatching the first of many lessons he'll give her. Then he takes a huge chunk of butter and starts melting it in a frying pan. Kate gasps.

"Cutie, everything you ever eat at a restaurant is dripping in butter," he says. "Stop thinking it will make you fat. It's delicious and essential. You get fat when you eat too much, not when you eat small portions of whatever you want. And preservatives in things like margarine and artificial sweetener make you fat. Not butter."

He whisks the eggs, adding some milk, and then pours them in the pan. In another pan, he cooks the vegetables, adding everything together once the eggs have started to bubble. Then he tells her to watch out and he flips his wrist so the eggs look like a pizza, turning in the air and settling down into a flawless omelet.

Kate applauds and he pulls her in for a kiss. "I've got plenty more to teach you," he says.

Today's *Wall Street Journal* announced that Blake's father has decided to resign from the bank, as if that were always the plan when he turned sixty-five. Blake had taken Justin Katz out for a drink and promised Justin the exclusive as long as he didn't mention that Blake's dad is being called as a witness for Mark Reed's prosecution. Justin didn't make any promises—he's too much of a pro for that—but he did well by them. He knows Blake and his dad can be very useful now and in the future. And on Blake's end, at least the story should shut Bethany up for the immediate future—or at least long enough for him to move off the couch in the living room and back to bed for a few nights until she finds something else to bitch about.

Blake's dad calls to thank him for helping with the *Journal* story. "You really think I should get into the restaurant business?" his dad asks when Blake mentions that Marco is looking for investors.

Blake says he knows it's risky but his dad can afford to make a few mistakes. Marco will probably find other investors soon enough. They have to act quickly.

"From Coast to Coast?" asks his dad. "That's not bad."

Blake says they should wait to see if Marco gets the television show with Zoe's dad before making any decisions about a new career.

"I like the idea of playing with money to feed people after all these years of sucking them dry."

Kate and Marco quickly move on from eggs. He teaches her how to glaze salmon with miso paste and pop it in the toaster oven for dinner. Wrap beets with aluminum foil after coating them with olive oil and sea salt. Roast them for an hour at four hundred degrees, but make sure they're cool before adding them to the lettuce, or else the salad will wilt.

"Patience and simplicity are the most important ingredients," he says. He demonstrates how to gingerly rope together the legs of a chicken with dental floss before roasting. "Like this," he says one night, guiding her fingers inside the chicken to remove the slimy cold organs. "Like this," he says, unfastening the ties after the skin is golden crisp.

For breakfast, he likes ordering sushi, what he calls "a perfect protein meal." And she starts joining him for workouts with his trainer in his building's gym. She's dropped ten pounds since she met him after learning how all the chefs stay slim. They eat big breakfasts and lunches and very small early dinners, usually a "family meal" with their staff, comprised mostly of leftovers. And when they go out to restaurants for dinner, they pick at a bunch of different dishes instead of finishing off any one plate.

If Kate had any other job, staying out late and sleeping in with Marco could be a problem, but no one has complained in the month since their first night together after Rao's. After all, if Zoe is to be believed, "chefs are the new rock stars" and "restaurants are the new dinner theater."

Don't you want to know if we're having a boy or a girl?" Danielle asks. By calling from a restricted number late in the day when he's distracted, she's caught Tim on the phone. *Manipulative bitch.*

"Danielle, I'm on deadline. Can we talk about this another time?"

"No, because you never call me back!"

A deliveryman with a stack of pizzas walks by, heading for the sports section. Tim's stomach rumbles, but the thought of actually eating anything makes him feel like puking. "I have to go."

"It's a girl," she says quickly. Tim doesn't say anything but feels the pores on his skin open up to suck in the greasy news. A girl. A little girl he'll have to protect from men like him. *If* the baby is really his.

"Do you want to hear some names I'm thinking about?"

"I'm sorry," he says, just wanting to stop hearing her voice. "I really have to go."

Tim is sure of one thing as he hangs up on Danielle. He's angry. And not just with her. He's just not sure if he's angrier that he's spending New Year's Eve alone *again* or that Zoe didn't invite him to St. Barts. Or that by not being invited there, he's being deprived of a week's worth of columns and contacts in the winter playground of the rich and famous.

But Zoe didn't exactly say he wasn't invited. She just said she was going away with her parents. Tim wouldn't have minded as much if he didn't find out from Kate that last year Zoe brought her now-ex-boyfriend from college. Some guy who went to prep school and is now working at Goldman fucking Sachs—at least that's what Tim came up with on Google. Tim has started obsessively researching the guy, wondering if there was a chance he'd be on St. Barts again this year, talking about golf and real estate with Zoe's dad. Tim even had his police source run a check on the Goldman golden boy, who, as it turns out, didn't so much as have a fucking parking ticket.

Tim flips through his chick-ionary. He may have to defensively date a few mattresses while Zoe's gone. But he realizes he's already paranoid that Zoe knows something about Danielle's pregnancy even though she couldn't. Only Marco and Blake know, and they've got enough secrets with Tim to keep their word. Still, you can't trust anyone.

"I'm definitely not going to sell you out," said Marco, who heard about it from his ex-hostess. "We all do things we're not proud of, but it doesn't mean we want to have to explain ourselves in the press."

vacation: work on location

The flight attendants in the first-class cabin to Aspen offer Kate and Marco mimosas with fresh orange juice, warm chocolate-chip cookies, and later, a meal served on china with silver utensils. Kate tries to remember the details so she can tell her parents, even though they're not thrilled she's dating someone they still call "too exciting."

"Just find someone nice," Kate's mother keeps saying when she calls on Sunday nights. "Someone who wants to help people."

"It's like dating Marco has become part of your job," says Nick, who wanted Kate to go skiing in Lake Tahoe with a group of their college friends, including Annie. "You're definitely getting carried away."

Kate pushes those thoughts away as she tucks into her lunch. Marco studies her hands while biting the inside of his lower lip.

"What?" she asks.

"You want the fork to hold the meat in place, with the prongs face-down," he says, putting his hand over hers and guiding her fork through the poached salmon in white-wine sauce. "Then cut with the knife."

Kate's embarrassed that she's been doing it wrong for twenty-two years—and wonders just how many people have noticed her unrefined manners.

"Don't worry about it. You're just a baby, you have plenty of time to do it right now," he says, pulling her in close. She falls asleep with her head on his lap, while he plays with her hair. They've been sleeping together at least three nights a week since Rao's last month—even though Kate usually wakes up before dawn to find Marco lying on his back, staring up at his stucco ceiling.

After they land, they settle into a suite at the St. Regis with a deep Jacuzzi tub and mountain views, and unpack their clothes. It's too late to hit the slopes, so they head down to the spa, where they get massages in the same room, side by side. Marco asks his masseuse to pay special attention to his shoulder. "I hurt it in a car accident years ago," he explains. The masseuse asks if the scar on his arm is from the same accident and he says yes.

Kate's shoulders tense up. "Breathe deeply," says her own masseuse.

What kind of accident and when? And why hasn't he told her? Why hasn't he told her about something that he still obviously carries with him?

The next morning at the slopes, Marco helps Kate fasten her new boots and affix her lift ticket to the jacket he bought for her. She hands him tissues and Chap Stick when he needs them. This is the way grown-ups vacation, she thinks. This feels right. Later, up at the lodge, he mixes up some chili and soup for lunch. "A cuvée," he says, presenting it with a smile.

The plus-sized talk-show host Star Jones is sitting by the fire in the lodge, next to an oxygen tank hooked up to her nose so she can breathe at the high altitude. Kate borrows Marco's BlackBerry to e-mail the item in to Lacey, asking for a fact checker to call the Jones's rep so Kate doesn't have to talk to her. She wants to pretend as much as possible that she's on vacation.

On the chairlift after lunch, Marco takes off his gloves to get a tissue and Kate sees the scar poking out. She almost asks him to finish what he started telling the masseuse yesterday. The words are about to roll off her tongue, but then she stops herself, knowing it could ruin the day. He's going to accuse her of "interviewing" him, which is what he does whenever she starts asking questions he doesn't want to answer. No, today Kate is just going to be Kate. Not Kate from the *Examiner*. Not someone worried about what she may or may not know and how she's going to find the answers.

"Is something wrong?" he asks, putting his arm around her.

She shakes her head. "I'm just cold." He rubs her arms, and even under all the layers she can feel his warm hands.

Back at the hotel, Marco finds out that he can't get Kate a seat at the socialite's dinner party where he's cooking tonight. She can only meet him there after ten o'clock.

"But at least we'll be together for the first kiss of the year," he says, kissing her on the forehead before heading out. "See you in a few hours."

Kate stays in bed, ordering room service in a big white robe and wondering what everyone else is doing tonight. When she calls Nick to wish him a Happy New Year, she can hear the party in the background. They're all making dinner and drinking beer in the hot tub. Instead of saying she wishes she were there, Kate tells him about the great powder on the slopes, the fancy suite, the talk-show host with the oxygen tank.

"Sounds like you're having a great time," he says. Kate suspects that he knows she's not happy about tonight's arrangement—she hasn't said much about Marco. "Just remember, it's all about who you're with, not where you are."

She can't decide if it's annoying or comforting that Nick is usually right. "How's Annie?"

"I don't know," he says.

"Isn't she there?"

He hesitates and then sighs. "She *was* here. But it didn't go exactly as planned. We hadn't seen in each other for a while and I guess we really built this up. We started fighting almost immediately over stupid shit like which mountain we were going to ski and what to have for dinner. It just seemed like we couldn't agree on anything. We felt like strangers."

"So what happened?"

"We had a big blowup when I told her that I couldn't move to California to live with her anytime soon."

"Doesn't she understand you have an important job?"

"No, not really. Annie can't seem to understand that anything is as important as her big law degree. So we had a huge fight, which everyone heard, and it was really embarassing. She has some law-school friends who also rented a house out here this week, so she moved over there and we agreed not to talk or e-mail for three months."

"Well, that sounds civilized. Do you think you can really do it?"

He takes a deep breath. "That's probably the saddest thing and the biggest proof that we're not in love anymore. I think it will be easy. I actually feel relieved."

"Well, I'm here for you if you need me," she says.

"Thanks."

Kate's not sure why, but she feels a little lighter, too. At least she won't have to fall asleep to music every night to muffle Nick's phone conversations with Annie.

She calls Zoe in St. Barts to tell her Nick's news.

"I'm not surprised," she says. "That relationship was so three years ago."

Kate laughs. "It's not like they were a fashion trend."

"Besides, admit it. Annie is self-righteous."

"Can't argue with you there."

"Where's your man? Why aren't you at some fabulous dinner party wearing white mink and cowboy boots?"

"First of all, I don't own either. Secondly, he's cooking at some party I wasn't invited to."

"That's bullshit. He's Marco Mancini, he can get you in anywhere. Have they seen his face on the new cover of *Gourmet*?"

Kate takes a bite of her room-service warm apple crisp with vanilla ice cream, which makes her feel momentarily better. "I'm meeting him there after the dessert course."

"Well, at least Marco's spending New Year's Eve with you," Zoe says. "As for me, I keep fighting with my dad. He won't stop calling Tim a scumbag and I keep saying, 'That scumbag is my boyfriend.' And then he asks me if I think *he's* a scumbag, and I say, 'Daddy, don't try the psychoanalysis bullshit on me.'"

Kate can't remember the last time Zoe sounded as smitten. Maybe Tim is keeping her attention because he's unlike anyone she's ever dated and, of course, because the relationship pisses off her dad.

Right before she hangs up, Zoe says, "You didn't hear it from me but . . ."

"Keep talking," says Kate, instantly alert. She's almost proud of Zoe for making it to the end of their conversation before blurting out a secret.

"Get ready to date someone really, really famous," says Zoe. "Marco got the show. They're going to run the pilot they taped a few weeks ago for the launch episode in February."

Kate feels a quiver dart under her skin but she's not sure if she's excited or scared.

Of course, tonight is the coldest night of the year. New Year's Eve is always painfully frigid, nature's warning for everyone to just stay home without any high expectations of finding a decent party. Tim's always in New York because Charlie goes to Miami for New Year's to be with one of his girlfriends there, and someone's got to cover the page. There could be an emergency, like a teen-queen catfight or a celebrity elopement. At least his name gets to be on the top of the page in bold for his mom to add to her clip collection.

Tim looks at the wrinkled tux hanging in the closet looking defeated and bored and imagines himself walking through the parties tonight, taking notes on napkins, and trying to find people remotely boldface whose stock is clearly plummeting because they don't have anywhere better to be on New Year's Eve. He considers staying in. He'll look at all the party pictures tomorrow anyway to choose a few for the page so he can pretend he was there.

Tim's phone keeps ringing. Mattresses, publicists, guys who can't get past velvet ropes with cash alone. Everyone wants Tim for easy access. No one is calling just to wish him a Happy New Year except his mom— and Danielle. He lets everyone go to voice mail. Let them all think he's at some great party, having too much fun to answer the phone.

He sits down on his couch, lights a cigarette, and flips on the television. Times Square is only six blocks away, but it looks like another planet, one made of glittery tiaras, balloons, and screaming, shivering, fat tourists. What's so great about a fucking ball dropping, anyway? The evil part of Tim wishes the ball would just explode, sending sparks through the crowd. Let them filter out to hell.

Fuck it. He's not going anywhere. Why go anywhere when he can have his beer and cigarettes delivered to his door? Besides, he sent the show ponies to clop around the parties, with explicit directions to call him if anything newsworthy happens.

Zoe left a bottle of Ambien and Tim washes down two with another beer, which he's using to chase the tequila he's almost done drinking. It's going to be a long night, but maybe he can make it a little shorter by falling asleep soon. At least he can say he didn't kiss anyone on New Year's and it won't even be a lie—if Zoe still cares. She'll come back either ready to dump him or desperate to see him. That always happens when you leave New York. Everything goes into focus and you make decisions you're determined to carry out for at least a week.

The stupid fucking ball is on almost every channel except one that has a documentary about that sick baby panda in China. Who cares? He flips back to the ball and mutes the television. He stubs out his cigarette and sucks down the rest of his drink, waiting for the familiar numbness, the heaviness, that deafening cloud to descend.

The dinner has just ended when Kate arrives. She can tell from the color of the scraps that Marco made his duck with cherry sauce. By now she knows almost every ingredient to all of his dishes. Women with fur collars and men wearing cowboy boots start gliding into a giant living room filled with overstuffed white furniture and deer heads on the walls. She can't find Marco but everyone's praising him. Calling him brilliant, *charming*, talented. "Those eyes!" they say. "That duck!"

Marco walks out a swinging door, poking his head through a new Ralph

Lauren brown cashmere sweater, eyes flashing. He gives her a quick kiss and hands her a glass of champagne. "This was the easiest thirty-four thousand I ever made," he says, grinning, and Kate wonders if he knows that his fee for tonight is exactly her annual salary—before taxes. "There's got to be some more clients in the room."

If anyone asks, she's supposed to say she's his assistant. "I can't have my client think I'm letting a gossip columnist in," he says, and Kate swallows hard, trying to get rid of that lump growing in the back of her throat. Why couldn't he just say she's his girlfriend? He flirts with his fans, complimenting their dresses and promising to e-mail them recipes. The most *charming* of hired help.

Kate spots Eve from *Vanity Fair* across the room—she's the only woman not wearing an appropriate Aspen outfit. Instead, she's wearing a short, simple black dress and a chunky silver necklace with her trademark massive vintage earrings that make her head seem larger than it is. Every short silver hair is in place. Kate wonders if she can get out of here without saying hi, without explaining she's Marco's private girlfriend and public assistant. But just as she decides to slink out of the room, Eve sees her and heads right over.

"Honey, what are you doing here?" she asks. "I thought I was the only member of the Fourth Estate to crash this party. And I pretty much had to bribe my gay date to bring me."

"My *friend* Marco snuck me in," Kate says, perhaps a little too quickly.

Eve looks a little surprised and asks Kate how she became friends with Marco. Kate invents a story about a mutual friend.

"He's very charming," says Eve, who seems to know she's not getting the whole story. "Can you believe he told me he was single?"

He told me he was single. The words echo through Kate's head. Eve knows what she's doing and seems to be enjoying it a little bit. Maybe she's punishing Kate for lying.

"Who is his ex-wife?" Eve asks, taking another stab.

Kate shakes her head. "He's never been married," she says. "He doesn't believe in it."

Eve raises her eyebrows. "Really?" she asks, and Kate nods again. "How interesting. Well, honey, take it from me. Better to find a keeper to just worship you. A rational marriage is a marriage that lasts. That's what all my smart friends did, and now they have babies and beach houses."

He told me he was single.

"Don't get me wrong. I've had my share of fabulous, exciting men. And let me tell you, it has been fabulous and exciting."

He told me he was single.

"But where am I now?" She's starting to slur her words a little and her red wine is sloshing precariously in her glass. "Spending another holiday with my gay friend. At least I've got the cover story this month. Angelina Jolie sent me a note to say she loved it. She's really stunning in person. Just stunning."

He told me he was single.

Why would both Eve and Lindsay think Marco had been married? He wouldn't hide that from Kate. He's not the type of person to be embarrassed or ashamed of being divorced, even if his family is Catholic. A divorce is not something people keep secret these days.

Eve squints her eyes. "Is that Kate Hudson?" She finishes her wine and heads back into the fray.

Kate slams down her glass a little too hard and it shatters on the table. At least it provides an excuse to get away. The whole room starts to look a little blurry, all fur and cashmere and cowboy boots blending together as she goes in search of someone with a broom or a towel. The big turquoise belt buckles and earrings, the smooth fifty-year-old foreheads and chunky diamond rings—suddenly everyone looks like Ivana Trump and Denise Rich, and then Kate realizes that they really are here. She tries to catch her breath but she can't. She wanders into a hallway, looking for a bathroom to hide in, to tell her reflection, *I'm going to be fine.*

Kate feels an arm wrap around her waist and she quickly turns around, stumbling into Marco's big, strong arms. "Hey, beautiful," he says, bringing her face up to his so she has to stand on tiptoes to meet his gaze. "What's wrong?"

She wants to tell him she doesn't want to say she's his assistant any-more. She wants to pretend they're invited guests tonight and not the hired help. She doesn't mention Eve, either, even though that's what's most bothering her. *He told me he was single.*

He leads Kate up two flights of stairs to a glass-and-cedar solarium filled with skylights that frame the snowy mountains glowing in the full moon. It's as if he ordered a customized romantic set. He pulls a bottle of champagne out of a bucket of ice and Kate recognizes it as the finest his restaurant carries, along with a tin of caviar, toast points, a container of crème fraîche, and a mother-of-pearl spoon. He spreads a blanket on the floor and proposes a toast "to us."

The salty eggs and smooth cream, the champagne and the toast mix into the kiss that keeps going, even after a roar rips through the house after the inevitable countdown. It seems impossible to Kate—time seems to be suspended up here.

His takes her face in his hands. "We love each other, right?" he asks.

"Right," she says, even though she's never said that to anyone before, and she's not sure it counts because he didn't say "I love you." It's more like an agreement. But still . . . It's a new year. Anything's possible.

About an hour later, they take a long bath at their hotel suite. Kate's still bothered by her conversation with Eve and decides to risk breaking the romantic spell of the evening by asking Marco why he told Eve he was single. After she poses the question, he starts rubbing Kate's feet.

"She's a legendary profiler of bachelors," he says. "If I got a profile in *Vanity Fair,* it would put me on a whole new level."

Kate blurts out that Marco got the show. She knows she shouldn't spread gossip from Zoe, especially where her dad's concerned, but right now she needs some kind of currency, some way to climb out of that cor-ner at the party. She wants him to feel like he needs her.

It works. He jumps out of the bath to grab more champagne from the mini fridge and they toast the show, they toast their *love.* "I'm going to be famous!" says Marco, clinking his glass against Kate's.

For the first time since they started sleeping together, he makes it through the whole night without waking, but he still wakes Kate up at one point, talking in his sleep. At first she doesn't know what he's saying.

"Me!" he shouts.

"What?" She tries to wake him up.

Then he half sits up and yells out, "Save me from myself!" The words are clear as an echo across a valley. Each word seems to hang in the air on neon signs.

She tries to wake him, to calm him down, to promise she'll do whatever he needs, but he quickly starts snoring again. *Did he really just say that?* She can't go back to sleep. She gets a glass of water and stands by the window, pulling the thick white curtains back a little. It's that sliver of time just before dawn, the stillest of hours. She presses her hand against the cold glass, leaving a smudge. The shadowy peaks seem much closer now, glowing the purest white before the first light, extra bright between the panes of glass foggy with her breath.

Considering he goes out almost every night of the week, New Year's Eve is a welcome excuse for a quiet night at home for Blake. He almost always spends it at his dad's house in Southampton. The icy ocean winds whip through town, blasting away the memories of sticky summer traffic, fights for the last newspaper at the cheese shop, the hung-over hedge-fund guys devouring the fresh tray of paninis at The Italian Café. In the winter, Blake rarely runs into any ex-girlfriends looking to upgrade from a cramped share house or publicists begging him to attend a lame lawn party where they make you use Porta Potties instead of the bathrooms inside the house.

Nothing happens on New Year's Eve in the Hamptons, and that's exactly what Blake likes about it. Bethany, however, who conveniently made up with Blake so she wouldn't be alone for the holidays, never stops complaining that they're not in St. Barts or Aspen or somewhere where she can show off that she's engaged to someone who can afford to take her to those places—if only he would want to. His dad usually throws a little dinner party, but now that he's on the list of controversial hosts, the phone hasn't even rung once and he doesn't seem the least bit concerned. Lindsay thinks she's too fat to be photographed out, so for once she's happy to stay home, too. Blake also wanted to be here because it's the last New Year's Eve without the baby, who will surely change everything.

The four of them pass out pretty quickly after watching the ball drop over Times Square. In the morning, Blake wakes up early and drives the old Range Rover into town to pick up some papers, on the off chance that any news broke. Maybe a benchwarmer reporter got a chance to show his chops while all the big boys were on vacation. You never want to get involved in a scandal around the holidays, when there's scant competition for news and people like Tim are manning the columns.

Blake also wants to know if there's any news about the baby panda in China, which he keeps dreaming about. It's a cartoon dream, in which he's trying to feed the little creature, but Bethany keeps trying to turn the bamboo into bracelets.

He smiles as he pulls into a parking spot right in front of the cheese shop and spots a full stack of fresh papers by the register. He'll have time to get through all four of them today. He buys two copies of each so there will be no fighting for favorite sections. As he's paying, he hears a small voice behind him say his name as if it were a question. He's surprised to see his cute fact checker, Alison White.

She brushes a piece of honey-blond hair out of her eyes and smiles, revealing a faint dimple in her left cheek. Blake thought those were extinct. Turns out they're just endangered. He realizes in that moment he doesn't even know the most basic information about her. Where is she going and where has she been and why hasn't he been paying more attention?

She says she's out here staying at a girlfriend's house, and she says *girlfriend* twice—probably so Blake will know she's single. She's got a stack of papers in her arms, too.

"I didn't know you ever got up before eight A.M.," she says. "And I would have thought you were in St. Barts or Aspen with all the other playboys."

Playboys?

"Early to bed and early to rise makes a country boy healthy, wealthy, and wise," he says for some stupid reason. She looks so sweet, he's worried he's going to start singing camp cheers.

"Or at least two out of three," she says with that cute little smile. He feels as if he's looking at her through a much-needed and stronger contact-lens prescription now that she's outside the office.

He says he's trying to catch up on the news and she doesn't say anything, waiting for him to say something more. Bethany always jumps on his words, never letting him finish a thought. Probably never listening, either. He tells her about his obsession with the panda and she looks surprised.

"I read everything about it, too," she says, her grass-green eyes widening. Why has he never noticed them, either?

He wants to invite her over to talk about the panda, to walk on the beach, to just sit across from him. He starts to invite her over but she says she has plans today. "Maybe when we're back in the city," she says, but he's a little worried that without this fresh light, she'll go back to thinking he's as weathered as he usually feels.

Later that day he tells his dad about Alison while they walk on the beach, bundled up against the cold and studying the ice patterns over the water.

"She sounds a lot nicer than Bethany," says his dad, who's been saying exactly what he thinks lately. "With all the money you're getting, your wife should at least buy you some happiness."

It's the day before deadline and everyone's starting to get anxious as the speed picks up around the *Examiner* office. Gavin's trying to close a news-breaking story and has enlisted a small army of fact checkers to transcribe his interviews, the most mind-numbing part of the job.

"Finished?" he asks one who's approaching their desks. The fact checker shakes her head and hands Kate a fax with her name written across the top of the page. It's a copy of an e-mail a real-estate broker from the Corcoran Group sent a client, urging him not to buy in Chelsea, a neighborhood full of "those gays" and drag queens and drug addicts. The sender of the fax has blacked out his name, but it's probably a competing broker. And, written across the top: "HE'S GAY!" Kate has actually taken the broker out to lunch and the rant doesn't completely surprise her. While they were lunching on the Upper East Side one time, an attractive black man came by to say hello, after which the broker said, "I know, he's *black*, but he's in *all* the right clubs."

Kate shows the fax to Lacey. "Report it out," Lacey says, looking interested. "Someone could easily make this up."

A few hours later, Kate's got the story. She's got the quotes and the confirmation and she's got a little buzzing feeling inside. She knows this could be it. Her first front-page feature. She owns this story and it's not an item. It's a perfect *Examiner* story. It combines money, power, and controversy—and you usually only need two out of three of those ingredients. She starts writing up her lede but stops to take a call, thinking it could be someone involved in the story.

"So, if I'm working on something about Marco that you may not want to hear about, do you want to hear about it?" asks Tim.

Kate has the distinct feeling that Tim is not calling about the media preview tape with a few episodes of Marco's show.

That buzzing she'd been feeling abruptly ends and she's suddenly got a knot in her stomach. He knows she can't resist hearing a secret, especially about Marco, even if it's going to hurt as soon as it hits her ears.

"I got a phone call today that you may be interested to hear about."

"I'm interested."

He pauses. "Apparently your randy restaurateur is married."

The knot tightens. "That's bullshit," says Kate, jumping on Tim's words. "He doesn't believe in marriage." *He told me he was single.*

"Well, I may have an explanation for that."

Kate's not sure if she's more upset about hearing something personal about Marco from Tim or about the fact that this could change everything.

"He's got this wife who lives in Italy who won't divorce him."

"No way."

"Do you really want to hear this?"

"Yes," she says quietly, cupping the phone to her ear. Label Whore and Lacey walk by and Kate fears they can hear Tim through the receiver.

"Okay, but it gets worse."

The knot twists.

"They were in a car crash in Italy years ago and he was driving. She was a big-time model, and she suffered serious scarring and burning to her face, so she could never work again. She never walked again, either."

Marco's scar on his arm suddenly makes sense. A *lot* of things are starting to make sense. That's the thing about hearing the truth. All the jagged pieces finally fall smoothly into place, even if the picture doesn't look the way you wanted it to.

"Suffice it to say he got out of town pretty fast, and now that this Christina is reading and hearing about Coast and the television show, now that he's at least fourteen percent famous, she wants more money and he won't give it to her."

Kate knows this kind of story is not something someone could easily make up. It's not on the list of things people claim when they hear someone's famous. She wishes there were a paper trail she could track, maybe a lawsuit she could dig up that would say otherwise, but she already knows it's true. There must be at least three sides to this story, but she can't help but feel sorry for this woman Marco hurt and left behind. If he could do this to her, what could he do to Kate?

Tim will only say his source had an Italian or maybe a Spanish accent. She was pretty breathy and spoke so quickly he had to tape the conversation and play it back to fully understand her. She said she just wanted Marco to pay his wife what she's owed, now that he has money for things like private trainers and drivers. The wife's parents have died and all their money is gone, mostly having been spent on her care, since she refuses to leave a secluded Italian hospital.

Whatever the story is, Kate's sure Marco doesn't want it in Column A tomorrow. She also doesn't want all those people who are impressed that she's dating Marco, people who read Column A religiously, to know her boyfriend may have done something like this. It can only hurt them both. Spinster probably hasn't been briefed on this part of his portfolio. It's up to Kate to do damage control. She takes a deep breath and swallows hard.

Kate says she honestly doesn't know anything about this, but she'll swap Tim something else if he kills it.

"Play on, player," Tim says, and Kate gives up the item about the real-estate broker. She rationalizes that the story could be scooped anyway, even though she knows she's probably the only reporter who got the fax.

"It's a deal," says Tim. Kate almost checks her hands to see if she sold off any fingers. "But Marco better hope that Charlie doesn't hear about it. I'm still on probation for covering Blake's dad's ass."

Next she has to go directly to the source. That's the only rational thought she has. She'll deal with Lacey later.

"I've heard that rumor, too," Marco says just a little too slowly when she finally gets him on the phone.

Blake's tuxedo collar is almost choking him. Time to cut back on the booze and splurge on the coke and cigarettes. It takes off about three pounds a day as long as you don't binge out when you're coming down. He's at a benefit at the Waldorf. His mother and Bunny Frank made him sit at their table, along with Bethany, Bunny's son Heath, and Heath's girl-friend of the month. She's the ultimate trump card for Heath, a trust-afarian who was always told he was a real catch. She's pretty, smart, has no discernible career aspirations, and won't be interested in marriage for about a decade. Best of all, she's a sophomore at Columbia. If Blake weren't too close to his potential subjects, he'd pitch a feature about the trend of Manhattan heirs handpicking their future socialite wives from the Columbia campus.

"She doesn't even know what the word *prenup* means yet," Heath whispers to Blake.

Bethany runs her hand over her gold chair and says, "Plastic piping," under her breath.

"Taaaacky," she adds, a little louder. "Can you believe people get *married* here?"

Heath runs his finger over his neck as if just the word *marriage* were a noose. Blake takes another bite of his chicken, trying to figure out the mystery sauce. At least he doesn't have to feel guilty about getting a free ticket. His mom actually bought a $25,000 table. But he does have to get quotes before all the rich idiots start trying to dance—that awful, inevitable hybrid of the white man's shuffle, the Electric Slide, and hip-to-hip grinding.

The auction starts, so they settle down, watching men make bids to shut their wives up. Blake's cell phone vibrates and he sees that it's his dad, so he picks it up since Lindsay is due this week.

"Rude!" his mother and Bethany, both of them alarmed, say in unison.

Blake walks out of the ballroom to take the call, and sure enough, it's his dad at the hospital. Blake calls Bethany on her cell phone and asks her to come out to the hallway.

"What is it?" Bethany hisses when she arrives there, stuffs her cell phone into her bag. "I was just about to get my picture taken by Sunday Styles!"

Blake says his dad has sent a car to pick them up and drive them to the hospital. Bethany's shoulders tense up.

"Are you kidding?" she says. "We can't just leave now. I'm doing serious networking with Heath's girlfriend. Her sister is an editor at *W*."

Blake looks at her closely, taking her flawless face in his hands.

"You. Must. Be. Joking," he says, letting go of her face and gently giving her shoulders a little shake.

She ducks out of his grip. "What is wrong with you? Why can't this wait another twenty minutes? The baby isn't going to just walk out of the hospital in the next few hours."

Alison White's grass-green eyes and little dimple suddenly pop into Blake's head. She probably loves babies and endangered animals and everything Bethany hates. It's always easier to end something when you think there's a possibility of starting something new with someone else. Someone like Alison.

"It's over," he tells Bethany, as if just those two words could explain how much he's wanted to breathe and sleep and eat on his own. He won't mind the memory of her so much once she's gone. Blake's sure of it. He can almost script all their future fights so why bother having them at all?

She says his name and tries to touch his face. Tears start carrying mascara down her cheeks. He's got to get out of here. By tomorrow, she will have spun a story about how she broke up with him.

"You can't just leave me here," she whispers in her wounded-animal voice. "What will people say?"

He starts walking away.

She yells out his name. "What will people say?"

"That I deserve better!" he shouts back at her, startling one of the clipboard girls. And then, just to be mean, just to say something people would remember: "With all the money I'm getting, my wife should at least buy me some happiness."

Kate knocks on the apartment door, expecting Marco to fling it open the way he always does, taking her in his arms for a kiss and pouring her a glass of wine. But this time he just yells for her to come in. Her pink dress is still hanging over the chair where she left it after a big foodie award ceremony the night before. Marco was anointed the new best chef in New York, and everyone told Kate she was "lucky" to be with someone so "charming."

He knew he had won before the ceremony because Kate had convinced the event's unsuspecting publicist to e-mail her an advance list of the winners. The tactic was not exactly unethical. Kate just e-mailed a request, saying she needed the information before covering the event in case she arrived late. "It's a busy night," she wrote. "There's a lot of competition for my coverage."

But last night feels like months ago. Now the apartment is dark and there's no sign of dinner, even though Kate's starving. She was waiting to eat with him. He promised he'd cook for her, which was probably her first confirmation that he's feeling guilty. These days he rarely even cooks in his restaurant kitchen because he's too busy doing interviews and meeting with investors. She fumbles to find the light switch, then sees his coat and bag on the hall table next to a stack of freshly printed business cards amblazoned with a new restaurant logo she helped him pick.

Kate finds him in bed with the covers pulled up to his chin. The television flickers white light across his face, practically sucking all the liquid out of his eyes. It looks as if he hasn't blinked for hours.

She lies down over the covers next to him.

"What do you want to know?" he asks, and his voice sounds as though it's recorded on a tape. Distant and anonymous.

"You should know by now that I always want to know everything, even if I shouldn't."

"You shouldn't," he says, and neither of them says a word for a few minutes. Kate watches the television. It's one of those dumb VH1 that air for months on heavy rotation shows about the fabulous lives of celebrities and Tim is on it, talking about Natalie Portman's new apartment in a new building in Gramercy Park. Kate almost ran an item about it herself, but the best real-estate source she inherited from Paul swore it was just a marketing ploy.

"How much do you really want to know?"

She takes a deep breath that looks like a yawn, but she's just having a hard time getting enough oxygen. "All of it."

Marco sighs and starts the story, the story he might have kept to himself if he hadn't climbed past 4 percent famous. He owes taxes and someone's coming to collect.

The story starts on a stormy night. "The kind of night when the pounding rain on the roof makes you want to stay in bed under the covers, listening to it wash over the streets and leave everything clean and still in the morning," he says.

It's a story that's already giving Kate goose bumps. She slides under the covers next to him.

"She wanted to stay home but I convinced her to go to a friend's party." He was driving fast because he'd made them late. "I was always late, even back then." Marco runs his hand through his hair. She?

"Christina—her name is Christina—looked perfect as usual. I can still remember her white sundress. It had these thin straps that kept falling down her shoulders. It was raining so hard I couldn't see the lines on the road." He pauses here, as if he's told this story many times before. He knows what to mention and what he can leave out. "She wanted me to stop, but I just started going faster. I told her she was being crazy. I said, 'You can't be the kind of woman who's afraid to drive in a storm.'" His chest rises up with a deep inhale.

"I saw the tree for just an instant before it fell on the car. . . . I thought I might be able to speed past it."

He takes a sip of water from a glass on the bedside table.

"The roof crumpled like aluminum foil. As soon as I heard her breathing, all I could think of was, At least I didn't kill her. At least I know that much is true. She had tiny silver bells on her sandals. I thought, At least she's moving. I suddenly had this kind of strength I never knew before or since, and I kicked off what was left of my door after smashing my arm through the window. My shirt turned red. Wet and sticky and red."

Kate doesn't know what to say.

He keeps going. She notices he's speaking quicker now, as if he wants her to have all of this, as if maybe he thinks it will make him feel a little lighter.

"When she looked up at me I screamed, even though I shouldn't have, even though that was the worst thing I could have done. Then she screamed and I could see her skull through the hole that used to be her nose. She screamed and the only thing I could think of was, Monster."

And that's the face and noise keeping him up at night all these years later.

He explains that her parents had always paid for everything. It was part of the reason he could afford to stay in Italy when he met her there while he was attending cooking school, with plans to move back to California and maybe open a restaurant in the Napa Valley. He came to New York instead, six years ago. He left once he knew she would live even if her life would never be the same.

He swallows another sip of water. "I couldn't bear it any other way," he says without looking at Kate.

The doctors said she would have permanent nerve damage. It would take years of cosmetic surgery and physical therapy to make her even vaguely resemble anything like her former self. "The doctor said the priority was to help her live pain free. I said that didn't appear to be an option."

Kate turns her head to look at him but he's looking at an invisible spot on the floor.

"Maybe if I made some real money, I could try to really help her . . ." His voice trails off.

Kate wants to forgive him. She wants to understand. She wants to believe he will help her. The accident wasn't his fault. But it's hard to find a shelf high enough to put the rest of it, a place where she won't be reminded every day of the part of the story he's tried to erase.

Kate has no idea what to say, but Marco asks her the one question she has an answer for.

"Will you help me bury this?" he asks, and she pictures them digging a hole in the dark and distant dirt.

Tim clears his throat and answers the phone. "Hi, Mom," he says, trying to sound better than he feels.

"Do you have a hangover?" she asks, already knowing the answer.

"Maybe a little." He walks over and raises the blinds, squinting at the sun. The snow on the ground makes everything brighter and harder to wake up to without feeling blinded. He turns away from the window and still sees black spots on the bedspread when he climbs back in bed.

She tells him she liked his story about the homophobic real-estate broker, who has since skipped town—the news editors bumped it up to the first section of the paper—and that she clipped it for her scrapbook, where she keeps all his articles.

"Why don't you come home for a few days? I'll help you get rid of that nasty cough once and for all. You just need some of my chicken soup. It always makes you feel better."

Tim's eyes water with the effort of trying to silence a hack. He takes a sip of water and lights a cigarette, inhaling silently.

"They've got to give you some time off. You worked Christmas!"

"Mom, I can't just take a vacation. I only get two weeks off a year."

"Well, why can't you get a job where you can keep more regular hours? There's got to be something else you can do, right? Something with less drinking."

Nothing she'd want to keep a scrapbook of. "You tell me."

"Maybe you could write a column for one of those men's magazines, maybe about fitness?"

"Mom, I haven't been to a gym in four years."

"But you used to be such a wonderful athlete! You were the captain of your high-school soccer team!"

He puts on his sunglasses and pulls up the covers. "I used to be a lot of things."

It's an icy morning when Kate stops by the designer Zac Posen's studio before work. Marco's stylist got the appointment for Kate, who needs a dress for the Oscars, coming up during the last weekend in February.

It's only nine A.M., but the studio is crowded with what looks like students sewing, sketching, and running around with arms full of bright fabrics. A bulletin board is propped up against a wall, covered with photographs of wild African animals and glamorous young women and men on safaris, and alongside the photos are swatches of zebra and leopard prints. Kate's greeted warmly by a short, smiling woman.

"We're all big fans of your column," the woman says, introducing herself as Zac's mother. His sister works there, too. Kate wonders if any of them know she's dating Marco and if it would matter. She likes that they want to dress her just for being her. It's the first time she's considered that she may not need Marco to get the things she sometimes wants.

Kate thought she'd be led to a mirrored dressing room with a plush carpet and an Italian tailor, kneeling with pins in his mouth. Instead, Zac's mom directs her to what must be the office bathroom, with a few old pairs of Manolos. She imagines that the starlets who often wear Zac's dresses on red carpets probably have racks of clothes sent to their apartments rather than using the bathroom here as a dressing room—and then she stops herself. Looking at her reflection in front of a rack of dresses she could never afford, she thinks, This should be enough.

"I want to see!" someone yells as he knocks on the door, and Kate knows it must be Zac. She has to suck in her breath when she zips up the dress and it *still* gets caught in her skin. She hopes she can get out of it alone.

"No," says Zac, shaking his head when she emerges. He looks about her age and he's wearing jeans and an old red velvet blazer. He looks her up and down. "Definitely no." He shoos her back into the bathroom, where she tries on a dress that reveals way too much cleavage. When she opens the door to show him again, he just shakes his head and hands her a long satiny gold gown. "This is the one," he says.

It's got silky gold straps over the shoulder and falls to her ankles in soft ripples. Kate twirls around for Zac and his mom, feeling like a princess.

"Perfect," he says, nodding.

"Perfect," says his mom.

They offer to messenger the gown to her apartment but she says she'll just take it with her—that way she doesn't have to mention that she doesn't have a doorman. Tonight she will try it on for Marco right away to make sure he approves.

Zoe agreed to go to a tasting with Tim and now he's wondering if she just wanted to try the restaurant. Lately she's been acting strange, canceling plans and not returning his calls. But she's already at the restaurant when he arrives, sipping a glass of white wine at the corner table.

She doesn't get up when he walks over to the table—just gives him a cool smile. He puts his cell phone on the table because he left the office before the column closed. He didn't want to be more than ten minutes late for Zoe. As soon as they order drinks, his phone vibrates, and before he can check it, Zoe grabs it.

She looks at the screen and a wrinkle creases in the center of her forehead. "So, are you going to tell me who Dan is or should I guess?"

Tim stays quiet. He knows what's coming.

"Okay, I'll guess," she says, raising a thin eyebrow. She looks as tough and unforgiving as a new pair of leather shoes. "I'm guessing that Dan is Danielle Marks, the mattress who probably wears red lace panties from"— she grimaces—"Victoria's Secret."

Tim downs the martini Zoe must have ordered for him in one big gulp while looking her in the eye. Fuck Kate. Marco must have told her and she must have spilled—but Zoe probably figured out the panties part on her own.

"And this Danielle was photographed sitting on your lap at Holly May's birthday party in a cheap red dress." Fuck WireImage.

"About five months later, which brings us to last week, she was photographed on the same Web site looking significantly fatter at a Liz Lange maternity clothes trunk sale. Something tells me she didn't just go off the South Beach Diet."

Zoe takes a breath and smiles the way her dad smiles at Tim. Miss Detective is feeling pretty smug. But still, she must have had help.

"What exactly did Kate tell you?" he asks, raising his voice. He has to know what he's working with.

"Nothing," she sputters, putting both her hands on the table and sending a fork clattering to the floor. "It was just a hunch. *Until now.*"

A waiter swiftly delivers a clean fork.

"You want to know why I'm mad?"

"Should we make a list?"

She brushes her long black hair out of her face, tucking it behind her ears. She's wearing the diamond earrings her dad gave her for her birthday.

"I'm not mad that you got some slutty girl pregnant." Zoe leans in close. "I'm mad that you thought you could hide it. You cannot hide a baby because a baby grows up to be a kid and then a teenager and then an adult. A baby can't get spun or swapped or buried."

She's right about everything and he tries to focus on his breathing. If he opens up his mouth, nothing but a sob will come out, and then she will have really won.

"I would have expected you to be more of a man," she says, standing up and neatly folding her napkin before placing it on her empty plate. "But I guess I expected too much."

Ever since Bethany moved out, Blake feels as if he bought the apartment next door and knocked down a wall to double his square footage. He happily eats in bed while watching television and leaves the sports section in the bathroom. He's been spending more time home, and tonight he even invited Tim over for takeout instead of going to a restaurant where they'd get too much free booze.

"Very civilized," says Tim when he sees the pizza and beer set out on the table with porcelain plates and cloth napkins.

"It's a new me," says Blake, who tries to show off photos of his new stepsister. At least he's still his dad's only son. And she's adorable, a cute, little, gurgling, smiley thing that likes to fall asleep on his chest. She makes him want one of his own. But Tim will barely look at the pictures.

Tim immediately launches into a tirade about Danielle being a "manipulative bitch" and how he's going to win Zoe back.

"Sometimes I fantasize about pushing Danielle down a flight of stairs."

"You can't be serious," says Blake, afraid that Tim is.

Tim pauses. "Of course I'm not serious, asshole."

But then something strange happens. Blake can see Tim's mouth moving and he can hear Tim's voice, but he can't understand anything Tim is saying. It's as if there's a white-noise box blaring in the room.

"Do you think that will work?" asks Tim, who's got a glob of tomato sauce in the corner of his mouth. Blake decides not to offer a napkin.

"Tim," he says. "I hate to be the one to break it to you, but I think you're going to have to start accepting that resistance is futile."

The invisible noise machine clicks off and Tim seems to be shouting. "What, is that a line from your new shrink? Don't you psychobabble me."

Blake shakes his head. "A baby is forever."

The tomato sauce drips down Tim's chin.

"I'm sorry, man. You're not getting out of this one."

it sucks to be a gossip
columnist in l.a.

(and never wear heels to a lawn party)

I am so jealous," says Zoe when Kate calls to say she and Marco have a stunning suite at L'Ermitage in L.A., even nicer than the one in Aspen. She tells her she can see the big billboard advertising Marco's new show from the balcony. The launch a few weeks ago was a huge hit with a record-breaking audience tuning in to watch him make risotto. Even the critics were kind. "A star is born," said the *Times* review. "Marco Mancini has an electric television presence that should appeal particularly to young women."

"It's crazy," she says, looking out at the massive picture of Marco advertising his show. *The Chef Women Across America Want to Take Home to Their Kitchens!* The only thing he's made in her kitchen is ice. But still, he's here with her. Kate always has been envious of Zoe's life, but now the roles are reversed and it makes her feel giddy, as if she's got a stack of birthday gifts to unwrap.

While Marco met with his agents over lattes in the lobby, Kate picked up two items while pretending to read magazines at the pool, where Julianne Moore, Patricia Clarkson, and Tim Robbins were hanging out. She thought she'd have to hide behind her *GQ* when she spotted Todd Slattery, but he came right up to her, smiling.

"It's great to see you," he said, obviously having forgiven her for her call about Harry Steiner's testicle. "I saw you check in with Marco Mancini. We love his show. Harry wants to set up a meeting with him. He thinks Marco has real big-screen potential." Kate promised to pass Todd's card on to Marco, and the white flag was raised. She could probably get a few items as commission. Todd is probably not the only source who's going to give her items here, now that she's linked with somebody currently at about 20 percent famous and climbing.

The only problem about the weekend is that Marco's also cooking at a fund-raiser on Oscar night, so he's not sure he can meet Kate at the *Vanity Fair* party, even though his new agent got him on the list. Kate looks at her laminated press pass for the party. It was delivered in a heavy bag from the magazine. She's only allowed to go from 11:15 to midnight, but even that she considers lucky. She only got invited after Lacey lobbied on her behalf with the magazine's special-events coordinator, who treats the party as if it were her only child's wedding.

Kate looks around the hotel room again. The big white bed, the soft pale pink walls, the gleaming big tub for two . . . The *Examiner* would never pay for a hotel like this, but just being seen here by a few publicists and celebrities has given her clout with people like Todd. They think she's one of them, and for this weekend she is.

"Hey, beautiful," Marco says, swooping in for a kiss when he walks in. She asks him what took so long.

He says his meeting turned out to include a twenty-minute date with the leggy blond actress Heather Grom in her trailer on the set of her television show. Kate feels her cheeks flush. It doesn't seem fair that she has to compete with noncivilians, especially a tall pretty one who always seems to be dating the new hot guy in the spotlight. A Starfucking Star. Last time Kate checked, the actress had been dumped by Heath Ledger and was dating Josh Lucas.

"Date?"

"Come on, cutie, don't get mad. Just think of what walking the red carpet with her could do to my celebrity quotient. It's not like I would actu-

ally date her. And she was really nice. I think she's looking to settle down."
He smiles. "Oh, and I thought you'd like this detail, and you can use it:
She once worked as an usher at the Hollywood Bowl!"

Is he kidding? He's not kidding. The *Examiner* is not the *Enquirer*. Kate
looks closely at his face. He seems jazzed, oblivious to any torment she's
enduring. "But it turns out her handlers—"

"Handlers?"

"She's got a small army of people who work on her image. They set up
the meeting or date or whatever and they timed it perfectly so she'd be in
makeup. She wanted to meet me because they like my image as a whole-
some, romantic bachelor. She even tried my Caprese salad dressing recipe!
Can you believe it?"

"No," says Kate, looking out the window at the giant billboard of
Marco. She bets those handlers wouldn't think he was such a great guy if
they knew about Christina. "And yes."

In New York, people read newspapers and magazines. They know bylines.
They want reporters around to write about them. In L.A., no one reads
anything but Condé Nast magazines and the occasional tabloid if they're
in it. It's a status symbol to keep the Fourth Estate waiting on line, and
there is no more humbling time for that than the Oscars.

This is the first time Charlie has let Tim go, and he quickly realizes it's
not likely to be half as glamorous as he always imagined it would. Charlie
expects Tim to file items every morning—a real fucking bitch with the
time difference. And it's always annoying to be at one of these award
show weekends. It's the same morons on the Sundance/Golden Globes/
Oscars/Cannes traveling circus.

Blake and Tim drive together from the airport, passing a massive billboard on Sunset Boulevard advertising Marco's new cooking show. It's a
picture of him making pasta with flour-covered hands looking huge as
they drive past it. Marco looks signficantly better in the picture than he
does in real life, and Tim wonders how much air brushing they did. Every

day, with every percentage point Marco gains, it becomes more likely that Charlie's going to hear about the wife and berate Tim for burying it. It's turning into a particularly good story. If he has a wife and if he really did desert her when she was disfigured and broke, does that still make him a desirable bachelor? Would the people in the fly-over states really want to learn how to cook a family meal or a romantic dinner from someone whose secret wife is begging for money to help fix the damage he caused? Doubt it. The skeleton could really throw a wrench in the network's marketing machine. Spinster's going to have to sweat for her next paycheck.

There's a fruit basket with a bottle of champagne on the table in the living room between their bedrooms at the Four Seasons, and after shaking the bottle up, Tim immediately uncorks it, spraying the big, fluffy white couches. He got the room free from a PR firm that's hosting a viewing party there and he requested an adjoining bedroom for Blake, whose magazine wouldn't allow him to accept such a freebie. *Vanity Fair* has sent over heavy gift bags with cosmetics and hats they've thrown on the floor. Blake picks out some expensive-looking beauty products and says he'll bring them back for Alison.

"The fact checker?" She seemed pretty dull when Tim met her a few weeks ago, but Blake keeps talking about her. She'll probably make him wait until the fourth date to fuck her.

In the gift bags are laminated parking permits and passes that allow them to attend the *Vanity Fair* party from 11:15 to midnight. Only the syndicated dinosaurs get into the dinner.

"That's bullshit," says Tim, pouring them each a glass of what's left of the champagne. Then he remembers the last time he trashed a hotel room and starts missing Zoe. "What are we, Cinde-fucking-rella?"

Blake opens the curtains, brightening the room enough for Tim to reach for his sunglasses. "Do you think they'd actually throw us out?"

"No way. It's bad enough we're not allowed to bring dates." At least Danielle can't get in.

Blake cracks open the terrace door and squints into the sun. "We should say we're movie producers."

Tim looks at his stupid laminated passes again. Forty-five minutes to work the party and he's not allowed to carry a notebook or a tape recorder? And he has to leave by midnight, when it'll just be getting good? No fucking way. These people have no idea who they're dealing with. Column A can make or break the party. By the end of the night they're going to be kissing his ass.

Kate and Marco walk past the clipboard chicks without even having to give their names before jumping on a golf cart that takes them up media mogul Barry Diller's long gravel driveway. When they reach the backyard, Kate's relieved she decided to take Marco's stylist's suggestion to dress casually and wear flip-flops—otherwise, she'd be sinking in the grass like everyone else. The sprawling yard is filled with Persian carpets and bright pillows, and impossibly famous people lounging around, talking about how they just hate Oscar weekend and they're relieved that they don't have to go to the "boring" award ceremony tomorrow night.

Barry's wearing a blue zip-up hooded sweatshirt, blue-and-white-striped pajama pants, and sneakers. "Now, that's famous," says Marco with a mix of admiration and envy. His stylist picked out his white linen shirt and designer distressed jeans. The blazer question took up much of the morning and he decided to carry it flung over his shoulder "just in case." Kate's wearing a new pair of striped alice + olivia pants that he said made her look skinny.

All the B-list agents are in suits even though the sun's beating down. It was raining yesterday and people are joking that Barry's rich enough to rent the sun for the party every year.

People keep coming up to Marco to say they love his new show and ask how it feels to be such a hit. Kate stands by his side, unsure what to say, unsure if she should mention *her* job, which is what got them into the party. Kate may as well be his handler for all she seems to matter. Only the Botoxed wives of the men who call themselves producers try to make conversation with her, about how "stressful" the weekend always is.

"I just spent a week at We Care to get in shape for the big weekend," says one wife. "And *voilà!*" She puts her hands on her hips and twirls around. "Ten pounds flew off." She leans over and whispers to Kate, "Nothing takes it off faster than daily colonics. You don't even have to exercise!"

Kate excuses herself and starts wandering through the party, wondering if the faces are familiar because she knows them or if they're just more than 4 percent famous. She finally spots Tim and Blake lounging on pillows, smoking and drinking. She's never been happier to see them and heads over.

"Where's your superstar boyfriend?" asks Tim.

Kate shrugs and sits down. "Being a superstar."

"Aren't you like his publicist now? Don't you need to handle all those fans?" asks Blake, looking over at Marco, who's standing next to Spinster (barefoot and holding a pair of strappy sandals) with his head thrown back, laughing with two guys in suits.

Kate throws a pillow at Blake and he laughs. And just when she's beginning to wonder if Marco's getting too famous to be seen with her, he looks right at her, winks, and holds up his finger. *He'll be here in a moment.* She smiles.

"Hey, aren't you guys supposed to be working?" she asks.

"It's too overwhelming," says Tim. "I feel like a fucking kid at a freak show carnival."

A waiter offers them a tray with four different kinds of desserts in little bowls. Tim takes one of each and sets them down on the grass.

"I feel like I'm in a movie about a party before the Oscars," says Blake, who's wearing his signature outfit. Kate finds this a comforting signpost.

Jack Nicholson walks by with Holly May in a short gingham skirt that Kate saw on the cover of the current issue of *Vogue*.

"I heard she got her tits from fat injected from her ass," says Blake. "Just like all those Brazilian models."

"Everyone's doing it," says Tim.

The snoops sit on their pillows, feeling the sun on their faces for the first time in months and wondering if the items will just fall out of the sky. Instead, the publicist Bottle Blonde, who invited Kate to the Dior shoe party all those months ago, runs up to them and starts complaining to Tim about Robin's item about her getting busted for doing coke with a starlet in the bathroom at a Golden Globes party.

"First of all," she says, struggling to keep her stilettos from sinking into the grass, "I've never done coke. Secondly, I still have that account. And thirdly," she says, raising her voice, "I wasn't even at the Golden Globes."

Tim reminds her that she went to the Golden Globes party with Charlie. Blake and Kate look down at the grass so they won't start laughing. A flicker of confusion mixed with determination passes over Bottle Blonde's face. She makes a motion like she's waving her hand to someone familiar in the near distance and quickly excuses herself, wobbling off toward the buffet.

Blake ends up standing next to Zoe's dad in the bathroom line in the smaller of the two houses on the property. At least Tim is a safe distance away, he thinks. Jack Miller is here for work. This is his job. He's not from this world and he's rich enough not to care what anyone thinks of him.

"So, I hear your friend and my daughter broke up," says Jack, rocking back and forth on his heels. He's wearing a khaki-colored linen suit with a white shirt. He fits in here as seamlessly as he does on the East Coast, a cultured chameleon.

"You've got good sources," says Blake, wanting to change the subject as quickly as possible. Blake hopes Tim won't need to go to the bathroom anytime soon.

Jack seems to get the hint. "Please tell me you're not still charmed by the randy restaurateur," says Jack, standing up straight and folding his arms across his chest. Blake thinks it's strange that Jack uses that old Column A moniker for Marco.

"I thought you would be the one most charmed by him," Blake says. "You've got a hit show on your hands."

Jack sighs. "You would think so, wouldn't you?"

Goosebumps appear on Blake's arms. It happens when he's about to get an item, even though this one will probably hit too close to home to be useful for anything but his personal files. Jack sighs, leaning against the white wall. "This is off the record"—he waits for Blake to nod before continuing—"but there's going to be a few changes in our spring lineup."

Blake hears the toilet flushing and hopes whoever's in the bathroom takes some extra time to primp. "Why?"

"I'm not your source on this, Blake," says Jack, rocking back and forth on his heels again. Before Blake can ask him anything else, Jack shakes his head. "You're the gossip columnist, you tell me what's going on."

Hollywood Prince walks out of the bathroom and Jack walks in. Blake's relieved that Robin scooped him on the item about the actor's kids buying drugs in Harlem because he wouldn't want to get yelled at here. He just smiles and says, "Nice to see you," which always throws people off because it suggests they've met you before.

Once Blake's in the bathroom, he calls his dad to tell him the show's being pulled off the air next month. He feels a little like an insider trader. Jack Miller didn't know that Blake's dad was considering investing in a chain of Coasts, and passing on the tip makes Blake feel almost as high as if he'd done a bump of coke, which he would do now if he had any. Instead, he pops two Sudafeds. His sinuses are clogged from last night's bender.

"Don't do the deal," Blake says. "Trust me."

As he walks back to Tim and Kate, Blake hears Marco's voice coming from the other side of the smaller house, the one not facing the party. He's laughing and a woman who's not Kate is giggling. Blake pushes himself against the house so he can peer around the stucco side undetected.

First he sees a swirl of a gingham skirt and then he sees Marco's white linen shirt. Blake quickly backs away from the house so he doesn't see anything more incriminating. He doesn't even want to carry the weight of what he just saw. Kate will figure it out soon enough. She doesn't need him to make her feel like she's playing catch-up, that she's the last to know. It's one of the reasons they all started doing this in the first place. They can only tolerate being the first, or at least one of the first, to know those things better left unsaid and unseen. This is one thing Blake wishes he didn't have the exclusive on.

On Oscar afternoon, Marco drops Kate and her gold gown off at the Four Seasons on his way to the Beverly Hills mansion where he's preparing dinner. He's making the duck with cherry glaze, and Kate can almost taste the sweet, soft meat that's been baking in the ovens since last night. By now she's learned that the secret to tender duck is letting the fat slowly seep into the meat.

He says he'll try to meet her at the *Vanity Fair* party if he can get out in time to catch her invite window. "I'll try to rush dessert," he says. "No one eats carbs here, anyway."

Kate goes up to the guys' suite to drop off her gown and then heads downstairs with them to a viewing party sponsored by Mercedes. They're supposed to show up and play nice with the publicists and at least run an item about who was there, even though anyone worthy of ink is at a better viewing party. The publicists are also offering free hair and makeup— hardly on a par with free Dior shoes. The bathrooms at every Oscar weekend event have makeup artists offering free touch-ups, which Kate has needed to help camouflage a breakout on her nose. She needs to look perfect in case Marco shows up at the *Vanity Fair* party in time for them to get their photo taken together.

Kate doesn't recognize anyone in the makeup room, but they all seem to know one another. Even though she's lost ten pounds since she started dating Marco four months ago, she feels pale and mushy next to all these tanned, toned women wearing pastel Juicy jumpsuits or designer gowns. At least Kate is working. Work is a comforting excuse. It sets her apart from the animals.

Kate goes up to Tim and Blake's suite to change into her dress.

"Wow, you look like a celebutante," says Tim when she emerges from the bathroom in the gold gown.

"And you look like you slept in your tux," says Kate, plugging in the iron.

"You know how to work that?" asks Blake, who looks perfectly primped for the big night in a tuxedo he actually owns.

Tim picks up the phone and calls the concierge. "Hi. No, I'm sorry, I can't hold." He grins. "This is Tim Mack from Column A." He pauses. "We are enjoying our stay here, thank you very much. But I would enjoy it a lot more if I could get housekeeping up here right away to help me iron my tux."

Tim hangs up and changes out of his tux into a pair of jeans and a T-shirt. "Come on, we're wasting precious open bar time," he tells Kate and Blake. "I'll get dressed later. It's not like anyone cares what I'm wearing anyway."

Kate doesn't get to actually listen to the television broadcast of the awards show. Instead, she spends most of the viewing party drinking and eating with Blake and Tim, who are trying not to get cornered by any publicists. A few hours later, en route to the *Vanity Fair* party, Tim calls Charlie to get a list of winners so they know what to ask the stars. It's confusing because the show is broadcast live, which means the whole thing is over by around eight P.M. L.A. time. Kate writes down a list, relieved she doesn't have to work alone tonight. She wouldn't have thought of making a crib sheet on her own.

The entrance to Morton's restaurant is flanked by paparazzi lunging over the velvet ropes like a thousand-legged octopus squirming on the seafloor. It's bright enough to be morning under all the lights.

A coterie of clipboard chicks direct them to another entrance. Their wattage apparently isn't high enough for the main entrance. Kate still feels the heat from the camera lights as they walk by and she hears a few lone *click click clicks* from photographers who don't know any better. Or maybe they're just betting that one of them will be embroiled in a scandal one day and their photos will actually be worth something.

This is the party she's wanted to go to ever since she started reading Zoe's *Vanity Fair* magazines freshman year of college. Kate had always imagined herself walking down this very red carpet, surrounded by stars holding statues, maybe meeting a handsome movie producer and living happily ever after, maybe in a house perched on an ocean-side cliff in Malibu. She never imagined it would make her feel like the hired help or, in Tim's poetic words, "like we were a trio of mangled midgets hired to juggle at the circus."

As she walks down the red carpet flanked by Tim and Blake, she suddenly feels something like a smooth pebble sliding down her hair, rolling off her gold dress, and softly clattering to the red carpet—which, it turns out, is nothing more than a thin cover over concrete. Kate grabs her necklace and, sure enough, one of the small diamonds just fell off. She should have never borrowed jewelry from Bethany.

Mission accomplished. Blake slaps his hand over his mouth and gasps. "Bethany's going to kill you." He drops to his knees to help hunt for the stray diamond.

"Ah, you could afford a couple grand to replace it, right?" says Tim, laughing. Kate doesn't look amused, so he drops down to join them on the red carpet, reaching around the stilettos as people try to avoid stepping on their fingers.

"Bingo!" says Tim, holding up the small shiny stone. Kate gives him a big hug and places the gem and the entire necklace in her purse. She wishes she didn't even try to fit in tonight. It's not as if anyone knows what she looks like, or she's celebrating anything other than being invited to the party for forty-five minutes. The *InStyle* reporters are certainly not asking Kate who dressed her.

They check their egos at the door, where the chief clipboard chick issues a stern warning: "If I see any of you with a notepad or a tape recorder, I'm going to have to throw you out."

Kate wonders if they've been invited just to feel inferior, and she's starting to panic that she hasn't gotten any good items tonight. She's got a column to fill, so she wanders off to try to eavesdrop while the guys get drinks at the bar. How do you look as though you're not working when you don't know anyone? It's much more intimidating than being a freshman at the senior prom. At least there she had a date to talk to.

Kate smiles at Sean Penn and tells Renée Zellweger that she looks great. What else is she supposed to say? It's not as if Kate's going to make any new friends here. Plus, it's getting hard to breathe. She wishes any of the New York party crashers—Shaggy, the baroness, even the guy in the Mets cap who invented dwarf bowling—were here to make her at least one rung up.

She spots Eve and Paul Peterson standing in a group of what must be other *Vanity Fair* writers. None of them look particularly glamorous, and they must all be wearing their own clothes, even though they could probably borrow whatever they wanted from any designer. Kate feels like a kid playing dress-up in her mom's closet, teetering in heels with a clown makeup face. The *Vanity Fair* group are choosing to dress their station, and that's something Kate suddenly decides is extremely smart and respectable. If only she knew that a few hours ago. Eve waves and Kate walks over, wondering if Eve really thinks Paul will ever leave his wife, or if being infatuated with him has just become her excuse for staying single.

"Don't waste time talking to us!" says Eve, who was invited to the dinner and doesn't seem to have a curfew. She thanks Kate for helping her research celebrity chefs for a potential profile, but explains it's not going to turn into a feature after all.

"We're just not sure this celebrity chef thing has legs," says Eve, who never asked Kate anything about Christina, making Kate wonder just how good a journalist Eve really is. But maybe that's the trick. Kate wonders if Eve was going to mention that Kate was Marco's girlfriend in the story.

"'Beware of the meteoric rise' is what we always say," adds Paul, who looks well rested, even tan and healthy. Getting off the gossip beat seems to have worked in his favor. His eyes are brighter, even bigger than Kate remembered.

When Kate tells Paul that he looks great, he returns the compliment.

"I hardly recognize you," he says, smiling and putting his hand on her shoulder. "It's like one of those makeovers you see only on television."

He's the only person who's ever been involved in the gossip world whose career Kate would like to emulate. He's got a loving family and a big contract at a serious magazine where he can do investigative journalism. However, he hasn't yet had a story come out, which prompted Lacey to say Paul was "failing upward."

Lacey was probably just bitter that Paul got a big raise and more clout, but still, how good can this industry get for Kate? What's the best-case scenario, and is that enough?

Eve nods, agreeing with Paul, her big vintage silver earrings swaying back and forth like hypnotic pendulums chanting *get out get out get out.*

"You should write the television treatment: How to Date a New Celebrity and Dress the Part," says Eve.

Kate wonders when Eve figured out that Marco was not single, and if it works for or against Kate.

Eve leans in closer. "Just make sure you have something to fall back on. What goes up can come down real fast."

Kate struggles to catch her breath. She tries to distract herself by looking around the party. It seems as though everyone has a clock on their foreheads to remind the guests not to waste too much time on one person. There are two big rooms with televisions suspended from the ceiling showing the red-carpet arrivals, just in case you're wondering if you should be trying to meet someone even more famous. The formerly Plus-Sized Pinup waltzes in, looking pale and gaunt.

"And honey, if it doesn't work out, at least you got a great new look," continues Eve, running a hand through her short silver hair. "For someone your age, that's harder to get than a new boyfriend, and it lasts much longer."

Kate pretends to cough so she can yawn to get more oxygen.

Get out. Get out. Get out.

Eve's eyes dart to the other side of the room. "Is that Nicole Kidman?"

Kate wishes Marco were here. He would know what to do, who to talk to, all the right things to say. Navigating this kind of event would be much less scary if she had someone at her side. Power coupling isn't so much a PR stunt as a survival strategy.

"Hey, Lois Lane," she hears before whipping around. It's Dylan Frye, the faded sitcom star whom she met after she crashed through the table at Lush all those months ago. He's wearing a black suit with a white shirt and a skinny black tie. "Need a date?"

He wasn't allowed to bring a date, either, and Kate wonders if they're the same percent famous, even though he used to be a lot more famous. Maybe it all evens out over time. Dylan steers her around the party, introducing her to a few agents and producers, people who also feel a little humbled, even if their perfectly primped dates look thrilled just to be in the same room with so many stars. Parties are like camping trips, thinks Kate—the pictures make it look a lot more fun.

Dylan waits patiently for her while she takes notes in the bathroom, and then they start doing another loop. She resists the urge to ask him for a personalized autograph she can show off to her high-school friends. But then she feels immediate disappointment that the reality isn't nearly as exciting as the fantasy.

There's no one left who would want to talk to them. Kate watches the queen clipboard chick throw Tim out after he tries to interview Hollywood Prince, probably about his son checking into rehab. Blake's nowhere to be found. Kate looks at her watch. It's almost midnight. She tells Dylan she should be finding the guys. She doesn't want to get thrown out, especially in front of Marco—if he appears.

Blake convinces the queen clipboard chick—whom he once slept with after a Hamptons benefit years ago—to grant him an extra fifteen minutes to get some decent short quotes.

"I hear you and Bethany broke up," she says, touching his forearm. If he didn't have it on pretty good authority that this one was thrown out of her share house that summer for stealing cash to pay off her Barneys debt, he would consider bringing her home tonight to take full advantage of the hotel room. But then there's Alison. Maybe she'll go out to dinner with him if he comes back and says he couldn't stop thinking about her. He wants to be loyal to his feelings and play this out because it feels right, not because he's following orders.

"I'll call you after we get back to the right coast!" he chirps to the clipboard chick, vanishing back into the crowd.

As Blake circles the room, he's spotted by an agent from New York he once met at one of Bethany's friends' obligatory dinner parties. The agent says Blake should consider turning the item he wrote a few weeks ago about the mysterious death at the banking heir's Palm Beach mansion into a book. Blake had tried to turn it into a feature for *Manhattan* magazine, but the editor said they needed him to focus on his column. When his dad heard about that, he used it as an excuse to harass Blake to try to freelance the story, as if he had the time for that.

"We could probably sell it for at least half a mil to one of the studios to option," says the agent, slapping Blake on the shoulder. Blake doesn't know the agent—or any agent—well enough to know if this is the kind of thing they say to every writer they encounter. But still, at least the possibility would mollify his dad a little for helping Blake get the contacts to report out that item. It makes him feel as if he's slightly levitating above this party, and the view isn't bad.

Maybe that's what he should do. Get out of the gossip game. The Palm Beach police still don't know how the body ended up in the closet. Blake heard about it from his boarding school friends and his dad got it confirmed by the octogenarian socialite who lives next door, who swears it wasn't a suicide.

He puts the agent's card in his tuxedo pocket—he's got to remember to remove it before sending the tux to the dry cleaner's—and says they'll set up a lunch next week. Maybe he could write a book about the murder that would get made into a movie that could even be nominated for an Oscar, and he could come back here feeling more like he belonged. He might even get invited to the dinner—with a date. That would show those publicist bitches.

A minor lightning storm erupts by the door: Holly May's big arrival in a clingy lavender-and-dark-green gown. Blake looks at his watch, feeling his chest tighten up with anger and then soften quickly into sadness. The randy restaurateur is living up to his reputation.

Kate's a little worried that the seams of her gold dress will burst from all the hors d'oeuvres she devoured at the *Vanity Fair* party, but she still doesn't take it off when she gets back to the hotel room, which looks far less glamorous at this late hour. She doesn't wash her face, either. She wants Marco to see her as she is. She throws the white blanket from the bed over her shoulders. California is always colder than she expects.

Even if Blake hadn't told her, she would have known by now. Almost every channel is running footage of the red carpet at the *Vanity Fair* party, and Kate watched Marco and Holly May holding hands twice already— probably along with her parents and coworkers and anyone else she bragged to about being here with Marco. Holly May in a lavender-and-dark-green gown that Kate recognizes from the Marc Jacobs fashion show. It's the spring line. Kate fingers her rumpled gold gown from however many seasons ago, a gown that felt extremely glamorous about seven hours ago.

As she usually does when she gets upset, she becomes compulsive and convinced she'll feel better if she has more information. Information equals control equals calm. So she turns off the television and logs on to the Internet, obsessively Googling Holly May, finding out her perfect body dimensions and how she runs six miles a day and brags about all the yoga poses she can twist herself into, even though Kate thinks the whole point of yoga is that it's not supposed to be competitive.

Holly May is a strict adherent of the Zone Diet, which makes Kate feel a little smug. Holly May did not go to college. More smug. Holly May has a multimillion-dollar contract with a leading cosmetics company and a new

$2 million Tribeca loft. More mad than smug. Time to step away from the Internet.

Kate catches her reflection in a mirror hanging on the wall. This is enough, she thinks. She got what she wanted. She dated someone famous and was invited to the *Vanity Fair* party on her own merit. But it was supposed to be more fun than this. She walks over to the mirror and stands close enough to see her breath fog it up, covering up the lower half of her face, making her vanish a little. In the reflection she can read the expiration date stamped on her forehead, and it's today.

Kate is disposable now that she can't do much more for Marco, now that she's not as useful as Holly May. Kate looks at the phone. If she had Christina's phone number, she would call her and apologize, even though Kate has no idea what time it is in Europe, or if that's even where she still lives. Kate would even want to see her, to study the damage Marco did to someone who couldn't walk away.

She goes back to the computer and starts Googling Christina Mancini but nothing comes up. If only she had a maiden name. She knows she should stop. Back away. Get into bed. Pick a pay-per-view movie. Order room service, even though she's never felt less hungry.

But her curiosity is killing her. Was it Christina who called Tim? If not, who is the woman with the foreign accent trying to air Marco's dirtiest laundry? And why has Kate been trying to bury it? She types in *Italy Marco Mancini family*. An old school photograph of Marco and a young girl with brown braids named Maria Mancini pops up, and Kate instantly remembers the date at Rao's four months ago.

My sister and I had a pretty big fight a while ago over a decision I made that she didn't approve of. It's a long story I don't really feel like getting into.

His sister is calling Column A. Kate just knows it.

She starts trying to research this elusive Maria Mancini, but she gets nothing else. His sister must have married. Losing your maiden name wipes out a whole history—for better or for worse. If only Kate could find her, she'd ask her dozens of questions. Mostly whether or not Marco regretted leaving Christina. Did he ever admit he was doing something wrong? Was his ambition the excuse? Will he ever help her?

She curls up in bed, sinking into the soft, cool white sheets. She's just going to take a little break to calm down.

It's 3:39 A.M. Two hours after Marco sent her a text message saying he was done working and and going to a big agent's annual after-party, where the press is always banned. Tim said it's always full of half-naked mattresses out in the grotto pool and lots and lots of really famous people high on coke.

She has to call someone besides Marco. She needs to hear a voice telling her what she already knows.

"Hello?" asks Nick, sounding groggy, and she pictures the faint morning light *tap-tapping* on his window. "Are you okay?"

"No." She swallows a sob. "I got carried away."

He clears his throat. "I know," he says slowly. "But it's not all your fault."

Now she's crying without trying to hide it. What good would finding Maria do, anyway? No answer would make her feel any better. "I should have known better."

"Kate, do you want to hear something that's going to be hard to digest?"

"Harder than Marco and Holly on the red carpet at the *Vanity Fair* party?"

Nick sighs, one last hiss of a seal he's been keeping tight for months. "Well, I didn't know about that yet, but I'm not surprised. Did you ever consider that maybe you're not the victim here? Maybe once you can see this all more clearly, you'll think that Marco was really your mistake. Chances are, one day you won't want anyone to know you ever dated him and he'll still be asking you for help every time he wants to kill or plant something in the press."

Kate nods even though Nick can't see her. "I just feel so stupid."

"Well, you should," he laughs, and Kate smiles. "You've been doing some seriously stupid shit. Confusing love with career advancement is pretty dumb."

She puts her head on the soft, cool pillow. The truth serum of Nick's voice seeps through every pore, stinging strong enough to be an astringent. All this time she thought she was doing Marco a favor by digging ditches in the dirt, covering up the old skeletons, providing shelter for the storm. All this time she thought he would appreciate her efforts and that they would also help her. But covering it up made it fester instead of vanish. Covering up made everything more complicated and less honest. Kate has made a very big mistake and she has no one to blame but herself.

"I just want to come home."

"You just tell me when and I'll be here waiting for you."

"Promise?"

"I promise."

She wakes up when Marco walks in around dawn, a rumpled silhouette in the pale light smelling like chlorine and champagne, with a splash of guilt. Her makeup mask has melted all over the pillow. So much for wanting Marco to see her dressed in her Oscars best.

"I know you were out with Holly May," she says quietly while he hangs his tuxedo in the closet. She's too tired to fight.

"Beautiful, that was just work," he says, sitting down and brushing her stiff hair out of her eyes. "I shouldn't have to explain that to you."

"Blake saw you with Holly May at the party after midnight, when you knew I'd be gone." It's an easier and calmer conversation than admitting she's angry he let her make this kind of mistake.

"I was still working," he says, biting the inside of his lower lip.

"You're a *chef*. You had a party to *cater*."

He stands up and Kate's relieved he looks ridiculous in boxers and black socks. If he looked handsome, she'd never be able to carry this through.

"If this relationship is going to work, we have to have an understanding," he says to her. "You of all people should understand the importance of exposure and networking."

Kate feels queasy, a little like she did after her first big meal at Coast. She gets up, walks over to the bathroom sink, and washes off her makeup, bruising the white fluffy towel beige and black before throwing it on the floor. She decides to stay in her gown. May as well take advantage of the loan. She doesn't tell Marco that Nick arranged for her to have a room at Pierre's hotel a few blocks away.

"I need more than an understanding," she says, because she doesn't think she can spend another night comparing herself to Holly May or worrying that if she hadn't helped hide Christina, she and maybe even Marco would be better off. Mostly she wants to get out while this is still something she remembers. Kate's already closing the hatches of her heart, but she doesn't want to forget.

She almost leaves it at that. Let him think this is about Holly or about wanting more. Let him think his ambition and passion were things she fell in love with and had to walk away from.

"I don't like the person you've become," she says.

"What are you talking about? I haven't changed at all."

Maybe that's the real problem. Maybe she's the one who did.

"It's going to catch up with you," Kate says, and his eyes go cold.

"You're not starting with me again about Christina." He turns off the light and the room goes pitch black, but she's never seen him clearer. "Come on, Kate, let's get some rest. In the morning this will all be clearer."

"It is morning and it is clear and I want you to give Christina the money she needs."

He shakes his head and sits back down on the bed. "What does something that happened a lifetime ago have to do with us now?"

She just stares at him, wondering if there's anything he could say to make this all better, wondering if in a few months he'll also think she was just part of some past life.

"Kate, that was so long ago. That has nothing to do with right now, and right now I need you," he says, softening a little. "You're my best friend and publicist!"

She switches on a bedside lamp. "I didn't sign up to be your publicist. And it has everything to do with me, with us, with right now."

Marco stands up and folds his arms across his chest. "Oh, I'm *sorry,* but correct me if I'm wrong here. Haven't *you* been enjoying the perks of building *me* up?" He waves his arms around. "This room. That dress. Did you actually think you got this all for being a *gossip columnist?*"

Kate starts packing up her things from the bathroom, resisting the urge to grab all the free fancy toiletries.

"You just don't get it, do you?" he yells. "You need me, too. Without me you're just a *gossip columnist*."

She puts her hands over her ears. She wishes he would stop saying that. Those two words keep knotting and kneading in her stomach.

Marco wants a fight because he knows he could win a war of spoken words. Kate's strongest when she's hiding behind a computer or a printed page. Real-time sentences sometimes scare her.

"You only can be with someone who you control," he says, and she wonders what's going to happen to his public image without her trying to control it for him. "That's what this is about. Control."

Kate shakes her head and swallows her tears. She says good-bye in a quiet, even voice that surprises her. He turns his back and she leaves him standing by the window, staring up at himself. *The Chef Women Across America Want to Take Home to Their Kitchens!*

They can have him. She wants someone of her own.

these people aren't your friends

Charlie calls in sick for the first time in over a decade the first day Tim is back after the Oscars. Probably a hot new mattress and a bottle of Viagra kept him up all night. His wife has already called twice looking for him. Tubby assigns one of the nightlife reporters from the features section to help Tim out, but he's still a little panicked that he can't pull off a column alone. He doesn't like being accountable.

The morning meeting is a firing squad of men in suits. They seem to enjoy shooting down ideas so much that he considers inventing a scandal with a starlet just to get them off his back.

"You call that a lead?!"

"My mother has better gossip about her bingo night in Miami!"

By 4:45, Tim still doesn't have a lead item and he starts panicking. He opens up his computer files of half-items, things that fell through, things they couldn't get past the lawyers, even though he's got to play it safe because he's still got that lawsuit looming. Nothing has magically material- ized since the morning. Tim stares at his phone, willing it to ring with some news. And then it does. Maybe I'm psychic, he thinks for a moment, but then again his phone rings pretty much every five minutes. He actually answers it and it's Spinster, sounding chipper enough to have just blown Brad Pitt.

"You didn't hear it from me," she says, and Tim rolls his eyes. She probably wants to trade him a free meal for a sighting of an expired celebrity at a new restaurant she represents.

Tim picks up his pen to take notes in the off chance that she might say something interesting. He avoids typing when someone's telling him something because they often get skittish if they hear the clanking of keys. Every now and then Spinster comes through, and he doesn't want today to be a PETA day.

But her news is about Holly May. "She! Has! A! New! Boyfriend!"

Tim half wishes Spinster were standing in front of him so he could throw something at her. "Let me guess, her new boyfriend happens to be your client Marco Mancini."

She ignores him and keeps spinning. "Did you see them walk the red carpet at the *Vanity Fair* party? Weren't they just *gorgeous*? I have some high-res photos I can e-mail you."

Tim doesn't tell her that he was passed out on the hood of their weekend Mercedes when this new *gorgeous* couple walked the red carpet. He doesn't say that Blake told him in the morning over Bloody Marys by the pool. Or that Tim and Blake ended up driving Kate to the airport, since she changed her flight to travel back to New York with them. Blake paid for her upgrade with his dad's frequent-flier miles. They fed her a cocktail of vodka tonics, warm chocolate-chip cookies, and Xanax until she stopped crying and saying, "It's not about Holly May."

"So what is it about?" asked Tim, knowing Kate was probably more upset that Marco was turning into a famous asshole, way past the 4 percent mark, and using her to spin his shit into bite-sized items.

"I can't do it anymore," she said, starting to cry again somewhere over Colorado.

"Do you want me to take him down?" asked Tim. "I'm happy to do it."

She took a deep breath and wiped her eyes with a corner of the scratchy airplane blanket. She didn't say yes but she nodded slightly and closed her eyes for a quick second.

"You deserve more," said Tim. Her nod was an invitation to suck the piss right out of Marco, and not a moment too soon.

"And he's headed for career suicide," added Blake. "Did you see that dumb commercial he did for the Home Shopping Network? And Holly May? She's not going to stick around when he hits the ground."

They must have said enough of the right things—a sort of lullaby—for before long she stopped crying and fell asleep. Luckily she missed the viewing of Marco's show on the airline's television. He was making risotto with the white truffles Tim remembered from the first time he ate at Coast all those months ago. There's nothing worse than trying to forget about someone when his image is plastered across the country. Blake even hid his magazine. The back cover was a photo of Marco in an ad for an espresso maker. The world was that guy's oyster, but not for much longer.

Tim tells Spinster that he'll see what he can do, but that item would certainly be sweetened if she could come up with something with a little more tension. "I'll call you back in an hour to follow up," she says.

What a useless bitch. Tim picks up a stack of papers from the floor by his desk and a scrap of paper flutters out. It's the number of that woman with the Italian accent who first told Tim about Marco's disfigured wife. Tim pictures this mysterious caller sitting somewhere near the ocean under a big white umbrella and wonders if she's hot and available. The number has the area code for Miami. He dials. She picks up right away, as if she were expecting his call.

"Marco is such a big shot now at the Oscars with that model," says the source, somewhere between a whisper and a hiss, "and he can't even help his wife?"

The source mentions Marco's well-publicized $250,000 deal with the espresso-machine maker to shoot a year's worth of ads. "Why doesn't he use this coffee money for her?"

Tim tries to get the source to give her name, or at least to confirm that she's not Christina, but she refuses. And yet he's still got enough to work with. Kate probably doesn't want to give him an assist.

"I'll only tell you this, I've known Marco longer than anyone," she says before hanging up.

While Tim's sitting at his desk trying to figure out how to get documents to back up this woman's claims, Tubby waddles over to remind him he's only got another hour before he's got to file his column. Fuck it. He doesn't want to dine at Coast again, anyway. It's not worth the risk of running into Zoe. Besides, she knows about Danielle now. There's no reason to protect Marco anymore. Use it or lose it.

He picks up the phone and calls Marco, who's about to be known for something much less glamorous than dating Holly May or being the chef women across America want to bring home to their kitchens. Build them up. Bring him down.

A month after Kate gets back from the Oscars, she tells Lacey and The Principal she wants to get out of gossip for good. Her fight with Marco still feels raw, and she wants to keep it that way so she won't repeat her mistakes.

Besides, Marco was her best source and she hasn't seen him since Oscar night. Maybe the fallout from the *Vanity Fair* party was her punishment for breaking the cardinal *don't sleep with the sources* rule. The Principal was right. It never works out in your favor. She doesn't want to ask him for anything ever again. Kate hasn't returned his calls. She doesn't want to help him spin the story about the network dropping his show or do damage control on Tim's item about Christina. Marco also lost his endorsement deal with the espresso maker and the Home Shopping Network stopped considering selling his line of cookware. Even Letterman canceled Marco's appearance. If Kate were his publicist, she'd quit just like Spinster did.

On Kate's suggestion, Lacey and The Principal agree to interview Robin to take over the column. Her stock rose when she broke the news last month about the head of the James Beard Awards being arrested for fraud.

"That's a story we should have had," said Lacey when it broke in the *Daily Metro*. They started talking about interviewing Robin soon after that. It's a story she knew Kate could have had if work were her priority while she was with Marco—and if her connections weren't as complicated. Robin's stock is also high because she's dating the New Literary Wunderkind, who's currently being featured in an ad for an expensive pen. Yesterday Column A ran an item—probably planted by her—about Hollywood Prince being "very interested" in the leading role of the Wunderkind's novel movie adaptation by Julian Joseph.

A few months ago Kate would have been jealous that Robin and her boyfriend were popping up in party pictures and being quoted talking about each other in the press, but the Wunderkind keeps saying he wants to move back to London and stay single forever, and the only gossip columnist to ever marry an ambitious boldface name ended up alone in a very good building on Park Avenue, with occasional appearances on morning talk shows for celebrity commentary.

But more than that, Kate wants out as much as Robin wants in. In the world of gossip columns, you can only get out—or at least get help—if you find your replacement. And if Robin works out, Kate could maybe get a better beat: The *Examiner*'s crime reporter just jumped to the *Times*.

Kate doesn't feel like going to any of the parties she RSVPed for tonight, so she heads home early. She doesn't want to talk to anyone, especially Joe at the newsstand, but she also wants to read magazines in bed, specifically the new *People*, which someone swiped from her desk before she could fully relish the picture of Holly May on the worst-dressed list.

"Hey, Brenda Starr!" shouts Joe as soon as she emerges from the subway stairs. "You're an appetizer. The best part of the meal!"

He holds out a page from a supermarket tabloid. It's a story about the women in Marco's life. Kate's listed as an appetizer, Wendy Winter is the main course, and Holly May is the dessert. Wendy's and Holly May's pictures are clearly publicity stills, as they're perfectly buffed and polished.

Kate remembers her photo being taken at the Tom Cruise premiere party at Cipriani about six months ago. Tim and Blake have been cut out of the frame. It's the only shot of her on WireImage.com—her arms look enormous and her hair is in her eyes.

"Doesn't do you justice, Brenda," says Joe, shaking his head. "A glamorous gal like you deserves better than that phony cook. What goes up that fast is going to hurt like hell when it hits the ground. I've read about it a million times!"

Every step Blake takes away from his editor in chief's office back to his desk feels lighter, as if his shoes had little air pumps in their soles. He just gave three weeks' notice and he's got a passport. The agent he met at the *Vanity Fair* Oscars party came through. Blake wrote a twenty-page proposal for a book about the Palm Beach murder. Writing more than 150 words was far easier than he expected, especially with Alison's help getting the facts straight.

"I'll trade you dinner anywhere you want any day when you can take some time to help me fact-check my proposal," he told her. "Just name the place and I'll get us an eight o'clock reservation."

"I don't care where we go," she said, flashing those grass-green eyes. "And I hope it's going to be a slow process."

But once he got started going, the words just started spilling out, as if they'd been corseted for years. The proposal was snapped up by the first publisher they sent it to, for a ninety-thousand-dollar advance. Blake doesn't even feel badly that he told the *Tribune*'s media columnist that he got six figures for it. Everyone rounds up. Today Blake feels at least 40 percent famous, and it feels fantastic. He just has to try not to get anxious about the distinct possibility that he can no longer write anything but gossip items.

Blake wonders if anyone will invite him anywhere once he's not a gossip columnist anymore. Or return his calls or give him a prime-time table at the new three-star restaurant. But now that he thinks about it, he's not sure he's going to want any of that again. The only access he needs now is into Palm Beach society, and his dad can help him there. Plus, Alison loves the beach.

Last night he gave her a yellow sundress after dinner in a cute little West Village café that she chose. He can't even remember the name of it or what he ate. He just remembers being happy there. He hadn't popped any Sudafed or blown any lines in weeks, and he could actually breathe through his nose and smell what he was eating.

"Your commission," he said. "And an invitation."

She laughed. "I don't need any bribes to visit you."

Then she let him kiss her for the first time. Maybe it's because she knew he was giving notice or maybe she had just wanted to make him wait, to be sure he was willing to change. To know he wanted to change. To be sure he was changing.

He's got to help his editors find a replacement, but he's a little stumped. Tim's too much of a liability for *Manhattan* magazine. They need someone who can blend in better. Kate could probably pull it off, but she wants to try out this crime beat at the *Examiner*. Breaking up with Marco seems to have soured her for good on gossip. And Robin's out, since she's going to replace Kate.

Blake flips through his Rolodex of 1,678 contacts. Not one of them could take over and he doesn't think he's being egotistical in thinking that. He's got to find someone with the right combination of skill, social savvy, ambition, and ethics. Someone smart and likable, someone who's not social climbing. A good reporter without too many sacred cows. Someone relatively uncorruptable but not naive. He scrolls through the list again. Nope. Not one.

Ripe's nightlife impresario gave Tim the club's VIP room for his thirty-fourth birthday last night, and pretty much every publicist in town showed up. The real ass-kissers even brought gifts for extra insurance. The club had cooled off and it was a desperate attempt to get some press, a lifeline, anything. Blake stayed late but left with his pretty new girlfriend, that fact checker Alison, who doesn't smoke or drink and is having an unfortunate boring effect on Blake.

Zoe didn't even call to wish him a happy birthday and Kate only stopped by for the first hour. She said she had a doctor's appointment in the morning. But Tiffany Gold came accessorized by two white toy poodles in a Birkin bag and her favorite gay decorator.

"Isn't this fuuuuuuuun?" she giggled, giving Tim a wet kiss on both his cheeks.

Sometime after midnight, while Tim was dancing with Robin, he took a close look at the crowd. Everyone looked a little familiar. There were the usual crashers like the baroness, who hit on him, and Shaggy. Label Whore and her new boyfriend, who was wearing a Gucci belt buckle. The publicists for Leo DiCaprio, Sarah Jessica Parker, and Heidi Klum. Even a few celebrities like Diddy, who likes to keep Column A on his side. But not one person Tim felt like talking to, even if he didn't have a sore throat from a particularly bloody coughing fit earlier.

"Do you think all these people are just here because you write Column A?" asked one of his high-school friends. Tim excused himself to get another drink. He needs to get nice and numb so he won't mind leaving his own party alone.

The next day, Charlie hasn't shown up by noon, when Tubby calls Tim into his office.

"Siddown," he says, and Tim sinks into the gray couch.

Tim should have showered. He knows he smells like last night's drinks and cigarettes. This is it. He's probably going to get fired. Maybe he can move down to Palm Beach with Blake, squat in the family's mansion for the summer. Tim would be good at that, as long as he didn't have to be held responsible for any of the facts. At least Robin helped him track down that driver of the Loathed Hollywood Lothario and clear that mess up. He'd never be able to do any serious investigative reporting on his own. There's no way he could handle that kind of long deadline, and he doesn't have the family connections to report that kind of story out. When you're churning copy every day, it's easier just to act like a machine on cruise control.

"Charlie's going to TV," says Tubby, tearing into a powdered doughnut.

"I can cover today, no problem."

"No, I mean he's going to produce one of those dumb-ass celebrity television shows. He's going, going, gone. He gave notice this morning."

Charlie's extra-long lunches recently in fancy suits and his letting Tim cover the Oscars now start to make sense.

"In this business, every door is revolving, and one guy's exit is an entry for some lucky kid like you who just happens to be in the right place at the right time."

I'm being promoted?

"We've got major reservations about letting you take over. I mean *ma-jor*. To be honest with you, we tried to get Robin back here to split the column with you, but she took a job at that bullshit money-losing paper before we could make her an offer."

For a moment there, he liked the idea of getting fired and moving down to Palm Beach with Blake. Picking up girls in pastel dresses and wearing monogrammed loafers. Maybe send Zoe tantalizing postcards. Postcards saying shit like, *The weather's great! Wish you were here!*

"But we've got no choice." Tubby sits back in his chair, folding his meaty arms over his chest, so his belly bulges out past his belt buckle. "And I'm going to tell you something else. Gossip columnists are a fucking dying breed. These kids with the blogs are killing you."

He waits for a reaction, but Tim is still trying to figure out if he's happy or sad.

"But!" says Tubby. "You're not dead yet, and Column A still brings in the highest ad rates and the most Web traffic. It's our brand and we need to keep it on top."

Tim wonders how much more money he can get for this. His current salary of sixty-five thousand isn't cutting it. Tim wants at least eighty-five thousand. He's going to have to start giving Danielle money.

Tubby takes another bite of the doughnut. "But try to think of a few names of people who can help you. I know you can't do this alone. No one expects you to."

Tim can't think of any. Not one. Dying breed. The last fucking unicorn. Before long, before anyone really notices, he could be gone from here, too, and maybe he won't be replaceable. The credits will roll. *The End*. But for now maybe this won't be so bad. Now he'll get all that shit Charlie got. Lots of first-class plane tickets, hotel rooms, dinner parties with celebrities who need the press, whatever the hell he wants from their publicists. Maybe even one of those $150,000-a-year "script consultant" fees from movie producer Harry Stein, who understands better than anyone that bribery buys protection.

"But! You're only getting this gig on one condition,"says Tubby.

Tim nods his head, thinking Tubby's going to say Tim's got to make it in on time for the morning meeting every day.

"The drinking has to stop. I'm serious. You're a liability. If I so much as smell booze on you like I do right now, you're out. And while you're at it, why don't you cut back on the smoking and kick that hack of yours. You always sound like a fucking dying horse."

Tim laughs. "That's like asking a pro ball player to win a championship without steroids."

Tubby doesn't even crack a smile. "You keep it up and I swear, Tim, I'm going to have management test your *piss* every morning."

A toast," says Blake's dad, raising his champagne flute. "To second acts."

"To second acts," chime Blake and Lindsay. Chris Flemming and Spinster are also there, and have brought along a draft of the press release announcing Blake's dad's becoming Chris's partner for his new $1 million restaurant in a Vegas hotel. His dad always said Vegas is a city built on piles of bills instead of bricks and mortar and he's getting in on the game.

As soon as Chris hired Spinster, she dropped Marco as a client, saying it was a conflict of interest—which is almost as honest as saying "It's not you, it's me." Blake could sense her disappointment upon hearing that he's getting out of the gossip industry. He's not doing her any favors any-time soon. Palm Beach may as well be Pluto.

"And to my son, *the author*," adds his grinning dad.

Hearing that word escape his father's lips makes Blake start panicking. What if he can't do it? What if he never finishes the book and has no job, no purpose, to come back to? The best thing about writing his column was that he could always deliver.

The sous-chef comes by to describe the dishes they'll be tasting. It all seems familiar to Blake, who only has Marco to thank for the palette train-ing. Every revolving door spits out a new sucker who never even saw the back of the last guy's head.

Blake goes to the bathroom, where he splashes some cold water on his face and tells his reflection, *Everything is going to be fine*. Better to try this and fail than get stuck. The worse-case scenario is that everyone stops paying attention to him, and that may not be so bad. On his way back to the table, he swears the hostess, a sexy Asian woman in a black dress, winks at him.

"Do I know you?" he asks her. She says she used to work at Coast, where she met Blake at the opening party.

"It looks like I was smart enough to pick a winner this time," she says, nodding at Chris Flemming and smiling like she's almost certainly fuck-ing him.

"How's your friend Tim?" she asks. "You know, I'm good friends with Danielle Marks."

The subtitles of their conversation tell the story of the baby.

"I don't know," says Blake. He's not sure he's going to be seeing a lot of Tim in the near future. Sometimes there is more weakness than strength in numbers. "For what it's worth, I tried."

She gives him a weak smile.

Then he bumps into Label Whore from the *Examiner*. She's at the bar waiting to be seated with a guy in an expensive Italian suit, and she doesn't look happy. Through her stiff, fat lips, she tells Blake that the hostess should know who she is and she shouldn't be kept waiting, especially after everything the *Examiner* has done for Chris Flemming. *They should know who I am.*

"It's too bad about Kate getting demoted," snips Label Whore, and he wonders if she actually believes her own spin. She'll probably say her date tonight wasn't rich enough for her when he doesn't call her again. "But we're very lucky to have Robin now and I want to do everything I can to help her." Blake's sure Label Whore is amply rewarded with free shit for her support.

Every straight brown hair is in place, her eyebrows are expertly plucked, foundation's been applied to make her skin seem smooth but ugly still radiates from all her pores. She probably didn't even pay for her own underwear. He wants to say she barely matters at all. She's never going to matter because everyone knows she's walking down a dead end.

Instead, he keeps it simple, giving her a big smile. "It must be nice," he says.

"What must be nice?" If her forehead wasn't shot full of Botox, it would be creasing like a Chinatown fan right about now.

"It must be nice," he says again, heading outside to call Alison to say he'll be at her place in forty-five minutes. "It must be nice!" he yells out one more time over his shoulder just to make sure everyone knows exactly who she is.

find your own replacement

Kate's phone hardly rings anymore and she feels compelled to hand over the good invitations to Robin, who's been nothing but nice now that they're on the same team. But she's beginning to feel a little invisible and slightly anxious that she may never break a good story again, that she may well vanish into purgatory, without even earning a graduate degree.

Kate's nights are suddenly free. Without a boyfriend or a job requiring party coverage, she's not really sure what to do. At least she has plans for tonight for a farewell dinner for Zoe. She's moving to L.A., mostly to get away from her parents now that they're officially separating. The blind item in *WWD* about her father's mistress was too much for her mother to take. The public embarrassment meant Zoe's mom would finally be able to score a settlement with enough cash to maintain her lifestyle—which softened the blow of having her age (fifty-eight) compared with the news-caster's (thirty-four).

"The last thing I want to be is a star in this courtroom drama," Zoe said. She's gotten a job in a talent agency as the assistant to some friend of her dad's. She says working at *Gourmet* was too fattening, even though the weight she's been gaining is more a result of her having given up speed. Zoe likes the idea of lunching with movie stars and finding a boyfriend with a studio deal and a beach house.

Kate's on her way to the restaurant downtown—not a new restaurant, and not one where the publicist is going to make sure they get a great table or a comped meal, just a favorite café with a garden. It's warm enough to eat outside tonight. She thinks she sees someone who looks like Marco on the street, but she realizes it's probably not him. She thinks she sees him almost every day, but it's just her imagination painting ghosts across the grids.

But this time it's really him. At first it's hard to catch her breath. Then she feels angry. What is he doing in Tribeca, anyway? Isn't there a red carpet to court tonight?

"Hey, beautiful," he says, and all at once Kate feels beautiful again. Just like that. That was always Marco's real talent. Charm.

"How are you?" she asks.

"Not quite as good as you, with your fancy new promotion." So, he's been reading up on her, too.

She wants to know if he sent Christina money and if he's speaking to his sister now that it was revealed that she was the one who called Tim on Christina's behalf.

"I sent Christina a generous check," he says. He can still tell what she's thinking. "Just in case you still care."

"I still care."

"And I talked to my sister and I think we're going to be okay."

"I'm happy for you," she says, even though *he* doesn't look happy. His eyes are puffy and ringed with pale lavender lines, a road map of tosses and turns.

"I'm pitching a new TV show," he says, sounding rehearsed. "But now that my publicist is working for Chris and you and Blake are off gossip, I don't know who to call anymore."

When she doesn't respond he continues, "It's a reality show about what makes a great chef, where the audience gets to vote. Like an *American Idol* for foodies," he says, and Kate wonders which agent came up with that tag line.

"You see, there are eight characteristics that make a great chef," he says, getting excited the way he used to about a new recipe. "There's personality, looks, charm, hospitality—"

"But," says Kate, cutting him off, "what about food? Isn't a great chef all about the kind of food he makes? How is the audience going to judge that if they can't taste the food during the show?"

Marco shakes his head, focusing those molten brown eyes on Kate's face, and they still feel warm. "The food is just one-eighth of it. The audience gets to vote on everything else to award the next great chef a job at a three-star restaurant in New York."

"I wouldn't care if a chef was fat and ugly and rude if he was making great food," says Kate, wondering when Marco started believing that his true talent was anything but cooking.

"Yes, you would!" he says, laughing, but Kate knows it's his nervous laugh. "Have I taught you nothing?"

He puts his hand on her shoulder and she tries to ignore the faint rush she gets, remembering his fingers rolling over her skin and the way his white stucco ceiling looked at night. No one will ever make her feel the way Marco did, but that may not be a bad thing. *Spoiled* is just another word for rotten.

"You taught me more than you'll ever know," she says. "I was your best pupil."

She walks away without turning around, even though she feels his eyes on her back. Zoe's waiting and she'll want to hear all the gossip about this chance encounter. In a few minutes, Marco will be boiled down into bite-sized pieces. *He's pitching a reality show!* More grist for the mill. It's easier that way.

But Kate can almost hear a hatch in her heart hiss. She doesn't trust herself to walk away, so she picks up her pace, almost breaking into a run.

Tim tried to go to bed early. He covered a downtown art opening and the dinner after at a yet-unopened, soon-to-be-trendy downtown restaurant. It was the kind of party that felt cool, like something out of a movie about downtown New York maybe a decade ago. He even got two items and a few lunch dates with potential sources. He drank tonic with lime all night so no one would know he was riding the wagon, as his dad used to call it. Charlie's been gone for two weeks—the longest Tim has been sober since high school.

He's even been going to the gym, finally using one of the many free memberships. Tim's finding muscles he forgot existed, and it feels much better to wake up sore than to feel as though his head is hammered to the bed.

His cell phone buzzes at 1:11 A.M. Zoe. She must be drunk-dialing. He takes her call, lying in his boxers with the sheet tangled around his ankles. It's a warm spring night and he's already dreading summer weekends alone in the city. As soon as he picks up the phone, she starts rambling, without even waiting to hear him say hello. She sounds like she wants to come over.

"Do you miss me?" she asks. He's not sure what game she's playing. Zoe doesn't believe in anything but the present, so why is she crawling back to the past?

Before he can answer she says she's going to miss him even though she hasn't returned his calls for a fucking month. Almost long enough for Tim to go ahead and run an item about her dad moving into Trump Tower with his mistress.

"I'm moving to L.A. tomorrow."

Tim pictures her sitting perched up on her white window seat, watching the empty cabs hunting Fifth Avenue for a fare. He wishes he didn't want her to come over.

"Will you visit?" she asks, slowing down to take a deep breath.

Fuck her. Tim wanted to be the one to leave her behind. Now everyone's leaving him and he's going to be the last one standing.

"Danielle came up to me at a party," she says, and his heart feels as if its chambers are filling up with ice. "She thought I could convince you to see her."

Tim doesn't say anything.

"I told her I didn't think anyone could make you do anything."

"That's one way of putting it."

"And what's the other way?" Her voice rises. "Why don't you tell me, because you know what? People are going to ask me and I'd like to have an answer besides that you're an asshole. This is not going away. Ever."

He wraps the sheet tightly around him. The moon must be full. It feels as though every light in his apartment is on. "Are you done?" There's no reason to take her shit anymore.

She sighs. "I guess so." No one says anything for a full minute. "Will you do me one favor?" she asks, and suddenly he knows why she really called. She probably would have left New York without saying good-bye if she didn't still need him.

"Could you try to go easy on them?" Her voice is starting to crack. "This is really hard on my mom."

Tim learned a long time ago not to make promises like the one she wants. And her dad never did anything for Tim but make him feel like he was clawing at the wrong side of the fence. But still. Maybe she'll come back.

"I'll try," he says, hanging up while Zoe's still talking. He turns off his cell phone and unplugs his landline for good measure. He pops the last of her Ambien and waits for that familiar numbness, that deafening cloud to descend.

The next day, Tim thinks about calling Zoe at least once an hour. He checks the flight times for the airline she always uses, trying to figure out when she'll be in the air. At six P.M., he finally breaks down and calls her. He wants to say good-bye. He wants to have a last conversation without promises or favors. He wants to try to give her an answer. But it goes straight to voice mail. She's already gone.

Later he meets Robin at a big movie premiere at the Ziegfeld. There's no sign of Blake or Kate or anyone Tim would want to sit with. In just a few months, all the faces have changed—except for the syndicated dinosaurs sitting in the front rows, of course.

After the screening, they get on a chartered bus to Cipriani, and as soon as they walk through the revolving doors, a waiter in a tuxedo hands Tim a

Bellini. He sucks down the sweet, fizzy peach concoction as if by reflex. What else is he supposed to do? He looks out across the crowded room, searching for the clipboard chicks to usher them through to the VIP area so he can get his quotes. He finishes another one after clinking his glass with Robin's. And then he remembers, I'm not supposed to do this. It sounds like a lie but he just hadn't thought about it before. Automatic pilot, he could try to explain to Tubby. The revolving doors are jammed now, full of people spilling into the party. No one else is getting out anytime soon.

Kate gets home before dusk, relieved to now have a line between work and play, even if she wasn't invited to the big movie premiere tonight and is slightly concerned that going home early without any plans may quickly lose its appeal. Still, she smiles as she kicks off her shoes. It's almost June, time to get her summer clothes from her parents' house upstate.

She sinks into the couch and turns on the television. Marco's a guest on a local news show. It feels like cruel and unusual punishment to have him projected into her living room. Breaking up with boyfriends in college was as easy as avoiding a bar or choosing a different floor of the library to study on. Her ex-boyfriends' omnipresence never existed outside the obsessing in her own mind. It's the best reason she can think of to stick to civilians from now on.

Marco is demonstrating how to make his famous oyster-and-uni dish, taking care to open up the raw oyster shells and preserve the liquid for the sauce, adding mustard seed and tomato water to balance the flavor. *Sweet, salty, sour, bitter,* he says. Four adjectives that now feel as if they're taunting Kate.

Sitting alone in the living room, Kate feels she's in a woozy dream, somewhere half underwater, where everything seems slow and murky, but her heart keeps racing. Just watching Marco scoop the slimy orange sea urchin from its prickly black shell makes her crave the nutty taste, the silky texture sliding down her throat. She suddenly, desperately, wants to call him. Instead, she calls the local sushi place and places a dinner order for her and Nick.

"Four pieces of uni," she says at the end of her order, hoping it will satisfy her craving.

The sushi arrives when Nick gets home and Kate lays it out on two plates, arranging the slices of fish and the rolls with rice the way Marco taught her. Mix up the colors. Make a paste with the wasabi and soy sauce first, then thin out the consistency with more sauce.

They eat on the couch, surfing the television channels. Holly May's being interviewed about a new line of bikinis, looking perfectly tanned, toned, and sunny. Kate can't bring herself to change the channel even though Nick says she should. The chipper interviewier asks Holly May about her love life and she says she's dating a musician with a new hit album—as if Marco never existed. Maybe that's why Marco keeps calling Kate. Maybe he's lonely. But finding out for sure is too risky because she's lonely, too.

"Sometimes love just surprises you," says Holly May, flipping her long blond hair and smiling sweetly.

"Starfucking star," says Nick, turning off the television.

The news of Holly's new boyfriend should bring Kate some satisfaction, but suddenly her face feels tight, as if some poison were trying to seep out. She moves her face around, trying to stretch out the muscles, which feel as if they're trying to burst out of her skin. She feels a little itchy and achy, too.

"Are you okay?" asks Nick, looking at her closely. He turns on the lamp and studies her face. "Your face looks swollen."

Kate rushes to the mirror and her reflection has slits for eyes, sinking in puffy pockets. He thinks she's having a reaction to the sushi even though she's never had any food allergies before. He makes her lie down in bed and presses a wet cold cloth over her eyes.

"Are you having any difficulty breathing?" he asks her while on the phone with his dad, a pediatrician.

She shakes her head.

"My dad says if you do, we have to get you to a hospital for an adrenaline shot."

"I hate hospitals!" she moans.

Nick hangs up and gives her two Benadryl with a glass of water and she crashes for the night.

The next morning, Nick takes her to an allergist who went to medical school with his dad and agreed to squeeze her in at 8:15 A.M.

"Wow, I even get a Town Car?" she asks, climbing inside wearing big black sunglasses because her eyes and lips are still swollen.

"Compliments of Pierre."

Nick reads old magazines in the waiting room while the nice doctor with gray hair and cool hands examines Kate.

She tells him she had sushi for dinner last night.

"Did you eat anything unusual? Or something that you've only had a few times before?"

She tells him about the uni.

"Are you crying because your face hurts?" he asks, pressing his fingertips to the most swollen part above her lip.

She just nods.

"Well, it could be a bad piece of fish, or some sauce," he says. "Or a new serious allergy to something omnipresent like seeds. But more likely it's the sea urchin. That's one of the few food that you can develop an allergy to after eating it a dozen or so times. You're body builds up the allergy."

He takes a plastic device with five little needle teeth dipped in various vials filled with liquid allergens—fish, sesame seeds, soy—and scratches the insides of her arms.

She remembers the sweet, salty, bitter, and sour flavors of oysters and sea urchin, the textures of ambition mixed with love and longing. She tries to focus on her breathing and stay still.

Most of the scratches remain red and flat, looking like the work of a playful kitten. But the one with the uni immediately swells up to a raised, throbbing red welt with a red ring around it.

"Your body is now rejecting the sea urchin," he says, examining the welt. "It can't tolerate any more."

The doctor says her face should be fine in a few days, but if she eats sea urchin again, her airways could close up. She should start carrying around something called an EpiPen, which he writes a prescription for, in case she accidentally eats something that may have touched sea urchin and she end up having a more severe reaction.

"You need to stay away from it," he says. "It could even kill you if you're not careful."

Even though her face is swollen and stiff, Kate's beginning to relax. She has a defense for the pain. A weapon, even. She's not going to repeat her mistakes. Something was built into her DNA to ward off what's not good for her. A warning sign, a red light, a flare on the freeway. Kate remembers the growths Marco told her about on the bluefin tuna in captivity. Maybe this is some way of her body affirming what she already knew. She was getting trapped, and escaping was becoming more dangerous and complicated.

Kate has never been a religious person but she prays she could pour water over the last year, take back every secret she spread. Heal Christina. Find a field of black orchids. Concoct a cure for the "never enough" epidemic.

"Be very careful what you put in your body, especially until your immune system is stronger," the doctor says, and Kate's relieved she's no longer a professional partier dining on hors d'oeuvres or dating a chef. She may have done this to herself, but at least she can change things.

Nick took the whole day off to take care of her, and on the way back home they stop at the newsstand to stock up on magazines.

"Your old boyfriend doesn't look so great now," Joe says, showing Kate the cover of *Women's World* magazine. Marco looks pale and bloated, with what he would describe as "carb face" after a night eating pasta. She almost wants to pick it up and read the interview but she keeps walking instead. There's nothing more to learn from him.

That night, Kate tells Nick the story of a meal she had that could represent each scratch on her arm. A map of all the flavors and textures she knows. The first big birthday cake she can remember with pink icing flowers. Salmon on her parents' grill for her graduation party. Caviar on a mother-of-pearl spoon at Coast.

Nick takes her arm and brings it under the lamp on the table next to the couch. The scratches are still pink, but they're beginning to fade. She's a little relieved, though, that the biggest scratch is still swollen and sore inside a circle. A reminder.

"Maybe this is lucky," says Nick, telling her to close her eyes. She feels him take her face in his hands and then softly kiss each puffy eyelid. Her skin has never felt smoother. She hears the music from the hookah lounge downstairs for the first time, wondering if it's this loud every night. Maybe they should find somewhere quieter to live. She has a feeling they're going to be staying in together a lot more.

She opens her eyes and looks at Nick. Kate knows this is a new beginning, a second act, one they could have never planned for, one they didn't know they'd have to come to New York to find. A beginning that's slowly, carefully coming into focus, as the millions of city lights ignite the sky all those miles across the river.

acknowledgments

Thanks for your support, inspiration and advice:

David Halpern, Sally Kim, Moby.

Toma Barylak, Drake Bennett, Jennifer Blumin, Zev Borow, Rachel Caplan, Jonathan Cramer, Jeff Dagowitz, Anne-Cecilie Engell, Gabrielle Finley, David Greenbaum, Vanessa Grigoriadis, Dan Harris, Alexandra Jacobs, Henry Leutwyler, Marshall Lewy, Tahl Raz, Meredith Scardino, Andrew Ross Sorkin, Jess Taylor, Jamie Whitehead, Laura Viggiano, and Adam Wilson.

about the author

Deborah Schoeneman has covered gossip, real estate, and society for the *New York Observer*, the *New York Post*, and *New York* magazine, where she's a contributing editor. This is her first novel.